On Dangerous Ground

Also by Lesley Horton
Snares of Guilt

On Dangerous Ground

Lesley Horton

ORION

First published in Great Britain in 2003 by Orion,
an imprint of the Orion Publishing Group Ltd

A CIP catalogue record for this book is
available from the British Library.

ISBNS: 0 75284 672 8 (hardback); 0 75284 673 6 (trade paperback)

Typeset at The Spartan Press Ltd,
Lymington, Hants

Set in Sabon

Printed in Great Britain by
Clays Ltd, St Ives plc

The Orion Publishing Group Ltd
Orion House
5 Upper Saint Martin's Lane
London, WC2H 9EA

For Andrew Taylor. For his support,
his encouragement and his faith in me.

acknowledgements

Many thanks to all who supported and helped me throughout the writing of this book. To Detective Chief Inspector Tony Hennigan (now retired) for his help with procedure and his discussions on policies and politics within the police service. My thanks also to Sheron Boyle, author of *Working Girls and Their Men* who gave of her time to discuss how young girls are groomed then worked as prostitutes.

Special thanks go to David Glover and Maureen O'Hara who gave of their time so generously to read and discuss the manuscript with me; to Joan Womersley who encouraged me through the bad times and to members of the Airedale Writers' Circle who were always there with their support.

My thanks also to my agent Teresa Chris, who was a hard task-master, for which I shall be ever grateful; to my patient editor, Sophie Hutton-Squire, and to Rachel Leyshon who corrected my mistakes and inconsistencies.

Finally I thank my husband, Brian, who was always on hand to keep me going.

prologue

The scream tore through the street engulfing everything in its path, drowning the sounds of the early evening traffic, the buzz of the lawnmowers and the laughter of the children splashing in their paddling pools. It was total and prolonged and finally, when it faded, it left in its wake a silence that bruised the warm summer evening, its shadow hanging over the neat suburban houses like an evil spirit.

Time hesitated and in the moments it took to register, the neighbours' senses sifted through the explanations their brains were giving to the sound they had heard. Then as suddenly as they had slowed, the minutes lurched back into their natural rhythm and the people abandoned their tasks to rush into the street, converging, gathering in clutches, establishing which house was disclosing its anguish.

'No. NO. NO.' The words filtered into the air, at first hardly discernible, then crescendoed into yet another scream.

'It's Clarissa,' someone shouted and as one of the crowd turned to run towards the house, the others followed, some rushing up the drive, others bounding over the low hedge to cross the parched lawn.

The front door was open. Those close enough could see Clarissa Braintree heaped on the floor, her forehead resting on the blue patterned carpet, her hands clasped around the nape of her neck. The cries had given way to a moaning, which sank deep into the thick woollen pile.

'Clarissa, what is it?' someone asked urgently.

Slowly, imperceptibly, she uncoupled her fingers and pointed up the stairs. Heads lifted and there, hanging from the top of the banister, was the body of a teenage boy swinging gently on a rope that had been tied firmly around his neck.

chapter one

Night patrol terrified PC Martin. The graveyard shift, they called it, and he'd never been keen on graveyards. He was not exactly new to the job, but he was still on probation, and the older officers had taken delight in teasing him with gruesome tales of working nights. He knew that's all they were, stories, but as he walked his beat, his nerves scuttered around his insides as though they had a life of their own, shadows loomed in front and behind him and his imagination worked overtime. If he hadn't been alone, had someone to talk to, it wouldn't have been so bad, but it was August, officers were on holiday and they were too short staffed to pair him up with anyone.

The duty inspector had been supportive and said he was sure Martin would manage on his own. 'I wouldn't let you go out by yourself if I didn't think so, and we're only a call away if you need us,' he'd said. Then, 'There'll be some drunks around, but if they're not a danger to themselves or anyone else leave them to their own devices. And,' he called as Martin was leaving, 'make sure you check the alleyways for glue sniffers and addicts.'

Bradford was a city of alleyways and in each one he entered the stench turned Martin's stomach. This one, the last in his circuit, had a name: Empire Way. There had to be a reason for that, he thought, but had no idea what it was. Anything less regal he couldn't begin to imagine. Shrouded between the back of the Copper Coin, a refurbished nightclub, a couple of restaurants and the high wall of the college car park, it was home to the city centre's drug addicts and the destitute, practised in a life that rendered them indistinguishable from the rubbish on which they slept.

He shone his torch along as much of the passage's length as he could see, before it curled around the bend of the hill. Cheerless and stinking of stale beer and rotting garbage, it was long and steep.

Muffled sounds from the club's disco seeped into the night air and the colours from the strobe lighting flickered through the grime of the windows. There was some light from the lamps high up against the eaves of the buildings, but it did little to relieve the gloom, throwing deep sections into darkness.

He moved cautiously, so cautiously that he caught the toe of his shoe in one of the cracks between the cobbles and stumbled. He let the breath he had been holding escape as he steadied himself against the rough stonework of the wall. Focusing his torch, he began again, sliding his way through the beer cans and polystyrene cartons.

A sound; a whisper; something.

It came from the bin liners huddled against the large wheelie bins. He turned his head sharply, shone his torch. Nothing. Nothing but the shadows cavorting in the tarnished light.

He swallowed hard in an attempt to pull himself together and threaded his way further up the passage, the beam of his torch catching at the piles of rubbish, illuminating them for a second or two before he moved on. The wheelie bins loomed large in the sea of garbage, casting their mischievous silhouettes along the ground and up the walls opposite. A dark shape ran from the water gully to his left and scurried across his shoe.

A rat.

He shuddered.

Unperturbed by human life, it tunnelled its way into the refuse. Suddenly it flicked round to sniff at something that had caught its interest. Martin stamped his foot and as it decamped he angled his torch in the direction of its flight, playing the beam on what at first sight appeared to be a sleeping druggie or a drunk.

But it was neither.

For a moment he remained motionless while his brain rationalised what his eyes were seeing, then reflex took over. He recoiled in horror and his stomach lurched at its first taste of violent death. Drenched in sweat, he took deep breaths to quench the nausea that threatened to relieve him of the meal he had eaten before setting out. He wanted to run, but his legs could barely hold him upright, let alone move. He stood, eyes closed, his breath coming in gasps. After what seemed like hours, but could only have been seconds, he forced himself to open his eyes and take in the scene.

A young girl, no more than thirteen or fourteen years old, was corkscrewed into the bed of waste, twisted as though she had been flung out like the trash that surrounded her. Her pants were stretched tight over her ankles and coagulating blood pooled between her legs. A dark patch stained her short skirt, but whether it was blood, urine or seepage from the mess that surrounded her, it was difficult to tell. Hypnotised by the image in front of him, Martin let his torch light up the rest of the corpse. A vicious wound covered the right side of her head and her skull had caved in. As he bent closer, she stared up at him, her eyes sightless, and he saw, stuffed in her mouth, the piece of old rag.

There is always a choice, Detective Inspector John Handford was to tell himself after it was all over. The question was whether, as he was driving himself and Gill home after their wedding anniversary meal and he caught sight of the young PC supporting himself against the wall, he had made the right one. He could have left the lad to radio in to the station. After all Central was no more than a few minutes' walk away. Someone would have been with him in no time. But Handford was there and in the young PC he saw himself some twenty-odd years ago. He had been punched in the stomach by a burglar making his escape, was winded and sick, and would have given anything for an inspector to pass by and help.

He slid the car to a stop against the kerb. Gill sighed and set her lips in a tight line. He'd seen that look before.

'I can't leave him, Gill, look at him. I promise you, I'll just check he's all right, and then I'll come back.'

'And if he isn't?'

'Then I'll radio in and get someone to pick him up.'

'Yeah.' Gill was sceptical, but smiled at him as he pulled himself out of the car and ran towards the officer.

Even in the glow of the orange street light, the constable's face was ashen. 'I'm DI Handford,' he said. 'What's the matter, son?'

Without looking up the young man pointed backwards into the alley. 'In there, sir.'

Handford turned to look at the entrance and the darkness beyond it. He held out his hand. 'Give me your torch.'

A few minutes later he emerged from the passageway, pale and solemn faced, and walked back to the officer. 'What's your name?'

'Martin, sir. She's dead, isn't she?'

It was an unnecessary question, but Martin probably knew that. 'Yes, she is,' Handford said. For a moment he leaned against the wall with him and breathed deeply in an attempt to rid himself of the vision. They were an incongruous pair. Martin – young, slight, his youthful features laced with fear, his uniform and helmet almost too big for him; Handford – taller, heavier, smart in the suit he was wearing for his night out. There were signs of ageing – the flecks of grey hair at his temples and the slackening jawline – but these added to, rather than detracted from the craggy good looks, which at the moment were blanketed with the incomprehension he always felt at a time like this. Although he'd seen his fair share of violent death over the years, it never failed to affect him. In spite of the questions, the answers, the reasons for the killings he had been given by perpetrators, he had never managed to understand how one person could take such extreme measures against another. And what he'd witnessed in that alleyway was extreme. He allowed himself a moment to think about it, then let experience take over, and as the horror faded, the familiar feeling of outrage took its place.

He tried to smother it, but as he turned towards Martin, his grey eyes were devoid of their usual sparkle and his question terse. 'Have you radioed this in?'

'No, sir, not yet.'

'Then do it, man. We need the duty inspector up here and an area car. It should have been the first thing you did.'

'Yes, I know, it's just that . . .' Martin pointed in the direction of the alley. 'It's the first time I've . . . I'm sorry, sir.'

At the sight of the man's expression, compassion wormed its way in and Handford remembered his own first body. He'd been a wreck, lost his breakfast at the crime scene and been given a telling off he'd never forgotten by the detective in charge. He shook his head. 'No, *I'm* the one who's sorry, Martin. You've done well.' He glanced at the pool of vomit. 'At least you waited until you got out here to throw up. Look, don't use your radio, ring in from that telephone box.' And in answer to Martin's puzzled look, he said, 'The press listen in on our radio waves; using the land line will keep them at bay for a bit.'

Handford watched him for a moment, then transferred his gaze to his wife. With a sigh he pushed himself away from the wall and walked over to the car.

No doubt his face said it all. 'I'm sorry, Gill, but there's a girl's body in the alley. I've got to stay—'

She interrupted him. 'Not another . . . ?'

'Probably. She's only young.'

Gill slid over to the driver's seat. 'When is it going to end, John? When are you going to catch him?'

'We will.' He sounded more confident than he felt. Three girls

5

dead and five months of investigation, without, it seemed, a glimmer of a lead. And now another. But it was nothing to do with him, he wasn't even on the team; it was down to the senior investigating officer on the case.

Detective Chief Superintendent Susan Forrester drove to the murder scene on automatic pilot. She'd been at home, crashed out on the settee in front of the television when her husband had woken her from a deep, though not entirely dreamless sleep.

'Phone,' he said shortly.

As she'd listened to the duty inspector, her heart had sunk into her stomach. Another girl dead. The press would crucify her.

Tony hadn't attempted to hide his annoyance when she'd told him she had to go out.

'Why you?' he'd said. 'Why not someone else for a change?'

'Because we have a killer out there murdering young girls and he's probably done it again and because I'm the senior investigating officer.' And because this is his fourth killing and because if I don't I'll be criticised for not taking the situation seriously enough. How many reasons did he want?

One or a hundred, it wouldn't have made any difference. 'He's not murdering young girls, Susan,' he argued, 'he's murdering embryo prostitutes and, let's face it, they'll hardly be missed. So it won't matter if just for once you say to hell with it and delegate the job to someone else. Look at you, you're exhausted.'

He was right, she was exhausted, but she pushed his words to the back of her mind as she drove and struggled to focus on the moment. She could have delegated. DI Noble was more than competent and he would be on the scene by now. Assigned to her from the Keighley division, he had been on the investigation from the beginning and was an experienced officer on whom she had to admit she relied more than a detective chief superintendent should. But there was also another senior officer there, a DI Handford from Central's CID, and she didn't want any suggestion from him that she couldn't be bothered to turn up. There were enough derogatory canteen comments about her suitability for the job as it was. Perhaps she was being unjust, but she'd never worked with him, didn't know him and wasn't prepared to take the risk. Senior investigating officers were not the most popular of officers. Although permanently based in a sub-division, they were not part of it. They worked only on major crime investigations with a chosen team of detectives and were resented by the station's CID because when a major incident came up, they pillaged the detective strength, leaving only the bare minimum to carry out day-to-day investigations.

As she neared the city centre, she prayed the press hadn't yet learned of tonight's discovery. They'd be round her like vultures if they had. Five months ago, they hadn't been too interested; the first deaths appeared unrelated and the media wasn't informed of the link between them. A few days of headlines, then as more interesting news surfaced, on to page four and from there into the 'Briefs'. When the third body was discovered, however, it all changed and with little evidence to back up their assertions, they began to draw their own conclusions. A serial killer was stalking the city, they said. He had to be; there were too many coincidences. All victims were girls, all of similar age and all found amongst the rubbish. They gave the theory credibility by nicknaming him the Trash Bag Killer, a misnomer since Bradford had long since stopped the use of black bags in favour of the large wheelie bins. But that didn't seem to matter, the Americanism added impact to the headlines, and now the editorials were beginning to ask if there was another Yorkshire Ripper on the loose, and whether the police were going to make the same mess of this inquiry as they had of that. A point that James Sanderson, the Assistant Chief Constable (Crime), had made forcibly when she'd been ordered to headquarters in Wakefield that afternoon.

'Are you making any headway at all, Forrester?'

No, she wasn't. She had nothing to help her make headway. She knew a lot about him, yet nothing about him. He was elusive, clever, organised, controlled and probably on a mission – a textbook serial killer. He murdered teenage girls, raped them with a blunt instrument after death and stuffed a rag in their mouths. Three deaths with the same signature, but he left no forensic evidence, no fingerprints, no fibres, no semen, no means of immediately identifying the girls, stripping them as he did of everything but their clothes. The girls were probably prostitutes, except she was not allowed to make that public. There *were* no child prostitutes in Bradford – and that was official. That gave this man the edge. It made tracking their identities and so finding him much more difficult. She didn't know where they lived or where they worked, for they had to work from somewhere because they certainly weren't on the streets. Out of sight, out of mind, so far as the council was concerned and therefore not raiding the city's social service or police budget.

But *he* knew and he was taunting the police with his knowledge, playing a game with them, her the more so because she was a woman – a hypothesis she hadn't articulated, but the ACC had hinted at. Would it be better, he had suggested, if someone else took over the case? Fresh eyes? A man's fresh eyes, he meant, but he hadn't spelled it out in so many words.

Close to the scene now, she glanced around. In spite of the lateness of the hour, people were milling along the pavements and in the streets, making the most of the current hot weather. She watched them and wondered how they could go about the business of enjoying themselves. She felt different from them, cut off, as if she didn't belong in their world. They were drinking, laughing, running, talking, oblivious that less than half a mile away a young girl had been brutally murdered, her body still lying where it had been dumped. A young girl who, again, for a few days, would be headline news until she was consigned to the inside pages when she would become as unimportant to them as she had been to her husband Tony.

Detective Chief Inspector Stephen Russell sipped his drink and watched his wife as she mingled with their guests in the garden. Natasha was furious with him and he couldn't say he blamed her. He'd been late for the drinks evening. He'd tried to apologise, but the fact was he didn't have a decent excuse. He'd forgotten; it was as simple as that. He'd had other things to do and he'd forgotten. He seemed to be forgetting a lot lately. So much on his mind.

Ten years ago it had been her smile that had drawn him to her. It still did. She was beautiful. A slim, elegant blonde who was intelligent and efficient, running as she did a successful PR firm in Leeds as well as being a perfect hostess. It showed at this evening's party, in the influential guests she'd invited. He was a lucky man.

A shadow loomed over him, breaking into his thoughts. The man, dressed in light-coloured trousers and a terracotta, open-necked, short-sleeved shirt, dwarfed Russell. His neatly dressed dark hair glistened in the heat and his deep-set eyes twinkled.

'She is beautiful, isn't she?' he said and grinned at his host. 'But you've been married to her far too long to be ogling her like that.'

Russell turned towards the voice. 'Andrew, you've made it. Good.' He looked round. 'No Rachel?'

Andrew Collingham sighed. 'No, she's still wandering the garden centres of Lincolnshire and doesn't expect to be back until late. I'm afraid that for my wife, buying bulbs for Mayfield Nurseries will

8

always take priority over anything else – even one of your wonderful parties.'

Russell smiled. 'Drink?'

'Please, my usual.'

Russell poured a whisky and handed it to him. 'I'm glad you made it.' They walked over to one of the garden seats.

'I'm only sorry I couldn't get here earlier,' Collingham apologised as they sat down. 'But I had to shower and change. I came away from City Hall like the proverbial lobster and drenched in sweat. That building may look impressive from the outside, but its air conditioning leaves a lot to be desired, particularly when council meetings go on for ever. And I tell you, the police committee is the worst. Your superintendent has got to be about the most long-winded man I have ever met; doesn't know when to shut up. He's not far off retirement, thank God, the sooner the better as far as I'm concerned.'

Russell made no reply. He and Collingham had known each other for nearly six years, but he still wasn't sure just how far he could go with him. He might be a good friend, but Russell always had the uneasy feeling that he could also be a weighty enemy. When it came to criticising one's superintendent, it was better to let Andrew make the comments and for him to say nothing. Collingham could draw his own inferences from the silences.

'You intend to put in for his job when he goes?'

'Yes, I'd like it, you know I would, but I'm not prepared to wait for ever. If something comes up elsewhere, I shall go for it.'

Collingham took a drink. 'I don't think you'll have too long to wait, Stephen. Can't say any more until it's official, but be patient.'

Russell's skin tingled. There'd been rumours circulating the station, but nothing confirmed. Now it looked as though it were true; Slater *was* retiring. More important than ever to stick with Collingham; an ally on the police committee had to strengthen his chances. He smiled to himself. Detective Superintendent Stephen Russell. He liked the sound of that – it had a certain ring to it.

Andrew Collingham said, 'Any progress on the serial killer, do you know, Stephen?'

Russell pulled himself back to the present. 'No idea; the serious crime team is nothing to do with us. You probably got more information at your meeting than I can give you. There are canteen rumours of course, but not much you can be sure of.'

'Your superintendent was saying nothing.'

'Well, that's probably because he knows nothing. The senior

investigating officer reports direct to the ACC Crime, not the divisional commander.'

Collingham turned to face Russell, his frustration plainly showing. 'It's our bloody city this killer is working in, Stephen. Surely we have a right to know what's going on. Certainly the council should have. He may only be killing prostitutes at the moment, but that's how Peter Sutcliffe started. What are we to expect? Child prostitutes now, innocent schoolgirls in a few months' time.'

'Prostitutes?' Russell made no effort to conceal his surprise. 'There's been no mention of them being prostitutes, not even in canteen gossip.'

Collingham drew the summer air into his lungs. 'No, and I shouldn't have said anything. It slipped out.' He lowered his voice. 'Chief Superintendent Forrester and her team know obviously, but we keep it out of the public domain and we stick to policy and don't go looking for them.'

Russell frowned. 'Surely that hinders the investigation.'

When Collingham made no reply, Russell continued. 'But they're at risk, Andrew.'

'Stephen, they're at risk every time they lie down for a punter.'

'But not like this.'

'Yes, exactly like this.'

'So, we should be finding them and protecting them, not pretending they don't exist.'

'Come on, Stephen, be realistic, even if we could find them – and that's a big if – can you imagine how much it would cost to put them in council care.'

'And that's all that matters, is it? The cost?'

The significance of the comment hung between them for a moment while, faint in the background, gentle music floated on the balmy night air, mingling with conversations and laughter. Their guests were enjoying themselves. Enjoyment in this part of the garden seemed to have lost its way.

Collingham angled his body so that he was close to Russell, a pulse of anger clearly visible beneath the tanned skin of his upper jaw.

'In an ideal world,' he said quietly, 'cost doesn't matter; in this one it does. So drop it, Stephen. Prostitutes we accept as a fact of life and if they don't cause trouble we let them alone. As for child prostitutes, if one comes to our notice we deal with her, but we don't go out looking. The Forrester woman knows to keep unnecessary details of the victims from the press; so far as they and the general public are concerned, he's killing schoolgirls. And that's probably better in the long run; keeps parents on their toes.'

He settled himself back against the cushions of the garden seat and drained his glass. 'And let's face it, if she doesn't hurry up and find him, he'll have moved on to schoolgirls anyway. So do me a favour and keep your ear to the ground. I want to know what's going on and whether Forrester is getting close. Because I tell you, if she isn't, then I want her out. And someone in who can find this bastard.'

Handford leaned against the wall and scanned the DI who had arrived some ten minutes earlier and taken charge. Detective Inspector Noble, five foot seven and well rounded, was a man who didn't wear his weight or the heat well. His corpulent belly pulled at the buttons of his shirt and sweat gathered in his armpits and down the small of his back, glistened on his close-cropped hair and ran down his face. A decent diet and regular sessions at the gym could do the man nothing but good, Handford thought as he watched him, but he probably didn't have time for either. Nevertheless, he was efficient and by the time his DCS hurried up the hill from the parking area behind the Alhambra theatre some ten minutes later, he had checked and secured the scene, noted the salient points from Handford and Martin, and accompanied the police doctor to the victim.

Susan Forrester couldn't have been much older than Handford's own DCI, Stephen Russell, but she was definitely more attractive. Tall and slim, her coppery blonde hair bounced off her shoulders as she half ran, half skipped towards him, and her black skirt and light-coloured blouse clung approvingly to her figure. Unlike Noble, she seemed to be dealing well with the heat, not a bead of perspiration clouded the clarity of her complexion.

'DI Handford?' she asked. 'I'm Detective Chief Superintendent Forrester.' Her voice was deep, almost sexy, but not quite. It came as no surprise to him; senior female officers often worked on the tone of their voice, so that it became richer and stronger, more authoritative.

'Ma'am.' Under the street light, he noticed that her skirt wasn't black, but a deep blue – the same colour as her eyes.

She looked round. 'It's very quiet here. I expected it to be buzzing with press.'

'I told Martin to report in from over there, ma'am.' He nodded in the direction of the telephone box. 'They won't have picked it up yet.'

She glanced towards the alley. 'You found the body, I under-stand?'

'No, not exactly. PC Martin found her. I drove up with my wife shortly afterwards. He told me where she was; I went to have a look. This is his first body and he's still a bit shaken, but he's done well.'

'I'll have a word with him later. Show me the girl.'

Handford led the way to the bank of leaking bin liners. Her body was as he had first seen it – twisted into the rubbish, the dingy rag spilling from her mouth. The doctor was working in the light of the dirt-splattered bulbs on the wall of the nightclub, topped up by the beam from a uniformed officer's torch.

As they approached, the doctor, a stocky man in his mid to late fifties, looked down. He straightened and raised his eyebrows, which were long and narrow and perched high above his eyes, giving him an air of perpetual surprise. 'Here we are again, Mrs Forrester.'

She tilted her head towards him. 'Are we, Doctor Jessop? Here again?'

'Oh, yes, I think so, Chief Superintendent, same injuries, same signature, similar crime scene.' He frowned. 'I just wish he'd choose to deposit them in a place more conducive to a man of my advancing years. I'm too old to go mountaineering over garbage sacks.'

She ignored the comment. 'How long has she been dead?'

'Not long, I shouldn't think. Probably no more than two or three hours.'

The rounded figure of DI Noble approached. 'It looks as though she was killed at the bottom of the alley,' he said, 'then deposited up here at the bins. There's evidence of both blood spots and drag marks.' His expression was serious. 'He's nothing if not consistent.'

Handford looked again at the victim. She couldn't be more than fifteen. About the same age as his eldest daughter, Nicola. When the killings had begun he had warned both her and Clare to stay with their friends and not to walk home alone. Either he or their mother would always pick them up. Nicola had mimicked him: 'And don't talk to strangers.' She was a good mimic and they'd laughed. But looking down on this girl now, he feared for them. No one seemed to know whether the man was an opportunist killer or a stalker, whether the victims had been in the wrong place at the wrong time, or whether they'd been befriended by him until they trusted him. Either way he was a threat to all young girls until he was caught.

Forrester turned to Noble. 'There's nothing much we can do here at the moment,' she said. 'Tent her body and tell the duty inspector to make sure the scene is secured overnight, two officers at each end of the alley. The operational support unit can begin house to house first thing and then when the scientists have finished they can carry out a fingertip search. I want the bastard this time, Brian.'

'Ma'am.' Brian Noble walked away, his mobile to his ear.

'Superintendent, I think our killer is getting careless.' Dr Jessop was holding up a small blue purse. 'It was in a pocket sewn into her skirt.' He bent down to hand it to her.

Opening it up carefully, she pulled out a small photograph, glanced at it then handed it to Handford. 'Do you know him?'

Black and white, it was slightly larger than that needed for a passport. One of the corners was creased, but apart from that it was in good condition. On the back was scrawled May 1987. Fifteen years ago. The picture itself was a head and shoulders portrait of a man, probably in his early twenties. There was something familiar about him – the rounded face, the straight nose, the cleft chin. But he couldn't quite place him, unless . . .

It couldn't be. It was ridiculous. He had to be wrong. Why should a dead girl have an old photo of . . . ?

He stared at Forrester.

'You know who it is, don't you?' she said.

'Possibly . . .' he faltered. He didn't want to say. 'I can't be certain, ma'am.'

'Who do you think it is?'

He made no reply.

'Inspector?' Her tone was insistent.

Worry lines creased his forehead. 'I've got to be wrong, ma'am, but it looks to me like Stephen Russell.'

'Stephen Russell?'

'My DCI. Crime Manager at Central.'

chapter two

'No, Deepak, please, not him. No, I hate him,' Leah Moorehouse screamed at the man towering over her. She grabbed at him like a child being forced away from its mother for the first time. 'No, Deepak, he's horrible. Please, no.'

Ignoring the fear in the fourteen-year-old's eyes and the tears staining her cheeks, Deepak Azam savaged her hands from him and bulldozed her backwards into the bedroom, slamming the door hard behind her, shutting her and the punter inside. His anger bubbled inside him like a hot spring and he leaned against the jamb. Then suddenly, ferociously, he banged his fist into the wall, denting the stoothing. She'd pay for that, the slag. For a while he remained still, calming himself, then he opened his palm on the crushed notes the punter had given him and began slowly, deliberately, to smooth them out. When they were to his satisfaction, he wrapped them around the wad from his pocket and thrust them back deep inside.

The action soothed him and he pushed himself off the wall to pace the narrow passageway of the flat, kicking open the door of each room as he passed it. The kitchen, where curdled milk stood in a bottle on the draining board, its sourness stinging his senses, the sitting room, with piles of rubbish on the chair and the floor, and the bathroom, where scum furred the washbasin and the toilet – each room was a mess. He'd given her a place to live and this was how she'd repaid him. She was filth. Worth no more than the men who screwed her. He glanced at his watch. They'd been at it only a few minutes. Half an hour the punter was allowed; if he needed longer the price went up.

Noises resonated through the paper-thin walls, a scream, a shout, then a thud as though someone or something had fallen on to the floor.

Then, 'You bitch. I'll teach you for that.'

The sudden sharp sound, a hand slapping against flesh, followed by a scream abruptly stifled into silence.

She was making him fight for it.

More screaming, more shouting, then silence again. Uninterrupted and prolonged this time.

He'd be using his strength now, holding her down, forcing himself on to her. And why not? He'd paid for it; he was entitled. In the end she'd give in. She still had spirit, he'd give her that. Spirit was good when she was out on the streets once she was sixteen, but not now. Now fear had to overwhelm spirit. Not fear of the punters, of the men who paid him money for her, but of Azam himself, of what he would do if she disobeyed him. And tonight she'd be getting the message once and for all. As soon as the punter left, he'd remind her of the consequences of not doing as she was told, give her a warning souvenir and tell her to expect him back tomorrow. Then he'd lock her in and let her sweat it out overnight. By morning she'd be so terrified, she'd show him the respect and obedience he demanded.

His watch read another twenty minutes left. God, he hated it here. The squalor, the musty smell of the damp, which seeped through the walls and the roof, and the boredom while the punter finished.

Restlessly, he paced the passage. He wished he could wait outside in the car, but he couldn't be sure who was watching. The police possibly, although they were easy to dislodge. Slap a complaint of racial harassment on them and they scuttled back to their lair like frightened animals. It was his rivals who worried him. He knew they were keeping an eye on him, looking to find out where he was working the kids. That's why he didn't come here too often, or to any of the other flats he had dotted round the city, but sent Varley or one of the others to let the men in and take the money. He'd built up a good company of women, with a useful sideline in girls, and he wasn't prepared for other pimps to take him out of the picture so that they could split his workforce between them. They were like lurking predators; he had to be permanently vigilant, could never let down his guard. They lived on their greed and their jealousy and were too stupid to realise they couldn't do what he did. Not one of them had the resources to groom girl after girl into prostitution. It took time and money. At best they ran two or three women each, five at the most and then only because of their muscle. Brains didn't come into it. The difference between him and them was that they were pimps and he was a businessman – he bought and sold. The commodity was immaterial. All he required of it was that it made him money.

That the girls were trash was unimportant too. They were no more than a product of the system that spawned them and of white parents who preferred their cigarettes, their nightly visits to the pub and their own enjoyment, to their children. By the time he got to the daughters, they were either runaways or had been dumped in children's homes. But carefully groomed, they were slaves to their vulnerability, and that was what he worked on, refashioning it into what they saw as his love for them and their love for him. Once that happened they were his – totally. Pick them up at twelve or thirteen, work on them and they'd give him a good twenty to thirty years of income – providing the heroin didn't get them first. Or the Trash Bag Killer.

The Trash Bag Killer had depleted his stock of young girls by three in the past few months and, thanks to him and the four he would lose to the streets once they reached sixteen, he was having to replenish quickly. Empty rooms earned nothing. So spirit or no spirit, Leah Moorehouse had to start working from Alice's tomorrow; he'd leave it to her to tame the kid.

The numbers on the dashboard clock clicked on to midnight as Susan Forrester and Brian Noble pulled up outside DCI Russell's home and climbed out of the car, disturbing the dust under their feet. Noble wiped the sweat off his face and gazed around. 'Look's like they're having a party,' he said.

Several vehicles were parked in the lane, and more stood alongside the curved lawns beyond the wrought iron gates, which closed the property off from the public. A series of lamps lit up the detached house and its garden, their poles intricately fashioned to match the scrolling on the gates. More lights illuminated the sky behind the house. Music penetrated the night air and the sound of conversation and laughter floated towards them.

Wonderful! Waking them up would have been bad enough, but gate-crashing a party! Forrester sighed. It made no difference. The ACC, James Sanderson, had agreed that she couldn't ignore the possible significance of the photograph found in the dead girl's purse, and if the man in it was Russell, then he had to be questioned now, tonight. It couldn't be left until the morning just because he was entertaining; by then, he might have been made aware of what was happening. She'd warned DI Handford not to contact him, but she couldn't be a hundred per cent sure he wouldn't. Russell was his DCI and there had to be at least a hint of loyalty between them.

'Come on, let's break it up,' she said.

They followed the drive to the rear of the house, the loose gravel crunching as it shifted under their shoes. Narrowing into a pathway as it skirted the side of the building, it finally opened onto a garden where some twenty or so people were standing chattering and laughing or relaxing on loungers. Away from the lamps surrounding the patio and the lawns, the remaining garden yielded to the darkness of the night. To the right, decorative iron tables held half-empty bottles, glasses and plates coated with the remains of the evening's buffet, and smaller tables and chairs were scattered around the grounds. The perfume from the roses caught at Forrester's senses, and she stood enjoying it for a moment.

A slim blonde was the first to notice them. She spoke briefly to the man with her, placed her glass on one of the tables and walked towards them, her welcoming smile barely disguising the air of puzzlement. 'Can I help you?' she asked. The fragrance of an expensive perfume hovered round her, combining with that of the flowers.

Forrester held up her warrant card. 'I'm Detective Chief Superintendent Forrester and this is Detective Inspector Noble. I'm sorry to come unannounced, but I need a word with DCI Russell.'

The woman held out her hand. 'I'm Natasha Russell, his wife. We do have guests, Detective Chief Superintendent, is it vital you talk to him now? Can't it wait?'

'No, Mrs Russell,' said Forrester, shaking her hand. 'I'm afraid it can't. If you would fetch him, please.'

Forrester's eyes followed her as she approached a group of drinkers deep in conversation. There was a sudden roar of laughter. Natasha Russell whispered in the ear of one of the men and pointed in the direction of the detectives. He placed his glass carefully on a nearby table and walked towards them. There was no doubt as to who it was. He was smaller than Forrester expected, but although he was older and his hair was beginning to recede at the temples, there was the same straight nose and cleft chin and a whisper of the same youthful looks of the man in the photograph.

'You wanted a word, ma'am?' Stephen Russell seemed more perplexed than concerned.

'Is there somewhere we could go that is more private than out here?'

His brow furrowed as the bewilderment bit deeper. 'Yes, come into the house.' If he was playing a part, it was a good one.

Russell led them along a path towards the open French windows and into the large lounge. The room was as immaculate as the man in front of them. Decorated in peach and cream it was furnished with two four-seater settees, a couple of easy chairs, several occasional tables and a state-of-the-art television and music centre. Forrester glanced down at her shoes, which had clambered over filthy bin liners and walked up a dusty lane, and hoped she would leave no speck of dirt on the pastel carpet.

'Please,' Russell said, indicating they should sit down. She attempted not to sink into the large cushions and Noble perched rather than sat. Russell, on the other hand, settled himself in the corner of the settee.

'How can I help, ma'am?'

Noble opened his notebook as Forrester pulled a small plastic wallet out of her folder and passed it over to Russell. 'Do you recognise this at all?' With anyone else, she would have played it by the book and started with his movements during the evening, keeping him waiting for the real reason for her visit. But she wanted to gauge his reaction before he had time to settle himself into the routine.

Russell took it from her and for a moment stared at the photograph it contained. 'Where on earth did you get this?' he asked, lifting his eyes and looking from Forrester to Noble and back to Forrester. Puzzlement rather than concern blanketed his face.

'You recognise it?' Forrester asked quietly.

'Yes, it's one of me.' He shook his head in bewilderment. 'It must have been taken fifteen years ago when I was at university or just after. Where did you get it?'

'It was in a purse belonging to a young girl.'

'A young girl? Who?'

'That was what I was hoping you could tell me. Her body was found in an alley about an hour and a half ago. According to the doctor she'd been dead for no more than a couple of hours at the most.'

He paled significantly as bewilderment remodelled into horror. 'A *dead* girl?' He was silent for a moment while he took in the information. Then, 'I don't understand. How did a dead girl come to have my photograph?'

'Again, Chief Inspector, that's what we were hoping you would tell us.'

'Well, I can't, ma'am, I have no idea.'

Forrester nodded and waited.

'You said she was found in an alleyway. Where exactly?'

Was the location important to him? 'On Empire Way,' she said in answer to his question. 'It runs behind a couple of restaurants and a nightclub a little higher up from the Alhambra theatre.'

For a moment he seemed even more unsettled. 'How did she die?' The tone of the question suggested he already knew the answer.

'She was murdered.'

His voice coiled into a tight ball. 'Is she . . . ?'

He didn't need to complete his question, she knew exactly what he was asking. 'Yes,' she said. 'She's the fourth.'

No one said anything and Forrester allowed the silence to deepen for a while.

Noble broke it. 'She was also carrying this.' He handed Russell the plastic wallet containing the newspaper cutting. 'It's a review of the street robbery initiative you instigated, from yesterday's edition of the local paper, I believe.'

Russell nodded. 'Yes,' he said flatly, and gazed into the distance, almost as though he had detached himself from the conversation.

Forrester leaned forward. 'The question uppermost in my mind, Chief Inspector, is why a girl of no more than fourteen or fifteen should be carrying around information about you and why she should keep it hidden in a pocket in the underside of her skirt. Can you suggest why she should?'

Whatever blood was left drained from Russell's cheeks. She guessed by now he was feeling sick. She was being hard, she knew, but police officers were difficult to break. He sat forward, rested his elbows on his knees and clasped his hands together tightly, the skin over his knuckles stretching white. 'No, ma'am, I can't,' he said quietly. Then he sat up and faced her, fixing her with a cool assessing stare. 'Can I ask you a question?'

'Of course.'

'We've never met. Who told you the photograph was of me?'

For a moment she prevaricated. 'We had the newspaper cutting.' And as he continued to stare at her, she said, 'Detective Inspector Handford was the first senior officer on scene. He thought he recognised the man in it as you.'

Russell's eyes narrowed. 'John Handford?' His voice flaked with anger.

'He didn't have a choice, Chief Inspector.' Forrester was on the defensive. 'The photograph was in the possession of a murder victim. What would you expect him to have done?' Her voice was cold.

He made no answer.

Abruptly, she changed her line of questioning. 'Where have you been this evening, Mr Russell?'

He stared first at one and then the other as if he didn't quite understand, then he flicked his tongue over his lips, a visible sign of the stress he was under. His voice, however, remained calm. 'I beg your pardon?'

'It's a simple enough question, Mr Russell. I want to know your movements this evening.'

'Why?' He was not making it easy for her.

She sighed. 'Just tell me.'

His eyes darted from side to side, fearful, and for a second or two he hesitated, as though he were trying to recall what he had been doing. 'I left work about nine . . .'

'Nine o'clock. Do you normally work so late?'

Again, he moistened his lips. 'Not usually, but I had to catch up with some paperwork.'

'You're based at Central, I believe?'

'Yes, ma'am, I'm Crime Manager.'

Forrester returned to the original line of questioning. 'Did anyone see you leave?'

'I don't know; I don't think so.' He paused, then added, 'The desk sergeant, perhaps.'

'Then what?'

'I drove home. We have guests as you can see and I was late as it was.'

'What time did you get back?'

'Half past nine, give or take a minute or two. The traffic is very light at that time of night.'

'And your wife can verify that?'

'Yes, and half the guests. As I said, I was late so I came directly into the garden to apologise before I showered and changed.'

'You're telling me that even though you were expecting guests, you remained at work?'

Once more the hesitation, slight, but perceptible. 'I needed to finish a report; it took longer than I expected,' he said.

'On a night when you had guests, you stayed behind to finish a report?' The tone of her voice suggested surprise.

'Yes.'

'What did your wife think about that?' Forrester was interested.

'She was furious.'

'I should think she was.'

Russell let his eyes drop away.

'Do you use prostitutes, Chief Inspector?'

He reeled as the unexpectedness of the question hit him, but just as quickly spooled back his composure. His eyes met hers, in them a mixture of resentment and contempt, and when he spoke, his voice was like steel. 'The answer to your question is no, ma'am, I do not use prostitutes.' Suddenly, as if it was the only way to contain his anger, Russell stood up, walked to the back of the settee then spun round to face her.

She looked up at him. 'Please sit down, Mr Russell.'

Russell remained quite still.

'Chief Inspector, sit down.' This time it was an order.

Hostility replaced outrage. 'No, Mrs Forrester, I will not sit down,' he said, his voice quiet and restrained. Placing his hands on the top edge of the settee, he leaned forward and let his eyes bore into hers, silent for a moment as he attempted to gain the upper hand. It was a trick they all knew, but a trick, she had to concede, he played with artistry. When he did speak, his words were carefully paced, his emotions controlled.

'You come to my house after midnight, you break up my party, you show me a fifteen-year-old photograph of myself and ask me about my movements this evening, and in so doing intimate that somehow I am involved in the death of a young girl. Then you ask me if I use prostitutes. I understand your reasons, ma'am, but I am not in an interview room, I am in my house and so are you, and I would be obliged if you would remember that and treat me with some respect.'

Silence hung between the three police officers, tangible; had Forrester stretched out she could have touched it. Russell was nobody's fool, he knew how it worked. He knew that when police officers were questioned, they were presumed guilty, never innocent. Their innocence came with proof. It probably had something to do with the service being seen to be impartial, not closing ranks, or perhaps with the knowledge that the officer could understand and play the game as well as the investigator. They couldn't be easily duped, because they knew how to dupe.

But a stand-off wasn't what she wanted and she glanced over at Noble who pushed himself out of his chair to stand next to Russell. 'Sir. Please,' he said.

The atmosphere lightened and Noble raised his eyebrows at his boss.

Forrester took the hint. 'Please sit down, Mr Russell,' she said. 'I do understand how you feel; this is hard for us all.' She waited while he returned to his seat in the corner of the settee. Eventually he looked up at her.

As her eyes met his, she said, her tone more sympathetic, 'If the girl is a victim of the serial killer, then it is likely she was a prostitute. If she was, I must ask myself, Mr Russell, why a young prostitute would have your picture? And unless you tell me differently, the only reason I can come up with is that you are one of her clients.'

At half past two that morning James Sanderson gave Forrester permission to research the background of Detective Chief Inspector Stephen Russell.

'Specific boundaries only,' he said. 'Personnel records, telephone and mobile records. No bank details, no questioning colleagues, relatives or friends. And let's keep it in-house; I don't want the press getting hold of it. We've too many allegations of corruption in West Yorkshire at the moment as it is, what with a superintendent facing charges of perverting the course of justice and a PC on an assault charge, not to mention the sex discrimination case we've just lost. Get someone on your team to do it. Who can you trust not to gossip? What about the fellow you were telling me about – Handford?'

Forrester didn't think so. 'He's not on my team, sir, and anyway he's only a DI.'

'You don't think he'd be up to it?'

'Oh, I'm sure he would, but it would be unusual and not fair on him. Russell is his DCI.'

'Possibly, but it seems to me he's everything he should be, experienced, discreet, sensible. He recognised the chief inspector from the photograph and he told you. He didn't keep anything back, nor did he warn him. Look, Forrester, I don't want to get someone in from another force, not for the moment at any rate. As I said, I'd rather play it low-key.'

'Even so, sir, an officer of lower rank investigating his senior; Mr Russell would be well within his rights to object.'

It was very late and James Sanderson's peppery nature surfaced. His voice rasped down the phone line. 'I wasn't thinking of asking his permission,' he said tersely. 'This is the first break you've had in four months, Susan; I would have thought, if you want to stay on the case, you'd grasp at anything. *I* don't like the idea that one of ours could be involved, but involved he might well be, and we need to know by how much. A senior officer a serial killer? God forbid. Can you imagine what the media will make of that? For goodness' sake, let's prove something one way or the other and soon. Give the initial research to Handford. If it gets too heavy, we'll pass it on. Tell him that, and at the same time tell him I'll see him in my office at noon.'

Stephen Russell made love to his wife that night. It was the first time since she had come out of hospital some eight weeks ago, when the ectopic pregnancy had stolen from them the chance of ever having children. She had been in such pain when she had been rushed into A & E, and had been so weak for a long time after the operation, that he'd been satisfied just to have her sleeping next to him. But tonight she wanted him and he needed her. He needed the release that lovemaking would give him. The questions, the lies, the evasions of the truth spun in his brain, mingling with an image of a dead girl and the prostitutes who brought back ghosts from the past – ghosts he thought he had laid to rest when he came up to York-shire. He had a lot to sort out, things that had happened then, things that were happening now, but his brain was saturated and he couldn't think straight. When Natasha had asked him what the chief superintendent had wanted, he'd said it was to do with work – he hadn't elaborated. He wasn't sure she'd believed him, but she didn't push. She was a police officer's wife and knew when not to ask questions.

He kissed her gently at first, then with a desire he couldn't control. Finally, his lips slid from hers and as his tongue traced her body, she arched towards him. They made love cautiously at first, then more passionately, and each time he thrust into her he neutra-lised the questions and the lies, erasing them for a while from his memory. When the orgasm came, his body and the person he had been fifteen years earlier seemed to explode into a myriad of little pieces, and he felt torn apart. He lay on Natasha for a while, exhausted, and she kissed him. Then, in silence, he slipped off her and rolled on to his back. She turned towards him, stretching her arm across his chest. He placed his hand on its warm flesh and lay staring through the darkness to the ceiling.

Gill was still asleep when Handford slipped out of bed at six-thirty the next morning, cursing as he did so the pool of apprehension that had lapped the edges of his mind, spawning a night of unease and misgiving. His dreams, if there were any, were forgotten, but the brightly coloured images of the dead girl and the monochrome pictures of a youthful Detective Chief Inspector Russell, which had floated in on waves of insomnia, were not. Now, fully awake, his consciousness homed in on the modern-day Russell: proud, at times arrogant and always sure of himself. Not the kind to put a foot wrong. But not a man he could say he knew. In fact, he didn't know him at all. When DCS Forrester had asked about him, he'd been unable to answer a single question. How could you work with a man for three years and know absolutely nothing about him?

The truth was he didn't particularly like him. He was so bloody self-assured all the time. He oozed confidence, which Handford felt was misplaced. It wasn't that Russell was a bad police officer, he wasn't. But he was no copper. He lacked practice for one thing, the practice of being out there amongst the villains. Like all fast-tracked officers, he'd spent his career keeping one foot on the accelerator of status and the other on the brake of experience.

Yet, in spite of his feelings towards him, Handford had wanted to warn the man about the photograph and once or twice had been on the verge of picking up the phone. After some deliberation he hadn't, aware that the reason had less to do with his loyalty to either his boss or the service and more to do with his loyalty to his mortgage provider. For a while, he'd talked about it to Gill. He was concerned Forrester would tell Russell who it was who had recognised him, and he knew it wouldn't go down well. Russell would take it as a sign of disloyalty – a personal insult even.

'You didn't have a choice, John. He'll understand that,' Gill had said.

Will he? Handford wasn't so sure. He shuffled into the bathroom. Even at this early hour the atmosphere in the house was tropical and both his stomach and his head were still feeling the effects of the anniversary champagne the two of them had drunk in bed last night. Turning on the shower, he stepped under the cool shards of water and soaped his body and hair with his large hands. The bubbles ran off him to gather at the drain where they challenged each other for the right to be first to disappear into the watery darkness. As he watched, Handford imagined them metaphorically washing away Russell's career. For unless he'd had a very good explanation, they would consider him a suspect, suspend him, question him formally, research his background.

Everyone had something to hide, even Russell, and as likely as not they would find it.

He shivered as the last droplets of water from the shower pinched at his flesh, and stepped out of the cubicle to wrap himself in his towelling robe and shave before returning to the bedroom. Gill was still sleeping soundly. He glanced at her, her head deep in the pillow, nomadic wisps of brown hair straying over her cheeks, and he wanted to make love to her again as he had last night, but it wouldn't be fair to wake her. She was on holiday from school and enjoying the freedom of sleeping on. So he dressed, stooped to give her a kiss and tiptoed downstairs.

In spite of the early hour, the sun shone through the kitchen window, its rays forming pockets of light on the work surfaces and the floor. The blue of the sky contrasted sharply against the green-leafed horse chestnut trees, which formed a barrier between the grounds of the local comprehensive and their garden.

Nicola was feeding the cats. Brighouse and Rastrick, named after Handford's favourite brass band, had their own method of bullying humans and the first person down in a morning was obliged to make sure their needs were met. As Handford entered the kitchen, Brighouse padded towards him to snake himself round his legs, uttering a silent miaou as he did so. He bent down to stroke the cat. 'I'm sure she's doing her best,' he told the animal. Turning to Nicola, he said, 'You're up early, darling, can't you sleep?' He thought she looked pale, but it could have been the early morning light in the kitchen

She bent down to put the dishes in their appointed places and walked over to the table to pick up a mug. 'No,' she said shortly. Then, 'The tea's still warm if you want some. Or I'll make you coffee if you'd rather.'

'No, tea's fine.' Handford unhooked a mug from the wooden tree and filled it from the pot. He poured in some milk and stirred. 'I'm going to make toast, do you want some?'

'No, thanks, Dad. I'm not hungry.'

She rested against the work surface, sipping her tea and watching the cats devour their food. Handford opened the bread bin, took out a couple of slices of bread, dropped them in the toaster and slid down the handle.

Once the cats had licked away every last morsel, they wandered over to the door to be let out. Nicola opened it for them, bending down to give each one a final stroke before they sauntered across the lawn to the shade of the trees where they would spend most of the day sleeping. Handford's eyes followed her, observing every movement. Where had fifteen years gone? It didn't seem two minutes since he had first held her in his arms, and now look at her – almost a young woman. She took after Gill, petite, attractive with dark curly hair and large brown eyes. The too-short night-gown she was wearing clung to the contours of her youthful body, defining her shape, but her facial features still held traces of the immaturity that belongs to childhood. Not yet a woman, but no longer a child, he wondered if she was aware of her vulnerability.

The toast popped up from the toaster and Handford spread the slices liberally with butter. 'Are you sure you don't want one?'

She shook her head. Then, 'Why do people commit suicide, Dad?' The question wasn't unexpected. The boy found hanging a few days previously had been a student at her school.

'I suppose things get too much for them and they see it as the only way out.' He took a bite of his toast, then asked, 'Did you know him well?'

'Not really. He was older than me, though I've seen him around.' She paused. 'Do you think he would suffer, hanging himself like that?'

Probably, thought Handford, but he said, 'I shouldn't think so.'

'You saw him, didn't you?'

'Yes, I went with Sergeant Ali.' He didn't want to say any more, to describe the scene, the boy, his distraught mother.

Handford changed the subject. 'How's Vishnu?' Vishnu Akram was Nicola's current boyfriend.

'Fine.'

He wanted to tell her not to get too involved with him because his future would already be mapped out and it wouldn't include her, but instead asked, 'Seeing him today?'

'Probably.' Concern clouded her features.

'What's wrong, love?'

When she didn't answer, he said, 'Come on, I've been your father for long enough to know when something's worrying you. Is it Vishnu?'

Nicola turned to the sink where she splashed water around her mug before placing it upside down in the drainer.

'Nicola?'

For a moment she seemed to freeze.

'Come on, love, it can't be that bad. And it takes an awful lot to shock me nowadays.'

A moment's hesitation, then she said, 'Why did Michael do it?'

That wasn't it. He had asked enough questions of enough people, seen enough vacillation over the years to know prevarication when he saw it. And Nicola was prevaricating. Michael's death had given her a route out from what it was that was troubling her. He allowed her her route.

'I don't know, Nicola. Exam pressure perhaps.'

'No, he doesn't do A-levels till next year. And anyway he was bright, everyone knew that. He'd have sailed through his exams.'

'Then there must have been something else. Whatever it was, he obviously didn't feel he could talk to his parents about it.' He planted a kiss on her forehead, then placing his hands on her shoulders he held her at arm's length and looked into her eyes. 'But as far as you're concerned, Nicola, nothing,' he emphasised the word as he repeated it, '*nothing* is that bad that you can't talk to your mother and me about it. Right?'

She nodded, but avoided his eyes. He wondered if she believed him.

He pulled her towards him, gave her another kiss and glanced at his watch. 'Now, I must go.' He smiled at her. 'Reports to write, villains to catch, and,' he scrunched his nose, 'Mr Russell to face.'

For the first time that morning Nicola chuckled. 'Oh, come on, Dad. Mr Russell's all right. In fact I quite like him, and I bet the WPCs think he's really cool. You're just jealous.'

Handford felt his heart sink and his mouth go dry as he said, 'I'm sure you're right, Nicola. I'm just jealous.'

chapter three

The roads were quiet early in the morning and Handford drove over the tops to savour the sight of the hillsides bathed in sunshine. He loved the scenery here, the ruggedness, the wildness, the Dales where the roads twisted and turned, rose high above sea level, then fell steeply into picturesque villages. He wouldn't want to live anywhere else. It was just a pity the accent was such a giveaway, particularly when he was with the likes of Russell with an attitude and a voice that oozed culture. Then his inferiority complex came into play and he turned into the archetypal northern plod.

He loaded a cassette into the player and let the sounds of the Brighouse and Rastrick Brass Band fill the car. He had been a member of a brass band himself before the police service had taken away his spare time, but occasionally he pulled out his trumpet or his saxophone and played for his own pleasure. He was a bit rusty, and he wasn't sure how much the neighbours appreciated it, but he'd managed a tune at the police Christmas party, with Sergeant Ali accompanying him on the piano. It had gone down well, and they'd both enjoyed it.

As he drove he tapped his fingers on the steering wheel in time to 'The Floral Dance' followed by 'The Knightsbridge March'. One day he would splash out and have a CD fitted and extra speakers maybe, let the music fully surround him. But even as a tape, it did him good, pushed the worrying niggles about Nicola to the back of his mind. It was probably nothing – a mixture of being fifteen years old and having boyfriend problems. Such things don't sit easily on a teenager. She would talk about it sooner or later, of that he was sure, or it would work itself out and she wouldn't need to say anything.

As the music slipped into the background, his mind wandered from his daughter to the girl last night. Judging by the large wound on her head, it was a cruel blow that killed her. She must have gone through hell when she realised the weapon was smashing down towards her. There were rumours that he beat his victims before he killed them and Handford couldn't begin to imagine the pain and the fear the youngster had suffered before she died. Nor could he imagine who would do something like that. What had happened in the man's life that had turned him into a killer of young girls? And how did he persuade them into a situation where he could strike without being seen or heard? Didn't they scream? Or try to run? Or was it so quick, so unexpected that they didn't have time?

For once, he was thankful it wasn't his problem. Detectives looked forward to being chosen for a murder investigation such as this, but this time he was relieved his only input was being there when the body was found. Once he'd handed his statement to DCS Forrester, he would be glad to be out of it. As it was, if Russell hadn't been suspended, he'd have a sticky time explaining why he'd appraised the DCS of the identity of the man in the photograph and why he hadn't at least warned him they were coming to question him. If he had been suspended, it would be up to him to keep the team together until a locum DCI was appointed. Either way he had the feeling it was going to be a difficult day.

The tape ended as he drove into Central's underground parking area. The artificial lighting contrasted sharply with the sun's brightness and he slowed to allow his eyes time to adjust. In one of the alcoves in front of him he saw Russell's car and his heart missed a beat. Whatever the outcome of last night's interview, Handford was going to have to face him this morning. As he climbed out of his own car, the cold subterranean air struck at his flesh and he shivered. Praying he wouldn't bump into the DCI, he climbed the four flights to his office. He'd write his statement for Forrester, then see Russell before the day began in earnest.

He was putting the finishing touches to the statement when a knock on the door roused him and a voice said, 'Can I have a word, boss?'

Handford beckoned Detective Sergeant Ali into the room. 'What's the matter, Khalid?' he said. 'Couldn't you sleep?'

'Too hot.'

'Even for you?'

Ali grinned. 'Yes, John, even for me.'

The smile was infectious and Handford returned it. Their relationship had changed since their first encounter late last year, which could only be described as stormy. Both men had felt insecure in each other's company, but professionalism – and Russell – had required them to tolerate one another, until, as the case they were working on progressed, toleration remodelled itself into a mutual, although sometimes uneasy, respect. For a moment Handford's eyes skimmed his partner. A couple of inches taller and considerably slimmer, Ali was younger and less careworn than his boss. His long, thin face bordered on handsome and today there was a glint of excitement in his deep brown eyes.

Handford had seen that look of animation before. Sliding the statement into a folder, he looked up. 'Come on then, Sergeant,' he said, 'I can see you're dying to tell me something, what is it?'

Ali sat down and pulled some papers from the file he was carrying. 'I didn't want to bother you on your wedding anniversary, but the post-mortem report on Michael Braintree came in yesterday afternoon. It's not suicide, it's murder. He was killed by a blow to the Adam's apple. He died of,' Ali turned the pages, 'vagal inhibition.'

His concerns about Russell relegated to the back of his mind, Handford rested against the chair. 'Vagal inhibition, what's that?'

Ali flicked through his notebook, scanning the information. 'According to the pathologist, he found evidence to suggest compression of the vagus nerve. It runs alongside the jugular vein in the neck and controls the slowing down of the heart. When the neck is compressed by something like a karate blow, it can cause stimulation of the nerve and the heart will stop. He said this is one of the silent kill methods taught to troops training in unarmed combat.'

'And he thinks that's what killed him?'

'More than likely.'

'And the hanging?'

'Well, the bruising from the rope suggests he was strung up almost immediately and the whole thing made to look like suicide.'

'So, we're looking for at least two people because it would need two to string up the body, and one or both of them has to be an expert in unarmed combat. I don't suppose it could have been an accident?'

'Not according to the pathologist.'

'Right. So someone from the army perhaps?'

'Or someone trained in martial arts. Anyone with that kind of training should be perfectly capable of doing it.'

Handford sighed. 'At a guess, Khalid, how many martial arts

clubs would you say we have in this city?' It was always the same; most investigations were nothing more than well-ordered, boring slog, looking for tiny clues in a morass of questions and answers in the hope that when cross-matched one or more of them might throw up a link with Michael Braintree.

'Seven. We're already on to it. Clarke visited two yesterday and got a list of members. We'll do the other five today. And we're also trying to find out how many soldiers with this training have left the army recently and live here or are on leave in this area.' He grimaced. 'I've got to say that needle and haystack are words that spring to mind with this one. Honestly, John, when I get a job like this, I wonder if I shouldn't have gone along with my father's wishes and remained a solicitor.'

Handford made no comment. He knew how hard it had been for Ali to shatter his father's dreams of his son making a career in law. Instead he said, 'Anything on Braintree's mobile yet?'

'No, guv, it'll be a couple of days. We could ask the lab to hurry it up if you like.'

'And double their bill? I don't think so. We'll wait.'

Handford glanced at his watch, picked up his statement, then pushed his chair back. 'Have his parents been told?'

'No, not yet.'

'They'll need questioning; you and I can do that this morning. We'll have a briefing first, get everyone up to speed. Organise it, will you?'

'Already done. Nine-thirty, after your meeting with Mr Russell.'

Handford's stomach churned. 'You've seen him?' He tried to sound casual.

'Yes, he was here when I arrived. He's been asking for you. Wants to see you as soon as you get in, he said. Seemed a bit on edge. Has something happened, John, anything I should know about?'

Handford walked over to the window and looked down to the square and towards the magistrates' court. Nothing was happening there yet, but in a couple of hours the place would be swarming as defendants, witnesses and victims passed through the doors or stood on the steps, smoking a last cigarette. The sun rising behind City Hall threw the square into partial shadow and, beneath him, Handford could see the remnants of the night before – the fish and chip papers floating in the fountains and the Styrofoam cartons dropped at the spot where the meal had been eaten. A few people were scurrying for their buses, but apart from them the day had hardly begun.

Except in his office.

He turned towards his sergeant. Should he tell him everything or nothing? For the moment he decided on the bare minimum.

'I don't know,' he said. 'Depends why he wants me. There was another serial killing last night and I was first senior officer there, so it might be about that. I'll tell you later.' He stepped towards the door and grasped the handle.

The sergeant persisted. 'I thought it was your wedding anniversary. How did you manage to come across a body?'

Hanford told him about the meeting with Martin. 'It was nothing. I waited until the SIO arrived and then I went home.'

Ali refused to let it drop. 'So why do you think the DCI wants to see you about that? They've not seconded you on to the team, have they?'

'No, Khalid, they haven't. Just leave it, will you?' He hadn't intended to be so curt. After a moment, he said more calmly, 'Look, I've got to go, I need to take my statement to the SIO. Do me a favour, will you? If Mr Russell asks again, say I'm not in yet.'

Leah cowered, her arms covering her head, waiting for the blows to stop raining down. She'd done wrong, she knew it; she'd not wanted sex with the man Deepak had shown into the room. She'd tried to get away from him, had pushed at him and fought with him, so that at one point he'd crashed onto the floor, but there had been so little space and in the end she'd had to give in and let him lay on top of her, penetrate her and thrust into her.

He'd been vile, sweaty, smelly. His belly had hung over his trousers, and when he'd unfastened his belt it had spilled out and the smell had become worse. His breath had rattled in his throat and then come in gasps with the effort of the sex, and at each gasp its foulness had made her feel sick. When he'd finished he'd rolled off her, complained that he'd paid too much to have to fight for it. Then he'd pulled off the condom and flung it at her, after which he'd dressed and left, leaving her clutching at the sheet, trying to control the retching.

For a moment or two, angry voices had filtered through the door. Then silence until Deepak had stormed into the room and punched her hard in the belly, leaving her doubled in pain. Then nothing, except for the click of the key turning in the lock. She had pulled at the door, cried and screamed to be let out, to go to the toilet, anything to give her the opportunity to explain. But she'd been left there, lying in his filth and eventually in her own, until morning.

She wasn't sure what time it was when she'd heard the key turn again and waited for the door to open. As it did so, the sun from the landing window streamed round the figure in the entrance. Deepak's shadow preceded him, growing longer with each step, until suddenly he was there, a thin, angular silhouette looking down on her.

'What the fuck do you think you were doing?' He yanked her upwards, pulling her towards him, then slapped her hard across the face. Usually he tried to avoid the face so that she didn't show bruises, but this time he didn't seem to care.

'He likes little girls,' he snarled. 'He likes you. He paid good money for you. Last night you didn't please him and he wanted it back. I had to promise him a freebie to calm him down.' He lifted his hand and hit her hard, each word heralding a blow more powerful than the last. 'I don't like losing money. Do you understand?'

She could taste blood in her mouth, could feel the skin on her face tightening as it swelled. Finally the punishment stopped and she pushed herself backwards with her heels until she felt the coolness of the wall through her T-shirt.

Deepak stood up, breathing heavily from the exertion. 'You're out of here,' he said, pointing at her with his finger.

She changed position and crawled towards him. 'No, Deepak. Please, no. It won't happen again. Don't send me away. I'll be a good girl.'

He took a step forward and bent over her, grabbing a fistful of hair in his hand, pulling her face up to his. 'You're bloody right you'll be a good girl; you're going to Alice's. She'll teach you to be a good girl, and if you don't want to be out on the streets, you'll learn. And until then there's no more of this.' He waved a wrap of heroin in front of her. She stretched up to the package, but as her fingers made contact, he snatched it away.

His eyes spewed venom. That look had never been directed at her before. She'd seen it aimed at the other girls who'd hung around him, trying to gain his attention; but she'd known they were wasting their time. It was her he loved, not them. Hadn't he given her his ring? His measure of commitment to her, his love for her. He didn't mean it now either, not really; it was just that she'd been a bad girl.

He dropped her back onto the mattress, stepped over to the wardrobe and grabbed the handle of the case. It fell heavily onto the bed, catching her on the shoulder.

Ignoring her cry of pain, he wrenched at the sheets under her.

'Wash these, they're bloody filthy,' he barked, 'and when you've done that, get your things together. Varley will drive you over to Alice's, so make sure you're ready. I want you working tonight. Understand?'

He made for the door, but before he opened it, he turned to face her. 'Leave the ring on the bed,' he said. 'I'll give it to someone who deserves it.'

Susan Forrester's finger slapped 'enter' on the computer keyboard and she rotated her chair to face Handford who was sitting opposite her. 'What do you know about this case, Inspector?' She seemed drained, bleached by a weariness that even the carefully applied make-up failed to disguise. He wondered how long she'd been at her desk.

'Not much, ma'am; just what I've read in the papers and what you told me at the scene.'

'And what you've heard in the canteen?'

He didn't answer, and she smiled at him as if she understood his reticence, then she placed her hand on the files in front of her and pushed them towards him. 'The investigation so far,' she said. 'A lot of paperwork for very little progress, I'm afraid.'

Handford frowned. 'I'm sorry, ma'am, I don't understand. Are you seconding me to the murder squad?'

'Not exactly,' she said. 'Look, let me take you through the case and then I'll explain.'

Not exactly. Unease mushroomed inside him. Either he was on the murder squad or he wasn't, and if he wasn't, why was she taking the time to discuss it with him? What was she up to?

Forrester pulled a batch of photographs from her own file and placed them in front of him. There were six in total: two of each victim, one in life, the other post-mortem.

'Until last night, he'd murdered three girls in four months: Beverley Paignton, Janice Thurman and Carla Lang. Beverley and Janice were fifteen-year-old runaways from care and Carla was fourteen and had been missing from home for about six months. According to the pathologist, and from the small amount of information we've been able to glean on them, it's very likely they were working as prostitutes.'

Prostitutes? There'd been no mention of that. An image of Russell and prostitutes blossomed in his mind and he knew he didn't want to hear any more. But the choice wasn't his. Short of getting up and walking out, there was little he could do.

'However,' the DCS was saying, 'if they were working, we have absolutely no idea where. They're not known on the streets, so that means a brothel. And if there is one operating, someone's keeping it very quiet, because it's not known to us. It does mean, however, there'll be more girls around – more potential victims. We think, although we can't prove it, that a man called Deepak Azam might be their pimp. Vice have never been able to pin anything on him and the older women are not talking. To all intents and purposes he runs a successful leisure centre in town. We're keeping an eye on him of course, and on the two bouncers who work for him, Dwayne Varley and Martin Johnson, both known to us.'

Handford nodded. 'Yes, I know Dwayne Varley – a vicious piece of work. Martin Johnson's more into petty theft though. I'm surprised he's taken up with Varley – way out of his league, I would have thought.'

'Unfortunately, we can't pour resources into continuous twenty-four-hour surveillance of them. And if we go too far without more evidence we're likely to have a charge of racial harassment slapped on us by Azam's solicitor. The best we've been able to do is to bring in two officers from the vice squad to investigate the prostitution angle: DS Michelle Archer and DC Chris Warrender.'

Handford didn't know Archer, but he was aware of Warrender, a detective with an unfortunate attitude towards anyone who wasn't white or male and who had once referred to Handford as a duff inspector. He'd probably be in his element on the vice squad.

'So far they've come up with nothing new,' Forrester went on. 'Realistically it doesn't make sense for Azam to be killing these girls. The punters pay well for the young ones. He'd be stealing from his own bank account.'

'I wasn't aware the killings involved prostitution,' Handford ventured. 'There's been nothing in the press.'

'No, and there won't be. We've been ordered to keep it quiet. Officially the city doesn't have child prostitutes.' Her tone was edged with sarcasm. 'The definitive police response is always that there aren't any because if there were we'd know about them. They're not on the streets, therefore they don't exist – and therefore they don't pull on the city's coffers. It's political and it's rubbish and it hinders our investigation. We can't talk to them because we can't find them, so we can't protect them, and since we can't publicise the information either, we can't warn them, and when they're dead it's too late. Even the older women won't help us, probably too afraid of reprisals from their pimp to co-operate, and in all honesty, I can't blame them; retribution is vicious in their world.'

She smiled at Handford. It lit up her face. 'Sorry about the soap box speech,' she said, 'but it makes me so angry. No one seems to care about these young kids, and the powers-that-be have our hands tied so tightly there's very little we can do, short of leaking what we know.' Her eyes held his and the smile played on her lips. 'That's not a hint, John.'

The pleasantry melted as she stood up and walked round the desk to perch on the edge. Dressed in a classically styled light grey suit and azure blouse and her hair arranged in a French pleat, she gave the illusion of being more severe than she had the night before and Handford decided he preferred her hair as it was yesterday, loose around her shoulders. A pleasant, but discreet perfume tempered the air. He recognised it. Gill had worn the same last night, and it had been the last thing his senses had held on to as he drifted into sleep. He recalled it with pleasure, allowing his thoughts to immerse themselves in the memory.

Forrester's words drifted into his thoughts. 'Each girl is killed in the same way, severely beaten with a wooden stick, although we've never been able to find it. Slivers of the same type of wood were found embedded in the wounds; they all had badly bruised backs, Janice and Beverley several broken ribs, and Carla a shattered clavicle. Whoever did this was punishing them quite viciously, probably for their lifestyle. Although how he knows . . .' She shrugged.

Against his better judgement, Handford found his interest growing. 'A punter?'

'Possibly.'

Handford let the information swirl in his brain. 'Do you think we're looking at another Ripper, ma'am?' he asked finally.

'I hope not,' she said with passion. She shifted her position. 'He doesn't mutilate them in the way Peter Sutcliffe did, and it wasn't the beatings that killed them. The final blows were to the head, as you saw last night.'

She slid from the desk and returned to her chair. She seemed on edge, unable to stay in one position for more than a few minutes. He felt sorry for her; she was under a lot of pressure.

'Each girl died close to where she was found, in alleyways, or in the case of Janice Thurman, in the grounds of a warehouse, but their bodies were dragged to the rubbish, where he left them. As far as we can tell, no attempt is made to alter the position in which they land, but before he leaves them he stuffs a piece of rag into their mouths. And that's something we're not giving the press. We don't need copy-cat killings. We don't yet know the significance of the rag, but on each one forensics has found evidence of the dead girl's vaginal fluid. He rapes them after death with some kind of blunt instrument, something similar to the wood type and shape of a gardener's dibble, the pathologist thinks. We think he cleans it after the deed with the cloth he crams in their mouths.'

'God!' Handford couldn't help himself. Sometimes he found it impossible to come to terms with the ways in which people brutalised and violated each other. A straight killing, a gun shot or a stabbing, bad as it was, was just not enough for some.

Forrester sighed. 'Yes, well, I'm not sure just how much God figures in this man's rationale.'

'You've never found the instrument?'

'No. He takes everything away with him; leaves us nothing – except for last night.' She paused. 'Which brings us to DCI Russell.'

Russell. For a few moments he'd forgotten him, and now that he was reminded his stomach began to churn. The computer sizzled as the screen saver came into play. Scrolls pirouetted silently across the screen, transmuting through the various colours, graceful, yet grotesque as they swirled in the blackness, like the tendrils of a sea anemone stirred by the rhythm of the waves. Simple, uncomplicated and far removed from the evil and squalor in which Handford had the uncomfortable feeling he was becoming increasingly embroiled. He swallowed hard. 'You spoke with him, ma'am?'

'Yes, I did. He agreed the photograph was of him, taken while he was at university or just after, but he had no idea why the girl should have it. He gave us an alibi of sorts. We'll check it out of course, but I suspect it's the kind of alibi we can neither prove nor disprove. We need more on him – and this is where you come in. I want you to research his background.'

His head jerked up and his eyes opened wide. So that was it. No wonder she'd said 'not exactly' when he'd asked if she was seconding him to the murder squad. The unease gave way to resentment. Not on the team, just someone to do the dirty work. Whatever he'd expected, it was nothing like this. What she was asking him to do was nauseating – and against the rules. He couldn't believe the matter-of-fact way in which she'd told him.

He wouldn't do it.

'I'm sorry, ma'am, I can't and won't do that; he's my DCI.' He was unable to keep the edge from his voice. 'You have no right to ask me.' He pushed back his chair and walked towards the door.

Forrester's voice iced over, stopping him in his tracks. 'I'm sorry too, Inspector, but you can and you will. And I'm not asking you, I'm telling you. I've spoken to the ACC Crime and he is in complete agreement; in fact, you were his suggestion. Take it up with him if you don't like it. You're to meet him in his office at headquarters at midday today.'

Handford stood, rigid, and there was a moment's uncomfortable silence as he attempted to control his anger. She'd been busy since last night, leaving him with no way out. His hand remained on the door handle, but he didn't attempt to turn it.

Finally, when she spoke, her tone had lost its hard edge. 'Do you know what's the worst thing about all this, John?'

He remained silent.

'It's the parents whose children have disappeared. They ring in, call in person, terrified – or sometimes hoping – that the dead girl is their daughter. Anything to end the nightmare they're going through. They bring photographs, ask to see the body – just to make sure. And for one family that girl could be their daughter, because they've warned us over and over again that they're convinced she has been lured into prostitution. But we're obliged to ignore it and tell them that it can't be so, because there are no child prostitutes in Bradford. Children go missing, parents scream prostitution at us, and we can't go looking because of a policy spawned by money. Try telling that to the Paigntons, the Thurmans and the Langs, John.'

Suddenly, Handford knew he couldn't escape. If he could have pressed the rewind button on life he would have done. Last night, he could have made the other choice and driven on, left Martin where he was, but he couldn't and he hadn't and even though he didn't like it, he was now part of this. He stepped back into the room.

Sensing his acquiescence, Forrester said softly, 'The ACC is right, there is a link between this girl and Mr Russell, and we need to know what it is. Look at the photograph; he must remember it. It's not like any I ever had taken at university, nor you, I suspect.' She was right. Most of his were of groups of friends clinging onto each other, pulling faces at the camera; the only one remotely similar was the official one taken after the degree ceremony.

'This photo is posed,' she continued, 'a head and shoulders picture looking straight forward. It is personal, taken specially.

We need to know for whom. Mr Russell is insisting he has no memory of it, so he's left us no alternative. It's rough, but it has to be done and for you to research his background discreetly will be better than bringing in someone from outside.'

Handford doubted that but didn't argue. Instead he asked, 'Does Mr Russell know that I was the one who identified him?'

Her eyes slipped away from his and for a moment she seemed embarrassed. 'Yes, he does. I'm sorry. He asked who recognised the photo.'

'And you told him?' He wished he could keep the bitterness out of his voice. 'And you're still asking me to research his background? If you don't mind me saying so, ma'am, it stinks.'

Senior officer once again, Susan Forrester held his gaze. 'Yes, it does, but it makes no difference. Look upon it as getting him off the hook if that's easier, whatever, it's not negotiable. Take it up with Mr Sanderson if you want, but so far as I'm concerned, the subject is closed. So, you can begin by telling me what you know about DCI Russell.'

Defeated, Handford sucked in a mouthful of air. 'I don't know anything about him, ma'am. He's not the kind of person to let his DI in, not into his personal life, anyway. He never talks about himself or what he does. As a senior officer he's professional, controlled, good at his job; but as a person, he's always . . .' he searched for the best word '. . . contained.'

Forrester grimaced. 'So is a pressure cooker, John,' she said pointedly. 'Until it needs to let off steam.'

chapter four

Handford marched into his room and slammed the door, his emotions in turmoil. Why, when he'd stood up and made to leave Forrester's office, hadn't he done so? Why had he stopped to listen? He dropped the files on his desk and slumped into his chair. She was good, he'd give her that. She hadn't even alluded to his feelings as a father, yet as she spoke, Nicola and Clare had insinuated themselves into his mind and he'd known he was beaten. The worst possible reason for a detective to get involved. By superimposing the victim on to one of his own, he'd lost his objectivity, the crime became personal and catching the perpetrator an obsession. Finally, she'd brought the parents into the equation, decribed them as fighting an impossible battle against an inanimate policy and immutable politicians and senior police officers. Oh yes, she was good. She had him well and truly hooked.

He ran his hands through his hair, his fingers twitching as they rode his scalp. How did this affect his relationship with Russell? Was he about to become an obsession? The DCS had painted an impassioned picture, but she hadn't suggested how he was going to face him. Presumably that was his problem. She hadn't suspended Russell; instead she'd given Handford this god-awful job and left the man he was screwing in situ, for him to face every time he walked along the corridor. She'd even got the ACC on her side. He'd expected a difficult day, but this was moving way beyond difficult.

He didn't want to research Russell's background, his secret life. He didn't want to know what Russell wouldn't want him to know.

Look upon it as getting him off the hook if that's easier.

He could, but doubted it would be any easier.

He picked up the files and opened the top one. Pictures of Beverley Paignton.

Young. Pretty. Dead.

At fifteen she'd probably had more experience of life than he'd had in all his forty-five years, been hurt more times than he ever had. Physically and mentally. The pimp, the punters, the killer, all moulding her life and her death. Perhaps that was the reason he'd agreed. Perhaps it was that she – and all the others – were outcasts in a city that should have protected them. Where did they fit on the scales of justice, he wondered. Victims or criminals? He knew where he'd put them. Perhaps *that* was why he'd agreed?

He picked up the scene of crime photograph. The rag spilled out of her mouth, the dingy material impregnated with her vaginal fluid. Could he look upon it as getting Russell off the hook? Anyone who could do that to a young girl, prostitute or not, didn't deserve to be 'got off the hook'. He deserved to be pinioned on to it. What if he *had* killed the girl last night? There was nothing to say he hadn't, and a photograph to say he might have. And if he had, he'd also killed the others. The signature said that.

Handford closed the file, unable for the moment to assimilate any more.

'Boss?' Sergeant Ali was standing in the doorway. He hadn't heard him knock or come in. 'We're ready for you,' Ali said. 'The briefing,' he added.

Handford hadn't realised that was the time, he'd been with Forrester longer than he thought. 'Right.'

For a fleeting moment he considered asking Ali to take it, but just as quickly changed his mind. The sergeant was suspicious enough, he didn't want to add to it, so he scooped the folders from his desk and walked over to the filing cabinet. 'I'm coming,' he said.

Ali stepped further into the room. 'Are you all right, John?'

Handford forced a smile. 'Yes, I'm fine. Just give me a minute, will you?'

Ali hovered. 'Are you sure? You don't look too good.'

Handford pulled out the information on Michael Braintree and locked the cabinet. 'For God's sake, Sergeant, I'm fine,' he snapped. 'I said, give me a minute; now will you do that, please?'

The briefing was short. Most of the basic actions had been organised by Ali the previous day. It was more a matter of bringing together what they knew and making suggestions for moving ahead.

Handford gave Ali a fleeting smile, the best he could manage, and asked him to run through the details.

41

'To all intents and purposes,' Ali said, 'Michael Braintree's death was a suicide. He left a note of sorts with a one-word apology, "Sorry", but no indication of why he had decided to kill himself. It was written on a computer, probably his, and printed on an inkjet printer, again probably his. No signature, just the message and only his fingerprints. The scene of crime officer found nothing unusual in the house, no strange prints, no sign of a brawl, and there were no defence wounds on the victim, in fact no suggestion of anything but suicide until the post-mortem.' He explained the findings of the pathologist. 'To be honest, we were just about to throw it back to uniform, when the report came through.'

Listening to the matter-of-fact way in which Ali had spoken had given Handford the opportunity to redress the balance of his emotions, forcing him instead to use his brain and his intellect. He thanked the sergeant and took over. 'As a result we've lost a couple of days, but at least we know we're looking for an expert in martial arts, someone who understands silent kill methods. There can't be that many in Bradford. Our difficulty is that there is little in the way of forensic evidence in the house, yet according to the pathologist he had to have been killed there, because the lividity and the bruising caused by the rope suggests he was hanged immediately afterwards.'

'It's an odd way to dispose of a body,' one of the detectives said. 'Why string him up? Why not dump him?'

'There've been a few lads hanging themselves just recently,' DC Clarke said. 'Just following the trend?'

A trend. A serial killer's trend. Handford pushed the itinerant thought to one side and forced himself to stay focused. 'Could be. Certainly it looks like they intended it that way. They use a silent kill technique, then they hang him with a rope, it's not something you carry in your back pocket, is it? They must have brought it with them, which means they probably had transport. That suggests intent.'

'Family?' Clarke suggested. 'His father owns an outdoor pursuits business – Dale and Fell. He'll stock rope. And I seem to remember reading something about him in the paper when they were doing features on local businessmen. Apparently he was in the army before he set up the first shop. Special forces, I think it said. He would have been trained in silent kill methods.'

'So it could be him, or perhaps it could be that someone wanted to throw suspicion on to him. Check Raymond Braintree out, Clarke, as soon as you can, please.'

'Sir.'

'But why?' Ali questioned. 'Why should anyone, least of all his father, carry out a premeditated murder on a seventeen-year-old like Michael?'

'Why indeed? That's the question we need to be asking,' Handford agreed. 'Premeditation suggests the reason behind Michael's murder must be serious – to someone at least. Something he was in to, something he knew?'

'Drugs?'

'Possibly.'

'Perhaps he threatened to shop a dealer.'

Handford turned to the pictures pinned on the board. A young lad smiled out at him. Dark, handsome, intelligent, with a future in front of him, a future any parent would be proud of. Yet there had to be another side to him. 'It seems to me,' he said, 'the only way we're going to make progress on this is to look at the victim. What is there in Michael's background that would cause someone to want him out of the way? Once we've found that, we may have more of an idea of why, and of who was responsible. So what do we know about him already? He was a student, preparing for A levels next year, wanted to be a doctor. Currently, there's no suggestion he was into drugs, not even socially, or that he went out drinking or spent his nights at raves and parties, but we mustn't rule it out. According to neighbours he was a nice lad who worked hard and generally kept himself to himself. Even my daughter who is at the same school said everyone liked him. Yet somewhere deep down there's something, and we need to find it, which means we'll have to dig until we do. I want everyone questioned who knew him – schoolfriends, teachers, relatives – everyone. And I want house to house. Let's see if someone saw or heard a car or a van outside the Braintrees' at the relevant time. Clarke, I want you to go with Sergeant Ali to question the parents.'

Ali looked up. 'But I thought—'

Handford knew exactly what Ali thought. 'You're with Clarke,' he said, silencing him with a hard stare.

The look of puzzlement on Ali's face didn't fade, but he acquiesced. 'Sir.'

It was a moment before Handford took his eyes off Ali. It wasn't fair, but he didn't want questions here and now. He was aware of the questions, but not of the right answers. And if he gave the answers he had, he didn't feel ready to cope with the arguments that would ensue, arguments for which he had no justifiable response.

The tone of the DI's voice silenced everyone for an instant, a silence that was broken when the door to the incident room opened. Handford looked up. Russell was standing against the back wall, his arms crossed and his eyes firmly on his DI. Even from this distance they were ice-cold blue.

In spite of himself, Handford felt a hot flush begin to bruise his neck and face. 'Sir,' he said, his voice a semitone higher than usual. He cleared his throat. 'Can I help you? Is there something you want to say?' He was babbling, he knew it.

Russell, on the other hand was controlled, contained – like a pressure cooker. 'No, thank you, Inspector. It's you I want to speak to. You've been quite elusive this morning. I thought if I came to the briefing I might stand a chance of catching you before you disappear again.'

Russell's door was ajar when Handford knocked. The smell of fresh coffee from his office penetrated the length of the corridor and Handford's mouth began to water. Even today, it seemed, Russell had kept to his routine of grinding a handful of beans and percolating his own coffee. Handford would have welcomed a cup, but he knew this was not to be a 'have a coffee, John' kind of session.

Russell was standing by the window, gazing out. Without moving, he told Handford to close the door. The office, as always, epitomised his personality. Technical and procedural manuals and carefully labelled box files were arranged neatly in the bookcase behind his desk, to the side, a glass-fronted cabinet held sporting and academic trophies and on the walls in mahogany frames were his degree certificates. The DCI was a lover of flowering and non-flowering houseplants, and had placed them round the room, watering them weekly from a brass watering can. The largest was a weeping fig, which had been nicknamed The Triffid by the less than respectful detectives because of the speed with which it had grown since it had been introduced into the station.

But today plants were the last things on Russell's mind. As Handford walked towards the desk, he swung round to face him. He didn't ask him to sit down. 'Tell me about last night, Inspector.' A simple request, controlled and composed, which cannoned into Handford and hit him full in the stomach.

He explained as calmly as he could how he had come across Martin and the girl's body, had rung in and stayed on the scene until DCS Forrester had arrived.

'I don't suppose you thought to let me know?'

'It wasn't our case, nothing to do with us. I didn't see the need to disturb you. I assumed I would be relieved once Mrs Forrester was on the scene, and that would be the end of it for me. It *was* my day off, after all.' He sighed deeply. 'I was in the wrong place at the wrong time, Stephen. No more than that. And I would much rather I hadn't been.'

But Russell had no interest in Handford's feelings. 'And the photograph? It didn't occur to you to tell me about that either?'

For a moment Handford toyed with the idea of saying he'd tried but couldn't get through, his phone was down – anything to take Russell's eyes from him and the guilt away. But he couldn't do that. Apart from the fact that he'd crucify any of his detectives who did the same, it wouldn't work. Russell would see through him in moments.

He looked away. 'No, I'm sorry. Mrs Forrester ordered me not to have any contact with you.' He'd like to have told him that he'd thought about it more than once, but that would exacerbate the situation, not alleviate it.

The DCI strode round his desk to stand only a pace away from Handford. 'Didn't you make her aware that you're my DI?'

Russell was smaller than Handford, but suddenly his presence seemed to dominate him. 'Of course I did, but not before Mrs Forrester had asked me if I knew the identity of the person in the photograph,' he said. He wanted to move, to expand his personal space. 'I recognised you, she realised I had and—'

'And you saw your chance and told her it was me?'

This wasn't fair. 'It wasn't a question of seeing my chance, Stephen. I had to tell her. The photograph was in a purse belonging to a dead girl.'

'Exactly, Inspector. A *dead* girl. My picture was on the body of a murdered girl, not one who'd been involved in a road traffic accident or who'd died of a drug overdose, but one who'd been murdered. And if I'm not mistaken, by the serial killer.'

Handford made no reply. He wanted to look elsewhere but at Stephen Russell, but the DCI's eyes held his like a vice. 'And I'm not mistaken, Inspector, am I?'

'No, sir, you're not.'

The atmosphere was solid, choked with coffee and mistrust.

Russell took a step backwards, then moved to sit behind his desk. 'So, even though it must have been obvious to you, that I was, at the very least, known to this girl, and possibly even a suspect, you still didn't think to contact me, let me know.'

Handford reiterated. 'I was told not to.'

'And you always do as you're told? I think I can remember times when you've disobeyed my direct orders.' Russell leaned forward. 'I could be a suspect in a murder investigation, Inspector. If the girl last night was a victim of the serial killer then I'm not only a suspect for her death, but for the others. Yes?'

Handford would have loved to have sat down, but it was obvious Russell wanted him in a position of weakness. So he stayed where he was and said, 'Yes, that's a possibility.' He took a deep breath. 'But if you are, Stephen, and I say *if*, then why haven't you been suspended?'

'Because at the moment one photograph is not evidence. But Mrs Forrester is not going to stop there, is she? She's going to research my background – she's probably got someone on to it already . . .'

Handford clung on to all the strength he could muster and prayed his expression gave nothing away.

'She's going to question my wife, my friends, my colleagues, search my house, and God knows what other indignities she's going to put me through. I'm the only suspect she has. Everyone knows that in all the months she's been on the case, she's come up with nothing. But now she has me, and she's going to stick with me and probably make me fit the facts.'

'No, sir, I'm sure you're wrong.' Handford wished he believed it himself.

'Well, she wouldn't be the first, would she? Remember the Ripper tape? They stuck with that through thick and thin, even moved the incident room to the north-east and when they finally caught Sutcliffe, I don't know how many years later, the tape and the Geordie had nothing to do with the killings except as a delaying tactic, a hoax. Well, I don't want to be a delaying tactic, I want this man caught as much as anyone. But I am not him; I did not kill her or the others.' His voice caught on the edge. 'I am not a murderer, John.' He let his head drop, and as he did so, his pride and his anger disintegrated, blowing into the air to dance with the dust motes sliding down a shaft of light that shone through the blinds. As he looked up again, the skin tightened apprehensively around his eyes but his voice was firm. 'I have no idea who she is or why she was carrying my photograph.'

Handford offered no comment. What could he say? I believe you, Stephen or – or what? I think you might have done it? Eventually, he said, 'Have you seen the body yet, sir?'

'No, Mrs Forrester and I are going to the mortuary later today.'

Silence descended on the room like a blanket, muffling all extraneous sounds. Handford walked over to the percolator. 'Do you want a coffee?'

Russell nodded.

He poured two cups and placed one in front of his boss. Close up, the man looked tired. It was obvious he hadn't had much sleep. There were dark purplish shadows under his eyes and his lids drooped heavily.

'She was a prostitute, John. I was asked if I used prostitutes. Can you see me doing that?'

Handford glanced at the photograph of the blonde smiling from the frame on his desk. No, not with her as a wife he couldn't, but you never knew.

'We don't know for sure she was a prostitute. It's possible the others were, but that doesn't mean she was. Mrs Forrester had to check, sir. She was only doing her job.'

Russell's expression tightened. '*We* don't know for sure she was a prostitute, Inspector,' he said coldly. 'For someone whose only involvement was to come across the body, Mrs Forrester seems to have taken you well into her confidence. What's going on?'

Handford felt himself whirling from confidant to adversary and for one wild moment, he thought about telling Russell everything, how they wanted him to research his boss, delve into his background. Let Russell do the complaining and him get on with investigating Michael Braintree's murder. But it was no more than a wild moment. 'What if' had crept in. What if Russell was the killer? Unimaginable, but possible. No one walked around with 'serial killer' tattooed on his forehead. The images of the girl last night and of the photograph spilled into his mind. He could talk to the ACC and try again to put his point of view, ask him to hand the task over to Complaints and Discipline or another force, but he couldn't tell Russell anything.

He studied the coffee in his cup. 'Nothing's going on, sir. I had seen the girl and the crime scene and she thought I might be interested in the background.'

He didn't know whether that was enough for Russell, but he doubted it – the man was not stupid. After a brief silence the DCI indicated that Handford should sit down, then he opened the file in front of him, his jaws working as he attempted to bring himself under control. Finally, he said quietly, 'About the Braintree murder. Where are you with that?'

Handford filled him in.

'Do the parents know yet?'

'No, Ali and Clarke are seeing them this morning.'

'You're not going yourself?'

The web became denser with every evasion and every lie. 'No, sir, I need to take the file on the street robberies over to the CPS.' He must remember to do that when he'd seen Sanderson. He moved on to safer ground. 'A couple of officers are checking out anyone known to be proficient in the martial arts, and I've got four on house to house and after that talking to everyone who knew him to see what sort of a lad he was. The trouble is his friends and teachers are not easily available because of the school holidays.'

'Perhaps if you'd treated the incident as suspicious from the first, you'd have been on top of it by now and wouldn't have lost precious time.'

Handford didn't know whether it was Russell's intention to be so hostile or whether it was his way of coping. 'We only got the pathologist report last night, sir. It looked like a straightforward suicide initially.'

'So it might, but you ought to know by now not to take anything at face value.'

Perhaps he shouldn't.

For the next twenty minutes, they discussed on-going and new cases, but as the briefing drew to an end, Russell's professionalism gave way again to nervousness. He flaked a piece of paper, letting the scraps drop like snow on to his desk.

'I had nothing to do with the death of that girl, John, I want you to believe that. I don't have the best alibi for last night, or indeed for the nights of the other murders.' He paused, his expression one of a man picking his way around a life spinning out of his control. 'Why should a girl I don't know have my photograph, and such an old one at that? I must have been at Cambridge when it was taken. Help me out here, Inspector, how did she get hold of it?'

Handford closed his eyes momentarily, not sure whose side he was on. 'I don't know, Stephen. Perhaps you swapped photos with friends before you left. I know we did. Think back. Who would have been most likely to keep it?'

For a fleeting moment, the DCI's expression sharpened. Knowledge of something or someone from way back? Maybe, but if it was, Russell wasn't about to divulge it. Instead he said, 'I don't remember giving it to anyone.'

As soon as Handford had left his office, Russell let his composure slip. How could it have happened? There was only one person who would have kept his photograph. He hadn't forgotten her, but neither had he thought of her for a long time. Now that he did, the memory was both pleasurable and painful. As he'd given her the photograph all those years ago, he'd pleaded with her not to take any notice of his father, begged her to stay with him. But she'd said she couldn't and he'd never heard from her again. Although he knew she'd joined a solicitor's practice in Norfolk, he'd respected her wishes and made no attempt to get in touch. For a while he'd hated her for what she'd done to him, and when he'd found that hating was easier than loving, the hurt had begun to diminish.

Had Handford believed him when he had said he didn't remember giving his photograph to anyone? He wasn't sure – he'd seen the look of doubt in the inspector's eyes. Would he mention it to Forrester? In spite of Handford's denial, she'd obviously taken him into her confidence and had more than likely questioned him about Russell. Not that he knew much. But if the man went to her with a gut instinct – and he might, older officers often worked on their instincts – then suspicion would mount that Russell had something to hide. At the moment there was nothing but the photograph, but when she began to research his background, his past would tumble out, and that was the last thing he wanted. Losing it had been a hard and painful journey, but he had done it and he was damned if it was going to be resurrected by anyone, least of all his colleagues. His past had to remain where it should be – firmly in the past, dead and buried. But now, if it was the photograph he'd given to her, then his past would return, the reason why the dead girl had it become clearer and the horror of her death more personal.

He pushed his coffee cup to one side, reached for the phone and punched in a number. The call was answered almost immediately.

'Andrew, hello, it's Stephen. Look, I need to see you. Can we meet? Lunchtime would suit me . . . Fine, I'll see you there.'

chapter five

A chill crept over Detective Sergeant Khalid Ali as he drove himself and DC Clarke to the Braintrees'. It seemed as though a dark cloud had covered the sun. He glanced into the distance. The sky was still a deep blue and the sun was shining brightly over the tops of the buildings. He accepted that the sudden wintry attack on his senses had nothing to do with the weather. It was inside him and it concerned John Handford.

Handford had been in an odd mood this morning, almost from the moment he arrived. Ordinarily he had a placid nature, only flaring into anger when he had good reason. This morning he was different. It had shown in his face when Ali had gone to the office to tell him they were ready for the briefing, and it had increased as the morning developed. Even in the briefing it had been there, hidden under the surface. And judging by his reaction when Russell had walked into the incident room, it had to do with the DCI. That the two of them didn't get on well was common knowledge, but it had never been allowed to affect either their working relationship or that of CID. Quite the opposite, for in public Handford tended to overcompensate by being extra polite, extra accommodating.

What *was* unusual was that Handford wasn't saying anything to anyone. Normally he was up-front, unless confidentiality was demanded, and then he would say so, but this time – nothing. Ali had tried to ask him when they'd met up at the drinks machine after Handford had seen Russell – a meeting that obviously hadn't helped his mood. The machine was playing up and kept rejecting Handford's fifty pence piece and he was becoming frustrated with it, slapping at it each time the coin dropped through. Ali had smiled at him, delved into his pocket and lent him another. Normally Handford would have smiled back and the atmosphere would have lightened immediately, but this time he hadn't. Instead, he'd pushed the new coin into the machine, dropped the rogue into Ali's hand and said, 'I'm not available between twelve and one. If there's anything urgent it will have to wait.'

Not available? Why?

Handford didn't elaborate, instead he picked up his drink and walked away.

Something had to have happened – something big. And whatever it was included and worried John Handford. Yet so far as Ali knew, the only incident in which the DI had been involved was the discovery of the body of the serial killer's fourth victim. Not enough, he would have thought, to cause this amount of pressure.

'Next left.' Clarke's instruction broke through his thoughts.

Ali glanced in the mirror and flicked the indicator to take the turn off the main road and into the suburbs. The sun began to catch the windscreens of cars travelling in the opposite direction and Ali pulled the sunshield down against the intermittent glare. Away from the rows of terraced houses the area was cleaner, litter free. The streets transformed into avenues, closes and crescents, and were tree-lined, the greenery adding to their charm as well as protecting residents from the searing sun. The immaculate lawns were edged with colour, spreading like velvet mantles in front of the stone houses. And it was quiet, so quiet. No children playing football on the road, no teenagers with nowhere to go and nothing to do hanging around street corners. This was Bradford's middle class.

Ali manoeuvred the car into Ridgeway Close and slowed outside number thirty-two. The detectives pulled themselves out and stood for a moment to take in the scene before walking towards the gate. The detached house seemed deserted, as though the family were on holiday. A Neighbourhood Watch sticker clung to the top corner of the patterned glass of the front door. Ali grimaced at the irony of it. There hadn't been much neighbourhood watching going on two days ago when a young boy was being murdered.

Clarke pressed the bell, its chime carving through the silence. Ali fidgeted, his concern over John Handford abandoned. The news he was bringing to Michael Braintree's parents meant he had to be focused. Compassion for a grieving couple was about to take a back seat, and he would be subjecting them to questions that would plunder their lives and, in the process, intimate that one or both of them might have had something to do with their son's death. He would dig into Michael's background while they stood by and watched as their son's privacy was invaded – a privacy they themselves had not been allowed to violate. It was possible that what was uncovered could taint their view of him for ever.

After a few moments a shadowy figure appeared behind the glass and Raymond Braintree opened the door. He had aged in the days Ali had known him. The professional man of two days ago had been crushed beneath the weight of events. His features were ashen and his hair had taken on a greyish hue. He was dressed in a pair of light-coloured trousers and open-necked shirt, but they were creased as though he had slept in them.

'Come in, Sergeant,' he said and opened the door wide enough to let the two men in. 'My wife is in the lounge. I'm afraid she's not really up to answering questions; the doctor came this morning and gave her a sedative.'

Mrs Braintree was dressed but stretched out on the settee, a pillow behind her head, a flimsy cover over her legs. Her features were strained and her eyes dulled by the medication. The room was untidy; signs of the scene of crime officers' examination were still visible as well as the Braintrees' attempts at acting out the rudiments of life. A tray with a plate of partially eaten toast sat on the small coffee table, cups half filled with a cold grey liquid had pushed aside the Lladro figurines on the alcove shelves, and a teapot, milk jug and two cups, the drinks in them almost untouched, stood on another coffee table next to the settee. The sun shone through the window, its rays reflecting off the words of sympathy on the cards set out on the sideboard, its light curling behind them, edging them in black.

Mr Braintree spoke again. 'I'm sorry everything is in such a mess. We slept down here last night, we couldn't go . . .' He pointed to the hallway and the stairs. He attempted some measure of control, but it was a moment or two before he could speak again. 'I want her to eat something, but she won't.' He looked up at Ali, his eyes pleading. 'Why, Sergeant? Why? Was it our fault?'

Ali indicated the nearest chair. 'Sit down, Mr Braintree,' he said kindly. 'I have something to tell you.'

His eyes met the detective's, a mixture of puzzlement and apprehension mingling with the sadness already there. He edged backwards to the chair. Mrs Braintree looked appealingly at Ali, as though she was willing him to tell them that the past few days had been a bad dream and suddenly everything was going to be all right.

'We've had the results of the post-mortem on your son and it appears he didn't commit suicide . . .'

Mr Braintree's head jerked upwards to stare at Ali. 'What do you mean, he didn't commit suicide? Are you saying it was an accident? That he was fooling about with a noose and somehow he slipped?'

'No, sir, I'm not saying that.' Ali moved towards a chair. 'May I?' he asked.

Mr Braintree nodded. 'Yes, yes, of course. Sit down, both of you, please.'

Ali sat on the chair facing Mr Braintree, Clarke on the window seat. 'The post-mortem suggests that Michael died from vagal inhibition,' Ali explained. 'That means he was struck with a karate-type blow to the neck. This stimulated the vagus nerve, which regulates the heartbeat, and Michael's heart stopped. He was already dead when he was hanged.'

The boy's father closed his eyes while he tried to grapple with the new information. 'I'm sorry, Sergeant, I don't understand. Are you saying that someone deliberately aimed a blow at Michael's neck and then strung him up to make it look as though he'd killed himself?'

'That's how it seems, sir.'

'But why? Who?'

Ali shook his head in mute apology. 'I don't know why or who yet, and I can only assume that Michael's death was made to look like suicide because three boys have hanged themselves in the past few months.'

'And Michael was going to be just one more? A paragraph in the newspaper?' Mr Braintree dragged himself from the chair and began picking up the dirty crockery. 'I'll get rid of these,' he said.

Clarke stood up and took the half-filled coffee cup from him. 'Sit down, Mr Braintree, I'll do this for you later.' He waited until the man regained his seat. 'I know this is hard, sir, but if we're to make any sense of what has happened, we need to learn about Michael, build up a picture of him, and the sooner the better.'

Raymond Braintree shuddered. The sun's rays burning through the large window did little to extinguish the suffering that blanketed the room.

'He was your only child?'

Michael's father nodded.

'And still at school?'

Mrs Braintree roused; she had made no comment since the detectives had entered the room, but now she said, 'Yes, he's doing his A levels. Maths, Chemistry, Physics and Biology. He wants to be a doctor. The teachers have high hopes for him.' She was still in the present tense, not yet ready to assign her son to the past.

'He must have been working very hard, he wasn't studying the easiest of subjects. How did he relax?'

'He likes to keep fit,' his mother answered. 'There's a leisure centre in town; he goes there once or twice a week, or round to Daniel's, his best friend. They listen to music, I suppose – that's what teenagers do. I'm not sure exactly. He never talks about it much – well, not to us anyway.'

'Daniel?' Clarke raised his eyebrows in a question.

'Daniel Emmott.' Mr Braintree seemed to have gained strength from his wife. 'I'll get you his address.'

As Clarke wrote it down, Ali asked, 'Did Michael have a girl-friend at all?'

Mrs Braintree feathered the corner of her eye with her fingers. 'No, nothing like that,' she said. Her hands were trembling as she caught hold of a frond of hair and curled it round her first finger, like a child does when drifting off to sleep. 'There are girls at school with whom he's friendly, but no special girlfriend. He's dreamed about being a doctor for as long as I can remember; he wouldn't damage his chances of going to university by getting too involved with a girl. His career is . . .' She hesitated as if she had suddenly realised what she was doing, 'was very important to him. He was even working at the supermarket so that we wouldn't have to bear all his expenses – it's a long training to become a doctor. He kept a bit back each week for himself, but the bulk of it he put in the bank. He'd saved about five hundred pounds. His bank book is up in his room.' Tears came and she looked imploringly at Ali. 'Please find whoever did this to my son, Sergeant.'

'We will do everything we can, Mrs Braintree. I promise you that.' He turned towards Michael's father. 'Can you tell me how Michael spent Tuesday?'

'Michael is seventeen, Sergeant, we don't question him about his movements. We were both out at work. He knows to get in touch if he needs us, but he didn't on Tuesday.'

'Could he have been with Daniel?'

'He could have been, or he could have been at the leisure centre.' Mr Braintree's voice suddenly turned to a strangled cry. 'I don't know, Sergeant, I don't know what my son was doing on the day he died.' And he banged his fist on the coffee table, the crockery jumping and a cup spilling its contents into its saucer.

Mrs Braintree threw off the cover and pulled herself from the settee, to hold her husband in her arms for a moment, rocking him like a baby. The ferocity of the action had taken him to the edge of his grief; his wife allowed its outpouring. Perhaps he would have preferred to drown in it instead, fill his lungs and cease to exist. But Mr Braintree was too strong for such luxuries. He had been a trained soldier, Ali remembered, and that training acted as a reflex to pull back his control.

Clarke handed him a glass of water poured from the jug on the drinks tray and his wife returned to her seat.

Mr Braintree took a sip. 'I'm sorry,' he said.

Now that he was more composed, Ali began again. 'Did Michael have any enemies at all? Can you think of anyone who would have wanted to do this to him?'

Mr Braintree's voice caught in his throat as he answered. He took another sip of water, then tried again. 'No, no one. Everyone liked him, at school, everywhere. He did have a problem, I think, with one of the men at the supermarket who picked on him a lot, made him do all the rotten jobs, pushed him around a bit, but Michael laughed it off and from what he told us, it seemed no more than that the other lad was jealous of him – you know, Michael being a student at the grammar school. I told him to tell someone, but he said it wasn't worth it. It never seemed that serious.'

Ali nodded. 'It probably wasn't, but we'll have a word anyway. Do you have the lad's name?'

'Michael only ever referred to him as Karl.'

Clarke made a note.

Ali wasn't sure whether Mr Braintree was ready, but he needed to reverse the questioning, turn it away from Michael and towards the victim's parents – victims themselves in a crime like murder, yet suddenly suspects. What he was about to ask would hurt – it always did. He tried to wrap his words in an innocent request.

'I'd like to go through your movements on Tuesday, Mr Braintree.'

Raymond Braintree stared at the detective. 'You want to know my movements. Why?'

'No more than a formality, sir.'

Slowly, Michael's father placed the glass on the floor, then pushed himself out of the chair to walk to the window. He stood gazing out for what seemed an age, then spun round to face Ali, breathing heavily as he tried to compose himself. The sun silhouetted him and he stood like an enormous shadow towering over the sergeant. The action was intimidating and had Ali countered it, they would have become adversaries and he didn't want that, so he stayed where he was and looked up.

Mr Braintree grappled with his emotions for a moment, then said, 'You think I killed my own son?'

'I don't think anything at the moment, sir,' Ali said quietly. 'I'm simply trying to piece together the day Michael died. I've got to start somewhere.'

In the man's eyes was a mixture of contempt and mockery. 'We're always being told that most murders are committed by family, aren't we? Well, Sergeant Ali, I'm not sure I'm prepared to be a suspect in my own son's death.'

'Mr Braintree, I will get this information one way or another, from you or from someone else, either here or at the station. I promise you it will be easier on you here. I would have thought in these circumstances you'd rather stay with your wife.'

Mr Braintree glared at him. 'That was below the belt, Sergeant,' he said. Ali's eyes slid away. The comment had been uncalled for, but he needed Braintree to answer him now, not at the station in a few hours' time when he'd had time to prepare.

A deep silence stretched into the room, adding to the grief already there. Finally Michael's father moved back to his chair and sat down. 'I run a retail business. I own a large warehouse on the outskirts of the city from which I stock my shops. You've probably heard of them – Dale and Fell.'

'They sell anything for leisure pursuits, don't they?' Clarke interjected.

'Yes, camping equipment, orienteering, clothing.'

'Ropes?'

Braintree sighed. 'Yes, Constable, ropes.' He turned from Clarke to Ali. 'Does that give you something to go on, Sergeant, make you feel any better? Because I can assure you, it doesn't me. I'll save you the embarrassment of asking. My son could have been hung by one of my ropes.'

'And was he?' An unnecessary question, which Ali knew was unlikely to get at the truth, and he regretted it immediately. The man's comment was no more than an attempt to release the hurt inside him. Ali ought to have known better and Handford would have admonished him for it had he been there. But sometimes he was unable to master the point at which his compassion as a man ended and his job as a detective began.

Mr Braintree's jawline tightened. 'He may have been, but not by me.'

Ali opened his mouth to ask another question, but before he could continue, Clarke broke in. 'You spent Tuesday at the warehouse?'

The DC's softer tones soothed Michael's father and his voice as he answered was calm. 'No, not all of it. I was there in the morning, then I drove up to the Grassington shop. I arrived around two o'clock.'

'You left Bradford at what time?'

'About a quarter to one.'

'Did you go for a particular reason?'

'Trade there is beginning to pick up after the foot and mouth ordeal. I went to talk over how we could speed it up.'

'Your business isn't doing too well, then?'

'It wasn't, but it's improving slowly. It wasn't just the farmers who suffered, you know. Anyone who ran a business was affected. Our trade fell by over fifty per cent, more in some places. I had to pour a lot of money into the shops to keep them afloat. It was tight, but as I said, things are beginning to pick up now.'

Clarke signalled to his sergeant that he had no more questions and Ali turned to Mrs Braintree. Throughout the past few minutes she had remained silent, colourless beside her husband's overt bitterness. 'Can you tell me what you were doing on Tuesday?'

At this her husband exploded. 'For goodness' sake, have you no pity? Look at her; does she look as though she could kill our son?'

'It's all right, Raymond,' she said. 'I work with my husband. I was at the office all day. You can check with our accountant, he was with me. My husband will give you his company address.'

Ali smiled at her. 'Thank you, Mrs Braintree. That's all for now, I think, although we may need to come back.' He pulled himself from the chair. 'However, before we go, I would like to take a look at Michael's room.'

'If you must. It's upstairs, first on the right.' Mr Braintree stood up and began to clear away the crockery.

'I'm sorry, sir, I'll have to ask you to come with us. I know it's painful, but we can't go through Michael's things without you there.'

The look of resignation that passed over the man's face said it all. The future of his family, which a few days ago had been three and was now, in the most awful way possible, reduced to two, was in the hands of strangers – strangers who could and would do whatever it took to get to the truth, no matter how much it hurt. He led them upstairs.

The bedroom was small, but well planned – a study room with a bed rather than a bedroom where he studied. A built-in work surface ran the length of one wall, shelves underneath it filled with textbooks and files. A computer sat at one end. On the adjacent wall was a wardrobe and a low set of drawers on top of which was a mini music centre. The speakers were supported on brackets high up above the bed. Anatomical posters covered the walls: the human skeleton, the muscles of the body, the brain and the circulatory system. Mr Braintree shrugged. 'He wanted to be a doctor,' he said.

The detectives worked silently and methodically, carefully fingering their way through the drawers and checking the wardrobe and shelves. Articles that caught their attention – a diary, letters, photographs – they placed in plastic folders. Ali found the bank book, glanced at it and slipped it into another folder; Mrs Braintree hadn't been far off in her estimate of how much her son had saved – the final total was £532.27. Clarke tipped the rubbish from the bin and smoothed out the balls of paper. Three of them he kept, the others he replaced.

'We shall need to examine his computer,' Ali said. 'I'll get someone to collect it, if that's all right with you.'

Mr Braintree nodded. Pressure was continuing to take its toll, argument beyond him as he watched Clarke ease the drawers out of their housing, checking the contents of each as he did so. Then he bent down to check the gap between the bottom drawer and the floor. He stretched an arm as far back as it would go, and dragged out a shoe box. Placing it on the bed, he sat down next to it and took off the lid. As the contents were revealed, he looked up at Ali.

More pain, if that was possible, flooded Raymond Braintree's features, bewilderment and disbelief etched into every crease. Inside the box were two packets of condoms, several small plastic packets of a substance that resembled tobacco, but was almost certainly cannabis, a packet of half a dozen white pills and a sheet of ten LSD tabs. At the back of the box was an A5 brown envelope. Ali picked it up, opened the flap and carefully pulled out a wad of banknotes.

Dwayne Varley came for Leah just before midday. When the key turned in the lock she held her breath. It was Deepak; he'd forgiven her, come to tell her he loved her and she could stay. But as soon as she saw Varley in the doorway, a smirk sliding across his lips, whatever hope she was clinging to receded.

She hated Varley. She didn't know how Deepak could have anything to do with him. He was a thug and not someone you messed with. His slight frame, fair hair, blue eyes and weasel-like features suggested he was a pushover, but anyone who believed that did so at their peril. Deepak had told her once what he did to punters at the gym when they became stroppy. That's why he employed him, to keep away undesirables. An Asian couldn't be too careful in this country, he said, it was necessary to buy protection and the man was cheap but good.

Varley swaggered into the room. 'You ready?'

She looked up at him. 'Deepak didn't really mean it, did he? He's not going to send me away.'

'Just listen to her.' She was sitting on the bed and he bent towards her. 'He doesn't want you any more. He's got another girl. A real looker. You're history.'

Leah pushed him away. 'That's not true,' she shouted. 'Deepak would never do that to me; he loves me, he doesn't want anyone else.' She pouted at him as she clambered off the bed and stood against the wall. 'You're jealous; you're only saying that because *you* can't have me.'

Varley's eyes narrowed and in an instant his hand shot out to grab her by the arm. He pulled it back and twisted it behind her until it was clamped solid against her back and she was pinned against his body. 'You still think so?' he smirked. 'I can have you any time I want. Now, if you like. Can't you feel me getting a hard-on?'

Leah fought to break free, but he was stronger and the more she struggled, the harder her body compressed against his.

He laughed. 'Come on now, little girl, you know you want to.'

In desperation she kicked out against his ankle, the toe of her shoe catching him on the bone.

He yelped and flung her from him. 'You fucking slag,' he shouted. She turned to run, but there was nowhere to go. As she tried to push past him, he grabbed her by both arms and hurled her on to the bed. 'This is what we do to slags,' he said. His body dropped on top of hers. Unable to move, she spat at him; the saliva catching him on the bridge of his nose. He pushed himself upwards, keeping one hand firmly on her and wiped the spittle off his face with the other. Then he shoved her deeper on to the bed. 'You like a fight, do you? Well, that's fine by me. It'll make it all the more fun,' and he firmed up his grip. His warm breath washed against her skin as he pushed his face into hers and forced his tongue into her mouth. With one hand he began to pull at her skirt and her knickers, and when they were round her knees he unzipped his trousers and fumbled inside.

'What the fuck is going on in here?'

Deepak loomed over them. Angrily, he dragged Varley off her. 'What the hell do you think you're doing?'

Leah pulled herself upwards. 'You bastard,' she screamed at Varley who strove to get his balance. He wiped his hand across his mouth, but said nothing.

Deepak turned on him, his finger punching the man in the chest. 'If you want to fuck her, Varley, you can, but you pay for it like the rest of the punters, do you hear? Now get her out of this flat and over to Alice's.'

Even though it was lunchtime the city centre pub was almost empty. The heat was stifling and those who could chose to eat their lunch in Centenary Square or in one of the parks further out of the city.

Stephen Russell was glad of the space. His office was claustrophobic and for the first time since he'd been at Central, the smell of percolating coffee clogged the atmosphere. He would have got out sooner, but had been ordered by DCS Forrester to make himself available should she need to question him again. Thus there had been little he could do but stay. In the event, all she had required of him was to visit the mortuary.

It was a waste of time, as he knew it would be. He couldn't give her what she wanted.

'*Do you know this girl, Mr Russell?*'

'*No, ma'am.*'

Not strictly true, but he wasn't about to tell Forrester. There would be no need if Andrew Collingham agreed to firm up his alibi. It was only a question of timing, nothing more. He would have preferred not to, but to get his friend's co-operation, he had to disclose the link between his photograph and the dead girl.

Russell leaned over the mahogany table towards him. 'I think she may have been trying to find me.'

Collingham glanced round before he spoke. 'And why should she want to do that? I'm sorry, Stephen, but none of this makes sense. Did you recognise her when you went to the mortuary this morning?'

Russell picked up a square of sandwich, but replaced it on the plate as though he hadn't the energy to eat it. He repeated the answer he had given to Forrester. 'No, Andrew, I didn't.'

'Then how can you possibly think she'd been trying to find you?'

'Because she might be my daughter,' Russell said in a low voice, his eyes firmly fixed on the plate of sandwiches.

Collingham stared at him. 'What on earth gives you that idea? I didn't know you had a daughter.'

'Well, I might not have, I'm not sure,' he said, 'but . . .'

'For God's sake, Stephen. Just tell me, will you?'

Russell's jaw worked, sucking at his next words as though he was cleaning them before he let them loose. Then, 'I gave the photograph to a girl I knew at university, just before I left. Catherine, Catherine Walsh. We met at one of the freshers' meetings on the first or second day there I think, and because we were both reading law we were together a lot. Eventually,' he stretched out his hand to his beer glass and began to run his finger round the rim, 'eventually we became – well more than friends.'

Collingham was impatient. 'You mean you slept together?'

'Yes.'

'And she became pregnant?'

'Yes, in our final year, a couple of months before we left Cambridge.'

'And you think the dead girl might be her daughter?'

'Can you think of any other reason why she would have the photo I gave to Catherine?'

Silence descended between them, each one playing with his own thoughts.

'You didn't want to marry Catherine, then?'

This wasn't what Russell wanted – to look back. Catherine had been his passion. It had taken him a long time to erase her from his life; and now he was frightened that with the answer to Collingham's question all the old feelings would be revived. 'Yes, I did want to marry her, but she left at the end of the term and when I tried to contact her, her mother said she had gone to work in a solicitor's office in Norwich. Catherine didn't want to see me again, she said. She wouldn't give me an address or a telephone number. I could have rung round all the solicitors in Norwich until I found her, if indeed that was where she was, but if she really didn't want to see me again, I felt I had to respect that. Also, I assumed she'd had a termination.'

'Why?'

'Because my father offered her the money for one,' Russell said bitterly, 'and when she didn't want to see me any more, I thought she'd taken it and run.'

'To the nearest private clinic, you mean?'

'Yes.'

'And now you don't think so?'

'No.'

'So why not just tell Forrester this? It will solve the problem of the photograph and put you in the clear.'

'Or give me a motive for killing the girl.'

'I don't see why.'

'Because the past could damage my reputation and that would be the end of a career that means a lot to me. Can you imagine what a journalist would make of it? *Senior police officer's love child murdered while searching for her father in the city.*'

'I think you're worrying needlessly, Stephen, but even if you're not, you've no motive for killing the others.'

'A serial killer doesn't need a motive, Andrew. The DCS is linking this girl's death with the others so there's got to be something they're not making public. I didn't kill her, I didn't kill any of them. But you know as well as I do that a denial won't stop Forrester. You couldn't expect it to. If she believes I might be involved, and at the moment she does, then she'll have to research my background, look into my movements at the relevant times and question Natasha. And that's what I can't risk.'

'Natasha knows nothing of last night?'

Russell shook his head. 'I told her it was a work problem.'

'Nor of Catherine?'

'No.'

'Why not just tell her?'

'Because at the moment she's vulnerable. She's not long been out of hospital and she might find the possibility of me having a daughter hard to handle.'

'Because of the miscarriage, you mean?'

'It wasn't a miscarriage, Andrew, it was an ectopic pregnancy. They had to take both Fallopian tubes. Natasha can't have children.'

Collingham stretched his hand out to give Russell's arm a reassuring squeeze. 'I'm so sorry, Stephen, I had no idea. I know how keen she was, well you both were, to have a family.'

'So you can see why I don't want Forrester on my back.' Russell leaned towards Collingham. 'I wouldn't ask if it wasn't important, Andrew, but I need you to give me a watertight alibi.'

'Like what? I didn't see you until I arrived at your house. I don't know what you were doing before that.'

Pain tightened Russell's features. 'You could say you'd rung me at the office at about nine o'clock explaining you'd be late for the party. You said yourself the meeting had gone on later than normal.'

'Surely I'd be more likely to ring Natasha.'

'Oh, come on, Andrew, please.'

Collingham took a drink and scrutinised Russell. Eventually he said, 'There's more to this than Natasha's feelings and your reputation, isn't there, Stephen?'

Russell offered no reply.

'I'll need a better reason than you've given for me to perjure myself. We're talking about a serial killer here.'

Russell acquiesced with a sigh. 'You'll have to trust my reasons, but I don't want Forrester researching my background or my present. That's all I'm prepared to say for the moment; I will tell you eventually, when the time's right for me, but not yet.'

After what seemed an age, Collingham shook his head. 'That's not good enough, Stephen,' he said. 'For whatever reason, Forrester sees you as a suspect and as a senior police officer you should be co-operating, not trying to build a false alibi. I'm a councillor on the police committee, you can't expect me to do anything to sabotage the investigation. And I've got to say that from where I'm sitting it seems that you're more interested in yourself than the wider issue – that we have a serial killer in the city. Don't you think that is more important? And if this girl is Catherine's daughter, don't you think she ought to know? At the moment the police have no idea of her identity and you do. Surely you owe it to Catherine to tell them? She'll be devastated, yet you haven't concerned yourself with her feelings or yours as a father for that matter. My advice is that you need to come to terms with whatever it is that's worrying you, stop using Natasha and your reputation as an excuse for refusing to tell the truth and talk to Forrester.'

He pushed his chair from the table, 'I'm sorry, Stephen, I can't help you with this.' Then without so much as a backward glance he walked from the pub, leaving Russell staring at his plate of half-eaten sandwiches.

chapter six

To suggest that Handford was nervous as he was shown into the Assistant Chief Constable's office at headquarters was an understatement. He hadn't felt such tension since the inquiry into his arrest of Mohammed Aziz for the murder of his sister a couple of years ago.

He had never met James Sanderson in person, but the brusqueness of his manner was well documented and even senior officers had been known turn a delicate shade of green when requested to join him at HQ. Yet, here was he, a mere inspector, about to commit career suicide by challenging what Forrester had insisted was the ACC's own order. Normally, he wouldn't have contemplated such a course of action, but this time he felt he had to make that final effort. Get himself out of the hole that had been dug for him. If it got him a tongue-lashing, so be it.

However, when James Sanderson took his hand and said, 'This is bugger of a situation, don't you think, Handford?' his resolve evaporated and the only words he could muster were, 'Yes, sir, it is.'

Sanderson turned to his secretary. 'Let's have some coffee, Eileen, and some biscuits. And don't look like that, I'll have one, no more. Handford here will keep an eye on me, make sure I do.'

The secretary left, casting a disapproving glance at her boss.

'She's worried about my weight, says I'm getting a paunch.' He looked down at his stomach and said, 'Do you think I'm getting a paunch?' And before Handford could weigh up the pros and cons of answering the question honestly or dishonestly, Sanderson broke in with, 'Well, maybe she's right. Come on, let's sit over here, it'll be more comfortable,' and led him to two deep-cushioned leather chairs separated by a rectangular coffee table.

Comfortably, if a little uneasily seated in the chair, Handford glanced around. The room was imposing, but not intimidating. Not unlike Russell's in some ways, although bigger and less cluttered. In fact it struck him that he had never seen an office so uncluttered, as though no work was ever done in here, that it was a set made for television appearances or meetings and that Sanderson actually performed his day-to-day duties somewhere else in the building, in the same kind of mess that jobbing officers were accustomed to.

The secretary returned carrying a tray with two cups of black coffee, a milk jug, sugar bowl and plate of biscuits. 'Rich Tea for you,' she said pointedly to the ACC as she placed the tray on the table, 'and I've put a couple of chocolate digestives out for the inspector.' Then she handed Sanderson the folder from under her arm. 'The file you asked me to bring in.'

As she left the room, Sanderson pushed the tray towards Handford, 'Help yourself to sugar and milk,' he said.

Handford poured milk into one of the cups but did not pick it up. 'Sir,' he began.

'Don't say it, Handford. I know what's on your mind; you want me to take you off this job. Don't look so worried, man. I expected it; in fact you wouldn't be the person I've been led to believe you are if you hadn't wanted that.' His eyes lost their twinkle as they steadied on Handford's. 'Well the answer is no, Inspector. You're staying on it.' He picked up his cup, then replaced it without taking a drink. He leaned forward, forearms resting on his thighs. 'Look, Handford, you're the same kind of copper as me. We've both come up the hard way – on the job. Neither of us has ever left Yorkshire, except perhaps for university and holidays. Call a spade a spade and all that. And because of who we are, I know you think it's not on that you should investigate your senior officer. Well, it's not on that a senior officer should be caught up in this kind of incident.'

'If he is, sir.'

'Quite, if he is. And that's just my point. That photograph may have nothing whatsoever to do with the killing; Mr Russell may have nothing whatsoever to do with prostitutes, of any age, or with the deaths of the girls. But he is involved somehow, innocently or otherwise, and for whatever reason, he's refusing to co-operate. So, I have a choice. I can suspend him, bring in someone from an outside force to investigate him or I can let you do it quietly and with discretion. If I choose the former, the press will surely find out, smoke and fire will come into it and, innocent or not, a promising career will be ruined, and worse still, it'll be all round your nick in how many minutes?'

Handford grinned. He was warming to the ACC. 'About ten, I should think, sir,' he said.

'Aye, if that. Now *you*, you can research his background quietly. If you come up with something big, I'll hand it over, but if you don't and it's all quite innocent, then no one else need ever know and you'll have done him a favour. You're an experienced and discreet officer – oh aye, lad, I've read your file – even with that bit of trouble you had a couple of years ago with the Asian community. You over that, by the way?'

Handford scrutinised his hands. 'Yes, I think so, sir. It took a while, but in a perverse kind of way, the fact that I have has probably more to do with the DCI than anyone. Although I doubt I shall ever forget Jamilla Aziz and her brother.'

'Then whatever it was that Russell did, it's probably time to return the compliment, and I can't think of a better way than finding out what's going on and getting him out of this mess. The inquiry got you out of your mess by exonerating you, showing everyone that you hadn't been persuaded from investigating the Aziz case as it had to be investigated, even though the community didn't like the outcome. Unfortunately for you, there was a racial aspect to it and we had to be seen to be doing something, so it had to be public. Russell's case is different. It needs to be carried out quietly and we need an officer who understands loyalty, will not shout his mouth off and has the tenacity to keep going until he has the answers. And that, Inspector, is you, like it or not.' Sanderson picked up a chocolate digestive and took a bite. 'Any arguments?' he said.

Defeated, Handford smiled. 'No, sir, no arguments.' And he took a Rich Tea from the plate.

'Right, now that's over,' Sanderson handed him the file, 'this is a copy of Mr Russell's personal file. It's fairly standard. Take it with you and keep it under lock and key. Lose it and I'll have your head. When you've finished with it we'll shred it.'

'DCS Forrester said I was to research only his personnel, telephone and mobile records. No bank details, no questioning colleagues, relatives or friends.'

'For the moment, yes, but use your discretion.'

'It's just that,' Handford hesitated, 'I don't know much about serial killers, sir, but from what I've read, in the early stages there can be a long stretch between one victim and the next, so it seems to me that four deaths in almost as many months probably means he's not new to it, in fact he's been killing for some time, more than likely in another part of the country. So far as I can see, it's a bit like being addicted to drugs; the more times the serial killer kills, the more often he needs to kill and the killings become closer together.'

'So, what's your point?'

'That if Mr Russell has anything at all to do with these killings, sir, then I need to go right back, at the very least to his years at university. I need to check if there were similar murders in Cambridge while he was a student and it also means I'm going to have to talk to people who knew him at the time. He could still be in touch with them, they may still be his friends.'

'Yes, all right, do it, but try to avoid people he's currently in touch with, if you can; if it looks as though you can't, let me know and we'll decide between us what's the best way forward. In the meantime . . .'

He pulled himself from the chair and walked over to his desk. Pressing the button on the intercom, he said, 'Eileen, get me ACC Crime in Cambridgeshire, will you?' Then he dropped into the chair behind his desk. 'I'll let Cambridge know what you're about, get them to trawl their archives for you. It's going to take a couple of days so if you've got to go there, then you're going to need someone to cover your back here while you're away. The last thing we want is it getting out where you are and why. DCS Forrester can help, but you could do with someone from your own squad to field the awkward questions. What about your sergeant? What's he called? Ali?'

No. No way.

Handford nodded. 'Yes, sir.'

'Does he know how to keep his mouth shut?'

'I think so, sir. Although, I'm not sure I'd want to burden him with this.' It was Handford's problem, one he would have to deal with. He was still annoyed with himself for being so abrupt with Ali. None of this was his fault. It would be unfair to bring him into it.

Sanderson leaned forward. 'One thing you're going to have to learn if you ever want to make DCI, Handford, is to be less nice and more thick-skinned. And,' he added as an afterthought, 'so will Ali if he wants to make DI. Anyway, do what you think's best, you know him better than me. Now, on your way out, Eileen will give you the authorisation slip to check Mr Russell's telephone and mobile records.'

The phone buzzed and he picked up the receiver. 'Thank you,

Eileen. Robert, how are you? Just hang on a minute, will you?' He placed his hand over the mouthpiece and, dismissing Handford, said, 'If Russell is involved, I'll have no compunction in bringing him down; if not, then we need to get him out of this with the minimum of fuss.' He nodded his dismissal. 'Keep in touch, John. Oh, and not a word to Eileen about the chocolate digestive.'

As Handford opened the door James Sanderson spoke to ACC Crime in Cambridge. 'Robert, I need your help, we've got a problem here . . .'

Alice was waiting for the girl at the gate. A slim, slightly busty woman, she admitted to being forty-five, but was probably nearer fifty. She was an attractive blonde, with a smooth complexion, which could have been genetic, but was probably a result of hormone replacement therapy and a well-organised regime of daily cleansing and nightly moisturising.

She hadn't had a bad life – first as a high-class hooker, serving the professionals, giving what they wanted at a price, and then as the owner of a successful bakery. She'd set up the brothel ten years earlier during a bleak financial patch when the bakery hadn't been doing so well, but, not wanting to give up the business, she'd needed someone to take on the initial grooming of the girls. It was then she'd met Deepak Azam. Of all the pimps who ran girls in the city, he was probably the most organised and reliable, and had the added advantage of being a respected businessman who owned a lucrative and legitimate leisure and health centre. At first he hadn't wanted to know, feigned disgust when she'd suggested he join her. She'd told him to stop pissing her around – she knew a pimp when she saw one. And he'd smiled at her and said, 'Let's talk business.'

Their understanding – for it could be no more formal than that – was that he kept her stocked with girls whom she trained and worked until they were sixteen and old enough to move to the streets, when he took them off her hands. The financial split was sixty-forty in her favour.

Azam was happy with the arrangement. The bakery was a good front for the brothel, in a good location where the girls could work unhindered. It stood back from the road, a double-fronted shop, shaded from the heat by a striped yellow and white awning. Wrought iron gates fitted snugly at each side of the house between the walls and the tall fencing, securing the privacy of the paths, which led to the back of the building and to the five bedsits inside. It was a lucrative little business, making most of its money from the lunchtime sandwiches sold to the workers from the industrial estate close by and the police officers from the sub-division station a few yards down the road. It amused Alice that they came in daily, in plain clothes and uniform to buy from her, exchanged pleasantries and jokes, but had no idea what was going on in the rooms behind. It didn't amuse Deepak Azam, but she didn't care.

Leah walked slowly towards her, leaning to one side as she carried her suitcase. She could see why Deepak had chosen her for grooming. He liked them small and slight with long blonde hair. As she approached, Alice noted the bruised cheek and tear-stained face. So he'd been free with his fists again – or was it Varley? Whatever, it probably served the girl right, but it would mean she might not work tonight, unless the punters fancied a bruised girl. Some did. There was no accounting for taste.

Alice guided her round to the back into the living area, but made no attempt to help her with her things.

'What's your name, luv?'

No reply.

Alice shook her. 'Come on, what's your name?'

The girl was sulky – only to be expected. 'Leah,' she said finally. 'Leah Moorehouse.'

'How old are you?'

Still clutching her suitcase, Leah stared at her. 'Sixteen.' There was an edge to her voice.

'Oh, yes. Minus how many years?'

Leah glared at the woman. 'I'm sixteen.' She spat the words out.

'Deepak doesn't take on sixteen-year-olds. Fourteen downwards is more his style. So, madam, how old?'

The girl banged down her suitcase, muttering under her breath. 'Mind your own fucking business.'

Alice didn't need to catch the words, she could have written the script herself. They were all the same when Deepak sent them, conceited and arrogant, as though, because they had been trained by him, they were something different. The kid'd be telling her next that he loved her.

With a sudden movement, she grasped Leah's chin and forced the bruising towards the light. Leah tried to pull herself away, but the grip was powerful and held.

'Gave you quite a slap, didn't he?' Alice said and released her hold. The blood seeped back into the imprint of the fingertips. Leah glared at her, eyes blazing, and for a moment Alice thought she was going to hit out at her. Then Leah turned away.

'He didn't mean it,' she snapped. 'It was my own fault. He didn't mean it; he loves me. He'll be back for me soon, you see. I won't be staying here long.'

Alice had had enough. She grabbed Leah's arm, her fingers digging deep again into the girl's flesh until it turned white beneath them. 'Now you listen to me, young lady. Deepak doesn't love you, in fact he doesn't care any more about you than the money you can earn him. And neither do I. You cross him and you'll get more than you bargained for – perhaps find yourself dead in an alleyway like those girls in the paper. They worked here, but they were stupid and thought they could get away. And that makes Deepak mad. So the sooner you learn not to cross him, do what he and I say, the less chance there'll be that you'll end up like them.' She didn't believe her own words, but she hoped the little girl sulking in front of her did. She pushed the point home. 'The sooner you answer my question, the sooner your life will be worth living. So, if you don't want a slap on the other side, you'll tell me how old you are.'

Colour had drained from Leah's face. 'I'm fourteen,' she said. Her manner still oozed insolence, but her voice wavered at the edge of the words.

Alice lessened her grip. At last the girl was frightened, and the longer she remained so, the more malleable she would be. 'Right, I'll tell you what happens now. You'll have your own room where you'll entertain the men. A hundred pounds a night is the least we expect from you, less than that and this will happen.' She prodded the bruise. Leah flinched, but made no reply. 'You give them anything they want, normal or kinky. You get twenty pounds and a wrap of heroin at the end of the week. If you want more drugs you buy them yourself – from Deepak. Not from anyone else, you understand. Anything you make extra, tips and the like, you give to me. Don't try to hide them, because you'll get nothing past me; I've been in the game too long. Oh, and it's up to you to make sure the punters use a condom; end up with some disease or pregnant because you haven't been careful and you're out on your ear. Make sure you've always got a stock because not all the men bother to bring one. Do anything wrong, upset a punter and the like, and there's no scag; do it again and there's a good hiding and no money. We provide clothes and food, but you clean your own room and you take it in turns with the other girls to do the cooking.'

Then she pulled Leah towards the window. 'See that house,' she said, pointing to a detached property the other side of the fence. 'That's where I live, in a flat on the ground floor. Upstairs there are five bedrooms, good bedrooms, posh ones. Punters who go there are those who pay to preserve their reputations. The solicitors, the doctors, businessmen, people like that. The sooner we can trust you, the sooner we know you can keep your mouth shut and the sooner we're sure you can satisfy, then the sooner you can work over there, in the meantime you'll stay here. You can sit in the garden if you're not working and, depending on your schedule, you can go into town. But if you think that'll be your chance to run off, then let me remind you of the girls in the alleyways.'

She glanced at Leah. If she hadn't been at it so long, she would have felt sorry for her. Whatever it was that had made this girl grow up quickly, she was still a child, but the men they served liked children, and she was probably better off here than living in some squat.

Alice picked up the suitcase and handed it over.

'Get used to it, Leah,' she said, not unkindly. 'You're a prostitute and you're Deepak's. He's not your boyfriend, he's your pimp. He owns you. Cross him and it won't just be a bruise on your face. Oh, and forget Leah, you're Jasmine from now on. Your name's on your door, third room on the left at the top of the stairs. Deepak's organised your first client, so get rid of that bruise, there's make-up on the dressing table. You've got half an hour.'

Handford drove into Wakefield to find a place to eat. He could have stayed at headquarters and bought lunch in the canteen, but the atmosphere there choked him. He needed to think and he wanted to read Russell's file away from other police officers, for in spite of the logical way Sanderson had wrapped up the reasons for digging into the DCI's background and the fact that he'd agreed, he still couldn't help but feel uneasy. If it all went pear-shaped and Russell found out, he could make a complaint and where would that leave Handford? He would be the one visible while Sanderson and Forrester sat tight behind their rank. Forget that he'd been following orders, that he had said he didn't like what he was being asked to do. It wouldn't be the first time senior officers had shaken off responsibility and let the more junior take the flak. Yet, like it or not, once he'd entered the ACC's office, he had run out of options. Not that he'd ever had more than two. Do it or don't do it. When he'd picked up Russell's file and taken the authorisation to scrutinise his telephone and mobile records, he'd said yes to the former and in the process had committed, if not professional, then certainly personal suicide.

He sipped his coffee and ate his sandwich as he read Russell's file. Mostly it was basic information. Stephen Russell, born 28 August 1964, only child; father Fergus Russell, mother Charlotte Russell, née Blackman. Attended the Rotherwood Preparatory School 1969 to 1975 when he moved on to a minor public school in Hampshire. Went up to King's College, Cambridge in October 1982 where he studied law and politics, graduating in July 1985 with a double first. He moved to London for a year to study for a Masters Degree in Business Administration and then joined his father's company, Worldwide Pharmaceuticals, as a junior executive. Two years later, in 1988, he left the higher echelons of corporate business and joined the police force. Reason: personal. His background had taken him into the accelerated promotion scheme and by the end of 1997 he was a Detective Chief Inspector. Handford could feel his hackles rising. *Nine years to reach my rank, a lot less than it took me.* Married Natasha Lavington – *Who else? Stop it, Handford* – in 1994; no children.

He had an almost unblemished work record, including a couple of commendations. The only blip was a reprimand and a fine for taking an unmarked police car home. He'd been on duty twelve hours, was tired and decided not to return to the station, but to drive home in the car he was using and bring it back the next day when he would pick up his own. In law, it was Taking and Driving Away and in theory he could have been charged, but it was hardly the first time a CID officer had done that, nor would it be the last. Just bad luck he'd been spotted by a vigilant DI.

Handford sighed. There was very little here to link Russell with the dead girl but two questions sprang to mind immediately: what were the personal reasons for leaving the lucrative world of business after only two years, a business, which presumably he would inherit one day, and why had it taken him so long to marry? Surely there had been eligible women at Cambridge – more than eligible probably – and he was a personable individual, charismatic even. Nicola thought so at any rate. Was it the career? Or did it have something to do with the photograph found on the body of the dead girl?

Handford closed the file. There was no doubt he needed to start in Cambridge and that would mean going there. Damn. He'd been hoping to cover everything on the phone from the incident room at Central; that way Russell need never know what he was up to, and Ali could be kept out of it. But even at this early stage, even though he hadn't yet left Wakefield, both were looking less and less likely.

chapter seven

Ali spread Michael Braintree's effects over the table in the incident room and let his eyes wander over them. What had they here? The component parts of a young man's life, but parts that made up only a fraction of the whole. The question was, which fraction? Certainly not the one his parents had been aware of, yet they had to be of importance for him to have hidden them like that. Important enough to be linked to his death? Condoms, drugs, money. Take each separately, perhaps not; take them together, then maybe.

Ali picked up the plastic wallet containing a strip of photographs: Michael and a girl, taken in a booth. One of them smiling into the camera, the second looking towards each other, laughing; the next licking an ice cream in a cornet and the last of them kissing, the melted ice cream trickling between their tightly locked lips. Probably not the kind of pictures he would have wanted his mother to see. Ali looked at them closely. No wonder Michael had fallen for her. She was attractive in a youthful kind of way; still a schoolgirl, with a schoolgirl sparkle, but in the smile, even with a rivulet of ice cream escaping from the side of her mouth, there was an air about her that the more discerning – or the more cruel – might describe as streetwise.

'Who do you think she is?' he mused.

Clarke perched his glasses at the end of his nose and took the photos from Ali. 'Someone he is at school with, or works with at the supermarket,' he suggested. 'But whoever she is, Michael's parents didn't know her.' He placed the strip on the desk and stretched over to pick up the diary. The bald patch at the crown of his head reflected the sun, the tanned skin contrasting with the silver-grey hairs surrounding it.

'He seems to have used his own code in his diary,' he said. 'It's nothing complicated – letters mainly. One of them could be her. H, probably, since it appears the most often, particularly since the end of July. Then there's DA, P, and a small p. DA is mentioned a few times – nothing startling, *meet with DA, seven o'clock*, that sort of thing. I doubt DA is the girl though, he'd be more likely to use one initial for her – she's got to be H or P. I don't think she's P, because he's written, "Persuaded H to go to P".' Clarke shook his head. 'P's something else, a club perhaps or a nightclub?'

'I wouldn't have thought so,' Ali interjected. 'Not if he had to persuade her to go.'

'No,' Clarke conceded. 'Further on he's written, "P some help but p useless". Small p is obviously different from capital P, and if one was some help and the other wasn't then maybe they're agencies of some kind.' He looked up at Ali. 'Counselling groups, night lines? Perhaps she was pregnant.'

'Perhaps,' Ali said. 'Put someone on to agencies beginning with a P, small and capital. See if she consulted any of them.'

'Right,' Clarke said absentmindedly as he pondered the rest of Michael's belongings. He picked up the pack of drugs. 'Do you think these might have been planted by the killer?'

'Doubt it, not unless he planted the cash as well. And that's hardly likely.'

'No. Was he a dealer, then?'

'Not according to the drug squad. They've never heard of him. Yet there's too much stuff there for his own use and anyway the pathologist said there was no evidence of him being a user.' Ali shrugged. 'On the other hand, there's also well over a thousand pounds in that envelope. He couldn't have made that kind of money at the supermarket, so what are we left with? He had to be a dealer of some kind and a good one at that if he hasn't been flagged up. It doesn't make sense, does it?'

'No, it doesn't,' Clarke agreed.

Handford put Forrester in the picture.

'There's a friend of Mr Russell's from his student days, ma'am, a Doctor Mark Neilsen, who's prepared to talk to me, but it's not something I'm prepared to do over the phone so I'm going to have to go to Cambridge. I've made an appointment for tomorrow morning. Mr Sanderson agreed that while I'm there, it would be worthwhile to look at similar unsolved crimes committed while the DCI was an undergraduate.'

'A good idea. A link of that kind could be useful.'

'Or the lack of one, ma'am,' he felt the need to remind her.

She took the point. 'Indeed, Inspector, or the lack of one.'

Handford didn't like the way she was expecting a result from his visit. She appeared to have already flagged Russell up as the killer. He had the uneasy feeling that Russell had been right and anything he found would be moulded to fit the facts as she had them.

'Has the victim been identified yet, ma'am?'

'Not yet. Her fingerprints aren't on file, she's not on the missing person's register, all teenage girls in care homes are accounted for and no one has reported their daughter away overnight.'

'And Mr Russell didn't recognise her?'

'He said not. He could be lying of course.'

There it was again – the suggestion that Russell was involved.

He caught hold of his anger and tried to reel it back in. But he couldn't keep a hold and said abruptly, 'I've never known him to lie.'

Forrester leaned towards him. 'Would you know if he had? Police officers are just as prone to lying as anyone else, particularly when they need to cover their backs.'

Reluctantly, Handford had to admit she was right. They spent a lot of their time with people in whose vested interest lay the ability to lie effectively and for some it rubbed off. He'd come across officers, senior and junior, who were better at evading the truth than most of the villains they apprehended. But he would take some convincing that Russell was one of them.

Forrester leaned back in her chair and swung it slowly from side to side. Eventually she came to a stop facing him. 'I know you don't like this, John, and I sympathise. But the fact is we may have moved into another league with this girl's death. The pathologist is not all that sure she was a prostitute. The hymen was badly torn but his guess is that it was done by the instrument with which she was raped. In fact, given the amount of damage, he believes she could well have been a virgin. So either the killer made a mistake or he wanted her dead for another reason, and for the moment we know of only one person who may have had a reason – Mr Russell. Like it or not, whoever killed that girl last night killed the others, because no one is aware of his signature except him and us.'

She picked up a statement from the top of the pile with one hand and her pen with the other. 'I need a result on this, John, and soon because there's no empathy for us out there. The top brass, the press, the police committee, even the city's MPs are on my back and they're not going to take no for an answer.' Her expression tightened. 'I'm relying on you, Inspector, to bring me back something to work on.'

As the door closed behind her, Leah dropped her case to the floor. Her eyes roamed the dingy room. The walls, which had once been cream, were stained with nicotine and the paintwork round the light switches was grimy where it had been constantly fingered. The drab sage-green curtains hung limp at the windows, the material wearing into holes along the edges where they had been dragged across to cut out the light. Opposite and next to the window stood a dark wooden wardrobe and squeezed between the back wall and the door were a dressing table and stool.

Leah pulled open one of the drawers. It was lined with an old newspaper. The black headlines leapt out at her. THIRD VICTIM FOR THE TRASH BAG KILLER. Alice had said the dead girls came from here, that he'd killed those who didn't do as they were told. The bitch. She'd done nothing but try to frighten her ever since she got here, and with this she'd managed it. Just like her mother's boyfriend did when she was young. 'If you don't stay in bed while we're at the pub,' he'd say, 'the ghosts and werewolves will get you.' Leah's imagination had gone into overdrive then and it was doing the same now. Images of ghouls or dead girls, what was the difference? She was sure Alice had lined the drawer with that paper on purpose. The fear she had felt as a child swept over her and she clawed at the newspaper. It tore under her nails and when all that was left in the drawer were the stains on the thin wooden base, she hammered the newsprint into a ball and threw it hard across the room, then, as exhaustion claimed her, her legs gave way and she slid down the wall, sobs racking her body.

What was she doing here? How had she ended up in this crummy room? Deepak said it was her fault. Everything had always been her fault. It was her fault her father had walked out; her fault her mother's new boyfriend had done those awful things to her; her fault her mother hadn't believed her. She should have kept it a secret like he told her. It was her filthy lies that had caused her mother to put her into care and her fault the foster-father had done the same things to her that the boyfriend had. But she'd learned her lesson – this time she hadn't told anyone. Instead she'd run away. No one came after her, but they wouldn't, would they? Who would want a bad girl living with them? The boy she'd met on the street said he knew someone who would. Deepak Azam. And he did. He'd looked after her, given her presents, taken her to places she'd never ever been before, given her his ring, made love to her.

Then he'd changed. Suddenly. Told her he wanted her to be nice to some of his friends. She'd known what he meant and said she didn't want to – she only wanted to love him. Instead of that pleasing him, he'd hit her hard in the stomach. So she'd done what he wanted and he'd been nice to her again, except when she'd run out of tampons and asked for some more money, when he'd flown into a rage and burned her with his cigarette so that she had marks all over her tummy and in her groin. Another time when she'd displeased him, although she couldn't remember how, he'd taken her out in his car to where the women were working and he'd called one of them over. As she'd bent down to his level, he'd grabbed a handful of hair and pulled her head into the car through the open window. Leah had blanched. An angry scar ran from the side of the woman's right eye across her cheek and to the corner of her mouth. The stitch marks were still visible. 'That's what you get if you don't do as you're told. Remember it.' And he'd pulled the woman closer for a better look before pushing her away so hard that she fell backwards on to the ground. Without a word, she'd picked herself up and returned to the street corner.

But, although she didn't mean to, Leah must have forgotten, because last night she'd tried to get away from the man he'd brought her. Afterwards, as she heard the key turn in the lock, she remembered and she slept fitfully, dreaming of the scar, which crawled like a snake over her body and around the burn marks as though they were some obstacle course. But she'd known that it was all her own fault.

Deepak hadn't sliced her face with a razor, instead he'd asked for the ring back. She needed to be taught a lesson. She knew that, because that's what you did to people you loved – taught them lessons. She had to learn to do as she was told, and that meant working for him, earning money for him. Yet, that was what she wanted too; she wanted him to be able to dress well, to wear gold jewellery and to drive around in a flashy car.

She lifted her head and surveyed the bed. It took up the bulk of the room. Next to it was a small table and lamp, its naked lightbulb a dull red. The wooden headboard rested against the wall. There the paintwork was chipped where it had banged or rubbed against it. At the top corners were knobs with lengths of cord wound around their necks. Instinctively, Leah knew what they were for and fear swamped her again. She took hold of her long blonde hair and drew it towards her mouth, chewing at it as she had as a young child. Deepak said she'd been bad; this was her punishment. Until she could prove to him that she could be good, she knew there was no way out. If she stayed, men would have sex with her night after night and if she left she would be living on the streets, open prey to the Trash Bag Killer.

Deepak was right: she was a bad girl, the worst there ever was.

Daniel Emmott watched the two detectives walk down the drive, then closed the door slowly behind them. He was shaking – not so much visibly, although he could feel the tremor in his hands against the handle. Rather, it was on the inside, as though a series of ripples were passing through him, running like waves to the sea shore, to be met somewhere around his stomach by others in retreat.

He walked through the spacious hall. A mahogany telephone table stood against the wall, the richness of the wood contrasting against the apricot-tinted wallpaper, and opposite, a wide staircase curled upwards. He glanced up it and shivered. Had Michael been as frightened as he was at this moment, or had it happened so quickly that he hadn't had time to think or feel? Daniel didn't know. He entered the kitchen, his flip-flops slapping on the quarry tiles. The glasses from which he and the two detectives had drunk their orange were still on the table, and almost without thinking he picked them up to swill them under the tap. His mother liked the kitchen spotless when she came home from work. Finally he wandered out into the garden and slumped down on the lounger. The sun was hot, but it gave him no pleasure. He picked up the personal CD player from beside the seat, fitted the earphones comfortably into his ears and turned up the volume as loud as he could bear in the hope that it would drown out the thoughts and fears milling around in his brain.

His father had come home from work at lunchtime and Daniel had sensed immediately that something was wrong. As he settled himself next to his son, his expression had fielded a mixture of emotions. He told him that Raymond Braintree had rung during the morning with upsetting and disturbing news, and that he had come home because he would rather Daniel did not hear it by chance. Then he'd told him as gently as he knew how that Michael hadn't committed suicide as first thought, but had been murdered. A painful silence had filled the garden, and to break it his father had tried to explain how Michael had been killed, but Daniel's brain had disconnected itself from his surroundings and the words hadn't penetrated. Before he left, Mr Emmott had warned his son to expect a visit from the police since Michael's father had told them of their friendship. But he had said not to worry – all he would have to do would be to tell them about Michael.

Tell them about Michael. That was the one thing he couldn't and wouldn't do. Dead or alive, he was Michael's friend and he couldn't be disloyal to him. But not only that, for his own safety, he couldn't do it. Michael hadn't just died; someone had taken his life – not accidentally, but deliberately. There was no way that Michael's death and the situation he had allowed himself to be drawn into were not linked, and because he knew of it, Daniel could also be a target. Mr Azam knew he was Michael's best friend, he'd seen them together at the leisure centre, even shaken hands with him when Michael had introduced him, and then acknowledged him each time they'd met. He hoped he wasn't being melodramatic, but whether he was or not his fear swallowed him whole. Money, drugs, girls, Mr Azam, Michael, then MURDER. The word swam in front of his eyes in big black capitals.

Daniel had warned his friend over and over again that he shouldn't do what Deepak Azam expected of him. But Michael had needed the money and Mr Azam paid him well. At first it had seemed harmless, charitable even. Daniel had tried in vain to warn him that there had to be more to it than Mr Azam was telling. No one was as charitable as that.

Michael hadn't listened. 'All he wants to do is to find them somewhere nice to live. I just look after them while he's doing it.'

Even when he was told to offer them drugs, Michael had mocked Daniel's fears. 'Everyone takes drugs nowadays,' he'd argued.

And he'd gone on earning his money, until he'd fallen for Hannah, the latest girl Mr Azam had asked him to 'look after'. Then suddenly, he'd acknowledged that Daniel might be right. Michael had panicked, gone to the coppers, but they hadn't listened, so he'd plucked up his courage and visited Mr Azam. Knowing Michael, he'd probably argued with the man, let slip what he thought he knew, even that he'd already talked to the police. He might even have said that he'd told Daniel. Whatever, he'd returned in an awful state. He wouldn't say exactly what had happened, just that he had to go away for a few days. He'd pleaded with Daniel not to talk to anyone about it, then rushed off. He hadn't even said goodbye. A few hours later he was found hanging. Daniel blamed himself. Had he thought for a minute that what Michael meant by 'going away for a few days' was that it was his intention to kill himself he would have told Mr and Mrs Braintree so that they could stop him, but he'd taken the words at face value. Now he knew he should have told them anyway.

But it was too late. Michael was dead and Daniel was frightened. There was no way Mr Azam must find out Daniel knew what Michael had suspected. The best thing to do was keep a low profile and pretend not to know anything.

So he had said as little as possible to the detectives.

'Michael was your best friend?'

'Yes.'

'Have you known each other long?'

'Ever since we went to the grammar school.'

'About six years?'

'About that.'

'You must miss him.'

'Yes.'

'Tell me about him.'

'He was just a mate.'

But that wasn't enough for them. They had sensed there was more.

Sergeant Ali had leaned forward, his face so close that Daniel could almost taste his breath. 'More than just a mate, surely?' he'd asked quietly. And when Daniel hadn't answered him, he'd pushed further. 'How much of a mate, Daniel? Enough of a mate for you to want us to catch his killers?'

The other had asked about the drugs and Daniel's face had told them what they already knew. At first he'd tried to protect Michael.

'He wasn't using,' he'd said defensively.

'Dealing, then?'

'I've never seen him dealing. It's easy enough to get drugs in school if you want them, but Michael wasn't selling and no one's ever asked me if he could get them.'

'But he had drugs?'

'No.'

The detective constable had raised his eyebrows as if to question the answer, and he'd had to admit that Michael had drugs. 'All right, then. Yes, he had drugs, but he wasn't dealing.'

'So why did he have them?'

'I don't know.'

'But you do know where he kept them?'

'In a box underneath the bottom drawer of the set of three in his bedroom.'

'You've seen them?'

'Yes.'

'What did you see?'

'Cannabis, ecstasy and LSD tabs.'

'And the money?'

Daniel had felt ground down. He didn't know whether the detectives were bluffing, or whether they really knew, so he'd nodded.

But the policeman didn't leave it there. 'So, if he wasn't using and he wasn't dealing, what was he doing and where did the money come from?'

Suddenly, Daniel couldn't take any more. 'I don't know,' he'd shouted, then pleaded, 'Please don't ask me any more questions.' Eventually, he'd been allowed to show the officers out of the kitchen. But the sergeant's words were still ringing in his head.

'We'll go, but we will have to talk to you again. You do know that, don't you?'

Then, as they'd moved into the hallway, the sergeant had pulled the plastic wallet containing the strip of photographs out of his file and asked if he knew the identity of the girl with Michael.

He'd told them that. If they knew who she was, they could question her instead and leave him alone.

'It's Hannah,' he'd said. 'Michael's girlfriend. Hannah Mellings.'

'I really don't want to do this, Gill, but I can't get out of it.'

When Handford had left Wakefield he hadn't wanted to see Russell so had taken the decision not to return to the station, but to go straight home. It had been easier to face him this morning before he'd thrown in the towel and agreed to research his boss's background, but now he couldn't. As soon as Russell saw him, he would realise there was something wrong. Handford had an expressive face and could divulge his feelings without uttering a word. It didn't happen with suspects, no matter what the crime. With them he was inscrutable, never gave away what he was thinking, but when he was feeling guilty himself it was a different matter. His lips compressed, his teeth clenched and the muscles around his jaw flexed. Russell would recognise the signs and Handford would have to explain, wouldn't be able to stop himself.

Gill was alone in the house when he arrived and much as he would have liked to have seen his daughters before he left for Cambridge, he was grateful Nicola was out with Vishnu and Clare round at a friend's house, and he could talk to his wife and articulate his fears and his guilt without risk of interruption. She handed him a coffee. He would have preferred something stronger, but he had a long drive in front of him and to combine his already clouded brain with whisky would have blurred his concentration.

'You don't really think Mr Russell is involved, do you?' Gill said.

'I don't know. When I saw the photograph last night, I didn't believe he was. I couldn't picture him beating a girl to death and then raping her and I still can't, but when you're dealing with a killer you're not dealing with his outward appearance, but with his mind, and I don't know anything of Russell's mind. According to both Forrester and Sanderson, he accepts that the photo is of him but he's refusing to co-operate. Why? He says he doesn't know who the girl is or how she came to have a picture of him and when I suggested he thought about who would have been likely to have kept one and possibly given it to the girl, he said he didn't know. But I swear he did. It was there in his eyes. He was lying, Gill. He's forcing us into investigating him and I don't know why.'

'Perhaps you'll find out in Cambridge.'

'Perhaps.' Handford leaned against the soft upholstery of the settee's back and closed his eyes. A pain pummelled at his head and all he wanted to do was sleep. Although it wasn't yet five o'clock, he was exhausted. This morning's talk with Nicola seemed to have taken place days ago and his wedding anniversary yesterday was way behind him, somewhere in the hinterland. Eventually he opened his eyes and pulled himself straight. 'Forrester suggested I look upon what I'm doing as getting Russell off the hook.'

'Then do that if it's easier.'

'I'm not sure it is. And anyway, I can't. To do that influences my opinion and I've got to be impartial, that's the only way to get to the truth. Once I start to let my feelings in, then I start to twist the evidence to fit them. That's what Forrester's doing at the moment. She's convinced she's on the right track. I can't blame her, it's the first bit of concrete evidence she's had, but she expects me to bring back information that will prove her right.'

'And if she doesn't get it?'

'I don't know.' He bent forward to take a sip of coffee. 'At least Sanderson is prepared to wait and see what I find out. He doesn't have expectations. If there's nothing, fine; if there's something, he's going to hand the job over to another force – which is what he should have done in the first place,' he added bitterly.

'I presume Mr Russell knows nothing of what's going on?'

'He knows how these things work so he's aware his background is likely to be researched, but he doesn't know I'm the one doing it.'

'And if he finds out?'

'Then I'm on very dangerous ground. He will complain, Forrester and Sanderson will hide behind their rank, and I'll be the one catching the flak.' He grimaced. 'It wouldn't be the first time I've been the whipping boy though, would it?'

Gill shook her head. She understood the implications as well as he did. She'd been there before, supporting him through an inquiry a couple of years ago, which had accused him of pouring fuel on the fire of racial divisions, when what he'd actually done was to arrest a young Asian lad for the murder of his sister. The community hadn't agreed with his findings and the younger members had rioted in the city.

Gill shifted her position to sit next to him and put her arm through his. 'This isn't fair, John. You've been put in a no-win situation.'

For a moment they sat in silence, both labouring with their own emotions. Eventually, Gill said, 'Have you told Khalid?'

'No.'

'John, why? You can't carry this on your own.'

'Because I know what he'll say and because I don't have a justifiable response to his argument, and because deep down I agree with him.'

'Then tell him that as well. He knows the system, he'll understand you had no choice.'

Handford doubted that. People always have a choice, he would say. Khalid Ali was a man with high ethical values, a man for whom loyalty was the basis of a relationship. He doubted very much he would understand.

'I'll see,' he said, and squeezed Gill's arm. He would have to call in on the sergeant anyway to let him know he wouldn't be available over the weekend should anything crop up. It wouldn't be fair on Gill to have to do the explaining if Ali rang him at home.

But Gill fixed him with a cool, assessing gaze that defied argument and a smile ran along her lips.

The inference was clear. 'All right,' he said. 'I'll call in on him on my way to Cambridge. See how I feel when I get there.' He leaned over and planted a kiss on her cheek. 'And that's the closest thing to a promise you're going to get.'

chapter eight

The drive to Ali's house took Handford out of his way, but it gave him time to think. He hadn't made his mind up whether to say nothing or to tell all. If the sergeant didn't know anything, then there were no answers for him to give should he be cross-questioned. Normally he looked forward to visiting the Alis, but burdening his sergeant with current events could be stretching their friendship and hospitality too far. He didn't want to break the tenuous thread of their relationship. Since that first invitation to dine with them last year, Ali's wife, Amina, and Gill had become good friends and the children loved Handford. They looked upon him as a favourite uncle, Ali said, and he had to admit that the feelings were reciprocated. It had also given the two of them a chance to become better acquainted, as people rather than as colleagues.

He pulled up alongside the gate. Although on a private estate, the houses were individual – not the usual box-type structures that builders often squeeze into their plots of land. Inside it was warm and welcoming. A real home. Handford was sure this was down to Amina Ali, rather than her husband, who spent even more time at work than he did – if that was possible.

She opened the door to him, her face lighting up in a smile. 'John, how nice to see you,' she said.

He kissed her on both cheeks, then stood back to admire her. Amina Ali was quite beautiful. The pale lemon salwar kameez she wore enhanced her slim figure, her brown skin and her long dark hair.

'As beautiful as ever, Amina,' he said. 'And looking so cool, too.'

'It's a myth, John. What I'd really like to do is strip off and lie in the shady part of the garden.' Her eyes twinkled. 'But don't tell Khalid, he'd be horrified that I even entertain such thoughts.'

'You can rely on me,' he promised. 'Actually, as much as I'd prefer your company, I'm going away for the weekend and I need a word with Khalid before I go.'

'He's in the garden with the children. You know your way. Would you like a drink, something cold perhaps?'

'A lemonade would be wonderful, if you have one.' Handford made his way through the French windows and into the garden.

As soon as the children saw him, they stopped what they were doing and ran over.

Seven-year-old Hasan grabbed his hand. 'Come and play,' he urged him.

'No, me, me.' Bushra, a couple of years younger than her brother, tried to pull him in the other direction. 'I've made some sandcastles, do you want to see?'

Ali, who had been stretched out on the grass, pulled himself up. 'Hello, John. This is a surprise.'

'It's a flying visit, but I do need a word.'

Amina came into the garden with two glasses of lemonade. She placed them on the wrought iron table. 'I'll take the children,' she said, 'then you can talk in peace.'

When they had gone, the two men sat down. 'What's so urgent it couldn't have waited until tomorrow?' Ali asked.

Handford took a sip of the lemonade. 'I won't be available tomorrow; I have to go away for the weekend.'

Ali frowned. 'You never mentioned it.'

'No. It came up unexpectedly. Anyway, I thought I ought to get up to speed with the Braintree case before I go. Anything of use from your visit?'

Ali described what they had found in Michael's room. 'He was into something, there's no doubt about that, but at the moment I've no idea what. If it wasn't for the fact that neither the drug squad nor any of the addicts we talked with have ever heard of him, I'd have said he was dealing. We spoke to Daniel Emmott who was edgy to the point of fear, but swore he knew nothing.'

'Did you believe him?'

'No, nor did Clarke. We'll go back again when he's had time to calm down. He did recognise the girl in the photograph, however. She's called Hannah Mellings, but other than that, he knew very little about her, not even where she lives. If we can find her, she might be able to tell us more.'

'What about Michael's parents?'

'They knew practically nothing about their son's current lifestyle except that he studied hard at school, had a part-time job at the supermarket and worked out at the leisure centre in the city. Not much considering he was their son.'

Thinking back to Nicola's refusal to tell him what was on her mind, Handford empathised with the Braintrees. 'Probably not,' he said. 'But he was at an age when he would feel that what he did was none of his parents' business.'

Ali sat back and his face darkened. 'I shall expect to know how Hasan is spending his time, even when he is eighteen.' There was a pious righteousness in the sergeant's expression that Handford had come to know well. He had little time for what he considered the liberal attitudes of some parents. They were wrong and he wasn't afraid to say so. 'It might be the Braintrees' way, but not mine. How can I protect my son if I don't know what he's doing and where he's going?'

Handford chuckled. 'Come and say that to me in eleven years' time. You might find your son has other ideas.'

'Hasan is Muslim; he will respect me as his father, he will know the difference between right and wrong, and he will do what is right.'

Handford would like to have disputed that since there was an increasing number of young Muslims in the city who were not toeing the line, much to the desperation of their parents who had no doubt felt the same as Ali when their boys were seven years old, but he didn't want to get into an argument. He led the conversation back to the case. 'Anything else?'

'Mr Braintree has access to the type of rope used and he's quick-tempered. Not very, but it's possible that if he knew what his son was up to they could have argued and he hit out at him. Probably didn't mean to kill him, but when he found out he had, he strung him up.'

'Have you any evidence for that?'

Ali laughed. 'Not a scrap,' he said. 'But it's worth looking into. Don't worry, John, I'll go carefully. I'll make sure I have Clarke with me at all times, he'll keep an eye on me.'

Clarke was the oldest man on the squad and as such tended to act as mentor and stabiliser for the team – he'd even been known to give Handford the hard word when he thought it necessary.

'Forensics are checking Michael's computer and also his mobile phone – but nothing yet,' Ali continued.

Handford drained his glass. 'You seem to have everything under control. I'll have to go, I've a long drive ahead of me.'

87

Ali cocked his head to one side like a bird and gave him a quizzical look. 'Where?'

Handford sighed. 'Cambridge.'

Ali couldn't hide his astonishment. 'Cambridge?'

'It's work, Khalid. I've got inquiries to make.'

'In Cambridge?' Ali drew in a deep breath. 'What's going on, John? You've been in an odd mood all day. Is it something to do with last night? You've been seconded to the serious crime squad?'

'Not exactly, no.' He was beginning to sound like Forrester, and just as 'not exactly' hadn't been enough for Handford, it wasn't enough for Ali either. He pushed further. 'What do you mean, not exactly?'

Both Gill and Sanderson had been right; he was going to have to tell him, if only to stop him asking around at the station next time he was in. If he did that, it would get back to Russell by default. He knew Ali; when something worried him, he was like a ferret, clinging on until he had the truth. That's what made him such a good detective. Handford sat down again, harbouring the distinct feeling that life was getting the better of him.

'This is for your ears only, Khalid. It's to go no further, do you understand?' Handford said seriously.

'Yes, if you say so.'

Handford related the sequence of events from coming across PC Martin to his interview with Sanderson. He left nothing out. As he talked, Ali's expression changed from interest to horror and then to disgust. He pushed his chair away from the table, stood up and took a few paces away from his boss. Then he turned to face him.

'This is rubbish, John. The DCI the serial killer? You can't be serious?'

'I didn't say I agreed with it. I'm having as much difficulty as you in coming to terms with the idea, let alone the facts. But there's no doubt the photo is of him or that it was found on the dead girl.'

'But why you? And why are you going along with it? Why did you agree to research his background? It's obscene.' He came back to the table and for a moment they stared at each other, Ali's expression a fusion of anger and disappointment, Handford's one of embarrassment.

'It was a direct order, I couldn't refuse.' The answer was shallow. Handford knew it and Ali knew it.

'You've disobeyed direct orders before.'

'But not from an Assistant Chief Constable. Have you any idea what Sanderson is like? He'd eat me for breakfast as soon as look at me.'

'And when the team finds out what you're doing, they'll have what's left of you for lunch.'

'And no doubt, you're going to be the one to tell them.' Handford realised he was shouting.

Ali's shoulders sagged and he slumped back on to the wrought iron chair. 'No. No, of course not.' He took a deep breath and let it escape slowly. 'I just thought better of you, that's all.'

Handford leaned towards him. 'Don't you think I haven't argued? I've spent most of the day arguing with both Forrester and Sanderson. But I was the one who recognised Russell from the photograph, I was the one who told the DCS. It has to be investigated and so does he, and so far as they are concerned, I'm the one to take on the background research. Experienced and discreet, that's what Sanderson called me. The fact is, Khalid, they want it kept in-house, and to them that means me. Their reasoning is that this needs to stay under wraps until I have come up with something that implicates the DCI or exonerates him. If it's the former, then it will be given to another force.'

'And if Mr Russell finds out what you're doing?'

'Then I shall be the scapegoat – not Forrester or Sanderson.' Handford concentrated his gaze on his sergeant. 'I hope you're not considering telling him.'

'No. But if he asks where you are, I won't lie for you.'

A conflict of impulses wrenched at Handford's stomach. It wasn't Ali's fault. He hadn't yet learned that sometimes in the police service you had to leave your principles at home. Perhaps he should ask Sanderson to have a word with him. He didn't know – that might make it worse.

Ali spoke, interrupting his thoughts. 'Have they no other suspects?'

'Not really. There's a possible – a man called Deepak Azam who is flagged up by the vice squad as a pimp. They seem to think he was the one running the dead girls. But, if he is, I can't see . . .'

As he spoke, Handford watched the fury mount on Ali's face once again. 'Don't be ridiculous!' The words exploded from him. 'What's the matter with these people? First Mr Russell and now Deepak Azam. My God, they must be desperate.' His eyes flitted from side to side, as though he were trying to come to terms with what he had been told, then they lighted on Handford. 'You know why, don't you? They see an Asian doing well for himself and the first thing that springs to mind is that he's a drug dealer or a pimp or both. Either way he can't be making his money legitimately.'

Handford frowned. An excessive reaction towards a possible suspect. It couldn't just be the fact that the man was Asian – even Ali knew the majority of the city's pimps were – unless . . . 'Do you know Azam?'

'Yes, sir, I know him.' He spat out the words. 'He's a good friend of mine – of the whole family. His father and my father are inseparable. We all meet up every week; Tuesday we're having a meal out.'

'Then I suggest that, given what I've just told you, you cancel it – or at least postpone it until we know more,' Handford said quietly.

'That's an order, is it?'

'No, it's a suggestion.'

'And what do I tell my father?'

'I think you know the answer to that, Khalid. You tell him nothing.'

'Yes, sir.'

Handford felt the coldness in his words and apprehension adhered to his nerve endings. He understood the problem this would cause for Ali. He had joined the police force against his father's wishes and had never been totally forgiven for it. Always he was having to prove to him that his chosen career was respectable. If it came to him having to chose once again between his loyalty to his father, when the involvement was personal, and his loyalty to the service, Handford couldn't be sure he would be able to do it.

The tension thickened and Ali's voice when he spoke was as taut as a violin string. 'You'll no doubt be passing this on to Mrs Forrester.'

When Handford didn't answer immediately, Ali said, 'Perhaps she'll order me to research my best friend's background.' The words overflowed with sarcasm.

Handford wasn't sure who Ali was getting at: Forrester, him or the system. 'I think you're the one being ridiculous now, Khalid. You know the score. Friend or no friend, it would be better for you not to be seen associating with him for the moment.'

'I'll think about it.'

'Do more than that. Talk with the vice squad. There are two of their team on the investigation, brought in specifically because of the concerns over Azam. DS Archer and DC Warrender.' Ali's eyes widened and Handford knew immediately that mentioning Warrender had been a mistake.

'Warrender? Central's token racist?' Ali had experienced difficult times with him. 'Brought in no doubt to make sure that Deepak is nicely trussed up.' Unmistakable emotions tightened his features. 'And *you* want me to talk with him? I don't think so, sir.'

Handford sighed. 'Do what you think best. Only whatever you do, make sure you have thought long and hard about it first.'

'Like you did when you were "ordered" to fit up the DCI?'

Enough was enough. Handford knew Ali was angry, but he wasn't prepared to take this. He stood up. As he did so, he saw Amina watching them through the French windows. 'I'll pretend I didn't hear that,' he said. 'I'll see you Monday.'

As Amina showed him to the door, she gave him a sad smile. 'It's obvious you've been arguing,' she said. 'Don't worry, John, whatever it is, he'll come round when he's had time to think.'

'I hope so, Amina. But he has an awful lot to think about.' He touched her arm. 'Help him, won't you?'

She closed the door behind him and for once, as he walked down the path to the gate, the house didn't seem quite so welcoming.

It was almost midnight. Leah lay on her bed, exhausted, but not ready for sleep. She felt dirty. She used to feel dirty sometimes when she'd been bad and Deepak locked her in the bedroom at the flat and she couldn't get to the bathroom. But not like this. Five men had had her tonight and she wanted to scrub herself clean, to get rid of them. And she hurt. The condoms had rubbed so much that she could have screamed out.

A head peered round the door. 'Hello. You new?'

'Yes.' Leah was too tired to talk, but the question had been friendly enough.

The rest of the girl came into view, surrounded by the pungent scent of a cheap perfume. Small and slender, her long dark hair framed the petite features. Her eyes were large and brown, like those of the spaniel that used to live down the road from Leah when she was a child. A scanty satin dressing gown hung from her shoulders. She had not tied the belt, or if she had, it had come undone and Leah could see the red panties, black bra and black stockings held by a red suspender belt. On her feet she wore a pair of shabby high-heeled shoes.

From the door, she scrutinised Leah. 'You finished?' she asked, then without waiting for an answer, said, 'You could do with some stockings. They turn 'em on good and proper. They can hardly hold it in.' She laughed as though it was a good joke she had told.

Leah pulled herself gingerly into a sitting position. 'I was wondering if I could have a bath.'

'Yes, if you want – or a shower. I'll give Alice her due, she likes us clean so there's always plenty of hot water. The bathroom's at the end of the passage and the shower next to it. You'd better be quick though, the others will be finished soon and then everyone will want the same thing, except for Debbie; she says she's always too knackered to bother. God knows why. Probably puts her whole heart and soul into it. I keep telling her not to work so frigging hard, but she takes no notice. Personally I lay back and fake it while they have their fun. It's easier that way and they never seem to know the difference. I'd have a television if Alice would let me, then I could watch it while they're doing the business. What's yer name?'

'Jasmine.'

'No, not yer working name, yer real name.'

'Leah.'

'Bloody 'ell, that's posh. Were you posh before you came here?'

Leah laughed. 'No. It was my grandmother's or my great-grandmother's name. My dad liked it.'

The girl threw off her shoes and sat on the edge of the bed. 'So where's yer dad now?'

'Dunno. Gone.'

'And yer mum?'

Leah shook her head. She didn't want to talk about her mother. 'What's your name?'

'Cindy. Jade to the punters. Got any cigs?'

'No.' Leah pulled herself to the edge of the bed, screwing up her nose as the pain struck.

Cindy was sympathetic. 'Hurt, does it? I've got some cream that'll do the trick. Give it few days and you'll hardly notice. Lisa was saying you're one of Deepak's.'

'He's my boyfriend, if that's what you mean.'

Cindy guffawed. 'Boyfriend! Deepak's no one's boyfriend. Ask Lisa. He had her before he had you, and I'm willing to bet he's got another lined up.'

'I don't think so. He loves me. He'll come for me soon.'

Cindy shrugged, then lay on her back across the bed. 'Have it yer own way,' she said.

It would have been good not to believe Cindy, but Leah couldn't shake off Dwayne Varley's sniggered words when he came for her. *He's got another girl. A real looker. You're history.* They'd been at the back of her mind all day, even when the men were with her. She feathered the bruise on her face with her fingers. It still hurt, though not as much as it had when Deepak had hit her. She'd done her best to cover it up with make-up, but it had turned a deep purple and was difficult to camouflage. She'd hoped the men wouldn't want her when they saw it, but Alice had been right, some of them preferred it. One man had stroked it before he lay on top of her. She shuddered, then squirmed her body down the bed to sit next to Cindy who scrutinised the injury. 'Deepak give you that, did he?'

Leah nodded, ashamed that it had been necessary for him to hit her at all.

Cindy must have felt her humiliation because she said, 'Don't worry, love, most of his girls arrive looking like they've gone four rounds with a Rottweiler. It's the way he gets rid of them.'

Leah smiled, half believing her, half not. 'How long have you been here?'

'Can't remember off-hand. I was twelve when I came, so about eighteen months, I suppose.'

'Do you like it?'

Cindy moved to prop herself up on her arm. 'It beats frigging school, and it definitely beats the squat I was in before then. It's warm and we don't starve. What more can you ask?'

'But the men, night after night?'

'Don't think about it. Let 'em screw yer, take their money, roll 'em if you can.'

'Roll 'em?'

'Steal their money. Pinch their wallet.'

'But don't they tell the police?'

Cindy laughed. 'What planet 'ave you been livin' on? They're not going to tell anyone, are they? They're shagging kids under sixteen. They'd get done if they went to the police.' She sat up. 'God, I could die for a cig. Are you sure you don't 'ave any?'

Leah shook her head. 'What do you do with the money?'

'We're supposed to give it all to Alice, but most of us keep some for ourselves. It's only fair, we're doing the bloody work. Just be careful where you hide it though, because she goes through your drawers every now and again and if she finds some, you'll get a good slapping. She can be a real bitch sometimes. She was a hooker, you know, before all this.'

'Alice was?'

'Yeah. Not on the streets, high class, with 'er own flat and everything. It was only the posh blokes she 'ad, paid 'er a mint, they did.'

She paused for a moment to reflect. 'I'm going to do that, set up on me own. In fact, if it wasn't for that frigging Trash Bag Killer, I'd 'ave been out of 'ere and done it already. But it's us he's after. All those he got worked here.'

'Alice says it's probably Deepak who's doing it,' Leah said.

'Nah. She's just saying that to frighten you. He's not going to kill us, is he? We're raking it in for him.'

'Alice said he killed them because they were trying to get away.'

'Yeah, well, they'd mentioned it a couple of times, but a lot of us do and he's never killed anyone for that before. He's got other methods 'as Deepak.'

'Like what?'

'Like you don't want to know.' The comment silenced Cindy for a moment and Leah wondered if he did the same to them as he'd done to the woman with the cut down her face.

Suddenly, Cindy sat up. 'I'll tell you what. We'll go shopping tomorrow.'

Leah shook her head. 'I've no money. Deepak took back what I had before I left. He said it would make me work harder if I had no money.'

Cindy smiled and tapped the side of her nose. 'Who's talking about shopping with money?' she said. 'There's other ways. You stick with me, girl, and I'll teach you more than any frigging school can.'

Sleep eluded Ali that night. He pummelled his pillow and closed his eyes in an attempt to drop off, but images of his boss and his friend catapulted around his brain as though he were channel-hopping television programmes. Eventually he got up and went down to the kitchen to make himself a drink.

When the first killing had come to light, he had hoped he would be assigned to the investigation; now he was relieved he hadn't been. The whole idea of Russell being involved was ludicrous and the bosses must think so too, otherwise he would have been suspended. If they hadn't done that, then they couldn't be sure enough of their ground. It was likely the photograph was all they had, not much on which to build a case of murder, although enough, he acknowledged, to begin the initial research into his background. But not by Russell's own DI. For John to accept the job was unforgivable. Ali had meant what he said when he told him he thought better of him.

As for Deepak Azam being involved with prostitutes, that, too, was ridiculous. Ali had known him for a long time; he was a hard-working, moral business and family man who was respected by everyone in the city; his wife, Shagufta, and his children wanted for nothing. This had to be a case of racism at its worst, the assumption that a wealthy Asian had to be a crook and was there-fore an obvious choice for scrutiny. But as he rinsed out his coffee mug, he knew it was unlikely. Following the race riots in the city and Lord Ouseley's report, everyone was working hard to build goodwill between communities. The police, more than any other organisation, were attempting to bridge the racial divide, so it would be unlikely that the vice squad would suggest, let alone accuse Deepak of such a crime without good reason. Something must have generated their initial concern, and he wanted to know what. Michelle Archer would be the person to tell him, sergeant to sergeant. Tomorrow, first thing, he'd look her up, find out the truth.

And if it were true, what then? How could he explain to his father the sudden decision to avoid the Azams? Perhaps he could demand confidentiality, then spell out what he had learned and ask him to stay away from the family, at least for the moment. Yet, Ali knew full well it wouldn't work; his father would never be able to break faith with his friend. If anything, his goodwill towards him would strengthen – as would his aversion to his son's choice of career. He would demand again that Ali resign and take up a position in what he had always considered a more acceptable sphere of the law. When Ali left university, he had gone along with his father's wishes to become a solicitor, but had hated it and had finally left to join the police service. His father had been devastated; it was not a suitable career for an Asian son. They had argued for many hours, but Ali had stood his ground and three days later had left to begin his training, his father's words ringing in his ears: 'If you do this, Khalid, you are no son of mine.' Much to Ali's relief, his father had stopped short of disowning him then, but now, this time, when there was a direct effect on the family and the com-munity, he might not be so understanding. Ali's loyalty would be more in question than ever.

Since Handford had left, he had kept quiet about what he had been told. But it was obvious he had been worried, stirring his food around his plate with his fork, but not eating at dinner and wandering the garden until it got dark. Amina had begged him to tell her what the matter was, had even asked why he and John had been arguing. He'd reprimanded her for that. Then he'd wished he hadn't, but hadn't apologised. Instead he'd told her to cancel the meal with the Azams for Tuesday. When she'd asked why, he'd said he would be too busy. Her expression suggested she didn't believe him, but she'd kept her counsel and said she would do it once the children were in bed.

He came to his decision as dawn was breaking. Not only would he talk to Michelle Archer, he would also go and see Deepak. The investigation into the killings was nothing to do with him so, at the moment, he rationalised, there was no immediate need for him to inform DCS Forrester of his relationship with Azam. Obviously he would tell her – if and when it became necessary. Nor could he see any need to inform the DCI. Michael Braintree's association with the leisure centre was as a member. It was procedure to make visits to places where a victim was known. Indeed a visit there was already on DC Graham's action list. Ali would go instead of him. It would look odd, a sergeant on routine questioning, but he couldn't help that. He had to know.

chapter nine

The next morning Handford stood at the porter's lodge at the gates of King's College and stifled a yawn. He had slept fitfully and for once couldn't blame the heat. For what seemed like hours he had lay pondering on his conversation with Ali. Amina had suggested that when her husband had had time to think he would come to terms with the problem, but Handford wasn't so sure. He could still see the contempt in Ali's eyes, and it concerned him that his sergeant's loyalty to his friend and particularly to his father might this time outweigh both his obligation to inform Forrester about his relationship with Azam and his desire to warn him of the direction the serial killing investigation might be taking. He hoped he was wrong. There was no room for misplaced loyalty in the police service, but in truth it was difficult to know what any one of them would do in this situation; the need to protect is a strong emotion.

The porter came off the telephone. 'Doctor Neilsen's on his way down, sir.'

'Thank you.'

Handford forced his thoughts away from Ali and back to Russell. He leaned against the wall of the porch, which was largely in shadow and cool to the touch. He let his fingers play along the rough stonework and visualised Russell here as a student. The scent of the newly mown grass from the college's lawn invaded Handford's nostrils and again he envied the man his time at Cambridge. There had been nothing wrong with his own university in terms of academic excellence, but a move from the city centre to the leafy suburbs would have vastly improved its image.

'Detective Inspector Handford?' A rich Oxbridge accent preceded the dark-haired man, who came towards him, hand outstretched. 'I'm Mark Neilsen.' His deep brown eyes were as warm as his hand-shake.

The voice and the appearance didn't match. Slightly older than Russell, Neilsen was small and stocky. His hair was tousled as though he had just got out of bed, and his over-large T-shirt swamped the khaki shorts peering from beneath. Handford, in light grey trousers and blue short-sleeved shirt, felt overdressed. 'It's good of you to see me, Doctor Neilsen.'

'Mark, please call me Mark. No problem. I thought we'd take a walk along The Backs if you don't mind. I've been working on my research since dawn and could do with the fresh air.'

He led the way across the lawned courtyard, past the chapel and through the grounds of Clare College. In front of them flowed the Cam and beyond that stretched The Backs, open grassland to the rear of the colleges, which, in spite of the heatwave, had not yet taken on the careworn texture of desiccated turf.

Handford said, 'You and Stephen Russell were students together, I believe?'

'That's right. Good friends actually, we corresponded for a couple of years after we left university, then, as so often happens, the letters dried up and we lost touch. We had rooms next door to each other, drank beers together, talked, laughed, put the world to rights, you know the kind of thing.' His mind appeared to drift into his memories. 'They were good times,' he murmured wistfully, then turning to Handford, he said, 'Are you going to tell me why you have come all this way to discuss Stephen?'

'We need to eliminate him from our inquiries.'

'By checking on his student days? Come on, Inspector, there must be more to it than that.'

Sometimes interviewing a person was like a game of poker – bluff and double bluff – and with some it worked and with others it didn't. Neilsen was one of the latter and Handford knew that with him the game wasn't worth the mental energy. He needed it straight.

'We've had a series of killings, young girls,' he explained. 'Always in the same way.'

'A serial killer, you mean?'

'Yes, it's beginning to look like that.'

'And you think this man is Stephen Russell?' Neilsen shook his head vehemently. 'Never in a million years, Inspector. The Stephen I knew was placid, unobtrusive, restrained, hardly ever provoked to anger, let alone violence. He was bright, intelligent, organised to the point of the ridiculous. He never did anything without considering it a dozen times. Now, does that sound to you like a serial killer?'

Handford sighed. 'Sadly, yes, it does. Serial killers often show themselves to be like that. They build a public persona that camouflages their real character. Our man is brutal, yet he's also clever and organised. He plans carefully, picks the time and the place, wants the girls found soon and makes sure they will be. Yet, in spite of the savageness of each attack, he has never once been seen, never once been heard and has left us no forensics.'

For a while, Neilsen remained thoughtful. 'So, how did you come to suspect Stephen? It can't be just because he may have the right profile.'

'No, of course not. And anyway, I'm not sure yet that he is a serious suspect. But we do need to eliminate him.' Handford took a deep breath. 'Look, I wouldn't normally pass on information like this, but the situation is unusual and I think you can help me more if you understand.' He stopped to take the plastic wallet out of his document case. 'The most recent victim was carrying a small purse sewn into the inside of her skirt. In this purse was a photograph of Mr Russell.' He handed it to Neilsen. 'As you can see, it's some fifteen or so years old and was probably taken while he was at Cambridge.'

Neilsen scrutinised it for a moment before giving it back. 'It's certainly Stephen,' he said.

Handford replaced it. 'I need to know who he gave it to, and how it could have come into the girl's possession. He insists he has no idea, but I think he *does* know, and isn't saying.'

'You said the situation is unusual, John. How exactly?' Neilsen was an intelligent man able to pick up on the inconsequential, apportion it some significance and then ask the right question. Handford took a deep breath, and exhaled slowly.

'He's a police officer, a detective chief inspector.'

Neilsen's eyes opened wide. 'No. Stephen Russell a police officer?' he said incredulously. 'We are talking about the same Stephen Russell, aren't we?'

Handford nodded. 'Believe me, Mark, I wish we weren't.'

Neilsen paused for a moment, and as Handford watched him, his blue eyes darted from side to side as if they were catching hold of past memories. 'The man I was at King's with,' he said eventually, 'was intending to be a high-powered executive in his father's pharmaceutical firm, not a police officer. Did he join the business at all, do you know?'

'Yes, for a couple of years, but then something happened and he left. I don't know what it was. The reason in his file said "personal" but because we're playing this low-key, I'm not allowed to speak to his family, and for the moment I'd rather not talk to him about it.'

Three skimpily dressed joggers elbowed their way past the two men, leaving the smell of their sweat in their wake.

Handford twisted round to allow his gaze to pass over Neilsen's face like a sensor. 'Can *you* think of any reason why he should leave?'

Neilsen offered no immediate reply. A frown creased his forehead and vertical lines ran down the centre to the cleft of his nose. For a few moments he seemed to be deliberating on whether to tell what he knew, and Handford left him to reflect. Eventually he said, 'I'm sorry, John, but I haven't been strictly honest with you in my assessment of Stephen.'

'Oh.' Handford raised his eyebrows.

'Certainly he was all the things I described, but there was another side to him. He had a tendency to moods, moods that were quite dark and filled him with anger. They didn't surface very often, but when they did they seemed to take him over. They were something to do with his parents, mainly his mother, I think, but he would never talk about it and I have no idea what it was that caused them, except that when it happened he always disappeared for a couple of days and no one ever knew where he'd been.'

Handford held his breath as he watched concern filter into Neilsen's eyes. He empathised with the don's reaction but tried to push the feeling away. Empathy was a luxury he couldn't afford, for he was painfully aware that had it been anyone other than Russell they were discussing, he would have relished this information as a possible breakthrough. Now, as much as he would have preferred not to have been made privy to it, Handford acknowledged that somehow and from somewhere, he had to learn more about Russell's darker side.

For a moment Neilsen studied the distant horizon, his thoughts elsewhere. Then suddenly, he seemed to pull back to the original question and said, 'As for his reason for leaving the firm, I can't help you with that, I'm afraid. When I knew him, he was full of the business, what he was going to do, how he would modernise. He wasn't a chemist, but with a good law degree, an MBA and his capacity for organisation, he would have taken the firm forward. Perhaps it was too much for the old man, perhaps he would have none of it. I do know he didn't get on well with his father, particularly after . . . well, after he left university. But even so, to join the police. Why not another company? It would have been more in his line, I would have thought.' Neilsen shook his head in disbelief. He pulled a handkerchief from the pocket of his shorts and wiped the sweat off his face. 'Do you mind if we sit down for a moment? This heat's beginning to get to me.'

Resting against the thick trunk of a tree Handford took in the view. In front of them was the Cam, already alive with boats and punts, and further away the imposing west end of King's College Chapel, the stained-glass window golden in the sunlight, the two spires contrasting against the deep blue of the sky. He wanted to tuck this picture away, take it back with him, unpolluted, if possible, by the image he was beginning to build up of his boss. He'd come here to get some answers about Russell, but he was likely to be leaving with more questions about a life, which, it had always seemed to him, fit neatly into business-like compartments. Yet it was rapidly becoming a life that was more messy, private and difficult to penetrate than anyone could have expected, least of all Handford.

'Tell me about him – as a student,' he said when they were settled.

Neilsen allowed a faint smile to cross his face. 'Hard-working, dedicated, something of a perfectionist. There was no doubt he would come out at the end of the course with a First. He knew what he wanted and how to get it.'

That sounded like the Russell Handford knew. 'His social life? What about that?'

'Well, work came first, but he did enjoy acting. I seem to remember he was particularly good in comedy roles.'

And that wasn't. The DCI wore his mask well. Perhaps they ought to persuade him into the police pantomime at Christmas – that would be a sight to behold. Handford sagged inwardly. It would be funny if it weren't so sad.

'Friends, girlfriends, what about them?'

'Yes, he was popular enough. Liked a drink or two, but never went over the top. I don't think I ever saw him drunk. Mind you, he could have been, I was drunk so often myself that I wouldn't have known how others were faring.' He paused for a moment. 'You know, looking back I wonder how I ever managed to get a degree, let alone a First.'

Handford smiled. 'Girlfriends?' he reminded Neilsen.

'Yes, of course, sorry.' He pondered for a moment. 'Only one, Catherine. They met in Freshers' Week, and apart from an occasional blip were together through their three years here. It looked at one time as though they would marry after they graduated.'

'Catherine, not Natasha?'

'No, it was Catherine. Who's Natasha? His present wife?'

Handford nodded.

'Pity. I had hoped that in the end Stephen would stand by her. They were head over heels in love, absolutely passionate about each other.'

'What do you mean, Mark, "stand by her"?'

'She was pregnant when she left Cambridge. She sat her finals and then left. Stephen wanted to marry her straight away, before the baby was born. His father, on the other hand, was against it. He demanded a termination, even offered to pay for it. Stephen was furious. I remember because we argued about it. He couldn't see that it would make sense, that to have a baby at that point would have meant putting her career on hold, and that would have been a waste. Anyway, as I understand it, she took the money and went home to Norfolk, presumably to have the termination, and Stephen went off to London to study for his Masters. That's when we lost touch.'

'Can you recall Catherine's surname?'

'Walsh,' Neilsen said. 'And as far as I remember she'd been offered a position with a solicitor in Norwich. In fact,' he was beginning to get excited, as though it were some game they were playing, 'you know, she's probably still there. There's a solicitor's office with the name Walsh on the window. I saw it the last time I was in the area and wondered if it was her. Let's face it, fifteen years on, she's almost bound to have her own practice. Anyway, it was a Sunday so I couldn't check it out, and then events overtook me and I didn't consider it again. It would be worth verifying, don't you think?'

Ali found Michelle Archer in the canteen. 'Can I have a word?' he said.

She indicated the chair opposite and picked up her sandwich. 'How can I help?'

'Deepak Azam. I've heard the vice squad have him flagged up as a pimp.'

'That's right.' She took a bite. 'Sorry about this; it's my break-fast.' She pointed at the teacake. 'Bacon,' she explained. 'So, who are you, and what's your interest in him?'

'DS Ali. I'm investigating the murder of a young lad, Michael Braintree. He was a member of Mr Azam's leisure centre. I'm going to visit him today – just routine inquiries – but I'd heard you suspect him of pimping and I wanted to check I had my facts right.'

Archer took another bite. A trickle of fat ran down her chin and she wiped it away with her serviette. 'Yes, you have. Not that we can prove anything, but then you hardly ever can with pimps. Anyway, we think he runs a covey of about twenty women.'

Ali attempted to keep his expression neutral, but he was having difficulty rationalising the information. None of what Archer was saying was possible, there was obviously a mistake. He would have known if his friend was involved in something so big, yet there had been nothing Deepak had done that in the slightest way aroused Ali's suspicion. He tried to keep his emotions in check and asked, 'What brought him to your attention?'

'Oh you know, a girl has let his name slip occasionally when she's been drunk or out of it on drugs. We've been keeping an eye on him for a few years now but never been able to pin anything on him.'

Ali flinched inwardly. If they'd been watching Deepak for so long, then they'd know he was a friend of his, yet there'd never been any mention of it, no one warning him off.

'Known associates?' he asked.

'Don't know. We never see him with anyone else but people who work for him. The chief constable could be his best friend and we wouldn't know. The trouble is we've had to stick to watching the centre and the women rather than him,' she explained. 'Otherwise we'll leave ourselves wide open for a complaint of racial harassment.'

'I can see that, particularly if all you have on him is the word of a few drugged-up prostitutes.' Ali hoped he didn't sound too scathing.

Her eyes flicked over him. 'I didn't say that *was* all we had on him, although to be honest it was until a couple of months ago. We were called out to an attack on a prostitute, Debbie Johnson. It was nasty, she'd been slashed from forehead to chin. Wouldn't tell us who'd done it of course. It could have been a punter or her pimp, but the fact that she didn't take the easy way out and say it was a punter led us to assume it was more likely her pimp.'

'And you think Deepak Azam is her pimp?' The words stuck in his throat.

'We didn't know for sure, still don't actually because she's not saying, but when we went to question her at the hospital, he was there.'

Ali's stomach lurched. 'With her?'

'Yes, sitting on a chair beside the bed. He disappeared as soon as he saw us of course. But ask yourself this, Sergeant Ali, why should Deepak Azam visit a prostitute unless he knows her or is working her, particularly as he was one of the people instrumental in having them removed from the streets in the first place?'

Ali let his eyes drop from hers. There was nothing much he could say. As Deepak's friend, he didn't want to believe her, but as a police officer, he had to put some trust in her judgement.

'So, why didn't you arrest him?' The question was a life-raft, nothing more, for he knew the answer.

'What for? Visiting a sick woman in hospital?' Her tone was scornful – no more than he deserved. 'We mounted a surveillance on the leisure centre for a while and on the women's designated site, but it was a waste of time. Seeing us had warned him off. The closest we got was a low-life called Dwayne Varley who works for him as a doorman and who collects the women's earnings each night. We could have followed him, picked him up, but it's Azam we want, and unless we actually see Varley handing over the money, we've nothing, and to charge Varley wouldn't be worth the paperwork. He's too thick to be running the girls himself, he's more a do-as-you're-told man.' She shrugged. 'There you have it. All circumstantial at the moment, but it doesn't take a rocket scientist to work out what's going on, does it?'

No, it didn't take a rocket scientist to work out what was going on, but then, Ali persuaded himself, he wasn't a rocket scientist, and he needed proof before he was prepared to alienate himself from family and friends. So when he left Michelle Archer he drove to the leisure centre. He parked the car and walked to the main entrance, contemplating the building as he did so. In former days the area had been the nerve centre of the woollen industry with massive warehouses rising on to the skyline, each filled with wool in its various stages of manufacture from sacks of waste to bales of export fabric. But as the decimation of the industry took hold and the merchants moved out, the buildings stood empty, a proud reminder of what they had once been. Eventually, in order to stop the rot, the council took over and the ground floors were rented out to dealers selling second-hand office equipment and electrical goods or for auctions of bankrupt stock. One or two snooker halls opened up to be frequented mainly by the work-shy and the school truants, and the drug dealers, prostitutes and petty thieves moved in. In spite of this, Deepak could see its potential. The district, which had once been the industrial hub of the city, had become a place to be avoided and the city and urban dwellers kept away. He wanted them back. He wanted them to reclaim it as part of their lives, he said. And he knew how to do it.

It would work, he told Ali. Central and within walking distance of the railway and bus stations and with a yard that could have been designed by the early planners with a twenty-first-century car park in mind, it was exactly right. The price had been well within his means too, for the council, wanting it off their books, were prepared to sell it at less than its market value. It would need a lot of work to turn it into a modern, purpose-built sports centre, housing a gym, squash courts and several large rooms for aerobics, martial arts, yoga and a slimming club, as well as the health food restaurant, but the building had something a new building couldn't offer, something money couldn't buy – history and tradition. Deepak knew how much the English honoured that, and when Ali had suggested it would be more sensible to buy land further out of the city where he could erect a purpose-built leisure centre, he had taken him to the front of the building. 'Look up,' he said, 'what do you see?'

Ali had been bemused. 'Nothing, except walls and a door.'

'And you a detective? Come on, Khalid, what do you see above the door?'

'The date.'

'Exactly. Eighteen-fifty. History,' he explained. 'Eighteen-fifty suggests tradition and if tradition is important to the people, then it's got to be a valuable asset to me.'

That was one of the qualities Ali admired in Deepak – his ability to know what would win people over.

And now, several years on, the exterior of the building, fashioned in local sandstone, remained a symbol of its glorious past, while inside it became a symbol of its modernity. Bright lights enticed punters in, rooms with lowered ceilings, subdued lighting and plush furniture persuaded them to stay. The well-equipped gyms, the squash courts, saunas, whirlpools and other facilities, as well as the expert trainers, aromatherapists, reflexologists and masseuses convinced them they were getting value for their money. There were yearly subscriptions for those who could afford them, half-yearly and three-monthly for those for whom money was tighter, and payment for individual sessions for those on limited budgets or for students and schoolchildren. As a result the clientele was wide and came from all classes, races and religions. Last year Deepak had been presented with an award by the Lord Mayor for his contribution to the multi-cultural ethos of the city. It was proudly displayed in the entrance to the building. The city was proud of him, the community was proud of him and Ali was proud to be his friend. Or at least he had been until he had spoken to Handford last night and Archer this morning. Now, he prayed his pride had not been misplaced.

The receptionist recognised Ali at once, smiled at him and said Mr Azam was in his office, but she was sure he wouldn't mind being disturbed. He took the lift to the top floor, which had been turned into the administration area at one end and a well-appointed flat at the other. Acknowledging the secretary as she opened the door, Ali walked into Deepak's office. Located at the canted end of the building, it was large and luxurious. The mahogany desk was the central feature. To one side of it was a state-of-the-art computer and at the other end of the room were two large leather chairs, a leather settee and a heavy mahogany coffee table. Imagining the bustling box in which he spent his own day, this seemed to Ali more like a gentleman's club.

Azam was working at his desk. A tall man, his handsome features were as clean and well cut as the navy blue trousers and crisp white shirt, which he wore open at the neck. Ali knew there would be a tie somewhere and that the suit jacket would be carefully hung in the dressing room in the flat. He knew also that in that dressing room were several articles of sports wear, which Deepak changed into before he went down into the centre, as well as a dress suit for the many formal occasions he attended. On the little finger of his right hand he wore a gold signet ring. His watch was a Rolex.

Azam pushed back his chair and walked towards Ali, his hand outstretched and a smile on his face. 'Khalid, this is a pleasant surprise. What can I do for you?' He waved his arm towards one of the visitor's chairs. 'Sit down. Can I get you a coffee? How are Amina and the children?' There was no doubt he was pleased to see him.

Ali refused the coffee. 'They're fine,' he said.

'Shagufta tells me you've had to postpone our meal.'

Ali shifted in his seat, the leather creaking as he did so. 'Yes, sorry – work. We're busy at the moment.'

Azam sat in the chair opposite him. 'You know your trouble, Khalid, you work too hard. Now, what can I do for you?'

'Business, I'm afraid, Deepak. I'm sorry to bother you on a Saturday, I know it's one of your busier days.'

'All my days are busy, I'm glad to say. But I hope I've still time for friends – and the police,' Azam added with a grin.

'We're inquiring into the death of a young boy a few days ago,' Ali said and held out his photograph. 'His parents said he was a member here.'

Azam studied it for a moment, his expression inscrutable, then handed it back. 'I can't say I'm aware of him, although that means nothing. He could well be a member, but obviously I don't know all of them personally. Just a minute, I'll check.' He stood up and walked over to the computer. 'What did you say his name was?'

'I didn't,' said Ali. 'But it's Braintree, Michael Braintree.'

Azam stared at the screen. He scrolled through the list of names, his eyes following them. The scrolling slowed, then stopped. 'Yes,' he said, 'here we are. Michael Braintree. He became a student member just over a year ago.' He lifted his eyes from the screen. 'Wasn't he the young boy who was murdered and it was made to look like suicide? I seem to remember reading something about it in the paper.'

Ali nodded. 'That's right.'

'Poor lad,' Azam seemed genuinely saddened. 'Well, Khalid, I'm not sure how, but if there is any way in which I can help you, I will. Is there anything else I can tell you?'

'Did Michael use all the facilities?'

'Our members are able to use whichever facility they want, although the younger boys tend to spend more time in the gym. Build up their muscles and their strength. You know what young lads are like.'

'When was his last visit?'

Azam leaned back over the computer and slid the mouse over its mat. His finger clicked the button. 'It was a Tuesday, 15 August, to be exact. He wasn't here long, only about three-quarters of an hour.'

That was the day the boy had died, but Ali didn't comment. Instead he asked, 'Morning or afternoon?'

'Morning, about 11 a.m.'

There was a silence for a moment while Ali made a note in his book, then he looked up and asked, 'Do you have security cameras here?'

'Of course.'

'And they are in all parts of the complex?'

'Not all parts. As you can imagine, we have to be careful where we locate them.'

'I don't suppose you have the tapes for that day?'

'Unlikely. I'll check, but it's doubtful. We only keep them if there's been an incident, an accident or a fall or something like that. Even our members wouldn't think twice about suing us if they thought they could get away with it. So we keep those tapes just in case. If it's down to us, we settle long before it comes to court.' He gave a short laugh. 'Usually quite generously, I have to say. If it isn't our fault then the tapes cover us against malicious litigation. However, there are few such occasions and there's been nothing in the last year or so.'

Ali stood up. 'Would it be possible to have a list of all present and past members?'

Azam gave him an old-fashioned look. 'In theory, no,' he said, 'they're confidential – and there's the Data Protection Act to think of. But since it's you and since you'd probably get a court order anyway, I think I can stretch a point, but it can't be now. I'll get my secretary to run one off for you and pop it into the police station tomorrow or Monday, if that's all right.'

'Thanks very much, Deepak, you've been very helpful.'

Azam smiled. 'Not at all, Khalid. It's interesting to watch you work.' He walked Ali towards the door of his office. 'Remember me to Amina and the children. Perhaps when you're not too busy we could rearrange that night out?'

Ali tried a smile. He hated deceiving his friend. 'I'll do what I can, but I'm not sure when that will be. Although from what Shagufta tells Amina, you're as busy as I am. She says you often spend the night here.'

'Sometimes, when it's late it's easier to crash out in the flat than it is to drive home. I try not to do it too often, Shagufta knows that.' He sounded cross, annoyed perhaps that his wife had complained. Or did he have another life – one that Shagufta knew nothing about? Or perhaps did know something about? Horrified, Ali lashed himself inwardly. What was he thinking of to bring Shagufta into this when he didn't even know for sure that Deepak was involved? He would be suggesting next that the children were part of it too. Even so, as ashamed as he felt, he knew he couldn't leave it there. He couldn't ask his best friend directly if he was pimping prostitutes, but he could try another road in. It might not get him all the way, but it would be a start.

'Just one last thing, Deepak,' he said as calmly as he could. 'I was talking to a sergeant in the vice squad this morning who was telling me they're currently watching a vicious piece of work called

Dwayne Varley. Apparently he's spending a lot of his time hanging round the prostitutes. I only mention it because she says he works for you.'

Ali watched Azam carefully. His lips tightened, and his words when he spoke were controlled, but he seemed more angry than concerned, for there were none of the tell-tale signs of apprehension that Ali was trained to look for. 'Yes, he does. He's a doorman, and a good one at that.' He took a step towards Ali, his eyes as hard as steel. 'It's kind of your sergeant to be concerned, Khalid, but to be honest I'd rather she minded her own business and left me to mind mine. As far as Varley is concerned, I'm only interested in what he does when he's here, not about his habits away from work. Having said that, you know how I hate prostitutes. Why else would I have worked so hard to rid my district of them? If it was up to our community, they wouldn't exist because no man would use them. It doesn't surprise me though that Varley does.' He smiled with his lips. 'However, I can hardly sack him for it, can I? So you go back to your police station, Khalid, thank your sergeant for the information but tell her that who I choose to employ is my business not hers.'

Leah didn't want to do this.

What if they got caught? What would Deepak do to her? Slash her face with a knife? Getting caught might deserve that kind of punishment.

Cindy lost patience. 'We're not going to get caught. I've done this loads of times, and I've never been caught.'

But Leah still didn't want to do it. She'd been nervous on the journey down into the city, and now they were here, she was even more nervous.

They'd caught a bus. A man got on with them and sat behind them on the top deck. Was he a copper? He had penetrating eyes like a copper that made you feel guilty even if you weren't. Did he know what they were going to do? She'd turned to look at him and he'd smiled at her. Then Cindy had started talking about a film she wanted to see on television. It was on late, but she'd asked Alice to tape it for her. Alice didn't mind doing things like that. It was an old one with Sylvester Stallone. She liked him, she said. 'He's really fit. I wouldn't mind 'im one night.'

Leah giggled. 'He's too old,' she said.

'Go on then, who would you want?'

Leah didn't know. She'd never been to the cinema and hadn't

seen much television since she'd run off from the foster parents. There hadn't been a set at the squat and after a couple of weeks Deepak got rid of the one from the flat. He'd said there were better things to do than watch television.

Cindy had got cross then. 'Deepak! He's all you ever talk about. Will you forget about frigging Deepak,' she hissed. 'You're doin' my bloody 'ead in.'

Although she'd tried not to, Cindy had said it loudly enough for Leah to be embarrassed and she'd looked round to see if anyone had heard. The man behind smiled at her again as though he understood, and self-consciously she'd returned it.

He got off the bus at the same stop.

Leah and Cindy wandered through the shops, looking at lipsticks, sticks of mascara, blushers and bottles of perfume. Anything Leah said she liked Cindy slipped into the bag she was carrying.

'Watch me a few times then you have a go,' she said.

Leah wasn't sure. It was still early, but busy enough for people to be milling round her. She felt conspicuous and glanced about a few times to make sure no one was watching. Once she thought she saw the man from the bus, but when she looked again, he wasn't there.

Cindy told her to stop. 'Stop bleeding looking round,' she whispered to her. 'You're drawing attention to yerself.'

Cindy made it look easy, but it wasn't. All she had to do, Cindy told her, was to slide the pair of earrings from the counter and let them fall into the bag. She had to be careful, the gap was narrow, open just wide enough for them to slither through. If they fell on the floor, she'd have to pick them up and put them back on the counter, make it look as though she'd dropped them.

The first time she tried was at the cosmetics counter. Fear numbed her fingers and as she slid the lipstick into her hand it slipped from her grasp and dropped onto the floor. She picked it up and put it back on the counter and then tried with a bottle of nail varnish. The same thing happened. But this time it bounced down, slid along the tiled floor and stopped at the feet of a shop assistant. The woman bent down and picked it up. She handed it back to Leah.

Leah could feel herself blushing. 'Sorry. Sorry,' she said.

She was no good at this. 'Let's go,' she said, but Cindy wouldn't have it. 'You've got to learn sometime.' So this time she went for earrings.

She'd just picked them up when she saw the security guard. Dressed in his beige uniform, the words 'Security Guard' embroidered in dark brown on his pocket, he walked towards them. Had he seen her? She was sure he had. Hardly daring to move or to put the earrings back on the counter, she clasped hold of them, her palms sweating. Suddenly he was next to her. She looked down at the counter as though she was scrutinising the jewellery, deciding what to buy, but she was sure he knew. Then just as suddenly he had gone past. Leah licked her lips and smiled nervously at Cindy who nodded that she should continue. Her heart beating hard against her chest wall, she tried again.

Close to Cindy.

Drop the earrings.

She was in the right place and they fell towards the bag, but this time caught on the zip and hung for a moment. Cindy shook it gently and they fell through. The silver foil with which the bag was lined rustled and it was then and only then that Leah let go of the breath she had been holding.

'Come on, let's go somewhere else,' Cindy said. It didn't do to stay too long in any shop.

The next one they tried was the ladies department of Next. There was a sale on and it was busy so no one had time to notice two young girls picking clothes off the racks. They came away from Next with some summer tops, although Leah hadn't been able to see how they could get them out of the store.

'They've got tags on,' she said. 'They'll set the alarm off.'

Cindy was scornful. 'Don't you know nothing? What do you think the silver foil's for? It stops the alarm going off.'

'How?'

'I don't know, do I? Does it matter?' she added impatiently.

Leah didn't suppose it did.

In British Home Stores Cindy fancied skimpy swimwear. She could lie out in the garden in it and get sunburnt. They fingered their way through the racks choosing what they wanted and Cindy had stowed away two bikinis, one for Leah and one for herself, before they saw the security guard, stealthily creeping up on them, his radio to his mouth.

Cindy shouted, 'Run' but Leah didn't need telling. She fled one way, Cindy the other. The guard chose Leah.

She ran fast.

She mustn't be caught.

If she were caught, Alice wouldn't forgive her, Deepak wouldn't forgive her. He'd slit her face with a knife. Tears ran hot down her cheek, her breath caught in her throat. She pushed aside shoppers who swore at her as they stumbled against the racks. The guard shouted out for them to stop her, but they were so busy keeping their balance that no one did.

Frantically, Leah looked round. She needed to get out, but she'd run away from the entrance. The stairs. Two lots and she wasn't sure whether the ones she chose were the ones that led to the restaurant or to the car park; she hoped the car park, because from there she could get to the road. Her chest was hurting now and her breath coming in gasps. She wasn't sure she could make it.

Then suddenly someone grabbed at her arm.

The guard?

No, he was still behind her, she could hear him shouting, 'Hold on to her, mate.'

Terrified, Leah was about to kick out as she had at Dwayne Varley. But the man said, 'This way,' and for a moment she stopped. 'Come on,' he whispered urgently. 'If you don't want to get caught, we need to go this way.'

It was a trick. He was a plain clothes copper. He'd take her straight to the cop shop. She struggled to pull herself away from him, but he held on tight, dragging her up the stairs. She kicked out at him, but missed.

'Hold on to her, mate.'

The guard was nearer now. Suddenly, her need to escape the man behind her was stronger than her fear of the one in front, so she stopped struggling and followed him up the steps, Once at the top, she glanced downwards and saw the guard frantically looking round, desperate to locate his shoplifter. It was too late, in seconds they would be gone. She let the man pull her up the last of the stairs, through the doors, across the car park and down the ramp to the back of the shop to freedom.

Together, they dashed across the road and up the hill to the Interchange bus station, looking, she was sure, for all the world like father and daughter rushing to catch a bus. Once inside, they stopped to catch their breath.

When he was capable of speech, her rescuer held out his hand and said, 'I'm Joe. What's your name?'

It was the man from the bus.

chapter ten

It was half past three in the afternoon when the duty sergeant rang through from the front office to tell Detective Chief Superintendent Forrester that Councillor Collingham was requesting a few moments of her time. He had some information for her, the sergeant said.

It was Saturday, she'd been in the station from early morning and had stayed on only in the hope she might hear from John Handford, although why she wasn't sure, since he'd got both her mobile and her home number. In fact she'd almost decided to go home, stretch out in the garden with a bottle of cold white wine and a trashy magazine when the telephone had rung. 'You'd better show him up,' she said with a sigh.

A few moments later Andrew Collingham entered the office. In spite of the heat he was wearing a dark suit, white shirt and tie. She stood up and held out her hand. Collingham took it. His handshake was light and sweaty, and she resisted the urge to wipe her palm down her skirt.

'What can I do for you, Councillor?' she asked as he sat in the chair she had pulled out for him. 'I understand from the sergeant that you have some information for me?'

Collingham settled himself comfortably, crossing one knee over the other. 'I want you to know, Chief Superintendent, that I have thought long and hard before deciding to come here today.'

'Yes, I'm sure,' she said.

Silence teased the air, almost as though it were playing a joke on those who waited.

'Mr Collingham?'

Resting on the leg that was crossed, his right hand held the left one loosely. A streak of sunlight squirming through a break in the blinds caught at his wedding ring and he blinked as the reflection snagged his eye. He shifted his hands slightly. Perspiration stood in droplets on his top lip, but his body language suggested confidence and control.

Forrester waited.

'Yesterday morning Detective Chief Inspector Russell rang me and suggested lunch. We met at The Vaults in the city centre.' For a moment Collingham was silent. He dragged at his bottom lip with his teeth, shifting the blood, which spilled back again when the pressure was released. 'He said he was a suspect in the killings of the girls. Is that so, Superintendent?'

Forrester's eyes glued on to his as, at the same time, a smile crossed her lips. 'Now, Councillor,' she said coldly, 'you know I can't tell you that. All I am prepared to tell you, and this is for your ears as a member of the police committee, not as a private citizen, is we came across evidence at the scene of the girl's murder that led us to want to question him. We are currently following up that evidence. Whether he is a suspect or not remains to be seen.'

Collingham's eyes narrowed. 'In that case, Chief Superintendent Forrester, perhaps I can take your inquiries a little further. Stephen's reason for our meeting was to ask if I would firm up his alibi for the night of the latest murder. He wanted me to say I had been with him or seen him or spoken to him at the time the girl was killed. He assured me he hadn't killed her, but said he needed a stronger alibi. One that couldn't be questioned.'

Forrester caught her breath. Russell had just moved himself a step closer to the centre of the frame. She controlled her excitement. 'And what did you say, Mr Collingham?'

'What do you think I said, Mrs Forrester? I said no.'

'Did he explain why he wanted you to do that?'

Collingham smiled at her. 'He did, but I'm not prepared to divulge his reasons, Chief Superintendent. You must ask Stephen.'

Forrester tried not to let her impatience show. She wanted to tell him that it ought to be all or nothing, but instead asked, 'Did he give you any idea as to where he had been, or what he had been doing?'

'No, none.'

'Had he been with a prostitute, perhaps?'

At first Collingham showed surprise at the question, then he laughed. 'I doubt it, Mrs Forrester. You're not going to find anyone more moral than Stephen Russell.'

'It was hardly the act of a moral man to ask you to give him an alibi when his own was weak, don't you think, Mr Collingham?'

'No, perhaps not. Even so, Stephen Russell with a prostitute? I doubt it.'

'And you won't tell us any more?'

'No. Anything else should come from Stephen himself. You'll have to ask him.'

Forrester stood up and walked around her desk. She perched on the edge, deliberately crowding Andrew Collingham. He uncrossed his legs and sat up straighter. As he passed his tongue over his lips, he looked up at her.

She smiled. 'You've whetted my appetite, Councillor Collingham, but no more than that. I don't know whether that was deliberate on your part, but I wonder why, if you weren't prepared to tell me everything, you came in at all?'

Collingham shifted his position again. His expression appeared to suggest he would have liked to stand up, move, lean against the filing cabinet, anything to give him back a level of control. Eventually, Forrester restored the status quo by slipping off the desk and returning to her chair.

Collingham relaxed. 'I'm a councillor, Chief Superintendent,' he said. 'What else should I do with the information I have, but give it to the investigating team? You think Stephen may be involved; he has asked me to do something an innocent person would never need to ask. What else would you expect me to do?'

She ignored the question. 'What are Mr Russell's views on prostitutes, do you know?'

Collingham threw her a look of disgust. 'You seem to have a one-track mind, Mrs Forrester,' he said critically.

'Oh, come now, Mr Collingham, you know as well as I do that prostitutes figure in these murders. We may pretend the young ones don't exist, but that's only for show – and for the budget of course.'

Collingham's lips compressed in anger. 'You have no right to question our policy, Chief Superintendent. You see only the narrow picture; we have to look at the wider one.'

'Even if the wider one results in the death of young girls?' Forrester leaned forward. 'The killer is deliberately targeting those who have been lured into prostitution, probably against their will. Young vulnerable girls who don't deserve the danger we are putting them in. Your policy is giving them to a killer who has a hatred of them, who needs to punish and kill them. I'm not asking about Mr Russell's views for any prurient reason, Councillor. His view of prostitutes may be significant.'

'In that case, I don't know. I imagine it's the same as any sane-thinking man.'

'And yours, what are yours?'

Collingham smiled. 'You think my view of prostitutes may be significant as well? However, if it's relevant to your inquiry – and I can't see how – I'll answer your question. I dislike them. They think nothing of propositioning men in the city centre, even in daylight. I've seen it myself. You, as a police service, ought to be doing more to stop them, and I, as a member of the police committee, will make sure you do. We will rid this city of prostitutes, that I can promise you. But we will do it inside the law, not with the carnage we are experiencing at present.'

'And when the young ones become older ones?'

'Them as well.'

Heat from the sun and from the passion of the last few minutes hung in the air. It insinuated itself into Forrester's lungs and she took a few deep breaths. Collingham sat, an expression of triumph on his face.

Suddenly Forrester said, 'Do you think Stephen Russell is the serial killer?'

For a moment the abrupt change in the questioning unnerved Collingham. At first he seemed flustered, shifted his position and recrossed his legs, then his experience on the hustings seemed to come into play and he said quietly, 'No, I don't think he is.'

'Then why *did* you come here today? He's a friend of yours, I believe.'

Collingham was more himself, calm but supercilious. 'I've told you,' he said. 'When Stephen asked me what he did, it was my duty to pass it on. But, I have to admit there are other reasons. The first is that I want him to tell you himself what he told me and you will no doubt be able to make him do that. I'm sure then that you will see nothing of importance in the photograph . . .'

Forrester felt her anger growing again. What kind of a police officer was Detective Chief Inspector Russell? It was in his own interest to keep the information about the photograph to himself, never mind in the interest of the investigation. If Collingham chose, he could tell every newspaper hack in the country.

'. . . also,' Collingham was still talking, 'were you around when the Yorkshire Ripper was at large, Mrs Forrester?'

She nodded. 'Just about. I was a teenager at the time he began, about eighteen when he was caught.'

'Well, let me tell you, for nearly six years he had every woman in the area terrified. They trusted no one, not their fathers, not their brothers, not their husbands, not their boyfriends. Rumours were rife. At one time, I remember, it was said he disguised himself as a policeman before he killed, so every bobby on his beat was mistrusted. Then it was said he was dressed as a woman – can you imagine what effect that had? No woman felt safe, and the more so when he turned from murdering prostitutes to murdering innocent females. Do you think I want this city to return to that? That is why I came to you, Chief Superintendent. I don't think Stephen is involved, but I'm not prepared to risk that he might be. So I told you what I thought was the significant part of the conversation I had with him, the rest you must get from Stephen.'

He stood up. He was completely in control now, the councillor with clout, and he knew it. 'If I'm wrong, then so be it. That will be between me and Stephen. However, Chief Superintendent, I can tell from your expression that you think I might not be.'

He held out his hand. Susan took it, marvelling at the man. With the expertise of any good detective, he had read her thoughts then, without her permission, had usurped her authority and ended the interview.

'I'll get someone to show you out,' she said.

It was late afternoon when Handford contacted Susan Forrester's direct number.

'John, what have you got for me?'

He described his conversation with Dr Neilsen and what he had learned about Catherine, the pregnancy and the split with Russell.

'Her full name is, or was, Catherine Walsh. She is, or was, a solicitor; Neilsen thinks that she still is and that she probably has a practice in Norwich. I'll go there on my way back, but it'll have to be Monday.'

The day was getting better and better. 'You think the photograph may have something to do with this Catherine Walsh?'

'I think it could do. I'm not sure how it came into the dead girl's possession, but it's obviously linked with Mr Russell and the link began in Cambridege.'

'Elaborate, please.'

He remained silent for a moment.

'John?' Forrester wasn't prepared to wait while he struggled with his conscience.

'Well, it's a long shot, ma'am, but if this woman is his former girlfriend, perhaps the dead girl is the baby who was to have been terminated; perhaps Catherine couldn't go through with it and continued with the pregnancy. Perhaps she had a daughter and that daughter found out somehow who and where her natural father was and came to Bradford to find him.'

'And perhaps she did find him, and perhaps, therefore,' Forrester added, 'Mr Russell knows more than he is admitting to.'

As she replaced the receiver, she smiled grimly. The hidden depths of Stephen Russell – an illegitimate daughter and a photograph. What life secrets were they concealing?

Assistant Chief Constable James Sanderson had been as good as his word and when John Handford visited Parkside Police Station overlooking the common land named Parker's Piece, he was given every assistance he wanted.

'We've been expecting you, sir,' the desk sergeant said and immediately rang through to the duty inspector who came down to greet Handford.

'The memo said you're interested in any undetected murders between 1982 and 1985,' the inspector commented as he walked Handford back to his office.

'That's right. I know it's a lot to ask given the short notice, but much as I would like to stay to explore Cambridge and its surroundings, I have to get back on Monday. I can trawl through the cases on my own, I don't want to take anyone from their duties.'

'Oh, I think we can do better than that.' The inspector picked up his phone. 'Tell Ted we're ready for him now. Yes please, in my office.'

He looked up at Handford. 'Ted Dimmock was our collator at the time, before we became electronic. And believe me, Ted is better than any computer, not only does he know what happened when, but he can tell you who the suspects were, their aliases, their blemishes, the names of their parents, brothers, sisters, aunts and uncles, even where they spent their holidays, I don't doubt.'

Handford laughed. 'Worth their weight, coppers like that. Computers might be quicker, but they can only give you what someone else has put in. If it's not there, you don't get it. Collators took a pride in knowing their villains.'

Ted, when he arrived, was in civvies.

'I hope I haven't eaten into your day off,' Handford said, shaking hands with him.

'It's no problem, sir. I don't often get the chance to hone my skills, so to speak. Not now with the computers taking over my job.'

He carried a number of files under his arm. 'I started getting these out as soon as the inspector here told me what you wanted. They're a bit dusty because they were in the archives, but they're all complete.' He turned to his boss. 'I thought we might use the briefing room, if that's all right, sir. It'll give us a chance to spread out.'

It seemed to make little difference whether the police station was old or new, big or small, in the north of the country or the south, certain rooms were always identical, and the briefing room was one of them. Tables set around the walls, a computer, TV and video, chairs left where they had been pushed when the last shift moved off, and pinned on the wall were rotas, maps and pictures of the most wanted and of missing children, some for quite some time. Handford scrutinised them, but none looked anything like their dead girl. Not that he expected them to, but it was worth a shot.

It was hot in here. The open windows let in the noise of the traffic along Parkside and suddenly the whine of a fire engine's siren blared above it all as it sped out of the station next door.

'They've been busy this summer,' remarked Ted as he spread out the files. 'This heat's left the area tinder dry. We're lucky we've not had a really serious fire.' He scrutinised the names in large black letters on each file. 'Right, there you are, sir undetected murders between 1982 and 1985. Five in total.'

'What I'm actually looking for are homicides of young, very young, women, probably prostitutes, who were killed during those three years, possibly by the same person. Are there any?' Handford psychologically crossed his fingers. Please don't let there be any.

Without hesitation Ted picked out three files. 'These are the closest.' He opened them, sweeping the rest aside. 'Prostitutes, but only one of them the kind of age you're looking at. They were beaten around the head and left for dead. Two had had it when they were found, the other died in hospital without regaining consciousness.'

Not quite what Handford was looking for. 'And the other two cases?'

'A child, found in a field. She'd been sexually abused, then strangled, and the other,' he opened up the file, 'was a man in his fifties, a lecturer at Magdalene. Found dead in the grounds. He'd been having an affair with one of the administrative staff. Her husband was the likeliest suspect, but we never managed to nail him.'

'Tell me about the prostitutes,' Handford said.

The constable pointed to the file nearest to him. 'The first was Jenny Marsden, better known as Sherry. Died 18 November 1982. Eighteen years old, had been a tom for a couple of years, been pulled in twice in 1981 for soliciting. As far as we could make out, she'd gone with a punter in his car. Never seen again, until her body turned up in a graveyard. She was a hell of a mess, not much of one side of her face left.'

He handed over the scene of crime photograph.

The dead woman, her dark hair and heavy make-up incongruous against the pallor of her skin, was lying over a gravestone, her face turned towards the camera, eyes staring, blood and dirt clogging deep wounds to the side of her head. She lay on her back, her arms flung to her sides and her legs splayed outwards.

'Had she had sex?'

'By the way she was lying it looked as though he'd done the business, then killed her. He must have used a condom though, because there was no semen.'

'Defence wounds?'

'No, that was what was surprising, there were none. He must have hit her from behind. There was bruising to her back and her shoulders, though.'

Handford fingered the next file. 'What about the others? The same or were there differences?'

Ted pulled a photograph from another folder. 'Kate Jennings, twenty-one. Killed October 1983. Bludgeoned again, and again there was bruising on her back. She was still alive when she was found slumped in the church porchway. They put her on a life support machine at the hospital, but the tests showed she was brain dead and after a couple of days it was turned off.'

'And the last girl?'

'Now, she's a bit closer to the age of victim you've been asking about. Lindsay Jefferson. Fourteen and a runaway. Came from Sussex. Usual story, father died, mother remarried, Lindsay couldn't stand the stepfather and ran away from home. Got in with the wrong crowd and ended up like that. We found her on a building site. Well, I say building site, it was rather the remains of the old than the beginning of the new. A chapel had stood there for years, but then was burnt down in an arson attack. The land was worth a lot and the trustees sold it off to a supermarket chain and were able to build a new chapel with the proceeds. Anyway, the builders were clearing the site to begin the work, and Lindsay's body was dumped there for all to see.'

The photograph showed the girl, foetus like, curled in the remaining vestiges of rubbish burnt by the workmen, her head lay on the charred residue, as though it were a pillow. It must have rained while she was lying there for her hair was plastered to the side of her face, which was blackened with the charcoal from the fire.

Handford replaced the photograph. 'Same MO?' he asked.

'Pretty much. She'd been beaten in the same way as the others, but it was the blows to the head that killed her.'

Handford hesitated before asking, 'And was she a prostitute, do you know?'

'No, idea. The pathologist said there was no doubt she was sexually active, but that's not unusual with runaways. If she was a prostitute she hadn't come to our notice.'

'And you think the deaths of these three were down to the same man?'

Ted sighed. 'Well, *I* certainly thought so, although I'm not sure the bosses did. No one wanted a serial killer on their hands, and the murders were a considerable time apart. The MO could have been a coincidence.'

Handford looked steadily at the police officer. 'But you thought so. Why?'

'Because of the places they were killed. In those days location wasn't considered part of the pattern, well, not like it is today. They were all beaten around the shoulders, and killed by blows to the head and all on church property. Yes, sir, I think it was the same man, some religious nut. Anyway the last one was February 1985; there were no more after that.' He returned Handford's gaze. 'If I were you, sir, I'd check out the locations of your murders, see if there's a pattern.' The constable began to pull the papers back into the files. 'Do you think you've a serial killer up in Bradford?'

Handford pondered the question. 'Yes,' he said finally. 'I think we have.'

'And you have a suspect who might have been in Cambridge during those dates?'

Handford laughed. 'Possibly. And that's all I'm going to say.'

Ted smiled. 'Don't take any notice of me, sir,' he said. 'I've been a copper for almost thirty years. I retire in a couple of months. I'm past caring if I upset an inspector or two. But the fact is that you'll get more information from me than most of the younger officers, CID or otherwise. I carry it around up here.' He pointed to his head. 'I don't need to rely on what's in a computer.' He paused again while he perched on the desk and crossed his arms across his wide chest. 'You know, sir, I'm willing to bet they'll still be asking for my help when I'm out on my boat or trying to get in a round of golf. I've forgotten more than most of these young 'uns will ever know.'

Handford sat with him, glancing out of the window as the fire engine returned to the station yard. 'Couldn't have been much of a fire,' he remarked. 'They're back already.'

The two men concentrated on the driver as he manoeuvred the appliance back into the shed. 'I'll need copies of these files, Ted,' he said, when the vehicle had come to a stop.

'Already done, sir. In the inspector's office.'

Handford's eyes widened. 'What all of them?' he asked incredulously.

'No, sir, not all of them. Only those I knew you'd want. The others are one-off murders, you wouldn't have come all this way for one-off murders. It had to be the ones that were linked, even if I'm the only person to think so.'

Handford shook his head. 'The force is going to miss you, you know.'

'You might be right, but I'll not miss it, not the way it's going.' He slid off the table and began to collect up the folders. 'By the way, sir, we thought the killer might be a student, particularly when there were no more killings after three years. Could be he's on your patch now?'

Stephen Russell poured his wife a brandy and suggested they sat somewhere more comfortable. She said she would prefer to see to the dishes before they settled, but he told her to leave them. He needed to talk to her.

'Let's go into the garden,' he said. 'I'll put the lights on.'

The day was fading and the evenings becoming shorter. The shadows the lamps threw might go some way to hiding his shame and embarrassment at what he was going to have to tell his wife. He tried to control his nerves as he walked through the French windows, and he hoped with all his heart that Natasha wasn't going to feel as betrayed as he had throughout his life and as he did at this moment by John Handford, a man he thought he could trust.

He knew his background would be researched, but not by Handford. At first he hadn't believed it, and would never have considered it had he not met Ali on the stairs leading to CID. He had made some comment about Ali working late, then asked if John Handford was about. The response to the question was as unexpected as it was unpalatable, for as innocuous as it was, Ali refused to meet his eyes.

'No, sir.'

'I thought he was on duty this afternoon.'

'He was, sir, but he asked me to take his place.'

'Why?'

Ali shifted his position. 'He said he had to go away.'

'Away? Where?'

Ali had looked even more uncomfortable. 'He's in Cambridge, I think, sir.'

As he nodded Ali's dismissal, the same physical pain he had felt when the doctor had told him Natasha would never have children had washed over him. Then it had been brought on through grief, this afternoon through anger and now through the sure knowledge that he might just be about to lose his wife. Handford was researching his background, starting in Cambridge and he was powerless to stop any of it. Even Ali knew, otherwise why did the man appear so flustered, ashamed even? Forrester had confirmed as much when he had tackled her about it, although she said she knew nothing about Ali. At that point he had said he would not answer any questions without his solicitor present, but it was no more than a gesture, a ploy to give him time, for he knew now he couldn't prevent his past coming back to haunt him. A past he was going to have to divulge to his wife and pray as he did so that it wouldn't drive them apart.

Natasha, cool in a cotton dress, sat down, her brandy in her hand, and smiled at him across the wrought iron table. 'Come on, then, Stephen, tell me. What's so important the dishes have to wait?'

Khalid Ali told his wife not to wait up for him.

'Why? Where are you going?'

'Out.'

'Out?'

'Yes, Amina, out.'

He wasn't prepared to say any more, or to put up with her questions. 'Just leave it, Amina.'

She had maintained her silence, but now as he drove to the designated site for the prostitutes, he could still see the anguish in her eyes and he hated himself for it. She was concerned about him and for him, he understood that, but he couldn't tell her where he was going or why. He wasn't even sure himself why. It was unlikely Deepak would be there, but he could talk with the women. Determine once and for all whether he was pimping them. He had to know, because if Deepak was living a life his policeman friend didn't know about, then this was the catalyst that would confirm whether or not Ali was able to put aside his loyalty to his race, his family and his friends, and remain faithful to the law, the police service and, most importantly, to himself.

chapter eleven

DS Michelle Archer shifted her position in the driver's seat of the unmarked police car and yawned. 'There's got to be a better way of spending a Saturday night at the height of summer than watching a clutch of prostitutes ply their trade,' she moaned.

DC Warrender grunted, his eyes firmly closed. 'Oh, I don't know,' he murmured.

The heat in the car was becoming unbearable and Archer began to wind the window down. 'Do you think Azam will show?' she said.

'I doubt it.' Warrender slipped further into the passenger seat.

Archer turned to look at him. 'And would you know if he did? You're supposed to keep your eyes open, Chris. You know, mounting a surveillance. Observing. Watching. With your eyes open.' She elbowed him in the ribs. 'There are times, Warrender, when you are a complete waste of space.'

Warrender rubbed his side and settled down again. 'If you say so, Sergeant,' he said.

'Warrender!'

He pulled himself up straight. 'For goodness' sake, Michelle, there's no point to this. Azam won't show, he never does. Why should he when he's got Varley to do his dirty work? If Forrester wants him for these killings – and in my opinion it's not him – then she's going to have to find a better way than this. She could begin by pulling in Varley for one. Or jumping on this lot, forcing them to tell us where the youngsters are. At least then we'd stand half a chance of nailing the bugger.' He leaned forward. 'Give me half an hour with them, and I guarantee they'll tell us.'

Archer turned to look at him, her expression as sour as an unripe fruit. 'You've already had your half an hour, Warrender,' she said. 'With the woman you went round the side of the factory with. Directing you to the fish and chip shop, was she?'

Warrender smiled. 'Something like that,' he said.

'Well, I just hope you washed your bloody hands before you bought our supper. If I end up with food poisoning, it'll be you I'll blame.'

She peered through the windscreen. The sun had set long ago, but the orange sodium of the street lamps, combined with the brightness of the moon, shed enough light for girls and punters. Two buildings of a derelict factory bordering the car park stood adjacent to each other, conjoined by the redundant chimney pointing like some phallic symbol high into the sky. At this time of night the structures loomed large in the gloom, casting deep shadows into corners and alleys, places where anyone could hide.

It was not the most salubrious part of the city, but it was the best the police and the council could come up with as a designated area for the prostitutes. Providing they kept to it and didn't wander over the other side of the road, they were safe from arrest, although not necessarily from lurking predators. The women had been moved here when their own street became too dangerous, when residents sent out vigilante gangs to frighten them away. Prostitutes had walked it for years, indeed so long had its name been synonymous with hookers and kerb-crawlers that had it been a country lane, ramblers would have had it designated a right of way. However, determined residents and a police service unable to guarantee the safety of the girls forced the council into the decision to give them a site where they could work. Whether the women were just as afraid in this venue as they had been in the old, the powers-that-be neither knew nor cared. They were street prostitutes, danger came with the territory.

A dozen or so were working. Archer watched them in their leather mini-skirts and scanty tops, tottering on high stiletto heels alongside the factory, around the concreted area between the two buildings and out into the road. In bad weather the rain formed deep puddles in holes where the surface had broken up; in the present climate they were dust bowls and as girls wandered, waiting, their shoes threw up clouds of grit and dirt from the dry ground. They smoked, incessantly, one cigarette after another.

Cars came and went, the occupants either dropping off or picking up. If the vehicle was empty, the nearest girl leaned into it.

'Ready for a good time, lover?' She didn't mention sex, that would have constituted soliciting.

If he was ready and the price was right, she gave a last drag on her cigarette, dropped the stub into the dust and ground it out with the toe of her shoe. Then, blowing the smoke from the side of her mouth, she climbed in to return about half an hour to an hour later. Not every punter wanted a women in his car and he would park up and follow her round the side of the factory or into the shadows. A quickie against the wall usually satisfied him.

'So,' said Archer, removing her gaze from the display in front of her. 'Why do you think Azam has nothing to do with the under-sixteens?'

'I didn't say that. He probably has, he's more than likely pimping them, but if he is, he's doing it in some place we don't know about, as far away from where he lives and works as it can be. He'll have them in a house with a madam schooling and chaperoning them. He'll hardly ever go near, just like he'll not come anywhere near here. It'll take a lot more than us watching a group of prosies half the night to catch him.'

'Like what?'

'Like frightening the shit out of him; letting him think that what we know is more than just suspicion; never getting off his back.'

'Oh yeah, and then having a complaint of racial harassment against us. That really would be a good move.'

'Well, it would be better than what we've got now.'

'And what have we got now, Warrender?'

Warrender's eyes held steady on hers. 'Four dead girls and bugger all in the way of evidence,' he said seriously.

A couple of cars cruised along the road, but didn't stop.

'A Sergeant Ali asked me about Deepak Azam this morning,' Archer mused.

Warrender looked up. 'I hope you told him where to go.'

'Why should I?'

Warrender shrugged.

'You know Sergeant Ali, then?'

'Worked with him at Broughton for a while and then on a murder inquiry at Central at the end of last year.'

'What's he like?'

'Like the rest of them, loyal to his own first.'

Archer gave him a hard stare. 'I meant as a police officer.'

'Good enough.' He looked as though he were about to say something else, but with her eyes still on him, decided against it. 'So what did he want?'

Archer relaxed. 'He'd heard we suspected Azam of being a pimp and wanted to know if it was a fact. He's making routine inquiries at the leisure centre for a case he's on – the murder of that young lad found hanging.'

'Then you can forget about proving Azam is a pimp. Ali will have given him the nod.' Warrender turned to face her. 'But I tell you this, Michelle,' he said, his tone serious again. 'Whether Ali warns him or not, if someone is knocking off Azam's girls, it won't be long before Azam starts to take matters into his own hands. He may or may not have any idea who's doing it, but if he decides it's a rival company, then he'll start to get his own back. And you know what that means. They'll begin by culling the women, then as they run out of them, they'll start on each other; you know, the old drive-by shooting. And who cares if innocent members of the public get in the way? Everybody's expendable to them.'

They fell into an uneasy silence. Normally, Archer hadn't much time for Chris Warrender. He was a prejudiced, sexist racist who was good at covering his back when it came to complaints. Nevertheless, this time she had to concede he had a point. If Azam was their pimp, it would make no sense at all for him to be killing the girls; it would be the same as burning money. And anyway, he had other methods of taming those he felt were getting out of line. The thought brought her back to her conversation with Sergeant Ali. At the time his request to know about Azam had seemed reasonable, but thinking about it, she wondered why he should be interested if all he was doing was checking on the dead boy's membership at the leisure centre. And why go to the top, why ask Azam himself? That smacked of more than routine inquiries. A receptionist could have told him what he wanted to know. Perhaps she ought to have another word with the sergeant.

Archer glanced over at her colleague. His eyes were closed. Again he was putting two fingers up at her authority. As far as he was concerned she hadn't any. But she did have elbows and, for a second time, she dug him hard in the ribs. He opened his eyes, gave a cursory look around and was about to resettle when a car neither of them recognised turned out its lights, crept towards the kerb and stopped. A young girl, probably no more than seventeen, wove her way towards it, her spindly legs offering little support. She leaned into the car for a moment, then pulled herself out, shouting 'Well, fuck you, mate.'

Turning to one of the other girls, she yelled. 'It's you he wants, Ros. Says I'm too old for him, the bleeder.' She turned back to the car, 'Just remember, you cocksucker,' she yelled towards the darkened car, 'you only get what you pay for. And you'll not get much from her.'

Unabashed, the second girl ambled towards the car, turning as she did so to express her opinion of her companion by stabbing the air with her middle finger. The punter opened the car door and she climbed in.

'Do we know him?' Archer asked.

'Never seen him before but, since he seems to like 'em young, I think we'll check him out.' Warrender spoke into his radio. 'Can I have a vehicle check,' he said, 'licence number Whisky, 583, Delta, Bravo, Juliet.'

A few moments later his radio crackled and the disembodied voice said, 'Whisky, 583, Delta, Bravo, Juliet is a dark green Vauxhall Vectra registered to Harbour Chemicals, Hill Top Industrial Estate. Not reported missing or stolen.'

'Received.' Warrender replaced the radio on the dashboard. 'Shit,' he hissed. 'A bloody company car, anyone could be driving it. Pity, it would have rounded off the evening nicely dropping him in it with the wife.'

DS Archer sighed. 'You really are a hypocrite, Warrender. You think nothing of unzipping your trousers when you feel like it, writing coded comments in your little black book when you've done and having a laugh with the lads afterwards. How many is it now, Chris?'

Warrender tapped the side of his nose and grinned at her. 'None of your business,' he said. 'But I get by.'

He was disgusting, and Michelle Archer was just about to say so when another car drew up at the kerbside and extinguished its lights. 'My, we're busy tonight,' she said. 'It must be the weather.'

Warrender opened the car door and pulled himself out. 'I'm sick of this, come on, let's have the bugger.'

Archer joined him.

They approached the car from the rear. Warrender crept up on the driver's side. He grasped the handle, pushed it down and snatched open the door. 'Come on, then, pal, let's be having you.'

As he saw the driver, jubilation spread across his face. 'Well, well, look who we have here,' he said. 'Detective Sergeant Ali, if I'm not very much mistaken. Come out for a bit of nooky, have you?'

It was late and the punters had gone, but, tired as Leah was, sleep evaded her. The flight from the shop had unnerved her and she couldn't help wondering what would have happened to her had she been caught. She had Joe to thank for her escape. She'd got back to Alice's at about two o'clock after he'd put her on the bus and Cindy arrived half an hour later, her bag bulging. *She* hadn't seemed at all concerned and had mocked Leah for being frightened of a security guard. It was all very well for her to scoff, she wasn't the one the guard had been after. What if he'd caught her? There was no saying what Deepak would have done to her, letting him down like that. At best he would have told Alice to beat her, at worst . . . she touched her cheek with her fingertips and remembered the woman with the scar.

She'd told Joe about Deepak – not what she did for him, but about him – what he was like, how much she loved him. And Joe had seemed to understand. He'd been really good to her, bought her a drink in the Interchange café and then they'd sat in Centenary Square talking. Joe wasn't like other men; he hadn't leered at her, or tried to look down her dress. Instead he'd let her talk and he'd listened to her, a bit like she supposed a priest would. She didn't think he was a priest though, because she was sure if he had been he would have tried to stop her shoplifting. And he didn't. In some ways, he reminded her of her father before he walked out on them. Her memory of him was hazy, but she'd kept bits and made-up bits, so that to her he was a whole person – the person she wanted him to be. Joe had said what she knew her father would have said, that if she ever needed to talk, she only had to contact him. He'd given her his mobile number just in case. Apart from Deepak, she thought, Joe was the only friend she had. And when she thought about him, the fear subsided. She *would* get in touch, because, like Deepak, Joe cared about her.

The weekend behind him, John Handford sat at the breakfast table in the hotel and made notes as he mulled over the past couple of days. The waitress hovered, wanting to know if everything was all right. It was more than all right, he told her, he didn't often get the chance to enjoy a full English breakfast. She smiled and left him.

In spite of his misgivings he had enjoyed Cambridge. Saturday, although productive, had not been a happy day, but on Sunday he'd switched off and become a tourist, delighting in the city and all it had to offer. He would have been fine wandering on his own, but Mark Neilsen wouldn't hear of it. They'd visited King's College Chapel and Handford had marvelled at the fan-vaulted ceiling, the painting *The Adoration of the Magi* and the beauty and colour of the stained-glass windows, which, he was told, he should look at in order, beginning at the north-west corner and moving east. In the evening they'd driven out into the country, terminating the journey in one of the many Cambridgeshire villages where they'd eaten a large ploughman's, washed down with several lagers in the beer garden of the local pub. Neilsen was driving and Handford wondered if he ought to suggest he didn't. But since Handford himself was probably over the limit, he decided to forget he was a police officer for once and settled back to enjoy the return journey and the conversation.

He flicked through the files Ted had copied for him. The deaths of the two prostitutes and the fourteen-year-old runaway may well have been the work of the same man. The crimes were carried out in the same way and there was a possible link in the crime scene locations, but whether there was a connection between these deaths and those in Bradford was questionable. The similarities began and ended with the choice of victim, the beatings and the final blows to the head. There was no post-mortem rape and no killer signature. The only link, if you could call it that, was Russell – and that was tenuous. In Bradford a dead girl had his photograph and in Cambridge he had been a student at the time of the murders, but then so had hundreds of others. Realistically, there was no concrete evidence to suggest the DCI was a killer. The dark moods worried Handford though. They were new to him, he hadn't experienced them at work. What he ought to do was talk to someone who knew Russell better than he did, discuss the moods, try to find out if there was a pattern to them. That meant family and friends, but the orders were clear – no family, no relatives, no friends. His hands were tied.

Handford pushed his plate away and reached for a piece of toast, which he spread liberally with butter and marmalade. While he was eating he read through Russell's personal file again. After Cambridge he'd gone to work in his father's business in Hampshire, some eight miles north of Winchester. He'd been there from 1986 until 1988 when he'd left to join the West Yorkshire police. Why? What had happened to make him do that? Had Russell and his father not seen eye to eye in the running of the business as Neilsen had suggested, or had he decided to move on again after another spate of killings? Like it or not, there would have to be a check on similar murders in the Winchester and Salisbury areas during the years Russell was working there. What had puzzled Neilsen was why Russell had joined the police service, and not a multi-national.

He had all the qualifications and it would have been better paid. Yet, for a serial killer, becoming a police officer would have its advantages, for he could keep himself in touch with the investigation without arousing suspicion. And that was something the more organised killers tended to do.

A piercing pain struck Handford between the eyes, adding to the dull ache behind them. For a moment, he had been establishing in his mind the basic actions needed to be carried out, in the way he would in any case. Russell had ceased to exist as his DCI and had become no more than a possible suspect to be investigated in the usual way. What was worse, he realised that the adrenaline had begun to pump and he was actually beginning to become energised by what he was doing. He picked up the half-eaten piece of toast and took a bite. This time it was like sawdust in his mouth, gritty and tasteless, and he swallowed rather than savoured it. He took a final slurp of coffee, pulled together the papers, pushed back his chair and left the dining room, returning to his room, from where he called Ali on his mobile.

'Something's come up,' he said, 'and I'm not going to be back until this afternoon. Cover for me as best you can; if it gets difficult, have a word with DCS Forrester.'

Ali sounded tense. 'I'm sorry, John, Russell knows where you are.'

'You told him?'

'I had no choice. He came in on Saturday and asked if you were in the station.'

'And you said, "No, sir, he's in Cambridge", I suppose?' Bloody man.

There was a moment's silence at the other end of the line, then Ali said, 'It wasn't like that. He didn't know we had changed shifts and he asked where you were. I did say I wouldn't lie for you.'

Anger mingled with apprehension. 'So, instead you told a suspect in a murder case where I was and what I was doing?'

'Not exactly. I just said you were in Cambridge.'

'And you think he wouldn't put two and two together and work out why?' Handford said coldly.

The temperature of Ali's tone matched his. 'I'm sorry, sir, but I can't believe Mr Russell is a killer, and I don't believe you do either.'

Handford tensed and his voice took on an ominous tone. 'It doesn't matter what we believe, Sergeant, there's a question mark over him at the moment and it has to be investigated.'

'But not by you.'

Ali's air of righteous self-confidence was too much for Handford. The man never knew when to stop. 'By anyone who is ordered to do it, Ali. And it's not for you to argue. You've told Mr Russell where I am, and by doing so, you've given him knowledge he shouldn't have. He's a possible suspect in a particularly nasty crime, for God's sake, and you've put him on his guard. At the very least I ought to report this to Forrester.'

Ali's breath exploded in small bursts over the phone, but Handford didn't give him time to calm down. 'I'll see you when I get back to the station. Make sure you're there,' he said and replaced the receiver before Ali could argue.

Not for the first time in their working relationship, Handford cursed his sergeant. He had a habit of making up his own mind about things, following his own path and hang the consequences, then leaving Handford to pick up the pieces. Well, this time Ali could be responsible for his own pieces.

When he felt calmer, he rang Sanderson.

Eileen answered immediately. 'Yes, Inspector,' she said, 'he's been expecting you. I'll put you through.'

He heard the click and then Sanderson's earthy accent.

'What have you got, Handford?'

John told him. 'I think we need to know whether there were any such killings in or around the Winchester and Salisbury areas between 1986 and 1988, sir.'

Sanderson was silent for a few moments. 'Yes, I agree. You go on to Norwich, see if you can find the Walsh woman and I'll talk to Hampshire police.'

'Sir.' Handford let the sigh of relief escape his lips. At least that chore had been taken from him.

'Anything else?'

He hesitated, then said, 'No, sir, nothing at the moment.' He knew he ought to have told him about Ali, but it would have been like informing on a mate without giving him a chance to defend himself first.

Sanderson's voice, when he spoke again, was softer. 'I know it's a bugger of a job, Handford, but you're doing it well. I promise you, if the information gets any worse, and it looks as though it might do, I'll pass it over. Now get yourself to Norwich, and Handford . . .'

'Yes, sir?'

'Drive carefully.'

*

Khalid Ali ended the call from his mobile phone and pulled out of the lay-by. He had never thought of himself as a hypocrite before, but with that call he had shown he could be as hypocritical as the next man. Saturday night he'd been caught checking on his friend. He'd be in trouble, he knew that. He hadn't been doing it officially, he was interfering with an ongoing investigation, and possibly, at worst, his presence could be construed as an attempt to warn his friend he was being watched. Warrender had been in his element asking him if he got a kick out of screwing a white woman and whether Azam had ever fixed him up with a little girl. At this point Archer had told Ali to go, with a reminder that it wasn't the end of it and she'd see him on Monday by which time she'd have decided what to do. Ali doubted she would have a choice. She'd have to report him because Warrender would make sure it was all round the station.

And following the conversation with Handford, Ali doubted he could expect his help either. He didn't have many friends at Central but of those he did, he counted John Handford amongst them – or he had, but just now John had been as cold as he'd ever known him. With good reason. Ali had screwed up by passing on information to a suspect and now by interfering with a case that wasn't his. Today wasn't going to be a good day.

He pulled up at the roundabout and watched as the traffic filtered in from the right. When there was a break he moved off, to be stopped a few moments later by the lights. This was why his father had not wanted him to join the police service – divided loyalty. In the past he'd managed to circumvent the problem but soon, he knew, he was going to have to face it head-on and make a decision, because if he didn't, it would bring him down, either within the police service or within his family and his community.

A car horn blasted at him, telling him the lights had changed and he turned left to drive down the side of City Hall, past the magistrates' courts and into the underground car park at Central Police Station. The darkness of the concrete walls and ceiling suddenly surrounded him, and as the sun was shut out from its depths, a chill ran through his body.

Michelle Archer was waiting for him and followed him into the building.

'Let's find an interview room,' she said in a voice that brooked no argument.

Ali walked behind her. She pushed open the door and stood aside. She was not giving him the choice.

There was no preamble. 'What the hell were you doing on Saturday night?' she said. 'I can't imagine you were there to pick up a prostitute.'

In spite of himself, Ali smiled. 'No,' he said.

She waited. For a moment Ali contemplated his fingers. 'I went to check out if what you'd told me about Deepak Azam was true.'

'And how did you expect to do that? We've been trying to pin him down for years now; what made you think you would have any better luck?'

'He's a friend.'

'Of yours?'

'Yes.'

'And you think he would have admitted to it just because you're a friend?' She ladled sarcasm into her voice. '"Oh yes, Khalid, I'll tell you what you want to know. I'm a pimp, of course I am."' For a moment she stared at him. She had the eyes of an interrogator, they worked into his conscience and sought out the guilt. 'Why didn't you tell me on Saturday morning that Azam was a friend?'

He shrugged. He could try to explain, but she'd never understand.

Her frustration plainly visible, Archer walked away from Ali. 'Did you see him at the leisure centre?'

Ali shifted his feet nervously. 'Yes. He told me what I wanted to know. It was just routine.'

She rounded on him. 'Have you never heard of the word impartial, Sergeant? Wouldn't it have been wiser, given what you knew and given that he is a friend, to have left well alone? Sent a DC along?'

Ali resented the slur on his professionalism. 'If you're worried I warned him about your suspicions, Michelle – you know, Asian to Asian – then the answer is no.'

Anger flared and Michelle Archer took a pace forward, her eyes narrowing. 'Don't play the race card with me, Khalid Ali. You're the one in the wrong here.'

Ali felt himself blush. 'Yes, I know. I'm sorry.'

'You should have told me straightaway of your relationship with him and then you should have kept well away. For God's sake, Ali, you know the rules.'

She was right, but he had to maintain some credibility. 'It's not as simple as that, Michelle. He's a friend. I had to be sure before I told my family to break with him. That's how it is in the Asian—'

'I said, don't play the race card.' She emphasised each word.

'This is not about your community or your family. This is about women being pimped and young girls, some as young as eleven or twelve, being groomed into prostitution by your friend. It's about child abuse and it's about whether or not you knew what Azam was doing and you were warning him, or whether you didn't and you were doing as you said and checking him out. But most of all it's about you thinking it's all right to let it go on while you decide which piece of your conscience you want to follow.'

Ali moved away from Archer. Inside he was a quivering mass. He would like to have told her she was wrong, that if the women were prostitutes it was because they were cheap and immoral, and if the girls were drawn into prostitution it was because their parents didn't care enough about them to teach them right from wrong. But he couldn't because even if it were true, Deepak was using their vulnerability, their trade and their misery to make money. He would like also to have said that he knew exactly where his conscience and his loyalties lay. But he couldn't do that either.

'I'd like not to have to pass this on, Khalid.' Archer's tone was softer now. 'But we both know I have no choice. I'll have to tell Forrester.' She grimaced. 'It's probably all round the canteen by now anyway; there's no way Warrender's going to keep his mouth shut about Saturday night.'

Ali stopped off at the coffee machine before going up to CID. He wasn't that interested in a drink, but he needed time to think. He grasped the Styrofoam beaker, and tried to steady his hands. Michelle Archer was right – he was going to have to decide which part of his conscience he was going to follow and in so doing acknowledge where his loyalties truly did lie. If he was to stay in the police service, then he had to accept that sometimes loyalty and job conflicted. If he couldn't cope with that, then he had to get out and admit to himself that for all these years he had been living a lie.

Outwardly it was a composed Sergeant Ali who walked into CID a few minutes later; inwardly he was still churning. Graham and Clarke were poring over pages of a computerised list, which spilled over the edge of the desk and on to the floor. He approached them, skirting the pile as he did so, then bent down to pick up some of the load. 'This from Deepak Azam?' he asked. For the first time ever, his friend's name stuck in his throat.

'Yes, it came in yesterday.'

'Found anything?'

'Nothing specific,' Clarke said. 'But he's got a motley collection of members.' He pulled the sheets through his hands. 'On the one hand there's Martin Johnson and Dwayne Varley . . .'

'They work for him, as doormen.'

'Their membership must be a perk then, because they're on the list.' Clarke manoeuvred the paper again. 'It's not all bad though, because here we have local politician Andrew J. Collingham, and here,' he pointed to a name, 'here's our fine upstanding Detective Chief Inspector, Stephen W. Russell.' He pondered for a moment then asked, 'What's the W for?'

Ali grinned. 'No idea,' he said.

Graham looked towards the sergeant. 'I wonder if they get together,' he mused, 'Johnson, Varley, Collingham and Russell? You know, for a game of squash and a beer afterwards.'

The telephone rang, saving Ali from thinking of a suitable reply. Graham picked it up. 'Okay, I'll tell him.' He replaced the receiver. 'Daniel Emmott and his parents are in the front office asking to see the officer who called at the house. That was you, yes?'

'Yes, it was,' Ali said thoughtfully. He had wanted to re-interview Emmott, but hadn't expected to meet up with him so soon. Perhaps now Daniel was ready to talk, tell the truth about what he knew, which would mean he must have come clean at home. Either that or his parents were here to complain about police harassment. You could never tell these days.

'I think you'd better be in on this, Clarke,' he said.

The front office was little more than a large expanse of brown tiles, with three blue metal chairs set against the wall to break the gloom and a curved desk across one corner. Behind the desk was an office and in front a lane mapped out by posts and strappings where members of the public were obliged to queue while waiting to be seen. Ali's shoes squeaked as he crossed the dry flooring.

Daniel Emmott was standing away from him, staring out of the large windows; his parents were perched uncomfortably on two of the metal chairs, Mrs Emmott clasping her handbag to her like a comfort blanket. He strode over to Mr Emmott, his hand outstretched. 'Mr Emmott?' he said with a smile. 'I'm Sergeant Ali. What can I do for you?'

The man stood up and took Ali's hand. 'Thank you for seeing us so early,' he said. 'But this couldn't wait.' He turned to the woman, still sitting, still clutching her handbag. 'This is my wife, and Daniel, as you can see, is over there.'

Daniel moved morosely from the window, as though he would prefer to be anywhere but where he was at this moment.

Ali nodded. 'Daniel,' he said. 'You remember DC Clarke?'

Daniel shrugged.

Ali ignored him. 'Look, let's go through, find an interview room.'

The desk sergeant broke in. 'There was a drugs swoop this morning and they're all taken, use 208.'

'Nothing else?'

'No, sorry.'

Room 208 was the worst in the building. Small, dark and the colour of old cardboard, it was meant for visiting journalists, but had been left to deteriorate over the years, probably in an attempt to persuade them to avoid it – use the telephone instead. In that way, if the questions became too searching, the officer could cut them short with the excuse that he had a meeting or someone needed his attention, and in theory the reporter would know no different. So, when 208 wasn't being used for its intended purpose, which was most of the time, it doubled as an interview room. Since there was no recording equipment in there, Ali often felt it the perfect location for the unscrupulous officer to disregard the Police and Criminal Evidence Act, knowing no one would be any the wiser. Indeed, those who used it, and there were some, often did so to intimidate or harass, let its atmosphere bear down before they began – the room did half their work for them. The problem with this tactic was that while it gave the officers the answers they wanted, it didn't necessarily furnish them with the truth. And it was the truth Ali wanted from Daniel Emmott.

One look at the sullen expression laced with apprehension suggested he was far too vulnerable to be subjected to the police station's darker side. If he was to talk, he had to be in the best surroundings.

'We'll use the DI's office,' Ali said.

Dismissing the temptation to ask questions as they walked, Ali led the way to Handford's office. Once there he pulled forward three chairs and invited the Emmotts to sit down. He sat in the chair behind the desk. Clarke remained standing.

Ali took the initiative. 'You have something to tell me, Mr Emmott?'

'Daniel has.' But before Daniel could say anything, Mr Emmott continued. 'I knew we lived in a depraved society, Sergeant, you have only to read the papers to know that, but until Daniel told me what he is about to tell you, I had no idea just how depraved. What is worse, what grieves me more, is that Daniel is part of it.'

The boy turned on his father. 'No, I am not. I told you I had nothing to do with any of it. It's just that you don't believe me,' he ended bitterly.

'I don't believe you were directly involved, Daniel; but you were mixing with people who were and that makes you part of it.'

'Not people, Dad, just Michael, and I did try to stop him.' He glared at his father. 'But I wasn't part of it.'

Mr Emmott leaned forward, his eyes penetrating into his son's. 'By doing nothing, by telling no one, you made yourself part of it, Daniel.'

Ali watched the exchange between the two. Although it was a fascinating spectacle of father–son relationships, it was getting him nowhere.

He broke in. 'Daniel, tell me what you told your father.'

The boy remained silent. He sat on his chair, bending forward, his forearms resting on his thighs, his hands clasped. His hair curled tightly towards the crown of his head, more tightly than anywhere else. Perhaps, Ali thought irrationally, that's where he will start to go bald later in life.

The sergeant tried again. 'Daniel?'

'For God's sake, Daniel,' his father intervened. 'If you won't tell the sergeant, I will.'

Ali pushed back his chair. 'I'm sorry, Mr Emmott, but this isn't helping. Perhaps Daniel and I can have a talk in private.' Without waiting for a reply, he got up and made for the door. 'I won't be a moment.'

When he returned he had Graham in his wake. 'DC Graham will take you to the canteen for a coffee. He'll take a statement from you at the same time.'

Norman Emmott stood, followed by his wife, but it was obvious he would have preferred to stay. As they made to leave the room, Mrs Emmott turned. 'Daniel's a good boy, Sergeant,' she said. 'I know he did his best to dissuade Michael, it's just that he wasn't prepared to inform on him to the police. That's not what best friends do, is it?' And she threw her son an encouraging smile.

The door closed behind them.

Ali repositioned himself in the chair vacated by Mrs Emmott. 'Perhaps it ought to be what best friends do, Daniel,' he said quietly. 'Especially if that best friend is in a mess.' Was he persuading himself or the boy opposite? Ali wondered.

'I'm not a grass.' The young man's voice was no more than a whisper.

'Sometimes, being a grass is the best thing. Perhaps if you had been, he would be alive now.'

Daniel's head jerked up at that. 'It's not my fault he's dead. It's not.'

He was trying hard to remain strong, but in the end he was only seventeen and not one of life's delinquents. He hadn't been brought up to cope with such knocks; probably the worst he had ever suffered was getting in trouble in school for not handing in his homework on time.

'I'm not suggesting you killed him, Daniel, but like your father said, by doing nothing, you did precious little to stop it happening.'

Daniel paled visibly. 'Don't you think I don't know that?' he said, glaring at Ali, daring him to contradict. 'I ought to, my father hasn't stopped telling me since I told him. But I did try, honestly I did.'

Ali waited a moment while the boy regained his composure. When he felt he was ready he said, 'Tell me.'

Perhaps it was the gentleness in the police officer's tone or perhaps Daniel couldn't take any more, but he looked directly into Ali's eyes. 'Michael was selling girls,' he said.

chapter twelve

Norwich's one-way system was a nightmare to those unused to it. For what seemed an age, Handford drove round the centre of the city, always ending where he began. Finally, he parked in the most central multi-storey car park he could find and walked the rest of the way. Neilsen had given him directions to the offices he thought may be those of Catherine Walsh, and Handford eventually found them down one of the steep side streets off the market square.

The offices were small, not those of a large practice. Nevertheless, they were well appointed and welcoming. The middle-aged receptionist gave him a wide smile as he entered and asked if she could help. The smile faded a little when he explained who he was, where he was from and that he would like a moment of Miss Walsh's time. He handed her his card.

'She has an appointment in half an hour,' she said with a pronounced East Anglian accent. 'Wait a moment, and I'll ask her if she will see you.'

She pushed herself away from the desk, walked towards the panelled door set in the wall to her right, knocked and disappeared. A few moments later she returned.

'Miss Walsh can give you about twenty minutes,' she said, and as Handford smiled his agreement, she held open the door for him.

The woman who greeted him was in her mid-thirties, tall, elegant and with the kind of beauty that only comes with maturity. Her dark hair was loosely pulled back and held in a wide slide in the nape of her neck. The navy suit she wore enhanced her slim figure and as she walked round the desk to shake his hand he could see how well the matching high-heeled shoes complemented her slim ankles and finely shaped legs.

'Good morning, Inspector,' Catherine Walsh glanced at his card, 'Handford.'

'Good morning, Miss Walsh. Thank you for seeing me.'

'You've come a long way, Inspector, it would have been churlish to refuse.' Her voice was cultured, authoritative, not unlike Russell's. She returned to sit behind her desk and indicated the chair at the other side. Handford sat down.

'Now, what can I do for you?'

'You were a student at Cambridge, I believe, between 1982 and 1985?'

The solicitor looked puzzled. 'Yes, I was,' she said.

'Studying Law?'

The puzzlement deepened. 'Yes.'

'Then when you left you came into a practice here in Norwich?'

'Yes.' Catherine Walsh leaned over the desk. 'I'm sorry, Inspector, I can't seem to grasp the relevance of your questions. Perhaps you should come straight out and say what you have to say. It'll be quicker that way.'

Perhaps he should. 'You were a friend of Stephen Russell, I believe.'

'Ah.' Catherine Walsh understood.

'A good friend?'

'No, Inspector, not a good friend, an intimate friend, as you probably already know or you wouldn't be asking. But Stephen is a friend I haven't seen or indeed communicated with for at least fifteen years. And to be honest, he is a friend I would rather not see again.' Her gaze remained steady on his. 'Now, does that answer your question and any other you may have wanted to ask?'

Handford smiled. Not only beautiful, but perceptive as well. The kind of woman he knew Russell would feel comfortable with.

'Thank you for your honesty, Miss Walsh, but no, not quite all, I'm afraid. I know you left him at the end of your final term at Cambridge and – I'm sorry but I also know you were expecting his child.'

She interrupted him. 'You seem to know an awful lot, Inspector, so before I answer any more of your questions or validate your thoughts, I think I'm entitled to be told why you've been digging into my background.'

'Not yours, Miss Walsh, Mr Russell's. You're part of it, so inevitably your name came up.'

'And the fact that I was pregnant?' She contemplated the blotting pad on her desk for a moment. 'That snippet of information must have come from Stephen's family, Stephen himself or from Mark

Neilsen, because as far as I know, they were the only people who were aware of it.'

Handford remained silent.

'Oh, it's all right, Inspector, you don't need to tell me. However, I would like to know why you're digging into Stephen's background. What's he supposed to have done?'

Handford left the question unanswered, reaching instead into his briefcase to pull out the plastic pocket containing a copy of the photograph. 'Obviously this is a copy,' he said, 'but did he give you the original?' He watched as her expression mirrored his own when he had first seen it.

'Where on earth did you get this?'

Handford shook his head. 'I'm sorry, I can't tell you, but it is evidence in an on-going investigation.' He waited a moment. 'Is it yours?'

She lifted her gaze. 'I did have one like it,' she said. 'But I don't have it any more. I threw it out when I married my husband four years ago. I decided then that the time had come to rid myself of the past, and that went out with the rest of the baggage.'

Handford took a risk. 'With *all* your baggage, Miss Walsh?'

She smiled. 'Well, no, not quite all. I held on to Hannah – Stephen's daughter.'

'Is it possible she wanted to keep his photograph? Could she have rescued it without your knowledge?'

'No, she's not a devious child. If she'd wanted it she would have asked and I would have given it to her. She's seen it, of course, but that was a long time ago and since then she's never shown the slightest interest in her biological father. Had she done so, I would have told her about him and let her meet him. But she hasn't, at least not yet. As far as she is concerned, Paul is her father; she loves him and he dotes on her.'

'Even though she's only known him for four years?'

'Hannah has known Paul all her life, Inspector. He was very supportive and in spite of the pregnancy, I joined the firm as soon as I left university. He's the senior partner in this practice; this is a satellite office, the main one is in the centre of Norwich. In this one we deal only with litigation and that's my expertise, which is why it's under my name. Paul and I worked closely together and, almost without our realising it, fell in love; I moved in with him when Hannah was six. We couldn't marry immediately. Paul was separated and the marriage was over, but his wife made him wait the full five years for a divorce. So you can see why Hannah looks upon Paul as her father, she's never known anyone else. Does that answer your question, Mr Handford?'

'I appreciate your frankness, Miss Walsh.'

'And I hope you appreciate that I will not keep Hannah from Stephen if that's what she wants. If and when she feels the need to meet him, then I will contact him.'

'You know where he is?'

'Yes, his mother keeps me in touch with what he's doing. She's promised me she'll not let him know we are in contact, although I think she hopes deep down we'll get back together again. It's nonsense of course, but if it gives her something to cling on to since her divorce, then that's fine by me.'

'She's divorced?'

'Yes, some years ago now.'

'Is she aware she has a grand-daughter?'

'No.' Catherine gave Handford a warning look. 'Don't even begin to judge me, Inspector. I know it's cruel keeping a grand-mother away from her grand-daughter, but I can't risk her telling either Stephen or her husband.'

'Because they believe you had a termination?'

'Yes. And because that part of my life is in the past, and that's where I would rather it stayed.'

'Can I ask why you didn't have a termination?'

Catherine frowned. 'This case must be very important for you to become so personal – in *my* office.'

Handford averted his eyes, a smile of embarrassment playing on his lips.

'But since you ask,' she continued, 'I might well have done, if Stephen's father hadn't interfered. Once he found out about the pregnancy, he decided the last thing his son needed was a young wife and a new baby, and he offered me money for a private clinic. Simply put, he wasn't prepared to have his son marry a woman who allowed herself to get pregnant out of wedlock; in his eyes that made me a whore.'

'And Stephen, did he agree with his father? About the termination, I mean.'

Sadness spread over her face like a bruise. 'Stephen always agreed with his father; that was one of his failings.'

Her voice fragmented as though the words were caught in her throat, and Handford wondered if deep down she still loved him. Perhaps love like theirs never really dies, but lies comatose waiting for the connection that brings it back to consciousness.

For a moment she struggled with her memories, then, by way of explanation, said, 'When I told him I was pregnant, Stephen wanted us to marry and have the baby. At the time, I wasn't sure, but we would probably have worked something out had we been left alone to do so. Knowing what his father was like, I will never know what possessed Stephen to tell him so soon, but once he entered the equation it was impossible. Stephen would never stand up to him, no matter what the man said or did. In fact so far as I can see, the only time he showed any backbone was when he left the firm and joined the police service.'

'Do you know why he did that?'

'I have no idea. Perhaps hatred overrode fear. Or perhaps he'd grown up. I don't know, but whatever the reason, I applaud him for it.' For a moment she was silent, the only sound the muted hum of the ceiling fan, then suddenly she said, 'It wasn't only his relationship with his father that decided me against staying with him. Stephen and I had some good times, Inspector, but there were some bad ones as well. He had dark moods and would go off for hours on end – sometimes staying away all night without a word. And afterwards, he'd throw himself into his work, studying as though his life depended on it. He never spoke about why he'd gone or what he'd been doing, although Mark Neilsen thought that somehow his mother was involved.'

'Could he have gone home, perhaps – to see her?'

'He could have done, but if that were so, why didn't he tell me? Why shut me out? Anyway, as much as I loved him, I didn't want my child to have a father who absented himself without explanation, and then locked himself away for days on end – better he didn't exist at all. Nor, or so I thought, did I want to be a single parent. So, I let him off the hook, said I didn't want to see him again and took the money Mr Russell offered. However, when it came to it, I couldn't end the pregnancy. The money for the termination is in a bank account in my daughter's name. After all, you could say it's really hers.'

Handford tried to keep his expression neutral, but he didn't like what he was learning about Stephen Russell. The dark moods had been confirmed and he wondered if they coincided with the deaths of the women in Cambridge, a detail it would be impossible to unearth. Although he would never have admitted to knowing the DCI, he was beginning to feel that his description of him to Mrs Forrester had been wide of the mark. Composed and contained yes, but never to the point of withdrawing into himself or of dark moods.

Then there was Hannah. He was beginning to get an uneasy feeling about her too. Parents didn't always know what was going on in their children's minds; unknown to them, she could have kept the photograph. Catherine said she would have asked had she wanted it, but if she didn't want to upset Paul, on whom she supposedly doted, then she might have taken it without her mother's knowledge. Could Hannah have been searching for her father? Could she be the dead girl? He looked round the room; there were no photographs of any kind, and it might be considered presumptuous, even strange, if he asked to see a picture of her. After all he was here to talk about Stephen Russell. But he needed to know.

'Where's your daughter, now, Miss Walsh?' His voice was as relaxed as he could make it.

'Staying with schoolfriends, in North Yorkshire.' Depending on exactly where they were, that was close enough to Bradford. 'They're camping somewhere in the Dales. I wasn't happy about it, but Paul said I had to let her go sometime and the family she is with is very responsible.'

Surely then, if the dead girl was Hannah, they would have notified her as missing by now, and her mother would be aware of it.

'Has she been in touch at all?'

'A couple of times, but we agreed she would only ring us on Wednesday evenings or in emergencies.' Handford relaxed. It was unlikely then that Hannah was the fourth victim. If she was missing at all, the family friends would have been in touch. Catherine smiled at him. 'It's hard,' she said, 'but I suppose you have to trust them sometime, don't you?'

A picture of Nicola flashed into his mind. She had seemed so vulnerable the last time he had seen her, leaning against the kitchen cupboards sipping her drink, and he worried again about her reluctance to tell him what was troubling her. 'Yes, I suppose you do,' he said almost to himself.

The solicitor broke his preoccupation with his own concerns. 'I'm sorry, Inspector, but I really do have a client in a few minutes. I wish I could be of more help to you, but I assure you I threw my photograph away. The one in your possession must have been given to someone else.'

Handford stood up. 'Any suggestions as to whom?'

'Ask Stephen.' She pulled herself from her chair and walked round the desk. Holding out her hand, she said, 'Do me a favour,

Inspector, don't tell him where I am, or about my daughter. If they are to meet, I would rather it was at Hannah's request, not his.'

Handford took her hand. 'I'll do my best, Miss Walsh.' He released his grip on her. 'Just one more thing, for the record. I assume Walsh is your professional name and not your married one?'

'No, my married name is Mellings, Inspector. Catherine Mellings.'

Michelle Archer swore under her breath.

Hell and damnation. Why did Khalid Ali have to be so bloody arrogant as to think the rules didn't apply to him? How dare he put her in this position?

Morosely, she flicked through the papers in her in-tray. Just how close to Deepak Azam was he? A friend? Or a friend and associate? And why hadn't anyone picked up on a link between them? Either their relationship was entirely innocent and they met only socially, or it wasn't and Ali had been very careful. And if he had, then without a doubt he knew about Azam's colony of prostitutes and had decided not to pass the information on. Why?

He's like the rest of them, loyal to his own first.

No, there was no way she was walking that road. Chris Warrender might, but not her.

'Michelle.'

She glanced at the copper-haired detective coming towards her. His smile had that knowing look he always reserved for dirt he wanted to dish.

Leaning over her, Warrender was unable to keep the triumph out of his voice. 'I've got it,' he said.

'Got what?'

He smiled again. 'The name of the pervert driving the company car,' he said. 'You know the one who preferred the younger girls.'

Archer shot him a look of contempt. She'd had no more than six hours' sleep over the past couple of days and was not prepared to play Warrender's games. 'So who was it?'

But the detective wasn't to be rushed. 'I rang Harbour Chemicals; they weren't forthcoming at first, wanted to know exactly why I wanted the information. I told them it was part of an ongoing investigation—'

Her patience snapped. 'For God's sake, Warrender, if you don't want my knee where it hurts, tell me.'

He bent over the desk, his face even closer to hers. 'Tony Forrester,' he said, his voice a stage whisper.

Tony Forrester. Should she know the name? 'Who's Tony

Forrester?' Then as the knowledge dawned on her, she said. 'You don't mean . . . ?'

Warrender straightened himself. 'I most certainly do,' he said, his grin stretching from ear to ear.

Pulling the nearest chair to the desk, he sat down and leaned forward. 'So, go on then, Michelle, what are you going to do?'

'Me? You checked it out.'

Warrender grinned. 'I know, but I'm not the senior officer here.' He pointed directly at her with his index finger. 'You are.'

She scanned Warrender's smug expression and knew exactly what he was thinking. Would she have the balls to tell Forrester herself, or would she be like most women and pass it on? He'd even be making a bet with himself. Two to one she'd give it to Noble, a thousand to one to Forrester and a hundred to one back to Warrender.

She'd love to take up the hundred to one shot, but she knew she'd be wasting her time. 'Well, I'm not going to Forrester, Mr Noble can tell her.' She pushed herself away from the desk. 'You're sure about this, Warrender? It's not just one of your sick jokes, because if it is . . .' She left the sentence unfinished, hoping he would pick up the warning in her eyes.

He did and held up his hands. 'I promise you, it's true,' he said, his voice more serious now. 'They gave me Tony Forrester's name; address same as the boss's. Check if you don't believe me.'

She could, but she wasn't going to. Let the DI do it, and while he was about it, he could check up on Ali, too.

In ten years of marriage Natasha Russell had never seen her husband afraid, except perhaps when she was rushed into hospital in such pain, but he was afraid now – for her, for himself and for their future.

She had decided to work from home today, but her mind wasn't on it. Last night had been traumatic; she'd learned more about her husband's life in the few hours they'd spent talking than in the whole of their marriage – not all of it attractive. As soon as he'd told her, she'd known what it would mean. The police were already delving into his background, at least John Handford was and Natasha knew that that hurt more than anything. The two men had little in common, came from different backgrounds and from the start had been cautious of each other, but Stephen also had a sneaking regard for his DI. Now that was shattered. She had said she was sure he hadn't taken on the task willingly, but Stephen had argued that even if he wasn't doing it willingly, he would be doing it well – that was the kind of detective he was. Whatever he found that could be construed as suspicious would become suspicious and from what Stephen had told her last night, there was much in his background to be suspicious about. Catherine, the pregnancy, the photograph, his parents, the immorality – particularly the immorality. All of this would come out and when it did, the police wouldn't care what damage they had done.

If only he'd told her earlier, not carried it with him all these years. He hadn't told her, he said, because he was frightened of losing her. Like he'd lost Catherine? she'd ventured, and he'd nodded. It had taken him a long time to get over Catherine, but in the end he had, he hadn't thought of her for a long time. If this hadn't happened, he doubted he would ever have thought of her again. Natasha had done that and he loved her so much.

She hadn't wanted Stephen to go into work until the interview, but he'd insisted. He was proud, too proud to let what was happening affect his responsibility to his work. His face was drawn and his eyes heavy as though he hadn't slept. He'd asked her over and over again if she thought he was a killer and she'd told him 'no' over and over again. She'd attempted to persuade him to tell Forrester what he'd told her, but he'd refused.

'Then at least tell her what you were doing on Thursday night. You don't have to tell her why you were there.'

He'd promised her he'd think about it, talk to his solicitor, take his advice.

As she'd watched him drive off, Natasha had felt all her strength from last night drain away. She wanted to be positive, but now, on her own, she didn't know whether her husband would be home with her tonight or in a police cell.

Susan Forrester was looking over her papers in preparation for the interview with Russell when Noble knocked. Her meeting with Russell at the weekend had been a farce. As soon as he entered the room, he'd demanded to know why John Handford was in Cambridge. She had refused to divulge the reason but he'd got it exactly right. He would, he said, make a formal complaint against her and she had replied that that was his privilege. Then, she'd told him she needed to ask him more questions. But he had refused – not without his solicitor present. A solicitor, it turned out, who was away until Monday. There was little she could do. Russell was not under arrest; she had to wait.

She glanced up from the statement she was reading. Noble looked serious, worried even. 'Yes, Brian, what is it? I can't give you long,' she said, but indicated he should sit down.

'Three things, ma'am. First, I've spoken to Sergeant Jensen who was on the front desk on Thursday and he told me DCI Russell left the station at about half past seven that night.'

'Not nine o'clock?'

'No.'

'And the sergeant's sure about that?'

'Yes, ma'am. Shortly after he'd said goodnight to Mr Russell a man came in demanding to see him to make a complaint about one of the detectives. Something about offensive language. When Jensen told him the DCI had left he wouldn't believe him. There was quite an argument apparently, but eventually Jensen managed to calm him down, said he would write the complaint in the book as well as leave a note for Mr Russell to ring him as soon as he got in the next day. The complaint is logged at 19.35.'

Forrester's lips compressed. 'No wonder he asked Collingham to tighten his alibi. If he left here at around seven-thirty and arrived home at nine-thirty, then there are a couple of hours unaccounted for. Add that to the photograph found on the girl's body and what DI Handford has found in Cambridge, I think we might have the beginnings of a case against him.' She leaned back and clasped her hands behind her head. 'What we could really do with is the identity of the victim. Are we any nearer on that?'

'No, not yet. Her fingerprints aren't on file and no one has come forward to report a missing fourteen or fifteen-year-old. Forensics say her clothes are of much better quality than those of the other victims and her shoes were made abroad, probably Scandinavia, but they're a style not imported into Britain. She could be a foreigner. At the moment we're checking on au pairs and students – it'll be an almost impossible task to check on all foreign visitors, but we'll do our best. What we really need to do is publish a picture of her.'

Forrester frowned. 'It'll have to be post-mortem then, and you know how much I hate doing that. Give it another couple of days, Brian, and then we'll see. Now, what else?'

'Well, it may be something or it may be nothing, but according to Michelle Archer, DI Handford's DS, Khalid Ali, is a friend of Deepak Azam.'

Forrester unclasped her hands and leaned forward. 'Go on.'

'We've not picked up on it before, and it's not clear just how much of a friend he is, but on Saturday morning he asked Archer whether it was true that we have Azam flagged up as a pimp. When she asked what his interest was, Ali said he was making routine inquiries in relation to a suicide turned murder he's investigating. She thought no more about it until she and Warrender were on surveillance at the designated site later that night and Ali turned up there. She didn't want to make a fuss at the time or to draw attention to themselves, so she told him to go home and tackled him about it this morning. He said Azam was a friend of his and he was only trying to check the truth of her information. But when she asked why he hadn't told anyone of his relationship with Azam, he became angry and played the racism card. More or less accused her of not understanding how it was in the Asian community. You know friends and family. It became quite heated by all accounts.'

Forrester, who had been listening intently while Noble was speaking, put her head in her hands. 'Oh, God,' she moaned, stretching out the words. 'First Russell and now one of his sergeants.' She pulled her hands away. 'Okay, one thing at a time. Let's get the interview with Russell over first, see what comes out of that, then I'll see Sergeant Ali. You have a word with him in the meantime and make it abundantly clear that he's not to leave the station or communicate in any way with Azam and when John Handford gets back, talk to him and let him know what's happened.'

'Yes, ma'am.'

She looked at her watch. 'You said there were three things.'

For the first time since he had come into the room, Noble appeared nervous. He shifted in his seat and ran his tongue over his lips. 'We've got the identity of the punter who asked for a young girl,' he said.

'Good. Who is it?'

Noble closed his eyes momentarily, then lifted his gaze to hers. 'I'm sorry, ma'am, but it was Tony.'

As her eyes widened and the colour drained from her cheeks, he said again, 'I'm sorry, Susan.'

chapter thirteen

Handford's office seemed to have chilled a few degrees.

'What do you mean, Daniel, "Michael was selling girls"?' Ali asked.

The boy backtracked. 'I don't mean he sold them like you'd sell vegetables, I mean he was paid to help them.'

'That's not what you said, your exact words were, "Michael was selling girls." '

'I didn't mean sell, I meant paid – to help them.' Daniel was emphatic.

'To help them do what?'

'Find somewhere to live.'

This was a long way from 'selling', yet Ali was sure it was what the boy had really meant and that 'paid to help them' was nothing more than a euphemism to protect his best friend.

'You're saying the girls were paying him to help them find somewhere to live?'

'It wasn't the girls who were paying Michael, it was someone else.'

'Who?'

'I don't know.'

'No?' Ali waited for a reaction, and when none came he wasn't sure whether to be relieved or even more worried. For a second, he wished he'd used Room 208. There he could have demanded the man's name and used the atmosphere to get it. But that wouldn't have been fair on Daniel; he wasn't the criminal here. Instead he said, 'Then, tell me, how long had Michael been helping these girls?'

'Not long.'

Ali pressed further. 'How long?'

'Since we went into the sixth form.'

'And the girls, who were they?'

'From children's homes or squats.'

'Then, surely Social Services would have been more able to help them?'

'No, they don't like social workers, and Michael said they would be better looked after by the man paying him than by Social Services, and anyway,' he hesitated, 'Michael needed the money – for university.'

The man paying him?

Deepak?

Ali avoided the issue. 'Are you telling me that Michael's reason for helping the girls was to pay his way through university?'

The boy raked a hand through his curls. A finger became caught in one of them and for a moment he diverted his concentration into freeing it, then he said, 'His parents were going through a bad patch what with foot and mouth and everything and he wanted to help.'

'And that was all?'

'Yes.'

'So, if all Michael was doing was helping out his parents and helping out the girls, why has your father dragged you in here?'

Daniel stared at Ali for a long moment, trapped between his need to remain loyal to his friend and the truth. Ali understood the boy's vulnerability – he was trapped in its clutches himself. Tension began to build again, thickening the already heated atmosphere. Clarke stretched over to switch on the fan.

Ali asked, 'Did his parents know what he was doing?'

'God, no, they'd have gone ape.'

'Why?'

'They just would.' Daniel was backing himself into a corner and he knew it. He leaned forward to make eye contact with Ali, defying the detective to argue. 'Michael just wanted to help, that was all; that's why he got the job in the supermarket.'

'But the money he earned there wasn't sufficient?'

He was on safer ground now. 'Not for five years at university. He'd have been lucky to save enough for five weeks on what they pay students.'

'So, how did he learn about the girls?'

Suddenly the safe ground had shifted and Daniel's expression suggested he couldn't avoid the inevitable. His eyes dropped away. 'One of the lads in school told him he knew a way of getting some extra money, said he knew someone who could help. All Michael had to do was to make friends with girls from children's homes and squats until this man found them a proper place to live. When he'd done that he would be paid.'

Ali leaned forward to reinstate eye contact. 'And what did you think, Daniel?'

He looked up. 'That it was iffy. I told him no one pays anyone to look after a complete stranger, unless they're going to get something out of it.'

'But Michael didn't listen?'

'No, he said not everyone was the same; some people liked to help others without getting anything back. This man is big in the city, a well-known businessman.' Ali's stomach lurched. He ought to ask his name now, but just as Daniel wasn't ready to divulge it, Ali didn't want to hear it, so he let the boy continue. 'Michael said the girls were unhappy where they were, and that, if anything, he was doing them a favour.'

'And that's what you mean by "selling"?'

Daniel's face tightened with pain. 'Yes.'

At last they were back at 'selling'. Now, as much as he would have preferred not to, Ali had to peel away the layers to unearth the identity of the buyer and the reasons for the purchase, although he was sure he knew, just as he was sure Daniel did. His heart beat against his chest wall. He also knew he ought to back out now, hand the questioning over to someone else, but a lot was lying on the boy's answers – both for the girls and for Ali himself. Logic told him there was more than one businessman in the city, that it wasn't necessarily Deepak, but the logic was trapped in the information from John Handford and Michelle Archer. With a conscious effort at self-control, he began again.

'Who was the boy, Daniel?'

'An Asian lad.'

'At your school?'

'Yes.'

Deepak had a son at the same grammar school. 'Do you know his name?'

'No, but he's in year nine.'

That would make him thirteen – the same age as Younis. Surely not. Surely Deepak wouldn't drag his own son into something like this. Get out now, before it gets any worse. No, it was ridiculous. Ali was allowing himself to be caught up in assumptions, the worst thing a detective could do.

He took a deep breath. 'Do you know him well enough to point him out to me if necessary?'

'If I had to.'

Ali leaned forward. He had to ask. 'And the man finding the places for the girls to live – do you know who he is?'

Daniel froze again. His tongue passed over his lips. The words when they came out were dry, as though forced out of a mouth as arid as the desert. 'I don't know,' he said, his voice no more than a whisper. Then, 'Can I have a drink?'

Clarke moved towards the door. 'Coke?'

'Anything, water will do.'

'I think we can do better than that,' Clarke said as he left.

Silence, broken only by the faint hum of the fan, descended over the room like a thick fog. Daniel took a deep breath. The questions had ceased, and for the moment he allowed a blanket of exhaustion to engulf him. Leaning forward, he rested his elbows on his knees and covered his face with his hands.

The real trick in this kind of situation was to recognise and accept the truth. Daniel would have to do so, as would Ali, even if the truth was unpalatable, even if it brought him in direct conflict with his father and the community. The sergeant moved from his chair and crouched down in front of him.

'Daniel, look at me. *Look at me.*' He waited until the boy returned his gaze. The eyes held little in the way of emotion. No sadness. No hatred. Nothing but fatigue.

'While we wait for DC Clarke to come back, I want you to think very carefully about naming the person who takes these girls. I think you know who he is and we need to know as well because we're going to have to talk to him.'

Daniel stirred. 'No, please.'

'Michael was your best friend, yes?'

The boy nodded.

'Then you should want to help.'

Misery flooded Daniel's face. 'I do,' he said.

'Well, the way to help is to tell us who this person is.' Ali stood up and resettled himself in Handford's chair. 'Think about it, Daniel. But don't say anything yet, we'll wait until Mr Clarke returns, then I'm going to ask you again.'

A few moments later Clarke reappeared carrying a can of Coke. He passed it to Daniel who opened it, the gas hissing out as though relieved to escape.

As Daniel drank, Ali could feel the pressure mounting and he took a couple of deep breaths in an attempt to settle his nerves, then when they were ready, he said, 'Now, tell me, who is this man?'

The boy's voice was ragged and the detectives had to strain to catch the reply.

'He owns the gym.'

Ali closed his eyes momentarily, then opened them to glance at Clarke. If his colleague had noticed the sergeant's reaction, he didn't show it.

'Which gym?'

'The one near the centre.'

'Do you know his name, Daniel?'

Daniel's voice descended into a whisper. 'Deepak Azam.'

A multitude of emotions crowded in on Ali. He would like not to have believed Daniel, but that, he knew, would be burying his head in the sand – and he'd been doing a lot of that lately. He had to accept now that Deepak was linked to Michael Braintree, whom he had paid to befriend vulnerable girls, and who, if Archer was right about him being a pimp, he was probably using as prostitutes. But Ali knew that was not all. Given the link they had uncovered, it wasn't beyond the bounds of possibility that Deepak could be involved somehow in the boy's death. Or was that his imagination running away with him? His mind was racing and he had to stop and become more analytical. The link between Michael Braintree and Deepak Azam was too strong to be ignored, as was the information given to him by Michelle Archer. He remembered the prostitute who had been attacked, Deepak seen at her bedside, her refusing to talk to the police, but not insisting it was some unknown punter who had slashed her face. Yet he couldn't see Deepak doing that any more than he could visualise him as a murderer. But, and the thought hit him with the force of a sledgehammer, he could see Deepak's bouncer, Dwayne Varley, doing both. Ali had never seen his friend raise as much as a hand in anger, but Varley . . . He had been fortunate his last stretch in prison hadn't been life. Good luck and good medical care had saved the lady he had beaten to a pulp when she caught him rifling through her things. The attack had been vicious. Yes, Dwayne Varley could commit murder. The awful question was, if he had done it, was it off his own back or on his boss's orders?

Daniel looked up at the detectives, his eyes no longer empty, but filled with fear. 'Please don't tell him I told you.'

Clarke reassured him. 'Don't worry, he won't hear it from us.'

At his words the atmosphere in the room softened, forcing Ali to push aside his own feelings and continue. 'I want us to go back to the beginning now, Daniel, and I want you to explain exactly how Michael found the girls to sell to Mr Azam.'

'He didn't, Mr Azam did, or at least one of his friends did.' Daniel was more confident now. 'I don't know his name, but he'd hang around outside children's homes or squats and when he'd seen one who was the right type, he would tell Mr Azam. Then she would be pointed out to Michael. All he had to do was to make friends with her.'

'How did he do that?'

'It wasn't difficult, he said. They liked being chatted up by a boy. To begin with they'd go to a coffee bar or somewhere until he got to know her. All they needed, he said, was someone to be nice to them for once. Eventually he'd buy her presents and tell her about the house that Mr Azam would let her live in if she wanted to get away from where she was; say he could introduce her to him if she wanted.'

'And what about Mr Azam, what did he do?'

'Nothing until Michael said the girl wanted to meet him.'

'What else did Michael do?'

'Sometimes, he would give her drugs; nothing heavy, a spliff or two first and then Es, or tabs if she was already using. Michael didn't really want to, but Mr Azam said it was no big deal, everyone was into drugs nowadays.'

'But no hard drugs, though, heroin for instance?'

'No. Some wanted it, but they had to wait until they were passed over.'

'Passed over?' It sounded like a death sentence.

'To Mr Azam, or one of his friends.'

Daniel sat up, took another swallow from the can and then a deep breath. 'All Michael had to do was to be friendly and spend some time with her until Mr Azam took over.' Daniel emptied the can of Coke then squeezed it into a crumpled mass.

Ali watched him, wondering if the action helped. 'When he had passed the girl over, then what happened?'

'To the girl, or to Michael?'

'Both.'

'I don't know about the girl, but . . .' He stopped.

'What?'

'Nothing.' Daniel stared at him, daring contradiction.

Ali didn't contradict. Instead he said, 'What about Michael?'

'He got his money.'

'How much?'

'Two hundred and fifty pounds plus fifty expenses.'

The information was given so matter-of-factly that it was hard to believe that they were talking about a trade in young girls.

'Mr Azam paid Michael three hundred pounds per girl?'

'Yes.'

Ali was aghast. If Deepak was prepared to pay out three hundred pounds a girl, then he was getting much more in return, which meant Archer was right and he was preparing them as prostitutes for either the home market or overseas. Whichever it was, it stank. Ali stood up and walked over to the window. He pushed it as wide as it would go. The noise from the traffic seeped into the room. Across the dual carriageway, the dome of the theatre stood out starkly against the deep blue sky. A removal van manoeuvred its way to the stage door, blocking the pavement and half the road as it did so. A theatre company preparing for the new season perhaps. Closer to the station, Monday morning shoppers crowded off the buses, and solicitors in dark suits and villains in jeans and T-shirts wandered across to the magistrates' court. Everything normal, except in here.

He turned from the window. 'A moment ago, when I asked about what happened to the girls, you were going to say something, what was it?'

'I told you – nothing.'

Ali struggled to keep his impatience at bay. He had to have it from the boy's own mouth. 'Come on, Daniel, you know what happens to them.'

'No.'

'Yes.' Ali played the yes-no game with his children at bedtime, but this wasn't a game.

Without warning, anger bubbled in Daniel. He jumped up and strode over to the door. 'I'm fed up with this,' he blustered. 'I'm off.'

But Clarke was too quick for him. Barring the way, he said quietly, 'Sit down, Daniel.'

'Let me out; you can't keep me here.'

Clarke stood his ground. At first Daniel tossed himself against the wall and crossed his arms, then after a few moments he walked sullenly back to his seat and dropped into it.

As though nothing had happened, Ali kept up the pressure. 'What is Mr Azam doing with these girls, Daniel?'

Fury etched deep into his features, Daniel fixed the sergeant with a look of hatred. 'Using them as prostitutes,' he shouted. 'Is that what you wanted? Is that what you wanted me to say? Is that what you wanted me to say?' Then, rocking backwards and forwards, he repeated over and over, the words just audible, 'I'm sorry, Michael. I'm sorry.'

Ali watched as Daniel, in deep pain, clung on to himself, and he knew how he felt. He wanted to do the same. He had forced both himself and an immature seventeen-year-old to confront the knowledge that a best friend – in Daniel's case, a dead best friend – was a dealer in the modern equivalent of slavery. Both of them had fought against it – and both of them had lost.

For Ali, Deepak Azam had become an unpalatable pill, which was slowly melting in his gut, leaving a bitterness that regurgitated with each question he asked and each answer he received. Azam – suddenly he was no longer Deepak – a pillar of society with an award for his good citizenship, an example to the community and a friend, was no more than a pimp, and the worst kind of pimp at that; one who not only preyed on and made money out of young girls, but who exploited a son's fears for his family in order to do it.

Ali took a deep breath and tried to rein in the cocktail of emotions threatening to overwhelm him. Whatever happened from here on, he mustn't let them spill over on to Daniel. He had his trust now, he couldn't afford to lose it. He tried to give him a reassuring smile, but he was unable to dampen down his emotions enough to do so. Instead, he crouched in front of him and touched him gently on the arm.

'Do you know that for sure, Daniel?'

Daniel looked up at him, his face streaked with tears. 'No, not for sure, but why else would a man like Mr Azam want to look after girls of their age and pay Michael three hundred pounds to bring them to him? For a start he never has more than one girl at a time, *and* he swore Michael to secrecy. He didn't want anyone to know, he said. Does that sound like Mr Azam to you? He's always in the papers for something that he's done. If it was above board, he'd be telling everyone. I said all this to Michael, but he wouldn't listen.'

There was no doubt Daniel was telling the truth. Ali had to accept that; the boy's reasoned argument mirrored his own. Ali's jaw worked as he spooled in the anger he felt for his friend. He cleared his throat. 'Tell me about Hannah. Was she one of Michael's girls?'

'At first she was, but Michael said she was different from the rest. More like him, you know?'

'No, I don't; explain to me. In what way was she like him?'

'Well, she had money for a start. And she wasn't in a home. I'm not sure where she lived, but she certainly wasn't in a squat or anything like that.'

'How did Mr Azam pick her out, then.'

'She was looking for someone, her real father. She said he was in Bradford, although I don't know how she knew. She had an old photograph of him and was asking everyone if they knew him. One day she asked Mr Azam.'

'And he decided Michael should befriend her?'

'He said it would nice for him to have a better class of girl for once.'

Rather, a means to an end; a better class of girl for a better class of men. Ali would have liked to stop the interview there, hear no more. It was nauseating and he thought for a moment he was going to be sick. He swallowed hard.

'Go on.'

'Michael fell for her as soon as he met her. He thought she was great and didn't want to pass her on to Mr Azam. He wanted to keep her for himself. He said he would go and see him, explain and ask for another girl instead.'

'One not so classy?' Ali couldn't keep the disgust out of his voice.

Daniel's features darkened, and he made no reply. Even he could grasp the assumption behind the question and what any answer would mean. Worse than that, he would have to acknowledge again to what depths his best friend had sunk.

'And did he?'

'Yes, but Mr Azam said he wanted Hannah. I think Michael must have argued or something, he was like that. Anyway when I saw him, he had a big bruise on his face, a burst nose and a cut lip.'

'Did he give you an explanation?'

'Just said he'd fallen, but I didn't believe him. I think Mr Azam had hit him, or had him beaten up or something.' His voice began to fade and he seemed to drift away for a moment, probably to replay the imagined scene in his mind. 'I tried to persuade him to tell someone about Hannah, but he said he couldn't; he'd thought about it, though, and he knew what he was going to do.' Tears began to cloud Daniel's eyes. 'It never occurred to me that he'd meant he was going to kill himself.' He looked up at Ali. 'Except that he didn't, did he?'

'No, Daniel, he didn't.'

'Was it Mr Azam who killed him?'

'We've no evidence to suggest that.' Ali knew he was doing no more than clinging on to a morsel of hope. 'When he realised what was happening, why didn't Michael come to us?'

'He did, but he said it had been a waste of time, no one had taken any notice.'

So Daniel wasn't the only one to let Michael down. Was this a metaphor of the times? Ali wondered. Paucity of caring dressed in a pin-striped suit or a uniform?

'When did he come?'

'About two weeks ago, something like that.'

'Who did he talk to?'

'Some copper in uniform. He said he would pass on what Michael had told him and someone would get back to him. But no one ever did.'

Clarke passed over an A4 piece of paper. 'I want you to look at this again, Daniel,' he said. 'It's a copy of a page of Michael's diary. Perhaps you can help with the code. H is obviously Hannah and DA, we know now is probably Deepak Azam. The small p is likely to be the police, because that fits in with what you said about no one getting back to him, but what about the capital P? Would you know what that means?'

Daniel studied it for a moment. 'It's probably The Project.'

'Do you know what that is?'

'Michael didn't say much about it, but I think it's a group that helps girls in trouble. I don't know how he knew about it, but he took Hannah there. He thought they might know what to do.'

Ali shook his head. Michael resembled a youth of seventeen going on thirty, and Daniel not far off. For both of them, their biggest problems should have been their A-levels and which university they were going to. Not the lives of prostitutes, whatever their age. He feared for Hasan and Bushra. How did you protect your children from life? Particularly when life threw information at you that you never knew existed.

Suddenly, he'd had enough. He wound up the interview.

'That's all for now, Daniel, no more questions. I want you to go with DC Clarke to make a statement of everything you've told us. Will you do that?'

Daniel nodded. He stood up and made for the door, eager to escape. But before he could do so, Ali said, 'One more thing, Daniel. Do you know where Hannah is now? We need to talk to her and to know she's safe.'

Tired as he was, Ali's immediate reaction following the interview with Daniel Emmott was to go to Deepak, seize him by the scruff of the neck and beat the truth out of him. But that, he knew, would give him only fleeting satisfaction, the police service a reason for sacking him and a good barrister the ammunition with which to destroy him, if and when it came to court. Instead he busied himself with tying up the loose ends.

While Clarke was taking Daniel's statement, he talked with Graham. It was important to check that the Emmotts' statement agreed with their son's. It seemed Daniel had left nothing out, unless there was something he hadn't told either his parents or the police. Ali didn't think so. He was fairly sure they had it all.

Finally, he went up to the canteen to thank the Emmotts for their time.

'What do you intend to do now?'

'I'll make some inquiries; verify what Daniel has told me.'

'Are you going to arrest Azam?'

'I'll question him certainly.'

'But not arrest him? Young girls are being abused by him.'

'Mr Emmott, we only have Daniel's word for that, and even he wasn't sure that was happening. But I promise you, I will make inquiries. Although I've got to be honest with you, I don't know of any prostitutes so young in the city.' He wasn't sure why he'd said that.

Norman Emmott pushed back his chair and stood up. 'That's because Deepak Azam is too clever for you. He recruits young boys to do his dirty work and then when they've done it the girls disappear. Michael certainly never saw any of his protégés again.'

Ali pulled back Mrs Emmott's chair and the three of them walked towards the door. 'I'll take you down to the foyer; Daniel shouldn't be long, you can wait for him there.'

They travelled down in the lift in silence. Once in the foyer, Mr Emmott turned on Ali. 'Do you know Deepak Azam, Sergeant?'

The question took Ali by surprise and he evaded it. 'A little.'

Maybe it was the tone of Ali's voice or the expression on his face – he would never know – but whatever it was, the answer he gave didn't satisfy Norman Emmott.

'And that's why you're not prepared to arrest the man. Forget that there are girls out there being abused by him and his friends at this moment.'

Ali tried to pacify him. 'We don't know that, Mr Emmott,' he said.

'No, and I doubt you ever will. Well let me tell you, Sergeant, if you won't do anything, I will. Michael is dead because of Azam.'

Ali made to protest, but Mr Emmott waved it away. 'I'm not saying he killed him personally, but it doesn't take a PhD to work out that his murder has something to do with this mess.'

The door leading to the back of the station opened and Daniel came through with Clarke. Mr Emmott walked over to him and put his arm round his shoulder to manoeuvre him to the main door. As they made to leave, his father dropped his arm and turned. 'I'm not leaving it like this,' he said. 'Do something, Sergeant, or I will.' And the door swung closed behind him.

Swallowing his concern, Ali went over to the front desk to look through the book in which all visits were recorded. The heat of the morning was penetrating the large windows, turning the area into a sauna. He shrugged off his jacket and rested it over the top of the desk. He found Michael's entry more quickly than he could have hoped, and it had been made by the desk sergeant who was currently on duty.

'Yes, I remember him,' Jensen said. 'He was in quite a state, so I got an officer down to talk with him.'

'From CID?'

'No, there was no one in, otherwise I would have. No, it was,' he ran his finger across the page, 'PC 3987 Foxton. He spoke to him for quite a while, I seem to remember.'

'Is he on duty now?'

The desk sergeant turned to inspect the duty roster. 'He was due in about ten minutes ago, he'll probably be in the canteen. Do you want me to ring up?'

Ali wasn't prepared to wait for someone up there to decide to pick up the phone. 'No, I'll go myself,' he said. He stepped over to the lift and pressed the button, then paced the foyer until it arrived, irritated it was taking so long

The canteen was full. A uniformed officer walked passed him, carrying a drink, a plate with a toasted teacake balanced precariously on the cup. He stopped her and asked her to point out PC Foxton. She nodded in the direction of a table where a group of officers were sitting deep in conversation. They looked up as he approached.

'PC Foxton?'

A fresh-faced young constable stared up at him. 'Yes, Sarg, that's me.'

'I'd like a word. Do you mind bringing your drink over to that empty table where we can talk.'

The constable threw a confused smile in the direction of his colleagues, pushed back his chair and followed Ali.

'I want you to think back ten days, Foxton,' Ali said when they were seated. 'You were called down to the front desk to talk with a young lad, Michael Braintree.'

'Yes, that's right, Sergeant. He was in quite a state. It took me a while to get out of him why he had come.'

'Tell me.'

'He said he was concerned about his girlfriend.' Foxton took out his notebook and flicked back through the pages. 'Hannah, her name was. He was worried that she was being made to become a prostitute. When I asked him how he knew, he said he just knew, but wouldn't explain any further. In fact he didn't really tell me much at all, but he was so anxious about her I said I would talk it over with a senior officer and someone would get back in touch. To be honest, it sounded a bit far-fetched to me.'

'But you believed him?'

'Well, actually, yes, I did, even though he wasn't clear in what he was telling me, and was probably keeping a lot back. But he was adamant she would be in a lot of trouble if we didn't step in.'

Ali's tone hardened. 'If you thought there was something in it, Foxton, why didn't you come and tell me when Michael Braintree was found dead?'

The officer's expression registered horror. 'Dead? I didn't know he was dead.'

'So where have you been for the past ten days?' Sarcasm was beginning to worm its way in. 'It's been in every paper.'

'Benidorm, Sergeant. I went on leave the day after I'd spoken to Michael.' He shook his head. 'Poor lad. Was it an accident?'

Suddenly Ali felt ashamed at his manner and when he spoke again his tone was laced with compassion. The news had obviously come as a shock. 'No, Foxton, unfortunately it wasn't. Michael was murdered, killed with a karate chop to the neck then hung up to make his death look like suicide.'

Foxton held Ali's gaze. 'It doesn't have anything to do with what Michael told me, does it?'

'That's what I'm trying to find out.'

Foxton shook his head. 'I should have done more. I had a gut feeling something was wrong, but I was going on holiday, I didn't have time.' He stared at his drink. 'He was a nice lad, you know, sincere, caring even. Seemed genuinely worried about his girlfriend.'

Not as sincere and caring as you imagine, Ali thought, but kept his opinion to himself. Instead he said, 'Don't blame yourself, Foxton; it wasn't your fault.'

'Then why does it feel as though it is?'

Ali couldn't answer. What Foxton was feeling now was no stranger to him. Eventually he said, 'Did you pass it on?'

'I had a word with my inspector first, but he said it was more a CID job and to take it to the DCI; let him make the decision about what to do.'

'And what did Mr Russell decide?'

'He said he'd never heard of any prostitutes of that age in the district and that the boy was probably worrying over nothing. He marked it for No Further Action.'

Try as he might, Handford was having difficulty concentrating on his driving. He'd already taken the wrong turning for Bradford and had had to make a long detour to get him back on the right road. He'd driven down to Cambridge worrying about Russell, and now he was driving back worrying about Hannah Mellings.

When Catherine had told him her married name, he'd had to think quickly and his gut reaction had been to make no comment. That Hannah was her daughter was not in doubt, but it wasn't certain that Hannah was the dead girl. Until he was sure, he was not prepared to put Catherine Mellings through the kind of pain experienced by families of murder victims. There would be time enough for that. At this moment she believed her daughter was enjoying a holiday in the Dales, and since the party she was with hadn't reported her missing, Handford couldn't see how she could possibly be the girl lying in the rubbish. Death had occurred Thursday evening, it was now Monday afternoon, and the murder had been well reported locally. Surely, if the family hadn't seen Hannah in all that time, they would have expressed concern to the police, asked to see the body even. Instead of which, they had rung her parents on the Wednesday to say they were having a wonderful time. It didn't make sense.

On the other hand, since she'd been carrying Russell's photograph, there had to be some link between the dead girl and the Mellings. So if she wasn't the Mellingses' daughter, who was she, why did she have the photograph and how had it come into her possession?

More confusing was that, according to Ali, Michael Braintree's girlfriend was called Hannah Mellings, and since Ali knew nothing about her nor had he had the photo-booth picture with him when Handford had called, there was no way of knowing if this Hannah Mellings was one and the same. If she was, then somewhere, somehow, there was a link between Michael Braintree and the killer, or between Michael and the young prostitutes – or both.

Could that be why he had been killed? Because of a link between

Michael and child prostitution – and if it was, who else was involved? The two names that had come up so far were Russell and Deepak Azam. The dead girl might have been a prostitute. There was link of some kind between Russell and the dead girl, and a more tenuous one between Azam and prostitution. Did they connect somehow, or was it just coincidence?

He needed to get back, talk with Ali, see the photograph of Michael's girlfriend and hope against hope that she was neither the dead girl nor Catherine Mellings's daughter because if she was either or both, Russell for one would have many more questions to answer.

It was lunchtime when Norman Emmott visited the Braintrees. When he arrived, he insisted he and Raymond go into the garden so that Clarissa couldn't hear what he had to say. There he had explained as gently as he could what Daniel had told both his father and the police.

Raymond Braintree stared at him. He couldn't believe any of it. Michael involved in prostitution – it didn't make any sense. He knew of Deepak Azam, most people did. He was an entrepreneur, a man who gave to charity, a man for whom money was not the most important thing in his life. He was the man who had done more to bring the Asian and white communities together than anyone. How could he do all that, and at the same time use children as prostitutes? He'd read about how these girls were groomed into the life, made completely dependent on the pimps who worked them, but to even think that Michael was involved was preposterous. Yet . . . yet it made some sense, however awful, of the money and the drugs.

'The worst of it is,' Norman Emmott said angrily, 'the police will do nothing. Michael is dead; they know he was being used by Azam and they intend to do nothing.' Norman Emmott paced backwards and forwards in front of his friend.

'Are you sure?'

'The sergeant said they would interview him, but he was dead against arresting him. They only had Daniel's word for it, he said.' Norman Emmott slumped on to the garden bench. 'Why should Daniel make up something like that, for God's sake?'

Raymond Braintree sat opposite him. 'I don't understand. Why would Sergeant Ali do nothing?'

'Oh, come on. He's like Azam, same race, same culture. Also he knows Deepak Azam. I tell you, Raymond, it stinks.'

Mr Braintree held himself rigid, a deep frown cutting through his forehead. 'So what do you think we should do? Go higher than Sergeant Ali? His inspector perhaps, or higher still?'

'No, Raymond. I don't, because I think it will be a waste of time. Azam is well respected and he's Asian. They'll be too frightened of being called racist to do anything.'

'So what do we do?'

'We go and see Azam ourselves and one way or another we get it out of him. I couldn't care less what colour his skin is – he's a pervert and he needs to be taught a lesson.'

'Leah!' For the third time, Cindy banged on the door.

Leah lifted her head. 'Go away.'

She didn't want to see anyone. All she wanted to do was push her face deeper and deeper into the pillow so that she couldn't breathe. Suffocate herself. End it all.

She hated everything. Alice, the men, Cindy, the other girls, the bakery, everything.

Today, for the first time since she'd arrived at Alice's, the punters had had her at lunchtime as well. Up to now they'd only come to her at night, but now, two days in, Alice had decided it was time for her to start pulling her weight at lunchtime, not leave it all to the other girls. One of the men had been Dwayne Varley. He'd asked for her specially. He'd had to pay like Deepak had said he would, but he'd made the most of it, got his own back for her kicking him and spitting at him.

'See ya, slag,' he'd sneered as he threw the notes at her. Then he'd left the room and whistled his way along the passage. The sickly sweet smells from the bakery had mingled with his sweat and Leah had jumped off the bed, slammed the door behind him and pushed a chair under the handle so that he couldn't get back in. Then she'd flopped on the bed and cried, silently at first and finally, as the despair hit, out loud. Too loud. Loud enough for Cindy to hear.

'Leah,' she yelled. 'Open the frigging door. I'll kick it in if you don't.'

She didn't have a choice. Cindy wasn't going away, and Alice would hear. Leah pulled herself off the bed. She dragged the chair from the door, pushed down the handle, then returned to sit on the bed, picking at the tissue in her hand.

'Aw, Leah, come on, don't cry.' Cindy sat next to her. 'It will get better.' She put her arm round Leah's shoulder.

For a while neither spoke, then Leah ventured, 'I hate it here.'

Cindy squeezed her shoulder. 'I've told you, it'll get better, and quicker, if you don't think about it.'

Leah pulled at the tissue some more. 'No, it won't.'

'It will, just do what they want and don't think about it. It's like being an actress on telly, pretend the punter's someone you like on telly or a pop star, pretend 'e's the one screwing you. Put 'is poster on the wall, then you can see 'im all the time it's 'appening. That's what I did at first. Now it doesn't bother me. Now I just let 'em get on with the business and think of me next fag.'

'I don't want to stay here.'

'Don't be daft, what would you do? Run away? You've done that once and ended up 'ere. And that's where you'll end up again if you run off, back 'ere, because Deepak will find you. Only when he's finished with you, you won't be as pretty as you are now.'

'Like the woman with the cut down her face?'

Cindy grimaced. 'You've seen 'er, have you? He shows 'er off to everybody.'

Leah hesitated before asking, 'Did Deepak do it?'

'Not 'imself, nah. He'd get one of his thugs to do it. Varley or somebody like that.'

The tears came again. 'I'm scared, Cindy.'

'There's no need to be scared. Alice won't let Deepak do anything to you, not while you're 'ere, but if you run away, she'll not be able to stop 'im. Honestly, you're better off 'ere than anywhere else. Look. I'll tell you what. I'll go and make us some tea. That'll make you feel better.' And Cindy hopped off the bed and ran out of the room.

Leah stretched over for another tissue. Cindy might tell her not to be scared, but it didn't stop her from feeling it. She never felt safe. She should have been safe when she was at home with her mother, and was until her father left and her mother's fancy man came and started to pet her and play with her. She'd thought she'd be safe when her mother put her into care; at least he couldn't get at her any more. Then she thought she was safe with the foster parents, until the husband had started to poke her. Then Deepak. She'd thought herself more safe with him than with anyone, and she still wanted to believe it. If she didn't have him to love her and to keep her safe, who else was there?

Joe perhaps?

Her mind slipped back to Saturday, to the man who'd saved her. He'd been nice. He'd given her his mobile number. She could ring him, talk to him again, he'd understand. She might even be able to tell him what Alice was making her do. Perhaps he could help her get away like he had from the security guard. She grabbed her bag and pulled out the piece of paper where he had written the number. Perhaps she could go out now and ring him, talk to him, tell him how much she hated it here and ask him to help her again. She pulled herself off the bed and walked over to the window. The other three girls in the house were stretched out in the garden, smoking. Lisa was there. She'd been one of Deepak's girls – or so she said. She was mean, was Lisa. She'd told Leah that Deepak was married with children. Leah had tried not to believe her.

She lifted her eyes from the girls in the garden and looked over at the other house. Perhaps it was better over there. Perhaps if she was good here, Alice would send her over there. But good wasn't always enough, was it? Her mother used to tell her she was such a good girl, but she'd still sent her away. Her foster father had told her she was good, when he was feeling her up. Deepak had said he liked her because she was good. At least, he had at first – until she'd turned bad.

'Leah, open the door, will you?'

It was Cindy with the tea. Leah shoved the piece of paper Joe had given her back in her bag and let her in.

Cindy was carrying two beakers, her tongue between her lips as she concentrated on not spilling the contents.

She handed one to Leah, who took a few sips, then clutched it tightly with both hands and held it close to her cheek. For a while she remained like that, the hardness and the warmth of the mug giving her comfort, then she said, 'How do you become good, Cindy?'

Cindy laughed. 'Good? Who the hell wants to be good? You'd 'ave to go to school if you were good, learn stuff that's of no use to anyone, be told what to do by snotty-nosed teachers.'

Leah shook her head. 'It can't be any worse than here.'

'Yeah well, you've not much choice.' Cindy's frustration was beginning to get the better of her. 'It's either 'ere, or a squat or some social worker taking you into care.'

Or Joe.

She hadn't mentioned Joe to Cindy and she wasn't sure she could trust her not to tell Alice if she did. But she had to talk to somebody.

'You know Saturday,' she hesitated, 'when the security man came after us . . .'

Cindy nodded.

'Well . . .' Leah told her about Joe.

Cindy listened without comment. 'Bloody 'ell,' she said when Leah had finished. 'You lucky sod. You telling me he just came from nowhere?'

'Not from nowhere. He must have been in the shop when the guard saw us. I think he was on the bus when we went into Bradford as well.'

Cindy frowned. 'You didn't tell 'im where you lived?'

'No, I only told him about Deepak. I didn't say anything about here.'

'Well, just you make sure you don't. He could be a cop.'

'No, he wasn't a cop. I'm sure he wasn't a cop.'

Cindy put her mug on the bedside table and kneeled up, looming over Leah. She raised her arms and waggled her fingers above. 'He could be the Trash Bag Killer,' she wailed.

Leah laughed. 'Don't be silly. He was too nice for that.'

Cindy resumed her position on the bed and picked up her mug. 'Well, just you be careful. People never do owt for nowt, you ought to know that by now; he's bound to want something. And don't let Alice find out about him, otherwise she'll knock 'ell out of you. And don't tell the others, they'll only be jealous and grass on you. Joe can be our secret, I'll not say anything.'

And as the two of them giggled, Leah felt better.

chapter fourteen

It was close to two-thirty when John Handford strode into Central's CID. There was a buzz of activity, but Handford wasn't interested. He walked over to Khalid Ali, who was working at his desk, and with no more than a cursory nod at the sergeant, said, 'My office, and bring everything on the Michael Braintree murder.'

There was much Handford wanted to say to Ali, not least to tear him apart for telling Russell he was in Cambridge over the weekend. This wasn't the first time Ali had had to be checked for discussing privileged information with a suspect he had decided was innocent. Normally, Handford kept it between themselves, but this time he would have to take it to Forrester. While he waited, he opened the mail. The first envelope contained post-mortem pictures of the dead girl.

Ali knocked and came into the room carrying a bundle of files. The sergeant's features were gaunt, there were dark circles under his eyes and his shoulders slouched as though he was overloaded with worry – probably concerned about his friendship with Deepak Azam, Handford thought, not unkindly. But along with his misdeeds, Ali's sensitivities would have to wait.

'The photograph of Braintree's girlfriend, let me see it,' Handford said, holding out his hand. He hoped he was wrong, but a thread linked her, the victim and Hannah Mellings and it would be too much of a coincidence if they were not one and the same.

Ali pulled the strip from the file and gave it to Handford. The girl giggled up at him and the apprehension that had tickled at his nerves since he left Catherine Walsh now sliced into his stomach like a scalpel. Even without the piece of rag in her mouth, she was the image of the murder victim. Attempting to keep his voice calm, he said, 'Have you had these blown up yet?'

'Yes, I did it straight away but they're not back yet. Why?'

'Because,' Handford pointed to the pictures, 'this is the girl in the alleyway.'

Ali stared at him and slumped on to the nearest chair. 'Are you sure?'

He wanted to shout, 'Of course I'm bloody sure,' but he kept himself in check and said, 'Yes, I am.'

Ali leaned his elbow on the desk and nervously fingered his lips, anxiety combining visibly with tiredness. 'I didn't know.'

Handford leaned towards him. 'Had you opened the internal mail, you would have done.' He threw the post-mortem pictures across the desk. 'You're supposed to keep up with things when I'm away.' He couldn't keep the censure out of his voice.

Ali picked up the photographs and shook his head. 'I'm sorry, I didn't have time.' And then by way of explanation, he added, 'I've been busy.'

Handford scrutinised his sergeant's face. He'd seen that look of sheepish embarrassment before and he knew Ali had been busy doing something of which his boss wouldn't approve. 'Doing what?'

When Ali didn't answer he repeated the question. 'Doing what?'

Ali kept his gaze firmly away from the inspector's, then he said quietly, 'I've been checking up on Deepak Azam.'

Handford groaned inwardly. Why couldn't the man do as he was told just for once? 'Checking up on him – how?'

Ali let out a long sigh. 'I talked to Michelle Archer, who told me more or less what you'd told me. I needed to check if Michael had been at the leisure centre on the day of his death, so I made a point of seeing Deepak at the same time.'

'And?'

Ali described the visit, then went on to relate the late-night surveillance of his friend and finally his embarrassment at being found by Warrender at the prostitutes' designated site.

Handford wasn't sure how he kept his temper. 'How stupid can you be, Ali? I told you to let someone in the serious crime team or the vice squad know of your relationship with Azam. I did not tell you to check him out yourself.'

When Ali lifted his eyes towards Handford's they showed neither avoidance nor guile. 'I needed to know, John; he's a friend.'

'And I suppose your reason for telling Russell where I was over the weekend was because he's a colleague?' Ali returned to studying the surface of the desk. 'I told you about the DCI because Mr Sanderson thought it would be a good idea; he thought I could trust you. *I* thought I could trust you.' Handford tried to keep his voice calm, but failed miserably. 'In situations like this your loyalty is to the service, you know that. If you can't hack it, Ali, then get out, because otherwise you're a liability.'

Handford swivelled his chair away from the sergeant and looked towards the window. There was little he could see from where he sat, except the deep blue of the sky and the dome of the theatre opposite curtained in gunmetal-grey scaffolding poles. That Ali had a problem wasn't in doubt, and it was a problem he was going to have to sort out sooner rather than later. He couldn't sit on the fence dividing family loyalty from the job for ever. Handford swung back. When finally he spoke, his words held a mixture of sympathy and warning. 'If it's any consolation, I understand why you did what you did, but this time you've taken a step too far. I can't condone it and I can't help you when Forrester finds out.'

Ali looked even more unhappy and took a moment to regain his composure. 'She knows, John,' he said eventually. 'At least, she does about my friendship with Deepak and that I have been checking up on him. Sergeant Archer must have told her. I've been warned to stay away from him and make myself available to see her when she's free.'

Handford felt the beginnings of a headache. Was all this his fault? Should he have left Ali out of it? He had told Sanderson he wasn't sure whether he ought to burden his sergeant with the information on Russell. If he hadn't done so, then Azam's name would never have come up.

'They are right though, John.' Ali's expression was one of someone who had just bitten into sour fruit and tears bubbled behind his words. 'Deepak is a pimp.'

Handford frowned. 'Go on,' he said.

The skin tightened apprehensively around Ali's eyes and he swallowed hard before describing his interview with Daniel Emmott.

Handford wasn't sure whether words of comfort were what Ali wanted nor was he sure they were his to give, so he asked, 'Do you believe him?'

Ali's tone was void of all emotion. 'Yes, I do. Deepak is running a brothel of under-sixteens somewhere in the city.'

'Did Daniel have any idea where they were being worked?'

'No. He mentioned an organisation called The Project, which helps prostitutes. They might know. Michael took Hannah to see them.'

'He didn't come to us?'

'He did, but the DCI decided there was nothing in Michael's complaint and marked it up for no further action.'

It was its very sparseness that made the interview room intimidating. The insipid paintwork, the four chairs, two on each side of the table, the recording machine and the clock – all were meant to cow the suspect and give the questioner the upper hand. Today the heat added to the pressure, the more so because the occupants were not dressed for the conditions, rather for the formality of the occasion; for no one doubted interrogating a senior police officer demanded formality.

Brian Noble was the first to speak. 'This is a taped interview with Stephen Russell timed at fourteen-thirty hours, Monday 19 August. Present are Detective Chief Superintendent Susan Forrester, Detective Inspector Brian Noble, Detective Chief Inspector Stephen Russell and Colin Armitage, Mr Russell's solicitor. Before we begin, Mr Russell, I must remind you that you are not under arrest and that you are free to leave at any time. I must also caution you that you do not have to say anything. But it may harm your defence if you do not mention when questioned something which you later rely on in court. Anything you do say may be given in evidence. Do you understand?'

'Perfectly.' Russell was plainly nervous, but his voice was strong.

Colin Armitage broke in. 'Before you begin, Chief Superintendent, Mr Russell would like to make a statement.'

The two detectives exchanged glances.

'Please, Mr Russell.' Forrester sat back, giving the chief inspector the platform.

Stephen Russell inclined forward, resting his arms on the table. For a moment he remained quite still, as though coming to a decision about what he was going to say. The fingers of one hand played with those of the other for a instant, then he sat back, but his eyes remained fixed on the table.

'I think, ma'am, I ought to apologise first for not being completely honest with you about my movements on the day of the girl's murder. I assure you, this had nothing to do with the killing, nor indeed did I. Because of its personal nature, I evaded the truth to protect myself and up to a point to protect my wife. She has been through a lot lately and the last thing she needs is to have to worry about me.'

The reason appeared flimsy, no more than an excuse, but Forrester made no comment. Instead she asked, 'So where were you, Mr Russell? I assume now you are prepared to tell us?'

'Yes, ma'am.'

His politeness was beginning to annoy her. 'So?'

For the first time he glanced up at her, and she saw how haggard he had become. He seemed to have aged in the past couple of days. The boyish features had been replaced by the careworn characteristics of a man for whom life had suddenly changed for the worse. The irate Russell had disappeared, his place taken by an individual more distressed and anxious than angry.

She didn't know the chief inspector well and hoped she wasn't being duped by him, and that this look was the norm when he was in a difficult position. She gave him the benefit of the doubt. 'Take your time, Mr Russell,' she said, her tone more sympathetic.

His expression, when he finally spoke, was ragged. 'I left my office last Thursday at about half past seven. I went to the leisure centre first for a massage, then I had an appointment with my counsellor at half past eight. I was with her until nine, after which I went home. We had guests, you will recall, ma'am.'

'And all you have said will check out?'

'Yes, ma'am. Vanessa is my masseuse at the leisure centre and my counsellor is Marion Hartley. She works at a private practice on Claremont.' He passed over a piece of paper. 'Her telephone number. I've already spoken to her and given her permission to answer any general questions you have about my consultation.'

'And this is the truth?'

'Yes.'

'So, tell me, why did you lie before?'

Colin Armitage broke in. 'I would have thought that was obvious, Mrs Forrester.'

'Not to me, Mr Armitage. Perhaps DCI Russell would like to explain.'

For the first time, Russell sat up straight. 'I am a Detective Chief Inspector, Mrs Forrester, and soon I hope to apply for the rank of Superintendent. I think my chances of ever being promoted would be lessened considerably if it was to be made public that I needed to visit a counsellor, don't you?'

'They would be considerably slimmer if you were to be arrested for killing four girls, don't you think, Chief Inspector?'

The tension in the room thickened as Forrester watched the play of emotions cross Russell's face: pain, fear, outrage. Anger at her, the same anger that had been in his eyes when he had insisted on her respect in his own home. Was he just a man ruled by dignity and pride, or was there something much more deeply entrenched in his personality?

'So, why are you visiting a counsellor, Mr Russell?'

He turned to his solicitor. 'Do I have to answer that? Surely my reasons are confidential?'

'Mrs Forrester, I cannot see what more information the answer to that question will give you. Mr Russell has told you where he was; he has given you permission to talk generally with Ms Hartley. She will confirm he was with her at the material time. Surely that should be enough?'

Forrester sat back in her chair. 'Normally, it would be, Mr Armitage, had it not been for information I was given on Saturday.' She turned back to Stephen Russell.

'I would like you to give me an account of your movements at lunchtime on Friday.'

Whatever dignity he had come in with was skimmed away with the question and for a moment his expression seemed to fall apart. He said nothing and Forrester watched him, the excuses, possibly the lies visibly spooling in his head. His shoulders dropped and he filled his lungs with air before exhaling. He seemed to accept that there was little more he could do but tell the truth.

'You mean my meeting with Andrew Collingham?'

'I gather you asked him to give you an alibi for the night of the murder?'

'Not to give me an alibi, just to firm up the one I had. I was at the leisure centre. I had hoped he would say I was there at the relevant time. He wouldn't. I'm sorry, ma'am. It was stupid. Andrew was right to come to you. I'll apologise to him when next I see him.'

Forrester had to admit that Russell played a good game; there was enough sincerity in his answer and his apology to make them acceptable. She honestly couldn't tell whether he was telling the truth or fabricating a series of lies.

'Can you account for your movements on . . .' She glanced at the sheet in front of her. 'The evening of 11 April? It was a Thursday.'

Russell flicked through the pages of the diary he had with him. He had expected the question. 'Apart from a massage and then a session with my counsellor at eight-thirty, there is nothing in my diary for that date.'

'Thursday, 13 June?'

'The same.'

'18 July? Also a Thursday.'

'Again, it's the same. I try to keep Thursday evenings free for my appointments with Ms Hartley. They are not easy, ma'am, and I need time to prepare myself before and sort out my thoughts afterwards.'

'These sessions, they make you feel angry, ashamed, what?' She sounded genuinely interested.

Russell considered the question for a few moments. 'When you are in counselling, Mrs Forrester, you delve deep into yourself, learn why you are what you are, what has shaped your life. It's tough and it's revealing, but more than anything it's exhausting.' He smiled at her. He seemed calmer now, almost mocking. 'If you think, Chief Superintendent, that when I come away, I have to expurgate my feelings on a young girl by killing her, then you are very much mistaken.' Russell pushed back his chair. 'Now, if you don't mind, I have given you my alibi, and I find the other questions unwarranted and intrusive, so since I'm not under arrest, I think I'd like to go.'

Forrester's expression was neutral. 'I can't stop you, Mr Russell, but I would be grateful if you would stay and answer a couple more questions.'

Russell glanced again at his solicitor, who shrugged as if to say that it was up to his client. Russell remained seated.

'Do you know a man called Deepak Azam?'

'The owner of the leisure centre? Yes, I do. Not well, but enough to pass the time of day.'

'Do you know anything of his activities outside the leisure centre?'

'He's something of a philanthropist, if that's what you mean. He's also eager to bring the communities together and works hard to that end.'

Forrester decided to take a risk. 'What would be your reaction if I told you we suspect Mr Azam of living on immoral earnings?'

If Russell was surprised, he didn't show it. 'I wouldn't believe you,' he said.

'And that he's probably running a brothel of under-age girls?' Forrester wasn't sure, but it appeared that anxiety had been replaced by curiosity in the man sitting opposite. It seemed he had almost forgotten that he was the one under suspicion. She needed to propel him back into the present.

'Or that one of your sergeants, DS Ali, is a good friend of his and probably knows exactly what he is doing – may even be part of it.'

He digested this in silence for a moment. 'I would ask you where your evidence was.'

'We have evidence, Mr Russell. Sergeant Ali has admitted to the friendship, but not before he was caught at the designated site for prostitutes on Saturday night. When asked by the two officers on surveillance why he was there, his explanation was less than satisfactory. We also believe that he has warned Azam of our interest in him.'

This time Russell couldn't keep the incredulity out of his voice. 'There must be some mistake, ma'am. Have you spoken to him?'

'Not yet, but I will.'

'And I'm sure he'll give you a complete explanation. Sergeant Ali is a good police officer and a good man.'

'I don't doubt the same would have been said about you five days ago, Mr Russell.' As soon as she had uttered the words, she regretted them and raised her hands in mute apology when the solicitor broke in with, 'Really, Mrs Forrester, I have to protest.'

She let her acknowledgement rest for a moment and then said, 'Do you know where the under-age brothel is, Chief Inspector?'

Russell rubbed his hand across his forehead. 'No, Mrs Forrester,' he replied emphatically. 'I do not know where the under-age brothel is. I didn't know there was one. I understood it was policy neither to acknowledge young prostitutes nor to go out looking for them.'

'And do you agree with that policy?'

'No, I don't. They are abused girls, and as such we should be protecting them, not pretending they don't exist. But since prostitutes of any age are not my remit, or that of my team, my opinion is irrelevant. They are the concern of the vice squad, or,' he added evenly, 'that of the serious crime team if the dead girls are from this brothel.'

Forrester pursed her lips. Russell was gaining the upper hand, the interview was beginning to spiral out of her control and she needed to get it back. She said coldly, 'One more question, Chief Inspector. To whom did you give the photograph we found in the dead girl's possession, and have you any idea why she should have it?'

Russell looked up again, directly into the chief superintendent's eyes. 'I expect you already know that, Mrs Forrester,' he said, bitterness smothering his words. 'I expect Inspector Handford has told you all you want to know. But just in case he has missed anything, I gave it to my girlfriend when we left Cambridge. Catherine and I had broken up and I wanted her to have it. And to save you the embarrassment of asking me, yes, she was pregnant, and yes, I think, although I don't know because no one ever thought to tell me, that she didn't terminate as my father expected her to, and yes, Mrs Forrester, it is possible that the dead girl, prostitute or not, is my daughter, but I can't be sure because I've never seen her.'

Waiting outside Forrester's office with Ali, Handford tried unsuccessfully to pull himself together. He held on to his hands, cursing his perpetual inability to control his nerves. In a situation like this, it seemed as though a small motor inside him fed paddles, which thrashed at his emotions to the point where he felt sick. That Forrester would be furious with Ali, there was no doubt, but Handford was having a problem ridding himself of the feeling that she would probably put some of the blame on him for confiding in Ali in the first place. That the suggestion – and he could honestly put it at no more than a suggestion – had come from Sanderson may not be enough.

Both men straightened as Brian Noble pushed open the double doors at the end of the corridor, holding one of them to allow Forrester through. Seeing Handford, she attempted a tired smile.

'John, you're back. Look, I can't see you now. Give your report to Brian and we'll set up a meeting when I've read it.'

She made to go into her office.

'I'm sorry, ma'am, but I need to speak with you.'

'Not now, John.' If anything she appeared more drawn than she had when Handford had last seen her prior to going to Cambridge.

He was emphatic. 'I'm sorry, but it's got to be now. I know who the dead girl is.'

She stopped in her tracks. 'You'd better come in.' Glancing at Ali, she said, 'And you are?'

'Detective Sergeant Ali, ma'am.'

She regarded him narrowly. 'I think you'd better join us as well.'

He avoided her gaze. 'Yes, ma'am.'

Once she was installed behind her desk and Brian Noble leaning in his usual place against the filing cabinet, Handford handed her the strip of photographs.

'Sergeant Ali found them in a box when he and DC Clarke searched the room of the young lad who was murdered last week,' he said by way of explanation.

Her lips formed a thin line. 'How long have you had these?' she asked as she passed them over to Brian Noble.

The question was not unexpected. Handford glanced at Ali. 'Today is the first time I've seen them, but Sergeant Ali picked them up from the victim's house on Friday.'

Forrester turned towards the sergeant. 'Who is the girl?'

'Hannah Mellings, ma'am. We'd been led to believe she was on holiday, camping in the Dales. But so far we haven't been able to locate either her or her friends.'

Forrester leaned over her desk. 'Well, you wouldn't, would you, Sergeant, since she's been lying on a mortuary slab since Friday.' Cold anger swamped her features. 'We sent her post-mortem photograph to every department on Saturday. Don't you look at the mail when Inspector Handford is away?'

Ali looked at Handford, hoping no doubt for some support, but when none was forthcoming he reverted to Forrester. 'I'm sorry, I hadn't seen them.'

Her eyes blazed at him. 'Have you any idea how much time we've wasted, Sergeant, trying to find out who she was? I've had officers on it who could have been better employed in other directions.'

Ali cleared his throat to speak.

She waved him to silence. 'No, don't even try to give me an explanation, because there isn't one. You've been negligent and your negligence has cost us three days.'

The afternoon sun seared in to the room, its rays catching Handford on the side of his face. He wanted to move, to side-step its heat, but he knew he couldn't. Instead he said, 'There's more, ma'am. Catherine Walsh's married name is Mellings and her daughter Hannah has taken Mr Mellings's name. However, since there were no photographs in her office, I can't be sure the girls are one and the same.'

'But it looks as though they might be?'

'Yes, it does. And because of what Sergeant Ali has told me of an interview with Michael Braintree's best friend, there may be some link with your investigation – through Deepak Azam.'

Forrester turned to Ali. 'I gather you know Deepak Azam?'

'Yes, ma'am.' His voice was no more than a whisper.

'Well, or just in passing?'

Ali swallowed hard. 'I know him well. We've been friends for a number of years and my father and his father are best friends. We meet up as often as we can. But I had no idea that he was involved with prostitutes. In fact, quite the opposite, he was instrumental in persuading the council to move them off the streets. It never occurred to me—'

'Obviously.' This time Forrester ladled sarcasm into her voice. 'Nor, it seems, did it occur to you to inform Sergeant Archer of your relationship with Azam when you spoke to her.'

He avoided her stare. 'No, ma'am.' As the silence deepened it appeared she wanted more in the way of explanation. 'I needed to be sure before I said anything.'

'So, you went to see him?'

'Yes, ma'am, but to question him about Michael's movements at the gym on the day of his death.'

'Ostensibly.' The word whipped across the room.

Ali made no reply.

Forrester persisted. 'When you were with him, did you mention prostitutes at all?'

Ali cleared his throat and Handford knew that his sergeant was about to dig his own grave. 'I told him I had learned from an officer in the vice squad that Dwayne Varley, one of his employees, was into using prostitutes.'

Forrester was holding on to her temper. 'What did he say?'

'He was furious and said who he employed was nothing to do with the police.'

'And you took that to mean?'

Ali's gaze was still concentrated floorwards. 'I thought his re-action excessive enough for me to accept what Sergeant Archer had told me was true.'

'But even that wasn't enough for you, Sergeant, was it? You had to check further, go and see for yourself. Never mind that you might be destroying any surveillance we had on him. Didn't occur to you to ask Michelle Archer first?'

Ali made no comment.

The look Forrester gave him could have frozen everything in the room. 'Sergeant Ali, if I were not so busy, I would begin the paper-work for an inquiry into your behaviour right now. Instead, I'll leave Inspector Handford to sort you out.' She leaned over her desk to fix her gaze on Ali. 'How could you have been so stupid, Sergeant? Do you know the damage you may have done to our investigation? And do you know how all you have told us looks? The fact that you have admitted to what you have done probably means that you are involved with Deepak Azam only as a friend. I hope for your sake I'm right, because if I'm not, I promise you I'll make time to set up an inquiry. In the meantime, you have nothing more to do with Azam, nor does your family. Do I make myself clear?'

'Yes, ma'am.'

She let the heat settle around her, then said, her voice restrained, 'Now, tell me all you know about Hannah Mellings and how she came to be linked with your murder victim.'

Ali explained the background to the investigation, as well as a concise description of the interview with Daniel Emmott. Forrester listened without interruption. When he had finished she said, 'The father she was looking for, have you any idea who this was?'

'Not until Inspector Handford told me of the relationship between DCI Russell and Hannah's mother.'

'And do you know why DCI Russell decided on no further action after Michael's visit?'

'According to PC Foxton, Mr Russell said he'd never heard of prostitutes so young and that what Michael was fearing was unlikely.'

'You haven't spoken to Mr Russell direct about this?'

'No, ma'am, not yet.'

'Then don't. Leave it to us.' She looked at her watch. 'It's three o'clock now. I want a full report on Deepak Azam. I also want copies of Daniel Emmott's statement and those of his parents. And I want them on my desk by four o'clock. And you discuss none of this with anyone except those of us in this room. Understood?'

'Yes, ma'am.'

As Ali closed the door behind him, Forrester turned to Noble. 'We'll pull Azam in tomorrow, see what he has to say for himself. Arrange it, will you?'

Noble nodded.

Finally, she concentrated her gaze on Handford. 'We've just finished interviewing DCI Russell,' she said as she handed him the tape. 'I want you to check out both his statement and the reason why he decided to go for no further action on what Michael Braintree told him.'

Handford felt his hackles rise again. He could understand why she wouldn't leave it alone, but he did think the time had come to pass over any inquiry into the DCI to another force. He opened his mouth to argue, but a glimpse at her expression told him this was not the time.

'Sit down, both of you.'

Noble passed a chair to Handford, who took it gratefully. Forrester looked at him. 'Are you absolutely sure this girl, Hannah Mellings, is the daughter of the Mrs Mellings you met in Norwich, John?'

'No, ma'am, I can't be. As I said, there were no photographs in her office, at least none that I saw, and it didn't seem appropriate to ask if she had any. At the moment all we have is what Daniel Emmott told us, that Michael's girlfriend was a Hannah Mellings who came from Norfolk and was holidaying in the Dales. That fits with what Mrs Mellings told me.'

'But, if you were to make an educated guess, would you say she is Catherine Mellings's daughter?'

'Yes, it does seem likely, although it worries me that, if it is her, no one has reported her missing.'

'Well, let's find out, shall we? Let's notify her parents.'

Handford was doubtful. 'Shouldn't we be more certain before we do that, ma'am? Try to find the family she's on holiday with. If we're wrong and it's not her, we're going to cause a lot of grief.'

Forrester didn't agree. 'No, John. The sooner we know for sure, the sooner we have a connection between the girl and Stephen Russell, and the sooner we firm up the case against him.'

Handford's heart slid into his stomach. She wouldn't let go. 'You think he's the killer?'

'I'm damned sure he is, but without a solid identification, I don't have any grounds to arrest him.' She smiled. 'So, who's going to tell them, us or the Norfolk police?'

Noble grimaced. 'The Norfolk police, I think, don't you? But . . .' He hesitated. 'I agree with John. Wouldn't it be better to fax a copy of the photograph to them first, ask them to check the girl's identity before talking to the Mellingses?'

Forrester fixed him with a hard stare. 'It will be a nightmare getting hold of someone in the school holidays who can verify her identity; it could be days before we know. Thanks to Sergeant Ali we've already wasted enough time, we can't afford to waste any more. Come on, Brian, wouldn't you agree that everything we have tells us that the body in the mortuary is that of Hannah Mellings?'

'Yes, I would, but . . .'

'Then we go ahead. Contact the North Yorkshire police, suggest they locate the family and find out why they haven't reported Hannah missing, then get on to Norfolk police and ask them to notify the Mellingses and get them up here.'

Handford returned to his office via the coffee machine. He was in desperate need of caffeine, although he knew it was the worst thing for the headache that was thumping in tune with his heartbeat. He opened his briefcase and took out the box of painkillers. Throwing two in his mouth he took a swallow of coffee. It was lukewarm but palatable. Wearily, he sat down behind his desk, pulled out the bottom drawer to rest his feet on and leaned back closing his eyes.

Life wasn't being kind. He was concerned for the Mellingses. Forrester was acting too soon. She ought to be more sure before notifying them, even if it meant another couple of days.

Then there was Russell. She was in too much of a hurry to acknowledge his guilt. The case against the DCI was vague at best, even a positive identification of the girl would not clarify it enough for a charge of murder. He picked up the cassette tape and pushed it into his recorder. Perhaps his alibi would give him an answer – one way or another – although he doubted it.

It concerned Handford that the inquiry was becoming personal, a vendetta against his boss, although he wasn't sure why. It could be that she was being squeezed from all sides for a result, but he had a feeling it was more than that. She wanted him guilty.

The telephone interrupted his musings. He picked up the receiver, his mind only half on the call. 'Handford . . . Gill . . .' He pulled himself up sharply; he'd promised he would ring her when he got back. 'Oh Gill, I'm sorry, I should have rung you,' he apologised. 'There was a problem here.'

'Well, you've got another one now, you need to come home.'

'I'm not sure I can just yet—'

'As soon as you can then.' Gill sounded upset. 'Please, John, let the job take a back seat just for once. I need you here.'

He was concerned; this wasn't like Gill, she was normally so composed. 'What is it? Is something wrong?'

There was a moment's silence, then a deep breath sighed through the phone into Handford's ear.

'Nicola is pregnant, John. She needs you; we need you. Please, come home.'

chapter fifteen

Khalid Ali glanced at his watch. Half past six. He ought to go home, but he was still smarting over DCS Forrester's reprimand and didn't feel much like moving from his desk. Warrender would be laughing over the fact that he missed the identity of the dead girl because he'd been so tied up with Deepak. He could hear him now: 'Told you so, they always think of their own first. As if they can't ever do anything wrong. They're blinded by their culture and as far as I'm concerned it's about time they went back to it.'

Was that what it was? Was he blinded by his culture, forced into putting family first by a father who, in his mind, still lived in the old Pakistan and expected his son to do the same? Was that why he'd missed Deepak's extramural activities? He tried to think back, to see if in the recesses of his memory he could dig out anything that should have warned him. He shook his head; nothing. They'd just been good friends, enjoyed each other's company – as had the rest of the family.

He dragged his hands across his eyes and cheeks. How was he going to face Amina with this? He'd been quite unpleasant to her since Handford's visit, as though it was all her fault. In trying to come to terms with the fact that Deepak was working prostitutes, he'd blamed the very people he should have been thinking of. With a sigh of resignation, he pulled himself from his chair and picked up his coat and his briefcase. Like it or not, he had to stop pre-varicating and go home, explain everything to her and to his parents and insist they mustn't see or associate with the Azams until the investigation was over.

He was almost at the door when the telephone rang. His first inclination was to leave it, but he'd been sloppy enough today. 'CID, Sergeant Ali speaking.'

It was the lab.

'Goodness me, you're working late,' he said when the woman at the other end introduced herself.

'There's a lot of crime about, did no one tell you?'

In spite of himself, Ali laughed.

'Actually, I'm trying to catch up on phone calls. The T-shirt in the Braintree case.'

'Yes?' The clothes Michael had been wearing at the time of his death had been sent for forensic testing.

'I think we may have something. There was quite a big patch of dried sweat on the front of it and it's not the victim's. We found two fair curly hairs as well. Since the boy would be a dead weight when they strung him up, it looks as though one of them steadied him with his head to stop him swinging. We've sent the samples away for DNA testing, do you want them fast-tracking?'

Ali swore under his breath. Under normal circumstances he'd have said yes and suffered the consequences, but not today. 'I'll have to let you know tomorrow,' he said, 'the DI's gone home and there's no one else to give authorisation.'

'Fine. If I don't hear from you by lunchtime, I'll use the normal route. In the meantime, you can be looking for a strong man with fair curly hair.'

'Thanks, there can't be too many of that description.' Indeed the only person he knew who fitted it and whom he could connect with Michael Braintree was Dwayne Varley – and Varley worked for Deepak Azam. All thoughts of his wife and his father momentarily pushed from his mind, Ali began to feel the excitement of a possible breakthrough. The bouncer would be at the leisure centre now, he could get hold of him there. It occurred to him momentarily that he was probably banned from the leisure centre given it was Deepak's place of work, but he dismissed the thought. DCS Forrester had ordered him not to talk to Deepak, but had said nothing about the centre itself or about talking with those who worked for him.

To hell with it; he had something that might take him a step nearer to Michael's killer and he was not going to wait. He was just about to set off when the telephone rang again. With a sigh he returned to answer it. 'Sergeant Ali.'

The voice at the other end sounded strained. 'Sergeant Ali, it's Daniel Emmott.'

'What is it, Daniel?'

'It's my dad and Michael's dad. They've gone down to the leisure centre. Since you won't do anything, they said, they're going to sort

186

out Mr Azam themselves. I'm frightened for them, Sergeant Ali. They don't know what he's like.'

Ali put down the phone, snatched up his case and ran out of CID. The stupid men. Why couldn't they leave it to him? He'd promised he would look into the allegations.

The roads were fairly quiet at that time in the evening and it took him no more than a few minutes to drive the short distance to the leisure centre. As he manoeuvred the one-way system, Daniel's words echoed in his mind: *Since you won't do anything, they're going to sort out Mr Azam themselves*. Ali banged his hand hard on the steering wheel. It was his fault. He should have made himself clearer, convinced them that he did believe Daniel and that if what the boy had said proved to be true, he would make sure Azam was arrested and charged. Instead he'd left it in the air with a vague insistence on evidence, and a distraught man and his friend were now out for revenge.

He pulled up at the side of the road next to the leisure centre and climbed out of the car. Quite a crowd had gathered outside and he waved his warrant card at the uniformed officer who was trying to move them on, then pulled open the heavy glass doors into reception. The two fathers had been there for some time and an officer inside was trying to persuade them to put down the weapons they were carrying. When Mr Emmott had said they would sort out Azam, he had meant just that. Deepak Azam was cowering in a corner in the reception area, blood seeping from wounds on his head and face. Raymond Braintree was towering over him, a baseball bat in one hand and a length of rope, fashioned into a noose in the other. Norman Emmott stood back, flailing his stick at whoever came near.

'What's happened?' Ali asked the police officer.

'I'm not sure how it began, but the one with the noose has accused Mr Azam of turning his son into a pimp, and of stringing him up when he wanted to back out of the arrangement. He's threatening to do the same to Azam, string him up, I mean. I've tried, but I've not been able to get anywhere with them. We need a negotiator, someone who knows how to talk to them.'

'And while we're waiting for one to materialise, we're going to stand by and watch him carry out his threat, are we?'

Staff crowded behind the far door that lead from reception into the centre itself, eager to get sight of what was happening. Dwayne Varley was amongst them. Much good he was in a crisis.

Ali spoke clearly but quietly. 'Mr Emmott.'

Norman Emmott swung round, his stick high above his head.

'Don't be silly, Mr Emmott,' Ali said softly. 'Put it down.'

The man didn't move. 'I might have known you'd come to protect this scum. I told you this morning if you wouldn't do anything we would.'

Ali glanced over to Azam. 'Are you all right?' he asked.

Deepak Azam attempted to shift his position, but as he did so, Raymond Braintree raised his bat higher in the air. 'Do I look all right, Khalid? Just get these maniacs out of my leisure centre.'

Keeping Norman Emmott in his sights, Ali spoke to Michael's father. 'This isn't right, Mr Braintree, and you know it. I'm not going to let you harm Mr Azam. More police are on the way and soon you'll have to give yourselves up. If we can settle it now before they come, I'm sure Mr Azam will not want to press charges; he knows what you've gone through and how upset you are.'

At this Norman Emmott exploded. '*He* won't press charges! *He* won't press charges! He's the pervert round here. Pimping young girls and teaching lads how to do the same.'

'You don't know that, Mr Emmott.'

'Yes, I do, and so do you.'

Ali didn't want this. If he made comment, he'd let Azam know he was under investigation and be back in front of Forrester and out of the service. If he didn't answer the man's accusation, there was no saying what he would do. He had to stop them, and he didn't want to do it by force.

He ignored the baseball bat and stepped closer. 'I told you I'll investigate and I will. But I can't do anything until you stop this and go home,' he said as quietly as he could. He hoped Azam hadn't heard him.

The two men glanced at each other, obviously unsure of what to do next. They had backed themselves into a corner from which it was becoming increasingly difficult to escape.

Ali stepped backwards. 'Come on, Mr Braintree,' he said. 'This won't bring Michael back and if I have to arrest you, what will happen to your wife? Don't you think she's suffered enough?'

Raymond Braintree cast a wild look towards his friend. 'Norman?'

Ali pushed home his advantage. 'It was Daniel who told me you were coming here, Mr Emmott. He's worried sick about what's going to happen to you.'

Norman Emmott relaxed his stance. 'And you, what will you do if we agree?' He pointed at Azam. 'Persuade him not to press charges and then patch him up, or will you arrest him?'

Ali ignored the question. 'Please go. Mr Azam will not make a complaint if you do. But if you stay here, I'll be obliged to arrest the two of you and I really wouldn't want that.' He hoped the men could see the rest of the message in his eyes.

They looked at each other for a moment, then Mr Braintree dropped the baseball bat and the rope, and in tacit agreement Mr Emmott let his weapon fall to the floor. Azam began to pull himself from the corner but Ali glared at him. 'Stay exactly where you are, Mr Azam,' he snapped as he bent down to pick up the weapons and the rope. He beckoned to one of the uniformed officers and handed them to him. 'Get rid of these,' he said. 'And take Mr Emmott and Mr Braintree home.' Finally, he walked over to Azam and pulled him roughly from the floor. He turned to the receptionist. 'Take me to the First Aid room,' he said and indicated to the other police officer that he should come too.

As they pushed their way through the doors, the crowd parted, first in silence and then, as the four passed them, a buzz of conversation broke out. Someone asked if Deepak was all right, but Ali held on to him and walked him quickly to the room marked First Aid. Once inside, Deepak slumped onto a chair. He turned to the receptionist. 'Get me a whisky, and one for Sergeant Ali as well.'

Ali shot him a look of disgust. 'Not for me,' he said coldly.

'Oh, come on, Khalid, don't look like that. I need a drink after what I've gone through, those men could have killed me.' He attempted a laugh, but pulled up short as the pain caught at him.

'I doubt it,' Ali said, little concern in his tone. 'But you've had a nasty bang on the head. We'll get you an ambulance.'

'No, I'll live.' The receptionist returned with the whisky. He took it from her and swallowed it in one gulp, then passed the glass back. 'Get me another, a large one.'

Ali looked on. He'd known nothing about Azam. Nothing at all. Everything about him was a sham, his religion, his lifestyle and his position in the community, even his friendship. He couldn't stay here; he shouldn't have been here in the first place. He turned to the police officer. 'You finish up,' he said and strode out of the room.

The receptionist accompanied Deepak Azam to his office. He thanked her and, insisting he would be fine, said she should get back to the front desk. As she closed the door quietly behind her, he slumped on to the settee. The wound had stopped bleeding, but his head ached and nausea was beginning to overtake him. Khalid was right, he ought to go to the hospital, just to be sure. Varley could take him later. Eventually he pulled himself up and walked over to a cabinet, opened it, took out a bottle and poured himself another whisky, which he drank slowly. He ought not to let the men get away with what they'd done and in normal circumstances he wouldn't, but the police would be suspicious if they were suddenly found beaten up or their houses torched, and a court appearance would mean them getting the opportunity to air their allegations in public.

He's the pervert round here. Pimping young girls and teaching lads how to do the same.

He didn't want that, enough people had heard it tonight. Most wouldn't believe it, not of Deepak Azam, but if it was reiterated in court, the magistrate might feel honour bound to pass it on for investigation. It stuck in his throat, but for once it would be better let it lie. And anyway, he had a bigger problem than two fathers who considered themselves in the big league.

I told you I'll investigate and I will. Obviously, Khalid Ali had not wanted to be overheard, thought he hadn't been, then he had ignored their question as to whether he was prepared to arrest his friend. The one thing he hadn't done was deny they were wrong. How much did Khalid know? What was he intending to investigate? Azam as a pimp? Azam grooming young girls? He cast his mind back. On Saturday Khalid had shown some knowledge of the women; he'd made out it was Varley who was involved with them, but even then Azam hadn't been convinced that what he was saying was no more than a friendly warning about one of his employees. Now he knew it wasn't. Ali had information, which had turned his allegiances from those to whom he should be loyal and over to the whites. Khalid had become the enemy, the pig, the white man. He would investigate his friend – or he would try to. The women, however, wouldn't talk – they were too dependent on Azam for their drugs – and if it seemed they were considering grassing him up, he only had to show them Debbie Johnson's scar. And as far as the young ones were concerned, the police didn't know where they were – otherwise they would have done something about them. No, he was safe. And in the end Khalid Ali would look both the fool and the traitor he was.

Azam stood up and poured himself yet another drink, gulping it down in one. Suddenly anger took hold and he hurled the glass at the wall, shattering it into small pieces on the floor. How dare Khalid Ali treat him like that? How dare he?

Breathing deeply, he went over to the telephone and punched in a number. When the voice at the other end answered, he said, 'Bring me a girl tonight. The one I sent over to you a few days ago, she'll do.' And he slammed down the receiver.

It was just about the worst evening of his life, Handford decided. Nicola pregnant. He didn't known whether to be angry with her or take her in his arms and comfort her, but as he approached the lounge door, he glimpsed her hunched on the settee. Hearing him, she turned her head towards him, her dark eyes filled with apprehension, and his anger dissipated and he almost ran to her and hugged her. 'It'll be all right, Nicola. I promise you it will be all right. We'll get through this one way or another.' They didn't talked about how, Nicola wasn't ready for that. It was enough she'd had to tell him and Gill. She needed to get over that.

Vishnu was the father, of course, although his family refused to accept it. 'Mr Akram wouldn't believe it's Vishnu's baby.' Nicola sobbed almost uncontrollably. 'He said I'm promiscuous and a whore, and that I've led Vishnu on, that it's all my fault. I'm not, Dad, I haven't. It isn't all my fault; Vishnu wanted to just as much as I did.'

For a while they sat, not saying much at all, until the telephone rang. At first he ignored it, but it was insistent. He pulled himself from the settee and barked 'Handford' into the mouthpiece. It was Ali. There'd been an incident at the leisure centre involving Azam, Handford had to go back in.

Gill argued. 'John, there are decisions to be made.'

'But not today, Gill. We all need time to come to terms with what has happened. Tomorrow will be soon enough to look at the options.'

'Will you be here tomorrow though?' Her tone was a mixture of hurt and anger. 'Or will I have to be the one who sorts things out as usual?'

A good question. Tomorrow the Mellingses were coming to identify their daughter. Tomorrow he would be busy.

'Don't worry, Gill, we'll find time.'

For his family and the job? He hoped so.

He met up with Ali in CID. There wasn't a lot to say once the sergeant had described the incident. He assured Handford that he had stayed with Azam for only the minimum amount of time. He didn't think he would want to press charges against Mr Braintree and Mr Emmott. 'He probably knows he's the one with the most to lose,' he said.

'And you, are you all right?' Handford met his eyes.

'I'll cope,' Ali said with a wry grin. 'At least, I hope I will. I've still got to tell Amina and my father.'

'Then go home. Leave the rest to me. We're pulling Azam in tomorrow anyway, so we'll look at the allegations then. And Khalid,' he said, a note of warning in his voice, 'I don't need to tell you not to have contact with Azam, do I?'

'No, sir, you don't.'

As soon as Ali had left, Handford went to find Forrester. She wasn't in her office and someone said they thought she'd gone home, but DI Noble hadn't and was in the canteen.

The canteen was almost empty, and Noble was sitting alone at one of the long tables. Like everyone on the inquiry, it seemed, the inspector wore an expression of abject weariness. Handford bought himself a coffee and went to join him. He filled him in on the evening's events.

'A pity it happened,' Noble said when he had finished. 'Mrs Forrester has enough on her plate, without this.'

'Something else has happened?'

Noble sipped his coffee. 'I haven't had the opportunity to tell you, but I had to tell her we picked her husband up for kerb-crawling.'

'Kerb-crawling?'

'Yes. I don't think I'd have bothered saying anything to her, we'd just have sent him the usual letter and left it at that, but according to Warrender and Archer he specifically asked for a young prostitute. Made something of a fuss with one of the other girls apparently.'

'So, they arrested him.'

'No, their brief was to keep the surveillance low-key, make a note of registration numbers and check them later. It turned out to be a company car. When Warrender rang them he was told it had been signed out in Tony Forrester's name. They'd no idea until then.'

Handford grimaced. 'I bet that made Warrender's day.'

'It did, but I've threatened him with everything I can think of if he breathes a word.'

'Have you questioned Forrester yet?'

'This morning. He denied he was in the car. Said he'd forgotten to sign it back in and someone else must have taken it out.'

'Did you believe him?'

'Not a word, and neither does his wife. They haven't got the best of marriages; he hates her job and she won't give it up, and this case isn't helping; she's never home.'

Handford sighed. 'Tell me about it,' he said.

'We're going to have to check him out; I don't think we've any choice. We've checked all other punters who have a penchant for young girls.'

'And Forrester, she's staying on the case?'

'Seems so. I told her she was compromising the investigation if she didn't hand it over to another senior investigating officer, but she wouldn't listen. She's determined to stick it out until we have Russell in the cells.'

'So she's still going all out to get him?'

Noble raised his eyebrows in response. 'She's sure it's him. Thinks she'll have it cracked in a few days.'

'And you?'

Noble shook his head. 'I don't think it's as cut and dried as she does. I'm not even sure Hannah Mellings is the fourth victim; which reminds me, since you've met Catherine Mellings, Mrs Forrester wants you at the identification suite with her tomorrow, eleven o'clock.'

Leah pulled her clothes out of the wardrobe. What to wear? Alice had taken her into the city and bought her some new ones, but they were for the punters, Leah knew that. The uniform of prostitutes. That's what Alice had said she was, that was what she was being trained for.

But not for long. Deepak had asked for her. She'd known he would, sooner or later. And it had been sooner, because he wanted her back. Alice had been wrong, the other girls had been wrong. She was still Deepak's girlfriend, he still loved her, he still wanted her. She had never doubted he wouldn't – well, almost never. All he'd been doing was punishing her for being bad. Now she'd shown him she could be good, that she would do anything for him, the punishment would be at an end. By tomorrow she'd be with him, permanently, and he would look after her as he had before.

Holding up the flimsy pastel blue summer dress Deepak had bought her, she decided that that was what she would wear tonight. He said blue suited her, matched her eyes. Her eyes were what had attracted him to her first of all – her eyes and her long blonde hair. When he'd given her the bag from the shop, he'd said she should wear the dress only for him. And she had; no one else had ever seen her in it.

She hung it carefully back in the wardrobe.

Pondering the rest of her clothes strewn on the bed, she considered whether to pack her suitcase now and take it with her tonight. It would save time in the long run. In the end, she decided she'd wait until the next day, then she'd ring Alice and tell her to send her things on. It would serve the old bat right to have to pack them up. Show her how wrong she'd been.

There wasn't time anyway; the first punter was due in a few minutes, so she pushed everything back in the wardrobe. Turning towards the dressing table, she picked up a packet of condoms and put it in her bag. They were for tonight, for Deepak. Then, opening the drawer, she pulled out three more packets for punters who hadn't come equipped. She glanced at the clock; five minutes and she would lie back and let them pump away inside her and pretend she was enjoying it. No, she wouldn't. Tonight, she wouldn't pretend anything, she'd just let them do it and leave. Because in a few hours they wouldn't be part of her life any more. She would be back with Deepak, and that was all that mattered.

She smiled.

For the first time in days she felt almost happy.

The children were in bed when Ali arrived home. Amina watched him walk down the drive. He was looking increasingly more tired, haggard even. She wished he would tell her what was wrong, for something clearly was. He walked into the kitchen and planted a kiss on her cheek. His meal was ready, she said, but it could wait if he wanted a shower. She'd have it on the table when he came down.

He shook his head and, taking her arm, said, 'No, leave it for a moment. I need to talk to you. Let's go into the garden.'

There was a sadness in his eyes that Amina couldn't interpret, 'What's wrong, Khalid? Please tell me.'

They walked through the French windows and into the garden and sat at the wrought iron table. The sun was beginning to set behind the trees, but it was still warm.

'Everything,' he said. He hesitated as if he was checking his words before he spoke them. 'But first of all, Amina, I must ask you not to see Shagufta again, or her children.'

She opened her mouth to argue, but Ali silenced her. 'Listen, please,' he said. 'I shan't be seeing Deepak and I have to ask my father not to spend time with Sohail.'

This time she wasn't to be silenced. 'For goodness' sake, Khalid, why ever not? What has happened? Has this something to do with your argument with John?'

'Yes, it's linked,' he admitted. She had known it. It had worried her ever since it had happened, the more so because Khalid had refused to discuss it. Now it seemed he was ready to tell her.

She listened in horrified silence as the events of the last few days enfolded. She tried to stop the tears, but they were too strong for her. Khalid put his arm round her and the sadness in his eyes deepened. 'I'm sorry, Amina, I would have preferred not to worry you with this, but there's no doubt it's the truth. Deepak is an evil man and I don't know why we didn't realise it before. When John told me I didn't believe him and I was very angry with him. But it is true.' He gave her a wry smile. 'I got an awful telling-off from the senior investigating officer today for not divulging my friendship with Deepak, and for checking him out myself. I'm still smarting from it. But I was so blinkered, so busy trying to prove them wrong, I didn't notice Michael Braintree's girlfriend was the girl found dead last week. It was my job to open the internal mail while John was away, but I didn't. Had I done so, I would have seen the post-mortem pictures and realised.'

Amina stroked his face. She couldn't judge him, enough people had done that already. 'Oh, Khalid, I'm so sorry, you must have had a dreadful day.' She paused, knowing she had to ask. 'What are you going to tell your father?'

Ali shrugged. 'The truth. And insist he keeps everything I have told him to himself.'

'He won't like that.'

'No, I know. He'll talk to me about divided loyalties again, and he's right, they are there. John can see it as well, although I think he understands – at least, to a point. Even so, he told me if I can't decide where my loyalties lie I should resign from the service.' He rubbed his face with his hands. 'I've thought about it all day. I can't be two people any more, Amina. As much as I don't want to, this has made me realise I have to choose between being myself or being my father's son for the rest of my life. It seems the two are not compatible.'

'And have you chosen?'

'Yes, I think so. I love and respect my father very much. He came to this country to give his family a better life and he has succeeded. But he's of the generation that hankers after the old culture, because he thinks it's the best. He may be right, but the fact is, it's not mine. Islam is my religion, but the culture he is part of is not mine. It can't be, I'm a detective and I have to be impartial, even with family and friends. My father will never understand that, but whether he likes it or not, as far as Deepak is concerned, it's what I have to be. I have to see him as he is. He's pimping white women and setting up children to be abused by those as bad as himself. He's preying on white boys who need the money to prepare the girls for him. But worse, I think, although at the moment I'm not sure, he's using Younis to bring these boys to his attention.'

Amina was horrified. 'Oh no, Khalid, no. Poor Shagufta. Can't I go to her?'

'No, Amina, not yet, I'm sorry. We have no way of knowing if she's involved. Perhaps later when it's all over.'

She stayed silent. This was so difficult.

Khalid grasped her hand and she felt his support. 'I know how you feel, but I can't go on living in two camps, Amina.'

'No, I know you can't, and I'm glad at last you've accepted it. It's been tearing you apart for too long.'

He stood up. 'Can the meal wait a while? I need to see my father.'

'Of course.' She gave him a long look. 'You won't change your mind, will you?'

'No, I won't.'

'Whatever your father says?'

'Whatever he says.'

As Susan Forrester sat in her office the next morning, her abiding memory of the previous night's events was not her husband's coldness towards her, nor his inability to look her in the eye, nor even the pain that had surged through her as he spoke, but the silhouette of the house, dark against the velvet blue of the sky as she had turned into the drive. A wave of unease had rippled through her as she glanced upwards to take in the geometric design of the walls, roof and chimneys outlined in the eerie half-light, and had felt its blackness razor into her isolation.

Now, she stared at the beige walls of her office and let the statement she was reading fall on to her desk as the replay became trapped within the confines of the small room.

She had parked next to Tony's car, almost glad it hadn't been the one he was driving when he'd picked up his prostitute, for in spite of his protestations to Noble and Archer, there was little doubt it had been him; he was too meticulous to forget to sign in a company car.

Tony had been in the lounge, slouched in an easy chair, his eyes staring at the blank screen of the television. In his hand was an empty glass.

'Tony?'

He glanced up but said nothing. Finally he looked away.

'Tony, I had to do it, I didn't have any choice.'

His gaze remained fixed on the television. 'Really?'

The coldness of his tone slashed at her flesh, and a chill threaded its way into her veins.

For a moment there was silence. Then, he steadied himself with the arm of the chair and stood up. He shuffled unsteadily to the drinks cabinet to pour himself a generous measure of whisky. He didn't offer one to Susan.

'Don't you think you've had enough?'

He glared at her. 'Don't tell me that I've had enough. *I'll* decide when I've had enough.' He took a large gulp. 'It's not every day your wife sets the police on you. I think I ought to drink to that, don't you?' He lifted his glass in salute before taking another deep swallow. 'You think I use prostitutes? Well, let me tell you, madam detective, I don't – though no one would blame me, with a frigid bitch like you for a wife. I don't get any at home, do I?'

The accusation hung in the air between them. She couldn't deny it. 'I'm tired, that's all. When this case is over—'

'There'll be another, and another, and another.'

He stumbled over to her, his face close to hers. The acrid smell of the whisky engulfed her. 'When I went to that church all those years ago, I thought I was getting a wife and eventually kids, not a herd of policemen.' He staggered backwards. 'Sorry, ma'am – officers – got to get it right.'

'You were, you have.'

'Not the kids, though; you're much too busy for that. Kids would mess up your career.'

A deep sigh escaped her. She watched him as he dropped into the chair. 'It *was* you in that car, wasn't it?' she said. 'It had been signed out to you, and not signed back in, and your car was here all night.' She paused. 'Did you think I wouldn't notice, Tony? I was worried sick. No phone call, no explanation as to where you were.'

He ignored the criticism. 'You shouldn't have sent those two to question me, Susan. You could have asked me yourself.'

She was asking now. 'Why a young one, Tony?' She had to know.

'Why not?' His head slumped forward.

'How young?'

He lifted his head and wagged his finger at her. 'Oh, no, you don't get me like that. I didn't pick up a prostitute, and you can't prove any different.'

He lay back against the chair. For a moment she thought the drink had taken over and he had fallen sleep, but suddenly he lifted his head and, almost sober, he blustered, 'Christ, Susan, you think I'm killing those girls?'

'No, no.' The last word trailed off.

'Yes, you do.' He stood up, his gait back to normal. 'You bitch. I'm one of your suspects just because you think I went with a pros-titute.'

'You asked for a young one, Tony.'

'But not that young. What do you think I am?'

Then she remembered. It hit her like a sledgehammer. 'When I was called out on Thursday night,' she said, her voice faltering, 'you didn't want me to go. You said someone else could take it because he wasn't murdering children, just *embryo prostitutes*.' She fixed him with a stare. 'How did you know the dead girls were prostitutes, Tony? That was one bit of information I hadn't passed on to anyone – not even you.'

chapter sixteen

It was late next morning when Leah woke. She stretched her arms above her head and turned to the man next to her. He was facing the other direction, but asleep, his breathing regular. His black hair was dishevelled, a clump near the crown standing upright; brushing wouldn't be enough, she thought, it would need washing before it would lay smooth to his head. The cut on the side of his face nestled in a darkening bruise. She'd told him he shouldn't get involved in stopping fights that punters started, he paid Dwayne Varley to do that for him.

She skewed herself round to lean her head on her arm. The sheets were silky, nice to the touch, better than hers on her bed. The top one had slipped down to below Deepak's waist, contrasting white against his brown body. He had such a beautiful body, such smooth skin. He hadn't said anything yet about her staying, but she knew that when he did, she would love living in this flat above the leisure centre. She would look after him, better than anyone had ever looked after him before; he'd never have reason to hit her or send her away ever again.

He'd made love to her with passion last night, hard and rough, but not like the men who came to the house. For them it was sex; for him, she was sure, it was love. She'd offered him a condom, but he'd said he didn't need one. 'When I make love,' he'd said, 'I do it without anything getting in the way.'

'But what if I get pregnant?' she'd asked. 'Alice said you wouldn't want me if I got pregnant.'

He'd laughed at her. 'That's if you get pregnant by one of the punters. Not by me, because you'd be carrying my child. Our child would be made in love.' Then he'd kissed her, forcing his tongue into her mouth.

She didn't kiss the punters, only Deepak.

She hoped she was pregnant with Deepak's baby. It would be everything they both wanted and make them so happy.

She stretched her head so she could look at the bright red figures on the bedside clock. Half past nine. The curtains were draped but not pulled all the way across the window and she could see the sandstone walls of the nearby buildings. A yellowy glow bathed the room. The flat was high up, on the top floor of the building. His penthouse, Deepak called it. She wasn't sure exactly what a penthouse was, but it sounded like somewhere where pop stars would live. Swanky but private.

Deepak stirred, then stretched. He turned towards her. 'You still here?' Then, 'What time's Alice coming for you?'

'She said about half past ten. But I don't have to go, Deepak. I could stay here with you.'

He laughed. 'I don't think so.'

Tossing back the sheet, he pulled his naked body into a sitting position and swung his legs over the edge of the bed. Without turning, he said, 'Get dressed, then make yourself useful; get me some breakfast. Coffee and toast will do. I'm going for a shower.' He padded across the room. 'Oh, and before Alice comes, strip the bed and put the sheets in the washing machine. Then make yourself scarce. It's not cold, you can wait outside for her.'

With that, he disappeared into the bathroom. Seconds later, Leah heard the water flowing from the shower.

Ali was leaving CID as Handford arrived.

'You look rough,' he said.

'Didn't get much sleep last night,' Handford replied.

'Nor me.' He paused for a moment. 'I told my father he wasn't to see the Azams for a while.'

'How did he take it?'

'Badly.'

They walked along the corridor together. 'I'm sorry, Khalid, we gave you a hard time yesterday,' Handford said.

'No more than I deserved. And anyway, it was a lot harder with my father.'

Handford opened the door of his office and stood back to let Ali in first. 'You know I've got to ask exactly what was said?'

'Yes.'

Handford indicated that his sergeant should sit down, then perched on the edge of his desk and waited.

Finally, Ali looked up at his boss. 'I told him Deepak was being investigated and that because of my position we should stay away from the family until it was over. He asked me what crime Deepak was supposed to have committed.'

'What did you tell him?'

'The truth. My father would take nothing less.'

'And?'

'He was in a difficult position. He wanted to believe me, but couldn't accept the accusation against Deepak. In the end he agreed, for my sake, not to see him until something had been resolved, but refused to alienate himself from Deepak's father. They have been friends for a long time and my father will not be disloyal. He promised not to disclose our inquiries.'

'And you believe him.'

'Of course I believe him, John; he's my father.'

Handford hoped he was right. Perhaps for once, Ali's father was experiencing the same conflicting loyalties and emotions that he had criticised in his son for so long. Perhaps at last he would understand, but that was an observation best left to himself. Instead he asked, 'And you, Khalid, how are you feeling?'

'Torn apart, but I will heal.'

Handford placed his hand encouragingly on Ali's shoulder, then moved to his own chair behind his desk. 'Where are you off to now?'

Ali smiled. 'To give Dwayne Varley his early morning wake-up call.'

'There's nothing like the personal touch,' Handford commented. 'Who's with you?'

'Graham.'

'Good.' Graham was a competent officer as well as physically able to cope if Varley turned nasty. 'Let me know what happens.'

'Will do.'

When Ali had gone, Handford pulled his briefcase onto his knee and took out a bundle of files. Families. Who needed them? He had enough problems with his own without having to worry about his sergeant's. And his had kept him up half the night. While Nicola slept, he and Gill had discussed the alternatives facing them until well gone three, and had come up with nothing more than what they already knew: their daughter could either terminate, or continue with the pregnancy and join the statistics of schoolgirl mothers. Adoption, they were confident, would be an unlikely if not unacceptable option. Hardly world shattering for four hours of discussion.

Dropping his briefcase on to the floor beside the desk, he slumped down in his chair. Without noting its contents, he gazed at his in-tray. They hadn't even been in accord as to what they should advise. While he favoured a termination, Gill had her doubts. She knew the problems having the baby would cause, she'd said, but equally she could empathise with the trauma their daughter might suffer if she terminated.

Wearily, he ran his eyes over Record of Interview sheets, results of TIE inquiries, forensic reports and internal mail that had been dropped into his in-tray, making notes as he did so to remind himself to follow up specific points, then, glancing at his watch, he picked up the night book and case files ready for the regular morning meeting with the DCI.

Uncertainty wormed away at Handford as he made his way to Russell's office. Too much had happened over the last few days in which he had played a part, and he was unsure of the protocol of such a situation. Since Forrester hadn't suggested the serious crime team take over the Braintree case, it was still on their books. Equally, Russell hadn't yet been suspended and was therefore still his DCI and as such entitled to be made aware of the link between Michael and the dead girls. But as a suspect in the major investigation, was he permitted to know what was going on? It was a mess, but not a mess of Handford's making, and if the senior officers insisted he continue to work in opposing camps, and neglected to offer guidance, then he, personally, had to keep the two as separate as he could. If they blurred at the edges, so be it. Nevertheless, he couldn't help feeling under siege and when he next spoke to James Sanderson he would insist that either he was taken off one of them, or the two became one and thus out of Russell's reach. In the meantime, discussing the Braintree case might go some way to clearing up why the DCI had marked Michael's complaint as 'no further action'.

It wasn't a comfortable meeting. The tension between the two men mixed uneasily with the aroma of the percolating coffee. Rays of bright sunlight seeped through the vertical slits of the blinds and particles of dust danced along the shafts slanting towards the floor. The fan hummed incessantly and the sound added to the fog in Handford's brain like a severe case of tinnitus. Russell sat at his desk, looking as though someone had pulled the plug on him. From the tapes of yesterday's interview it seemed likely he knew the dead girl was the daughter he'd had by Catherine Walsh. But to be sure he would have to wait for formal identification, and the wait was draining him. When he saw Handford, he smiled briefly. It was a smile that didn't make it to his eyes. He offered Handford a chair, which the inspector sank into gratefully.

The two men got down to the work without preamble.

There had been few crimes committed overnight and they quickly assigned them to specific detectives. Of the jobs that were on-going, two were close to completion, and in three others the officers seemed to have hit a dead-end. The rest were progressing favourably.

'What about the Braintree murder? Is Ali making any progress there?'

Handford prevaricated. 'Some,' he said. He explained where Ali had gone. 'It's possible that Dwayne Varley is involved in Michael's death. Forensics found a patch of sweat and two fair head hairs on his T-shirt. They're currently being DNA tested.'

Russell pondered the information for several moments, then suddenly the plug was pushed back and light flickered as he regenerated into the senior officer that Handford recognised.

'Then shouldn't you wait for the results before interviewing him? As I see it, Dwayne Varley is only a suspect because he has fair hair. If I recall correctly, house-to-house revealed nothing. No one had heard or seen anything on the day of Braintree's death. The nearest we have to strangers in the area is a woman in the next street who said a blue van was parked close to her house at the relevant time. She hadn't seen it drive up or drive away and she didn't take the registration number. She thinks, however, she might have heard a squeal of brakes mid-afternoon, but she can't be specific about the time, although when she checked, the van had gone. And all that, quite miraculously, leads us to Dwayne Varley. Something of a leap of faith, don't you think? Tell me, does he have a blue van matching that description?'

During the tirade, Handford had let his gaze slide onto the files. 'No, sir, but there is one registered to Martin Johnson, a known associate of his. And both he and Varley work at the leisure centre. We'll get it in and let forensics go over it.'

'You'll need more evidence than Varley has ridden in it to link him with Braintree's murder.'

'I'm aware of that, sir.' He could feel his temper rising.

'So, Inspector, tell me, why Dwayne Varley in particular? Apart from his fair hair, of course.'

'Because of his link with Deepak Azam.'

A deep silence filled the room. Russell stood up and walked

towards the window. He pulled open the blind, throwing a sudden ray of sunshine across the room. Handford shadowed his eyes with his hand.

Without turning, Russell said, 'How does Deepak Azam fit into the Braintree investigation?'

Handford placed his files on the edge of the desk. He needed time to formulate his answer.

'Coffee, sir?' he said, walking over to the percolator.

'Please.'

As Handford handed him his drink, he described Ali's interview with Daniel Emmott, the incident at the leisure centre and finally his sergeant's involvement with Azam himself. 'He says he's sorted that out now and that neither he nor his family will be seeing Azam again. Although obviously I won't let Ali have input into any of the interviews we might have with him.'

Russell had barely moved from the window while Handford was talking, but when the inspector had finished, he returned to his chair and sat down. He placed the cup and saucer in front of him and gazed at the brown liquid as though he was scrutinising it for inspiration.

'You have evidence to back up all you've been told by the Emmott boy?'

'Not yet. The vice squad have suspected Azam of pimping for some time although they've never been able to pin anything on him, but the information we got from Daniel seems sound enough. Obviously it will be checked out, but even you must admit, Stephen, it would take someone with a hell of an imagination to make up something like this. The fact that Hannah was Michael Braintree's girlfriend adds some credence to it.' He fixed Russell with a cool assessing stare, the kind of look his boss had often used on him. 'She was in exactly the right situation for a pimp of this kind to home in on. She'd been asking about your photograph for days, she could easily have shown it to Azam. He may or may not have recognised you, or she might have told him that the man in the photo was her father. But either way, if he is what we think he is, he would have picked up on the fact she was vulnerable. All he had to do was to watch her, make sure she was what he wanted, then pass her over to Michael. Unfortunately, Michael fell for her and since by this time he had some notion as to what Azam was doing, he tried to get her and himself out of it by coming to us.'

Russell picked up his cup and took a sip. 'This affects my position, doesn't it?'

'Yes, I'm afraid it does. It doesn't look good that you marked up Michael's information for no further action.'

Handford hadn't meant for the comment to sound hostile, but from the way his boss's lips compressed, he knew it had.

After several moments, Russell looked at Handford. For the first time, there seemed to be a nervousness clouding his eyes, although when he spoke his voice was firm.

'Michael had not told the constable very much,' he said, 'just that he thought his girlfriend was being lured into prostitution. He refused to say why he thought that or give any details as to how it was being done or who was doing it. There was nothing to go on.' He hesitated. 'Also, there is no indication at all that girls so young are working as prostitutes in the city.'

'And if there had been, you'd have done something. But since there wasn't, you did nothing. Not even after he had been murdered.'

Russell regarded him narrowly. 'I don't make the policy, Inspector; I only implement it.'

'And you always go by the book?' Handford drained his cup, the coffee suddenly as bitter as his tone.

Russell ignored the question. 'You think my explanation thin, don't you?'

'Yes, sir, I do. If I'd come to you with the same thing, you'd have bollocked me good and hard, and I'd have deserved it.'

'Probably, but I wouldn't automatically have suspected you of killing the young girls, which is what this is all about, isn't it?'

'Along with everything else – yes.'

But in truth, it wasn't enough; any detective worth his warrant card could tell you that. Everything they had was circumstantial. To be sure of Russell's possible involvement in the deaths, they needed forensic evidence, witnesses, a confession even. They had none of these and there was only a vague suggestion of motive and opportunity. Yes, the explanation was thin, but that didn't mean it wasn't honest. Questions rattled around in Handford's brain. There were so many, but for the moment it wasn't his place to ask them. Instead he let Russell digest what had been said.

Handford stood up and placed his cup on the tray housing the percolator. 'I shouldn't tell you this, Stephen, but Catherine is coming in with her husband to identify Hannah's body this morning. I don't know whether she wants to see you, or if you want to see her, but if Hannah *was* your daughter, and from what Catherine told me, I'm sure she was, maybe the two of you ought to talk. And . . .' He paused.

'Go on.'

'I think it's Mrs Forrester's intention that after the identification you will be asked at the very least to take some leave, possibly suspended.'

Leah sat on the steps outside the leisure centre waiting for Alice. She was determined not to cry, even though it was the thing she most wanted to do. Deepak hadn't wanted her; he'd told her to go.

I could stay here with you.

I don't think so.

He'd laughed at her.

She didn't want to believe it; she'd gone to him last night to make love to him. Please him. And still he'd told her to go.

Now, while she waited, hunched up, arms wrapped around her knees, the constant hum of the traffic negotiating the steep roads that led in and out of Bradford's centre built up in her head and she decided she would go away. London perhaps. Then Deepak would be sorry. He'd come looking for her, just like she imagined her mother had come looking for her after she'd run away from the foster parents. She hadn't found her, but Leah was sure she *had* come looking – just not in the right places.

City Hall clock chimed ten. Alice wouldn't be long now. She watched the people passing by, going about their business. Not one gave her a second glance or asked her what she was doing. No one cared. She turned her attention to the traffic again, car after van after bus after lorry, all travelling in or out of the city. She could jump in a van or a lorry, hide away, let it take her wherever it was going. There was a small white one across the road with nothing behind it. Its back doors were open, planks of wood hanging out, a white cloth tied to them. It had stopped to drop someone off. If she could climb in the back without being seen, she could hide herself and go wherever it was going. Anything would be better than Alice's, having to listen to the girls' sneers and their shouts of 'I told you so', being nice to the men.

Determination engulfed her and she pulled herself from the step, but she was too late, the van moved off and she'd missed her chance. She drifted back to the entrance to the leisure centre and sat down again, pulling her knees up to her chest. The door of the café across the road opened and she caught the odour of the food. It reminded her of the bakery smells, and she tasted the stench of the men and the sweat and the sex and Cindy's acrid perfume and she felt sick. She buried her head deep into her knees to shut them out, but they percolated through the flimsy material of her dress. It had been no more than a silly dream to think she could jump in an open van and disappear from here. They wouldn't let her go, they'd search until they found her. The vision of the woman with the scar and the headlines about the killer murdering girls who tried to run away from Deepak crawled into her mind and fear wrenched at the knots in her stomach. She didn't have a choice. She'd have to go back. She lifted her head and as she glimpsed the drivers in the cars and lorries and the passengers in the buses, she wondered what it would be like to taste the freedom she'd been running towards all her life.

As she watched, a car sped up the hill faster than the others. Suddenly, it slewed across the road and skidded to a halt. It was on yellow lines and in a bus lane, but it didn't seem to bother the three men who clambered out. A bus driver hooted at them; then, when they ignored him, he opened his window and shouted obscenities. A man from the car ran towards the bus and pulled something out of his breast pocket, holding it up to show to the driver.

She froze. Coppers. Coppers in plain clothes. Come for her. To arrest her for being a prostitute.

One of them shouted, 'Leave it' to the man by the bus. She moved off the step and tried to hide herself against the wall next to the door. But she needn't have worried because, like everyone else, they showed no interest in her. She might as well have been invisible.

Five minutes later they returned with Deepak, one either side, clasping him by the arms. He skewed his head round and called to someone out of sight, 'Get my solicitor, and let one of the community leaders know I've been arrested. Tell Iqbal Ahmed, he's the best.'

In anger, Leah made a grab for the arm of the police officer nearest to her. 'Leave him alone, you pig.' Another pulled her off. Then as they pushed Azam in the car, she shouted, 'You racist pigs. Leave him alone.'

But they took no notice. As they bundled him into the back seat she screamed out, 'Deepak!' But he mustn't have heard, for he didn't even look back as the car turned round and sped down the hill into the one-way system. She slumped on to the step and this time let the tears come. What had happened played and replayed in her head like a video tape and she cried even more because there was no one to reset it or tape over it.

Her head deep in her knees, she didn't notice the figure who came towards her until she felt someone grasp her arm. She looked up, expecting Alice.

'Hello,' Joe said and he smiled at her.

Dwayne Varley's flat was on the seventh floor of the Harold Wilson block, not more than five minutes' walk up the road from the leisure centre. Although on a hillside, as was all inner city housing, the area had been cleared in the sixties and the ten tower blocks were constructed to accommodate an ever-expanding population. It was hardly an estate, just a set of tall rectangular buildings perched on a sloping piece of land, but at the time they were up to date and considered very suitable for the post-war and upwardly mobile population. As the decades passed, however, the upwardly mobile moved into more salubrious suburban dwellings and the flats were let to less directionally diverse tenants. Inevitably and eventually, the neighbourhood became the domain of the petty criminals, vandals and drug dealers. Which was one reason why Dwayne Varley had been given a flat there when he came out of prison.

Ali grimaced as he surveyed the buildings. The outside walls of the blocks were covered in dirty pebble-dashing, which had broken away at the base where it had been kicked or had missiles flung at it, as well as on each floor where satellite dishes had been fitted. Paint flaked from the rotting window frames and doors, and on the balconies washing hung on short lines or was draped over the iron railings. The area around each building was grassed and litter strewn, and used as a cemetery for supermarket trolleys, the bulk of which had been appropriated as the means of ferrying around stolen goods, and then disabled by the removal of their wheels.

Graham and Ali tiptoed carefully across the grass, unsure of what they might step in, and, holding their breath, entered the ground floor. As expected, the lift was out of order, so they were obliged to climb the seven flights to Varley's flat. The stairs and passages were dark and the acrid smell of urine adhered to the walls, the floors and the spaces in between. Condoms and syringes mingled in the corners of the landings with the vomit, the polystyrene cartons, the remains of takeaway foods and the squashed drinks cans. Concerned residents refused to clear them for fear of disease, and suffered the smell, the pollution, the foraging cats, dogs and, lately, rats for which the debris seemed to be a perpetual delicacy. Occasionally, someone complained to their councillor, who passed on their complaint to the council. Quoting the Health and Safety Act, the cleansing department declined to send in men, but a spokesman for the council said that soon they would pull the blocks down and build more desirable dwellings. It had been part of every political party's manifesto that eventually all tower blocks would be demolished. Annually, the same promise was made in the context of votes and the elections, and once the elections were over, in the context of the budget. Electioneering was soon forgotten when the budget was set.

It was early and, much to Ali's relief, the landings were deserted. Very few of the tenants held down a day job; some worked nights, although not necessarily in legal occupations, and since the school holidays were not yet over, most of the occupants were probably still in bed.

A quiet knock failed to rouse Dwayne Varley, so Graham banged hard on the door.

'Come on, Varley, we know you're in there. Come on, open up.'

A series of grunts followed by a series of expletives heralded Varley's egress from sleep and his desire to return to it. The detectives waiting outside heard the key being turned in the lock and watched as the door opened as far as the chain would allow. As soon as he saw Graham and Ali, Varley made to push the door closed, but Graham was too swift for him and his large foot filled the cavity.

'Fuck off.'

'Now that's not very nice, Dwayne. Not when we've come all this way to see you.' Graham pinned a smile to his face.

'What do yer want? I've done nowt.'

'Just a little chat, nothing more,' said Graham, his smile widening. 'Now come on, open this door and invite us in. The council wouldn't be happy if I had to break it down.'

'Well, move yer fucking foot then.' The detective obliged and Varley shut the door to remove the chain from its housing, then jerked it open.

His fair curly hair was tousled, and he was dressed in a vest and shorts, which would have benefited from a visit to the launderette. A small crescent moon dangled from one ear and the tops of his arms sported convoluted tattoos. As he regarded the men out of sleepy eyes, he scratched first at his scalp and then at his stomach, allowing the vest to ride up to show off his firm abdominal muscles. He stood back to let the two men in.

The sun had not yet worked its way round to the west side of the block and the flat was dark. Ali peered into the shadowy gloom. Varley switched on the light and the detective wondered if it would not have been better to save the electricity. The small hallway reeked of poverty; much of the wallpaper was streaked with a substance Ali wouldn't have wanted to identify, and the rest had been torn off as though someone had begun to strip it ready for decorating. Cardboard boxes were piled up against one wall and dirty shoes and trainers rested against the skirting board. The stench emanating from the kitchen could have come from anything, curry and chips or a greasy fry-up. Whatever it was, it smelled as though it had been there for some time. What was the betting that the sink was piled high with dirty dishes? Or perhaps Varley only ever ate from Styrofoam cartons.

'Living as well as ever, I see,' Ali remarked.

'Yeh, well, if this is the best the poxy council can give us, I can't see why *I* should bother with it.'

The men followed him into the sitting room. A voice from the bedroom called, 'Who is it, Dwayne?'

'It's that Paki cop and another one.'

'Then get rid of 'em and come back to bed.'

'Still with Marilyn, then? I'd have thought she'd have seen the light by now,' Graham said. 'Still working in the pub down the road, is she?'

'What of it?'

'And you, you're a bouncer for Deepak Azam?'

'So?' Varley's irritation was beginning to show. 'Look, what do you want? I've done nowt and you can't prove as I have.'

Ali smiled. 'Actually, Dwayne, forensics has moved on a pace since you were last sent down, so I think we might just be able to prove you've done something. But in the meantime all we want is a look round your flat and a little chat.'

Varley opened his mouth to protest, but Ali cut him short. 'If you prefer, I can take you in and question you at the station, but I don't think it will go down very well with the parole board, do you?'

Without waiting for a reply, Ali nodded at Graham. 'Now, Mr Graham's going to have a look around, while we talk. You don't mind, do you?'

Varley's mouth opened again, but, watching Ali, he decided against the comment he would have preferred to make and said, instead, 'Well, just don't make a mess.'

'I'll try not to,' Graham promised. 'Perhaps you could ask Marilyn to get dressed? I wouldn't want to embarrass her.'

'Get yerself dressed,' Varley shouted without moving from the spot.

'Fuck off,' she replied.

'Fuck off yerself.'

Graham shrugged. 'Still as much in love, I see,' he murmured, and began to check the room's contents.

Ali settled himself on the edge of a chair, resisting the urge to sweep it clean with his hand. 'Tell me, Dwayne, what exactly do you do for Azam?'

'Anything he wants me to.'

'Like?'

'Like I stand outside and stop those what shouldn't be there from coming into the centre.'

'Like you did last night?'

'I'd gone for a leak when they came in, otherwise they wouldn't 'ave got in.'

'What about Martin Johnson? Does he work for Mr Azam?'

'Yes.'

'And Mr Azam knows about your records? That you're both on parole?'

'He says it doesn't matter; everyone deserves a second chance.'

'And a third and a fourth,' remarked Graham, his head in a cupboard.

Varley threw him a malevolent look.

'So, what else do you do? Apart from standing at the door.'

'Anything he wants me to.'

'Picking up the earnings from his girls?'

'What girls?'

'Oh, come on, Dwayne. The girls he looks after.'

Varley took a cigarette packet from the mantelpiece and pulled one out. He placed it between his lips and struck a match. It flared and he lit the cigarette, the tobacco burning bright for a moment as he pulled at it. Carefully placing the extinguished match behind his ear, he said, 'I don't know nothing about no girls, and you can't prove as I do.'

'Well, do you know Michael Braintree, then?'

Varley ought to have been used to the police method of interrogation, the number of times he had been a party to it, but the change of direction took him by surprise. He played for time. 'Who?'

'Michael Braintree. He was a member of the leisure centre.'

Varley drew again on his cigarette. 'Him and a few thousand others.'

'He was murdered last week. A karate chop to the front of the neck. It was in all the papers.'

'Don't read the papers.'

'You read these though, don't you?' Graham appeared with a clutch of magazines. '*Martial Arts, Body Building for Men*.' He threw each one on to the settee as he read out its title. 'I bet you can't get some of these from WH Smith's, or this video from the local video shop.' He held it up. '*Martial Arts Six – The Silent Kill*. This yours?'

'Never seen it before.'

'So what's it doing in your video recorder?'

'You put it there, you're trying to fit me up.'

'You know a lot about martial arts, Dwayne?'

He looked at the officers, as if weighing up the reasoning behind the question. 'Some.'

Ali smiled at him. 'Oh, come on, Dwayne, don't be so modest. I'd heard you're a black belt.'

'So?'

'A karate chop to the neck, isn't that a method of silent kill?'

Varley remained silent, obviously not wishing to incriminate himself.

Ali stood up. 'I think we'd better continue this conversation at the station, don't you?'

Varley floundered. 'You can't do this. I haven't done nothing. I didn't kill that lad.'

Ali grabbed him by his vest. 'Get dressed, Dwayne. You can tell it to the tape. Go with him, Dave.'

Graham pulled a face, which indicated that he would rather not, and grabbed the man by his shoulder to push him towards the bedroom.

'Come on, Dwayne,' he said, 'let's get dressed.'

Handford glanced at his watch. Time to check Russell's alibi before going down to the mortuary. For the DCI's sake, he'd decided to play it as low-key as possible and to phone both Vanessa at the leisure centre and Marion Hartley at the consulting rooms, instead of going round in person.

Vanessa was eager to help. Yes, Mr Russell had visited for a back massage on the day in question. It takes about half an hour, so he would leave just after eight. No, she'd no objection to letting the police have a list of her clients for last week. Was it to do with the poor dead boy? Such a nice boy, too; anything she could do to help catch the person who'd killed him, she would. 'Do you want me to bring my appointments book into the police station in my break so you can have a look?'

'That would be very helpful, Vanessa. I may have to keep it though. It could be evidence, you understand.'

'No problem, I always keep a duplicate anyway, just in case I lose one; I'm such a dizzy person sometimes.' Joining in her laughter, he thanked her for her co-operation.

Marion Hartley, however, was not so forthcoming. She was prepared to accede to Mr Russell's request, she said, although she couldn't see why it should be of interest to the police.

Handford made no comment; he was already beginning to dislike the woman. 'Perhaps you could tell me what time Mr Russell arrived for his appointment on Thursday evening and what time he left.'

'His appointment was for half past eight; he was with me for half an hour until nine. If you wish to see the book for verification, I am more than happy to show it to you.'

'Thank you, Ms Hartley, that will be most useful. I'll send someone round for it. You'll be given a receipt and I'll let you have it back as soon as possible, although that might not be for some time.'

A heavy sigh transferred from the woman on the other end into Handford's earpiece. 'I said you can look at it, Inspector, not have it. All my clients are in this book, and their identities are confidential. I'm going along with you because Stephen asked me to, but I've got to say it's against my better judgement.'

Handford swallowed his growing annoyance with the woman. 'I'm not interested in who your other clients are, Ms Hartley . . .'

'In that case, you don't need the book. If, however, you are determined to have it, then you'll have to get a warrant.'

I might just do that. 'Nevertheless, Ms Hartley, I will need to see it.' He could feel her disdain feeding down the phone line. 'I'll come myself later – and if necessary, I *will* get that warrant.'

She was not at all fazed by Handford's threat. 'I'll expect you then. Try to make it on the hour or the half-hour since those are the times of the change-over of clients. I'm not prepared to leave them so if you come at any other time you'll have to wait.'

The police force is now a service, he reminded himself, be nice. 'I'll make sure I do that,' he said. 'Perhaps you could tell me – where exactly is your clinic? On Claremont, Mr Russell said.'

'That's right, Inspector. Claremont is on the left-hand side up the hill opposite the university. You can't miss it; it's only about four minutes' walk from where that girl was killed last week.'

*

Detective Inspector Noble worked on his reports while he waited for Deepak Azam's solicitor. He was sure the man was being tardy on purpose and he knew that when he finally arrived, he would demand a lengthy consultation with his client.

The telephone rang beside him. He picked it up and put the receiver to his ear. 'Detective Inspector Noble.'

He listened while the man on the other end introduced himself.

Noble smiled. 'Hello, Bob, and how's North Yorkshire these days?' he said.

'Probably quieter and less fraught than West Yorkshire, if what we read in the papers is true. Why don't you get yourself a transfer?'

'No thanks. I'll stick with fraught; it's likely more interesting.'

'Probably. But just to prove we're not only into marauding sheep and cock fighting, we've managed to find your family for you. Do you want us to bring them over?'

'No, that won't be necessary, they can find their own way.'

'You may want to change your mind when I tell you . . .'

Noble listened with mounting concern.

'Okay, bring them in and now,' he said and banged down the receiver.

Shit, shit, shit.

He fingered in a number.

Forrester's mobile was turned off. He tried Handford's – ditto. He rang the mortuary.

'Sorry, I can't get hold of them just now, they've gone into the viewing suite. I'll ask one of them to ring you when they come out.'

Shit.

Handford and Forrester stood back as the sheet was about to be lifted off Hannah Mellings's face. Catherine clung on to her husband's arm. Paul Mellings grasped her hand, his knuckles white. In a moment they would see their dead daughter, know for certain she was gone from their lives. Any drop of hope they had clung on to would be shattered.

What could the two of them say that would make it easier for them? Nothing. No platitudes, no words of sympathy, no promise that they would catch the man who had done this dreadful thing. Nothing would stem the pain except . . .

'This is not Hannah.'

Paul Mellings turned to them, relief giving way to sudden anger, like it does when a child you had thought was missing walks in the door.

'You bastards,' he said quietly. 'You bastards, couldn't you have made sure before you put us through that? This isn't Hannah; this isn't our daughter.'

chapter seventeen

'Leave us.'

James Sanderson barked his order at Handford and Noble, who were sitting across the desk from Susan Forrester.

In unison they murmured, 'Sir,' and slid back their chairs.

'And don't leave the station.'

The door closed quietly behind them.

Sanderson took one of the chairs vacated by the inspectors. 'This is a bugger of a mess, Mrs Forrester,' he said quietly.

Sanderson was at his most dangerous when he was quiet.

'Yes, sir, it is.'

'And it's your bugger of a mess.'

He'd no need to tell her. 'Yes, sir, I know.'

'I gather we now have the identity of the dead girl?'

'Yes, we do.'

Sanderson was becoming impatient. 'Do I have to guess, Superintendent?'

Susan stifled a sigh. 'No, sir. According to the Mellingses, her name is Jenny Broomfield, fourteen years old, the daughter of their long-time friends, Andrew and Lisa Broomfield. Up until a couple of years ago, she lived with her mother just outside Norwich. Her father works for a company in Sweden, and comes home only periodically; Jenny and her mother used to join him during the holidays. Then her mother died in a car crash and rather than move his daughter to Sweden, it was decided to keep her at school in Norwich where she had her friends, and let her live with the Mellings during term-time. Holidays are generally spent with her father, or if that's not possible, as with this year, then with his sister, Alison Broomfield, who lives out at Cottingley. Miss Broomfield works for an academic publisher in the city and normally there isn't a problem about Jenny staying with her. However, a few days into the school holidays, she was unexpectedly asked to go to America, one of the original party had fallen ill or something. It wasn't possible to take her niece with her, and Jenny said she would join Hannah and her friends in the Dales.'

'But she didn't.'

'No. She stayed to look for Hannah's father. The two girls were good friends, almost inseparable, told each other everything and when Hannah explained about her natural father, it seemed the obvious thing for them to try to find him. Somehow Hannah had got hold of the photograph, probably when her mother thought she'd thrown it out, and then a few months ago when she overheard Paul Mellings saying that Stephen Russell was working in Bradford, she knew where to start looking. It seemed like fate to them, Hannah going to the Dales and Jenny staying with her aunt. They would take his photograph and ask around. Unfortunately for Jenny, it fell to her to do the asking because Hannah couldn't get away from the campsite.

'Why she took Hannah's name is unclear, but it may have had something to do with her not wanting to bump into anyone who knew her aunt. Hannah thought that perhaps she'd got the idea from a bag she'd lent her since it had her name inside. It's one of those small ones that can be worn on the back, a bit like a rucksack. It wasn't found with the body, so we can only assume the killer took it as a souvenir. It seems that when her aunt went off to America, Jenny continued to live at the house in the evening, and trawled the city during the day for Hannah's father. It must have been around this time she met Michael Braintree.'

'So the aunt thought she was with the Mellingses and the Mellingses thought she was with the aunt?'

'That's what it seems like, yes.'

He leaned towards her. 'Have you any idea how hard I've had to work to put all this right? Mellings is a solicitor, knows all the tricks in the bloody book, and more besides. If he sues, he'll win.' Sanderson let the last comment ride in the air for a moment. 'For God's sake, woman, why didn't you make absolutely sure before you pulled them both from Norfolk? You had her photograph, couldn't you have faxed it through, or is modern technology beyond you?'

Susan glared at him. 'Everything we had suggested Hannah Mellings was the dead girl, sir; the photograph, the statement from Daniel Emmott, even the information from DCI Russell, everything.'

'Except confirmation.'

'That's what the identification is for.' She hoped that didn't sound petulant, she hadn't meant it to. Sanderson took it as argument.

'Don't push it, Superintendent,' he growled. 'You've been less than diligent, and you know it. You don't bring parents all the way from Norfolk without doing everything you can to be ninety-nine per cent sure, particularly,' he leaned further forward, the expression in his eyes revealing his hostility, '*particularly* if those parents are solicitors.' He barked out the last word.

She couldn't stand to look at him any longer and instead surveyed her fingers, long and slim with perfectly manicured nails, her wedding ring dark against the fairness of her skin.

'You've been negligent, Chief Superintendent.'

'Yes, sir, I know; but now, for the first time, I have more to go on. I have the description of her bag, which we will circulate, I have useful information about the child prostitution and I have suspects.'

Sanderson stared at her. 'You are joking. You don't think that after this you can continue to head the investigation, do you? Mellings would crucify us. No, Forrester. You made the mess, you live with the consequences, and the consequences are that you go.' He took in a deep breath, and when he spoke again his tone had lost its bite. 'Look, Susan, just go quietly. You're owed some leave, take it.'

She raked her fingers through her hair, which hung loose to her shoulders. She hadn't had either the time or the inclination to arrange it in a French pleat this morning.

'Sir—' she began.

'Don't bloody argue with me, woman; you're off the case, and that's an end to it.'

The uniformed officer placed the tray on the desk in front of Sanderson, Noble and Handford.

'No biscuits, lad?' Sanderson complained. 'Go and find some biscuits.'

The officer looked puzzled, no doubt wondering where he was meant to get them from, and if it was the canteen was he supposed to pay for them himself?

Handford threw him an understanding smile. 'Try CID, Constable, there's a tin in there. Tell whoever is in that I've sent you.'

'Thank you, sir,' the constable said and withdrew gratefully.

Sanderson picked up one of the cups and liberally spooned in some sugar. 'I'll lay it on the line for you two,' he said. 'I haven't a senior investigation officer who's not snowed under at the moment, and to start picking a new team without a leader would be suicide. We've had enough with one officer attempting hara-kiri, without the job lot of you doing it. Handford, since the Braintree murder is linked, you and your men on the inquiry join the team, and you and Noble take over the day-to-day running of the two cases. I'll fill in as SIO until one becomes free.' He stopped stirring, placed his spoon in the saucer. 'You wouldn't believe it, would you? Not one senior investigating officer who has the time to step in. And they try to tell us there's not as much crime about.'

There was a tap at the door, and the constable entered with a plate of biscuits. He placed them next to the Assistant Chief Constable.

'That's better, lad. We'll make a policeman of you yet,' he said and picked up a chocolate digestive.

When the officer had left he continued. 'So far as I can see, you've been running around like headless chickens for the past four months, so let's stop that and put some common sense into this investigation.' He waved his biscuit in the air. 'Let's have a look at what we've got, then prioritise. Inspector Noble, you start.'

Noble reviewed the previous cases, describing the lack of evidence and witnesses, then turned to the murder of Jenny Broomfield. 'He, whoever he is, has probably made his first mistake. For whatever reason, he's either assumed she was a prostitute the same as the others, or he's moved on. Or he had another reason for killing her and will go back to prostitutes later.'

'Or she was always his original target and the others were killed to confuse us,' Sanderson broke in.

'Possible, but unlikely, sir. Firstly he would have to have known who she was and that she would be in the city during the school holidays. He began killing some four months ago, and four months ago Jenny wasn't sure where she'd be for the holidays.'

'So, we're back to a serial killer who hates prostitutes, and may have made a mistake, or may have watched Jenny being lured into the job by either Deepak Azam or by Michael Braintree and decided to stop her before she began in earnest, so to speak.'

'That seems likely, sir.'

'Could it be Mr Russell, Inspector Handford?'

'I hope not, sir.'

'I hope not too, Handford, but that wasn't what I asked. Could it be him?'

Handford blushed at the mild rebuke. 'It seems to me, sir,' he said, 'that there are a lot of coincidences surrounding Mr Russell, and not that much hard evidence. I agree with Brian. He would have to have believed Jenny was in the city *and* that she was his daughter. Yet, according to Mrs Mellings, it's more likely that he accepted she'd gone ahead with the termination all those years ago. It seems to me, sir, if he has killed the others, then Jenny, Hannah and the photograph were bad luck – and I don't buy that.'

'Nor do I, so what does that leave us with?'

'Well, sir, firstly, Mr Russell lied to us about his movements on the evening of the last killing and then asked Andrew Collingham to firm up his alibi. Then he avoided the issue of the photograph and who he had given it to. Understandable in the circumstances, but not very wise. I . . .' Handford hesitated.

'Come on, Handford, I appreciate he's your boss, but if there's something else, let's be knowing.'

Handford straightened in his chair. 'I rang Marion Hartley, his counsellor, earlier, and she verified he'd been with her between half past eight and nine. The only thing is . . . the clinic is on Claremont, and Claremont is no more than a four-minute walk from where Jenny was killed. He could easily have left his car in the clinic car park, met her, killed her and driven home for the time he said.'

'What about his movements at the time of the other killings?'

'A massage followed by a session with Ms Hartley.'

'What, each time?'

'It seems so, sir.'

'What the hell's the matter with the man? Do we know why he needs to see a counsellor?'

Noble broke in. 'He refused to tell us in interview, said his reasons were confidential.'

'Nothing to do with prostitutes, then?'

Handford shrugged. 'I don't know, sir.'

'Fair enough. We'll leave it for the moment. Anything else?'

'Just that Mr Russell was at Cambridge at the time of the prostitute killings there. I don't know how much that means. Except for one, the women killed were older than our girls, but serial killers often begin with one set of victims and refine as they go along.'

'Motive? What would be his motive?'

'Difficult to say, sir. Something that happened in his childhood, which came to a head in Cambridge.'

'In that case, I may have something.' Sanderson seemed to be enjoying getting back to grass roots. 'First of all, I checked with Winchester; there were no prostitute killings during the time Russell was working there with his father. However, the ACC Crime said he seemed to think there was something concerning the Russells, but couldn't remember exactly what it was. You need to contact a Chief Inspector Greenaway who knows all about it.'

'Sir.'

'And if it's unfavourable to Russell, then I'll have to suspend him. I can't leave it any longer. The Chief Constable's coming back from the Far East tomorrow, he'll want to see some positive action. And once that happens the press will surely get hold of it. So move with speed, Handford.'

'Sir.'

'Now, Azam. How involved is he with these girls, and is he a pimp?'

Brian Noble replaced his cup on the tray. 'I'm sure he is. We've got him in at the moment; he's with his solicitor. Although to be honest, we have about as much chance of proving anything as knitting fog. The women won't tell on him, either for fear of a beating, or because they rely on him for their drugs, and we have no idea at all where the young girls are being worked, except that it's not on the streets. And as things stand, if they're not on the streets, they don't exist.'

'What about this Project place?'

Handford broke in. 'I've asked Detective Sergeant Ali to go along there this afternoon. He'll find out what he can.'

'So Azam might be a pimp, but is he a killer?'

'I don't rate him as the serial killer, sir,' Brian Noble said. 'If he was going to kill prostitutes, it would be ones from another camp. To kill his own, particularly the young ones, would be like robbing his own bank account. It could be a rival pimp wanting in on Azam's act, but we have absolutely no evidence against any one of them.'

'What about Michael Braintree's murder?'

Handford took over. 'That's a very definite possible, although I don't think for a minute that Azam did it himself. We should have the forensics back on the hair and sweat on Braintree's shirt. I'd put my money on them belonging to Dwayne Varley. If it was him, the chances are Martin Johnson was involved as well. They both work for Azam, ostensibly as bouncers. He knows of their records and is likely to use that knowledge to his advantage. However, whether we'll ever get either of them to grass on him is questionable.'

'At the moment then, Russell and Azam are our only suspects for the murders of these young girls. Neither are what one might call prime.'

Brian Noble exchanged glances with Handford.

Sanderson hadn't missed it. 'What?'

Noble straightened in his chair. 'We have another, sir. Tony Forrester.'

Only the hum of the fan broke the uneasy silence that descended while Sanderson digested what he had just heard. 'Tell me he's not who I think he is.'

Their silence confirmed his suspicions.

The skin tightened around Sanderson's eyes. 'So, Mr Noble, why do you consider him a suspect?'

Noble explained what Archer and Warrender had seen and heard on surveillance. 'I'm sorry, sir, but the man in the car was Mrs Forrester's husband. There's no doubt, I'm afraid.'

'Why a suspect, why not a kerb-crawler? Perhaps he's not getting any at home and nips out when his wife's not looking. Could he be doing that?'

'He could.' Brain Noble ladled loathing into his voice. 'Tony Forrester is the type of man who thinks screwing women is a bit of fun. He doesn't care how much he hurts his wife, or the women he uses for that matter. It wouldn't be too bad if he stuck to prostitutes, all they want is his money, but he doesn't. I think deep down he hates women, likes to see them suffer.'

'Enough to kill them?'

'I don't know, sir. All I can say is heaven help the one who gets the better of him – sexually, socially or financially. I guarantee he'll screw her into the ground.'

'I gather you don't like him?'

'No, sir, I don't, and I can't think of one good reason for his wife to stay with him.' Noble took a deep breath. 'Unfortunately we have more information than the kerb-crawling for a young prostitute. After she'd seen you, Mrs Forrester came to me and said she needed to make a statement. It may be something or it may be nothing, but it appears that on the night Jenny Broomfield was killed, he was furious his wife was being called out yet again for dead girls whom, he said, had been nothing more than embryo prostitutes in life. That was confidential information.'

'And you're sure she hadn't told him?'

'She insists not. And,' Noble added defensively, 'I for one believe her.'

Sanderson gave a half-smile. 'All right, Mr Noble, you've made your point. I admire your loyalty, but don't take it too far. Treat him like you would any other suspect, bring him in again, put Mrs Forrester's information to him, see what he says, then set someone on to researching his background. Now, anything else?'

Handford shuffled in his chair. 'Yes, sir. I'd like to look at the location of the deaths. The collator in Cambridge believed there was a religious connection to the prostitute deaths there. If the same man is operating here, the scenes of crime might be linked somehow.'

'Then do it, Inspector. I'm not into psychological and geographical profiling, although I'm not so much of a dinosaur that I haven't heard of it. I just think it's expensive for too little information. But, I'll grant you, we've got precious little else at the moment, so let's go with whatever our gut feeling tells us to.'

On his return to his office, Handford found Andrew Collingham pacing the room.

'Why have you arrested Deepak Azam, Inspector?' he demanded abruptly. 'I've just spent the best part of an hour on the phone with Iqbal Ahmed, who was told that three of your officers manhandled Mr Azam through the leisure centre and into their car. Three, Inspector! I would like to know why you had to go in so mob-handed and indeed why you had to arrest him at all. You do know he's a community leader, one of the most respected men in our city – Asian or white?'

'I'm sorry, Mr Collingham, I can't discuss a case with you or an arrest. Suffice it to say we had our reasons and Mr Azam was needed to help us with our inquiries.'

'And has he helped you with your inquiries?'

'Not yet. We've been waiting for his solicitor who has now arrived and is consulting with his client. When they are through, we will talk to him.'

Collingham rounded on him. 'You know what this means, don't you? What has happened will do nothing for race relations. The Asian community are up in arms about the arrest and the youth in particular are likely to protest in a way that could well disrupt the city.'

Handford sighed. He didn't need this. He'd had enough of riots and mayhem to last him a lifetime, but he wasn't going to be threatened by one. 'Then, you must go back to Mr Ahmed, Mr Collingham, and ask him to stop them. You and I both know he has that level of influence. Now, if you'll excuse me, I am very busy.' He opened the door. 'I'll get someone to see you out, sir,' he said.

Ali's interview with Dwayne Varley was going nowhere. The man was suffering from terminal amnesia, a condition that often besets petty criminals who think that to remember nothing means the police can prove nothing. Unable to recall where he'd been or what he'd been doing on any of the dates Ali had put to him, he was lounging on the chair, his hands behind his head, the picture of insolent disinterest.

'Sit up, Varley.'

He obeyed, but slowly, as though it were all too much trouble.

'Where were you on the afternoon of Tuesday the fifteenth? Come on, Dwayne, it's only seven days ago.'

The duty solicitor shifted in his chair. He was as bored as the rest of them. 'I think my client has answered your question, Sergeant,' he said wearily. 'Mr Varley is unable to remember. He has told you that at least four times. If you have no witnesses or indisputable evidence, I think you are going to have accept his answer.' He didn't add, 'And let us all go home,' although Ali knew by his expression that was what he was thinking.

The fact was, he may not have indisputable evidence now, but he should have by tomorrow when the results of the DNA from the hair and the sweat were expected back. The problem was what to do with Varley in the meantime. He probably had enough to hold him on suspicion while further inquiries were made. Varley was a black belt in karate, was cognisant in silent kill methods, even had a video on the subject, knew the victim and had a strong link to Azam and, according to Archer, to the covey of prostitutes, and was on parole. It was enough – just – to keep him in the cells over-night, if only to prevent him from disappearing into the under-growth.

Interview room two was claustrophobic. It smelt of sweat and aftershave. Handford swallowed hard to rid his throat of the biting acidity. Warrender, who sat next to him, remained inscrut-able, his eyes never leaving the two men opposite. If it was meant to disturb them, however, the attempt was an abject failure.

Handford would have preferred Warrender to have been left out of this. His views on the Asian population were well known, albeit covertly hidden in deed rather than word. Ali had been the butt of his hatred from the moment they'd met. Luckily, not only had he coped with it, he had waited patiently until an opportunity arose when he was able to put Warrender firmly in his place. That said, Warrender was a good interviewer and could lead a suspect round to what he wanted without any sign of bullying or harassment. He had also been on the vice squad for some months and had more knowledge of Azam's pimping than anyone else.

To his credit, Deepak Azam ignored all attempts at rattling him. He sat, cool in the heat, denying everything, his denials interspersed with accusations of racism and aggression. He appeared neither upset nor disturbed by the situation he was in. His solicitor, Anwar Rafiq, a suave gentleman in a well-tailored pin-striped suit and sporting a heavy gold watch and ring, demanded to know where the evidence was that his client was a common pimp.

Handford remained silent; he didn't have to tell the solicitor anything, not yet.

But the solicitor was not to be put off. He glanced down at his notes. 'Procuring prostitution, I think, is the other reason for his arrest. Where did that come from?'

'Information received,' Handford replied abruptly.

Anwar Rafiq persevered. 'This informant? Has he or she a name?'

Handford proffered a smile. 'You know better than that, Mr Rafiq. I don't have to divulge the name of my informant.' *You'd have a field day if you knew he was dead, and it was his seventeen-year-old friend who had passed on the information. Even if you've considered it, admitting it would dig your client in too deep.*

They sat for a moment, digesting the facts, until Azam broke the silence.

'Inspector,' he said, his tone laced with boredom. 'I am a Muslim, and as a Muslim I do not approve of the practice of prostitution. It is a sign of immorality in the women who enter into it. It is a sin, and as a Muslim, I could not condone, let alone take part in such a sin. Indeed, so abhorrent do I find the practice that I was a party to having these women moved from the area in which they worked and in which my community lives.' He smiled, his teeth white and perfectly formed. 'I think that alone answers any "evidence" you think you have against me. Many people will vouch for my integrity and my morality, members of your community as well as mine.' He sat back in his chair as though waiting for applause.

'Someone hasn't, otherwise we wouldn't be here,' commented Warrender.

'Then, Detective Constable . . . Warrender,' Azam raised one eyebrow, to question the accuracy of the detective's name, 'you either have a racist on your hands or someone who is jealous of my success – or both.'

They had reached an impasse, and Azam was beginning to dominate.

Handford felt Warrender stiffen next to him. They needed a change in direction before the constable did or said something that would wreck the interview.

Shooting Warrender a warning glance, he said, 'You could be right, Mr Azam, but either way we are obliged to investigate.' He picked up the photograph of Michael Braintree. 'Now, do you know this boy? I am showing Mr Azam a photograph, exhibit KA 4,' he intoned for the benefit of the tape.

Azam glanced at the picture. 'I do now, Mr Handford. Sergeant Ali asked me about this boy a few days ago. He said he was a member of my leisure centre. I know now that he is Michael Braintree, the young man who was murdered. But as I told your sergeant, and as I will tell you, I have many members in my centre, some of whom are senior police officers, so it's understandable I don't know all of them. Indeed, I was unaware of both the boy and his death until your sergeant appraised me of them.'

Handford had to compliment the man on his knowledge and use of the language; he would have made a good solicitor himself. He had the ability to threaten without being overtly threatening.

'Do you know Dwayne Varley?'

That damaged. Azam allowed his tongue to flick over his lips, the first sign of lurking apprehension. 'Should I?'

'Martin Johnson?'

'I repeat, Inspector, should I?'

'They work for you, Mr Azam, they're your bouncers.' Handford sat back and steepled his fingers while Azam whispered in his solicitor's ear. Anwar Rafiq nodded.

'I believe I do know them.'

'Then you know of their criminal record and that they're both currently on parole?'

'Yes, they were both absolutely honest with me when they applied for the jobs.'

Absolutely honest – that must be a first for those two.

Azam continued. 'I admired that in them and was happy to take them on. There's no law against it, is there, Inspector?' he asked innocently.

'None at all, Mr Azam, but there is a law against asking them to carry out illegal activities for you.'

The solicitor's eyes flashed in anger. 'Inspector, really. First you arrest my client on suspicion of living on immoral earnings, then you suggest that he is somehow implicated in the death of a boy he doesn't know, and now you are asking us to believe that he is the guiding hand behind any illegal activities his employees may be involved in. This has got to stop.'

An hour later, Handford left the interview room hot, angry and frustrated. Azam had given nothing away. They were no nearer the truth than they had been when they had brought him in. He doubted very much the man was the serial killer, but that he had had a hand in Michael Braintree's death and that he was pimping a clutch of older prostitutes and maintaining a brothel of younger ones were distinct possibilities. He could only hope when Dwayne Varley realised they had, fingers crossed, DNA evidence that could put him at the scene, he would forget his gratitude to Azam for giving him a job and chatter away like a four-year-old. He held out less hope that his women would inform on him. They would be too frightened of retribution or of not getting their regular fix to make any statements.

Mr Rafiq had demanded his client was released and, since he could think of no real reason to keep him, Handford agreed, providing, he said, Mr Azam surrendered his passport.

chapter eighteen

At The Project Ali held out his hand. 'Thank you for agreeing to see me at such short notice, Mrs Townsend.'

The young woman smiled, dimples forming in her cheeks as she did so. 'Paula, please. Mrs Townsend makes me sound old, and I'm desperately trying to cling on to my twenties.'

She led the way into the house, then turned. Small and almost anorexically thin, she wore jeans and skimpy white top with shoulder straps too narrow to hide the wider black ones of her bra. 'There are no women here at the moment, so I'll give you the grand tour, if you like.'

Without waiting for a reply, she moved smoothly to the room to their right.

'The lounge, sitting room, whatever you like to call it.' Stale cigarette smoke hung in the air. 'I know it smells foul, but I promise you, we only allow cigarettes in here; no drugs, not even dope. In fact we try to persuade the girls off drugs, get them on to programmes or into rehab units. Sadly, we're fighting a losing battle; their pimps have them both hooked and frightened. The best we can do is to limit the damage by providing clean needles.'

Ali glanced around. The light beige paint of the walls had darkened over time, and the carpet that had once been green was now threadbare. A few cheap pictures hung on the walls, but the windows stood naked, no curtains to frame their features or blinds to deter peeping toms. The furniture comprised two settees, a couple of armchairs, which had seen better days, a small table and a series of old wooden cupboards leaning against the wall, their catches broken, doors swinging open.

Ali grimaced.

Paula sensed his thoughts. 'It is pretty dire, isn't it? But we've had to beg, borrow and steal most of what we've got, and when you do that, you get cast-offs.'

'Where does your money come from to run this place?' Ali asked.

'A small percentage from Social Services, the NHS Trust and West Yorkshire Police, the rest we have to find ourselves. We do have charity status, but we can hardly go out rattling tins. Can you imagine the reaction if we asked for money to help local prostitutes?'

Ali smiled. 'Vividly,' he said. 'What about the house? How did you acquire that?'

'One that no one else wanted. It's had a chequered career, but the neighbours think it's reached the depths now. Prossie Manor they call it. It was built by a minor businessman just before the turn of the century. When his immediate family died out, it was sold as a home for retired ladies and gentlemen. That went into receivership, and the Salvation Army acquired it as a hostel. When they needed somewhere bigger, it was passed on to us. We pay a nominal rent to some distant descendant of the original owner and hope that when she dies, and she's currently touching ninety, they don't decide to ditch it. Given the opposition to us, I'm sure the executors, whoever they are, won't think twice about moving us on. Still . . .' She shrugged resignedly and led Ali out of the room.

At the end of the corridor, a door stood half open, giving sight of a small kitchen and an old cooker. The cupboards, what Ali could see of them, were painted a bright buttercup yellow.

She began to climb the staircase to the upper floor, taking the steps two at a time, her mop of curly black hair bouncing as she went. Ali followed.

'I hope you didn't mind me asking you to come so late, Sergeant, but this is the best time for us. As I said, the majority of the women are out working now, catching the early evening punters. It's better they don't see you; they're not that keen on police.'

Even if he hadn't heard similar sentiments before, Ali couldn't have taken exception to Paula Townsend's remarks, for she exuded a warmth that transcended acrimonious words.

In its former life, her office had been a bedroom. The original mahogany fireplace remained in situ, dark against the grubby white paintwork. In the recess to the left was a filing cabinet and to the right, shelves stacked with cardboard boxes. The rest of the furniture consisted of a desk, an office chair, two newish upholstered seats and two shabbier easy chairs. Incongruous amongst them was a computer system and printer. 'Donated by a far-sighted benefactor,' Paula explained. 'To be honest, I don't know what we'd do without him.'

'If you get money from the various departments, then you must be managed by a board,' Ali said.

'Yes, three officers, and a committee on which there is supposed to be a council member, someone from Social Services, from the NHS Trust and from the police.'

'Who's the police officer?'

'No one at the moment. Sergeant Price was volunteered on to the committee some years ago by his inspector, but he retired in March, and they haven't given us a replacement. To be honest if it wasn't for Councillor Collingham, who's also on the police committee, we wouldn't have any input at all from your service.'

She waved him to one of the easy chairs. 'Can I offer you a drink?' she said. 'Coffee? Tea?'

'A cup of tea would be very nice, thank you.'

She busied herself with the kettle and the mugs on the small table near the window. 'Now, how can I help you, Sergeant?'

'In two ways. Firstly,' he said, holding out a photograph of each of the dead girls and one of Michael, 'do you know, or have you had any dealings with these girls, or with this boy?'

She took the pictures from his hand. 'And the second way?'

'I want to know about the young prostitutes.'

The kettle switch clicked off and steam rose as Paula filled the mugs with the hot water. She handed one to Ali. 'Help yourself to milk and sugar,' she said, then moved to sit behind her desk.

As she studied the photographs in her hands, a frown darkened her previously sunny features. 'These are the dead girls,' she said. She glanced up at him. 'I'm concerned it's taken you so long to get round to us, Sergeant Ali.' The smile trickled from her voice. 'You must have known they were working as prostitutes.'

Ali shifted in his chair. Her tone registered disappointment in him, as though it were all his fault. He sat in front of her, cradling his mug in his hands. Perhaps he ought to tell her he wasn't on the team four months ago, and even now he couldn't be sure that he was officially. Yet, as he formulated the words, they felt like an excuse, and he sucked them back.

Spreading the photographs out to face him, she said tightly, 'These three were definitely working, had been for some time. This one, Hannah,' pointing to Jenny, 'wasn't, although her boyfriend,' she touched Michael's picture, 'was afraid she was being lured into it.'

For the first time in minutes, Ali made eye contact. Keeping his voice level, he said, 'If you knew all this, Mrs Townsend, why wait for us to come to you? Why didn't you come to us?'

Had he hoped to wrong-foot her, he was disappointed. She sat back in her chair and swivelled it to look out of the window, although the only view afforded to her was that of the branches and leaves of a chestnut tree and the chimneys of the house opposite.

'The first three were dead,' she said finally, turning back to him and meeting his gaze. 'There was no point. I couldn't have told you anything about them that wasn't in the papers, except that they were working. For me to come to you would have meant police trampling all over us, and for the sake of our other clients, I wasn't prepared to risk that. Instead, when any of the younger girls came for help, I warned them to take care, to stay as close to home as they could and to go out in twos, not alone. It wasn't much, but it was more than you were doing. Hannah, on the other hand, was different. She wasn't working and what we discussed was confidential. I can't break confidences.'

'Perhaps had you done so, she would still be alive.'

Paula Townsend countered him angrily. 'And perhaps if you had taken Michael seriously she'd still be alive.'

The air swirled with passion. '*You* did nothing, so don't blame me,' she threw at him. 'Our service is confidential and I'm bound by that unless the client gives me leave to pass her information on. Hannah didn't, so I advised her and Michael to come to you. After all, you're here to prevent crime, aren't you? I didn't see much attempt to prevent Hannah's death on the part of the police.'

Ali sat in silence. He hadn't come here to be told off for the shortcomings of his bosses, but he couldn't blame her.

'I'm sorry, Sergeant,' she said, reeling in her emotions. 'It's not your fault alone, but it makes me so angry. These young girls are being abused daily, and you do nothing.'

As she turned all her anger and frustration on him, he wondered if she were aware of the policy regarding the girls. He levelled his gaze at her. 'We do nothing, Paula, because they're hidden. If we could find them, we would. They're not working the streets and we don't know where they're being kept, and I'm willing to bet you're not about to tell me. The police work by rules too; we have to have a complaint before we can do anything. No one has made that complaint.'

'Michael did.'

'Yes, but he told us nothing; not what was going on, or where, or who was doing it, or even his own part in it. All he said was he thought his girlfriend was being lured into prostitution. He didn't even bring her with him. She's the one we needed to make the complaint. Without her we had absolutely nothing to go on.' He put his mug down and sat forward. 'Surely, sometimes the information you get about these girls comes to you piecemeal and you have to wait until the jigsaw starts to come together before you can act.'

'Yes, sometimes.'

'Well, it's the same with us. We have to wait. That's what we were doing with Michael's information.' A white lie and he knew it, but he wasn't prepared to accept all the blame. He looked at her pleadingly. 'Come on, Paula, the girls are dead; surely, you can break their confidences now, and what you tell us just might help us find the person who is killing them.'

'I don't agree that because they're gone I can discuss what they told me. Confidentiality is a difficult concept, Sergeant, which causes me much heartache, but it's not something I play around with. However, I will tell you what I can. To begin with, the names they gave me were not their own, certainly not those printed in the papers anyway. When they start work, they're given their working name; that's the one I got. That's the one they all give me.'

'Where do they work?'

'I have no idea; they don't offer me their addresses or telephone numbers, you know. Eventually, however, if I'm careful, they'll confide in me, tell me what's been happening to them. And it's always the same story, Sergeant. The girl may be in care or a runaway, or she may be living in an unhappy home; whichever, she's emotionally vulnerable. And it's that vulnerability her would-be pimp feeds on. Once he's chosen his victim – and I use the word advisedly, because, believe me, she is a victim – she's befriended by a boy close to her age until she's ready to be groomed by the pimp, at which point she's introduced to him. Initially, he doesn't act like anything other than a caring boyfriend; he spends time with her, takes her out, spoils her, buys her clothes and jewellery, then eventually gives her a ring, which he says binds her to him. He puts her in a flat where he begins a sexual relationship with her. By now she's totally dependent on him, has lost whatever friends she had and is isolated from whatever family she had. The crunch comes when he asks her to have sex with one of his mates – to pay off a debt, he says. She agrees; it's a way of showing her gratitude. But then he demands that she continue to prove her love for him by having sex with other men. He's paid for her services; she isn't. So without realising it, she's become a prostitute. Once that happens, he dumps her and sends her to live in the house with the other girls, where she services eight, nine men a day – sometimes more. The stupid thing is, she continues to look upon him as her boyfriend and thinks one day he'll take her away from it all.'

Ali placed his mug on the edge of the desk. His mind was reeling. He tried to imagine Deepak doing everything Paula Townsend had described, and yet, although he accepted the truth of it, he couldn't hold the pictures in his head. Deepak Azam had fooled his best friend and the Asian and white communities as easily as he had fooled the girls. Now Ali had to admit it to a stranger, although even now, he felt the need to water the facts down by demanding more concrete evidence.

'I don't doubt what you're saying, Paula, and I'm horrified by it, but what you've given me is not hard evidence, and that's what I need. Everything you have at the moment is anecdotal, nothing concrete; no names, no dates, no addresses, nothing but their stories.'

Paula threw her arms in the air in astonishment. 'What's the matter with you? Surely, these anecdotes as you call them warrant investigation? There are enough of them. Corroboration by volume; that's the legal term, isn't it? Do something, Sergeant. Please.' He caught her gaze, the frustration gone, her eyes like a spaniel's, a mixture of pleading, hopeful, persuasive. 'These girls are neglected, wrapped up in a parcel and stuffed on the top shelf where they're forgotten. They need to be plucked off that shelf, and this is the best opportunity you'll get – to do it while you're investigating the murders.'

Ali sighed. He was being manipulated, and he knew it. 'I'll do what I can,' he said finally. 'But don't expect too much. The best lead is Michael and he's dead. If you could tell me where the girls are being worked, or give me concrete evidence as to who is pimping them?'

'I'm sorry, I can't because I don't know. They never name their pimp. Although . . .' She hesitated.

'What?'

'The woman who watches over them once they begin working is called Alice. I don't know anything about her or where she lives, but,' she flashed the smile she had greeted him with, 'I'm sure, Sergeant Ali, it's not beyond your capabilities to find her.'

*

Leah hadn't been able to express in words how relieved she'd been to see Joe; instead she clung on to him and cried.

'Come on now, Leah,' he said as he stroked her hair. 'It can't be as bad as all that.' Then he looked down at her tear-stained face and smiled. 'It is though, isn't it? Is it Mr Azam? I saw the police take him.'

'I tried to stop them,' she wept.

'I'm sure you did, and I'm sure he knows you tried,' he said. He pointed across the road. 'There's a café over there, let's have a cup of coffee, unless you'd like some breakfast, because I bet you haven't eaten, have you?'

How did he know that? How did he know Deepak had expected her to make him something, but had not offered her any? She smiled at him – the first time this morning. 'I'm not hungry,' she said. 'But I would like a drink.'

'Come on then, we'll have a chat, then I'll get you a taxi to take you home.'

'No,' she said. 'You don't have to do that. I have a friend coming to pick me up.' She didn't tell him who her friend was, only that she was called Alice.

There was a big window in the café and they sat beside it so that she could see Alice arrive. When the car drew up, he reminded her of his mobile number and said if she needed to talk again she only had to ring. Then, before she left him, he said he'd try to find out what was happening to Deepak if she wanted. She nodded.

'I've got appointments tomorrow,' he said. 'But I could meet you in Centenary Square about eleven o'clock, I ought to be through by then.'

'That's all right. I can be there at eleven, but I have to be back by one.' She had a punter at one.

On the journey back to the house, Alice asked her if she'd had a nice time. She made it sound like she'd been to a kids' party. Leah said yes and tried not to cry.

'The police came for Deepak.'

'Yes, I heard.'

'I tried to stop them taking him.'

'You shouldn't have; you don't want to get noticed by the cops. Deepak'll be all right; he can take care of himself.' Alice sounded unconcerned, but she bit her lip and frowned and the rest of the journey was made in silence. She didn't even ask about Joe, who he was or what they had been talking about, which was fine for Leah, because she didn't want to have to tell Alice anything.

Now, back at the house, Leah sat on her bed, her emotions in turmoil. On the one hand she wanted out, wanted to get as far away from Deepak as she could, but her instinct at the leisure centre had been to fight the coppers who'd tried to take him away from her. She supposed she still loved him. She knew she had a pain in her chest whenever she thought about him. There'd been a video she'd seen once called *Love Hurts*. Perhaps it did. Fumbling in her purse, her fingers searched for the piece of paper on which was the eleven-digit mobile number Joe had given her. She wondered if he'd been able to find anything out yet. Not that she could ring him from here, Alice wouldn't allow it.

The house was silent and she guessed the rest of the girls were making the most of their free time in the garden. The heat in her room stank. Scrunching up her nose, she scrambled off the bed to open the window. Men smelled, and their smells lingered – their sweat and their alcoholic breath. Sometimes it was so strong she could taste it when it wasn't there, like she had outside the leisure centre.

She dragged off the dress Deepak had bought her and threw it on the bed. She'd so wanted to wear it for him last night, now all she wanted to do was to tear it into little pieces, but she daren't – not yet; not until she was sure she was safe from Deepak's anger.

At least Joe understood.

She smiled at the thought of seeing him tomorrow. Whatever they said about her and Deepak, they could never say the same about her and Joe. Joe was a real friend and with Joe she felt safer than she'd ever felt before.

'Dad.'

Handford turned to see Nicola hesitating at the door of the dining room, a mug of coffee in her hand. A map of the city was spread out over the table and for the past twenty minutes he'd been bending over it, trying find some link between the scenes of crime, although if there was a pattern, he was damned if he could see it. The best he could come up with was that the bodies had been deposited within half a mile of the centre.

'Are you busy, Dad?'

'No, love, just frustrated, with a head like a mushy melon.' He took the mug from her, sat down on one of the dining chairs and stretched out his legs. 'Come and talk to me.'

Nicola walked over to stand next to him and put an arm round his shoulder. 'Are you really mad with me, Dad?'

He placed his free arm round her waist and smiled. 'Not *really* mad, darling, just a little bit mad,' and he gave her a squeeze. He hadn't done this for ages; there'd never seemed to be any time.

'I'm sorry, Dad.' Her voice faltered.

'Don't be sorry for growing up, Nicola. I ought to be the one who's sorry – for not being there when it was happening. I swear you were a little girl the last time I looked. Your mother's right when she complains I let the job come first; fathers shouldn't miss out on their daughters' lives. If I'd taken more notice, I might have seen this coming.' He moved his arm. 'Come on, sit with me for a while. This,' he waved at the map, 'can wait.'

Nicola pulled up a chair. 'Vishnu's gone. His father's sent him to London to live with relatives,' she said.

'And that makes you unhappy?'

'I love him, Dad. It's not his fault, at least not only his. I'm just as much to blame.'

Handford wished he could go along with that, but he couldn't, and he knew that was the father in him talking.

'How did you find out he'd gone? You haven't been to his house again?'

'No, his brother came over this morning. He shouldn't have done, and his father must never find out, but he thought I'd want to know.'

'That was kind of him.'

'They're a nice family, Dad, just different. You can't blame Vishnu's father for wanting to protect him.'

'No, Nicola,' Handford said grimly, 'but I can blame him for not letting Vishnu take responsibility for his actions. You're having to.' He straightened in his chair, formulating as he did so the question he had to ask, even though he dreaded the answer. 'Have you made a decision yet?'

'Not yet.' Tears glistened in her eyes. 'I keep thinking I have; I decide to have a termination, then I think of it as a baby, and I want it. Then my mind goes back to me and what I want to do – get my exams, go to university, and I know I'll not be able to do that with a baby. So then I decide to terminate, and it all goes round again.'

Handford placed his mug on the table and moved from his chair to kneel in front of her. He hugged her tight. 'Oh, Nicola,' he said, his throat constricting, 'I'm sorry I can't tell you what to do, I wish I could. But it's such a personal decision and whatever you path you take, you're the one who has to walk it and ultimately live with it. I'd give anything for it to be my problem and not yours, but it isn't and it can't be.' He pushed her away from him to look at her. 'You do know though, don't you, that we – me and your mum – are always here for you? You can talk about it whenever you want, night and day if necessary, and ultimately we're with you, whatever you decide.' He paused for a moment. 'Just promise me one thing, Nicola. That your decision will be a proper one, not a non-decision. In other words, you don't put it off so that time has made it for you.'

'I won't do that, Dad, I promise.'

Handford moved back to his chair and grasped hold of his mug. 'Aren't you having one?'

Nicola pulled a face. 'It makes me feel sick,' she said. She turned to the map. 'What are you doing?'

'Trying to find a pattern to the murders, but I can't.'

'Are the red dots the places they were killed?'

'This one here,' he said, pointing to one, 'was where the last girl was found.'

Nicola scrutinised it with him. 'There used to be a church there, you know, a long time ago. Well, not there exactly, that was where the Alexandra Hotel was, and the Empire Cinema. They're gone now, but somewhere round there was where the Octagon Chapel was.'

'The Octagon Chapel?'

'Yes, it was closed down in about 1820 because it was unsafe. The church built in its place was where the Arndale Mall is now. So that's gone as well.'

'How do you know all this?'

'It was in the local history part of our GCSE course. A man came to talk to us in school. He's a lecturer at the college and his hobby is local history. He gives talks all over the city and outside. He was really good, ever so interesting. According to him, there are lots of places in Bradford that have religious significance, more than you'd ever know.'

'Nicola, do you have your notes on this?'

'They'll be in my room somewhere. Do you want me to get them?'

'Please.'

Nicola dashed from the room and he could hear her running up the stairs and her bedroom door as it slammed shut.

Handford felt a tingle of excitement, tempered with anxiety. The Cambridge prostitutes: Jenny Marsden, eighteen, found in a grave-yard; Kate Jennings, twenty-one, in a church porchway; Lindsay

Jefferson, fourteen, on the site of a former chapel; all beaten around the shoulders, all killed by blows to the head and all on church property.

I think it was some religious nut.

Is that what they had, some religious nut? A religious nut called Stephen Russell? God, he hoped not. Come on, John, keep it in perspective. It's probably no more than coincidence that Jenny Broomfield was found close to the site of a former church, and very likely that the other crime scenes are not on land that had once been sacred. But . . .

Nicola rushed back into the room, waving an A4 ringbinder. 'I've found it.'

'Right, let's have a look at the others.'

Nicola opened it at a neatly drawn map.

Handford said, 'Beverley Paignton was found in an alleyway between two sets of shops, just above Rawson Square.'

Nicola found it. 'That was the site of Christchurch. It was built as the first parish church in 1815 and had gardens, which stretched right up from Kirkgate. The teacher said that at the time Bradford was one of the fastest-growing cities and the church was becoming an obstruction to the flow of traffic, so the council bought it in 1879, pulled it down and made a through route from Darley Street to Northgate.'

'What about the land up Great Horton Road where the second girl was found?'

She traced her finger up the drawing of the road. 'The Bell Chapel. Built in 1809 as a chapel of ease to the parish church. It's still there, but it's a warehouse now. Do you know that the gravestones from the churchyard were made into the boundary wall?'

Handford didn't know, and at that moment he wasn't that interested. But he smiled at his daughter, pleased to see her so animated.

'Is that where he put her, near the gravestones?'

Her father shook his head. 'No, next to the bins. Okay, Nicola. Let's try the third scene. Carla Lang found at the side of a pub in Ivegate. Don't tell me there used to be a church there, on a hillside like that.'

Nicola turned back to the map and them flicked through a few pages. 'No, no church. But John Sharpe was born close to it.'

'Who on earth was John Sharpe? I've never heard of him.'

'He was the Archbishop of York in the 1600s. So I suppose you can say he was religious.'

'Yes,' Handford echoed thoughtfully. 'I suppose you can.'

Was this the pattern? That all the girls were deposited as close to God as the killer could get them without using an existing church. Dumping them close to or amongst the rubbish was a indication of what he thought of them in life; making sure that the site had a religious significance was what? His way of giving them absolution? In all but one of his murders the Cambridge killer had used existing churches. If he and the Trash Bag Killer were one and the same, then he had done as Handford suggested earlier and refined both his choice of victim and of location.

'Nicola, can you remember the name of the man who came into your school to give this lecture? I'd like to talk with him. Get a list of his students.'

'I wrote it down somewhere.' She turned the pages. 'It's Andrew Collingham.'

'The councillor?'

'I think so. Yes, he must be because one day he said he couldn't stay to talk to us afterwards because he had to go to a council meeting.'

Handford sighed.

Councillor Andrew Collingham; friend of Stephen Russell.

chapter nineteen

The next morning, Handford made two phone calls. The first was to Andrew Collingham.

'I wonder if you can spare me a little of your time this morning, Mr Collingham. I'm quite happy to come to you.'

The councillor was brusque. 'Is it important, Inspector? I've a meeting at eleven. Exam results are out tomorrow and we're having a planning meeting at the college. God knows why, since there's not a lot we can do without the results, but the powers that be insist.'

'It is important, sir. I really do need your help. But it isn't something I can discuss over the phone. I can be with you within the half-hour. I promise I'll be gone in plenty of time for you to make your meeting.'

'Very well, Handford. But I warn you, any signs that I'm going to be late and I'll cut you short.'

'Yes, I understand.'

Handford was just about to replace the receiver when Collingham said, 'By the way, Inspector, I'm glad you saw sense and released Deepak Azam. The situation could have turned nasty.'

Handford swallowed his annoyance with the man and said, 'Yes, sir. It could. I'll be with you soon.' Then he cut the connection before Collingham was able to comment further.

The second was an internal call to Stephen Russell.

'I have to go out, sir; would you mind if Sergeant Ali took my place at our briefing this morning?'

'No, I suppose not. Tell him I'll see him at nine.' The man sounded tired.

'Thank you, sir.'

Again he was about to replace the receiver when Russell spoke. 'Before you go, John, has Catherine left the city, do you know?'

Handford's voice softened. 'No, Stephen, she hasn't. She and her husband are waiting for Jenny Broomfield's father to arrive. I think he's due into Leeds Bradford airport at about ten. They're bringing him straight here.'

'Poor man.'

'Yes, poor man.'

For a moment neither spoke, then Russell said, 'Do you think Catherine will see me?'

'Do you want her to?'

'I'd like to see my daughter at least.'

Handford refrained from commenting that since the man was under suspicion for killing Jenny, it was not a good idea. Instead he said, 'Everyone's very upset at the moment, Stephen, Hannah especially. I'd give it a day or two if I were you.'

Like many of its councillors, Andrew Collingham preferred to reside outside the city boundaries, although he worked and carried out his civic duties within them. Instead his home was perched high on the edge of the moors close to the village of Baildon. Wonderful in summer, thought Handford as he pulled up in the driveway, but a hell of a place to live in winter.

Collingham was in the garden, a mug of coffee in his hand. He greeted his visitor with, 'Do you think this weather is ever going to break? Our lawns are parched. My wife insists she's going to water them, but I tell her it would look bloody bad if a councillor's wife was fined for using a hose pipe while there's a ban on. One law for them and another for us, the papers'd say.'

Handford hadn't realised just how strong Collingham's Yorkshire accent was. It hardly seemed noticeable when he was making speeches or electioneering, and it certainly hadn't been that obvious when he was chastising Handford for the arrest of Deepak Azam. It was interesting that out of the public's gaze, the councillor gained as much relief from shedding his public accent as he did from shedding his tie.

'Your wife's a keen gardener, sir?'

'Oh, more than that, Inspector, she's a landscape gardener, has her own business. I tell you, she won't let me do anything in our garden but admire. And if I dare to touch any of her tools, you'd think the world had come to an end.' They walked towards the house. 'Still, you didn't come here to talk gardens, and I do have a meeting.'

'Actually, sir, it's your interest in local history I want to discuss with you.'

At first Collingham showed some surprise, then an unexpected wariness crept into his eyes. 'Why?'

Before Handford could answer, they entered the kitchen, oppressive in the blaze of the morning sun.

'We'll go through into the sitting room, it'll be cooler there. The sun rises on this side of the house, and in this weather the kitchen's like an oven in the morning,' Collingham said as he placed his mug in the sink. 'Do you want a coffee, by the way?'

Handford shook his head as he looked around him. The room was homely, yet functional, designed as it was to emulate the country cottage kitchen; the Aga, the oak units and a wooden table in the centre, which reminded Handford of the teacher's table in his primary school. He ran his fingers along it.

'It's wonderful, isn't it?' Collingham said. 'I bought it when one of the old schools was closing down. It was the teacher's desk. I got it for a pound. Cost me more to varnish it than it did to buy it, but I doubt you'll find anything quite so sturdy nowadays.'

They moved through into the hall and from there into the beamed sitting room. Collingham waved Handford to a leather-covered chair.

'Now, why have you come here to discuss my interest in local history, Inspector? It seems an odd thing to do. I'm intrigued.'

Handford sat forward and explained what he had discovered. 'Ever since I joined the team investigating the killings, I've had a gut feeling there had to be more of a pattern to the murders than the fact the victims were prostitutes.'

Collingham looked interested. 'Go on,' he said.

'Well, I couldn't see it; not until last night when my daughter pointed out what you'd told her class about the religious significance of many places in Bradford. All four girls were found where there had once been a church or in the case of Carla Lang whose body was dumped in Ivegate, the—'

'Birthplace of John Sharpe, one-time Archbishop of York. You've got a clever daughter there, Inspector. I'm flattered she remembered my talk. Most of 'em look bored stiff. No interest in the past, kids today. Still, since she seems to have filled you in, I just wonder what more help I can be.'

'There are three things I'd like from you, Mr Collingham. Firstly, a list of all the students who have attended your local history classes, plus a list of the schools where you have delivered your lectures, as well as the names of the history teacher or teachers who were involved in the lessons. Then, if possible, I'd like information on other such sites in the city. Whoever it is will kill again; serial killers tend not to stop until someone stops them. If the location is part of his signature, then just for once I'd like to try to be one step in front of him.'

Collingham's eyes widened. 'Christ, Handford, you don't want much. It'll take me a while to get it all together, but I'll do my best. I'll have a go at it tonight and drop it off at the station tomorrow.'

'That would be great.' Handford stood up. 'I understand local history is your hobby; you don't teach it at the college, then?'

'No, building studies and CDT, that's what we'd call woodwork, but it's CDT nowadays – Craft, Design and Technology. I haven't always been a teacher, though; I started out as a builder. Served my apprenticeship with one of the big multi-nationals and travelled the country. I've worked on some big sites,' he said spiritedly. 'That was before I met my wife of course.'

Handford laughed. 'That does tend to clip your wings, doesn't it? Do you have family, Mr Collingham?'

The councillor shook his head. 'No, Inspector, my wife and I married rather late – too late for children.'

'Brothers, sisters?'

The smile that had lit up Collingham's face a moment before faded. 'Two brothers and a half-sister – product of my mother and her lover,' he said bitterly.

Handford hid his embarrassment with an apology. 'I'm sorry, sir. I didn't mean to intrude.' He shouldn't have asked.

'No, no, Inspector. I'm sorry for embarrassing you. It's just that even after all these years, the whole sorry episode makes me angry. It split my life in two at the time – all our lives in fact, mine and my brothers.' He stood up. 'And you, Inspector, do you have children?'

'Two girls. Nicola and Clare.'

'Well, let's hope they never cause you pain.'

Handford desperately wanted to change the subject, and as they reached the door, he turned. 'You're a friend of Mr Russell, I believe?'

Collingham stiffened again. 'That's right. We've known each other for a good few years.'

'Can you tell me, sir, is he interested in local history?'

'Stephen? Not a bit. His eyes glaze over as soon as I mention it.'

'So, he wouldn't know about the sites of religious significance?'

'Funny you should ask that, because that's the one part of local history he does know something about. We walked them together when I was preparing a pamphlet on them for the library. In fact, he helped me write it. Yes, Handford, I'd say Stephen knows all of them.'

Handford returned to the station feeling as though the whole world weighed heavily on his shoulders. Every bit of information he procured seem to dig Russell deeper and deeper into the killing of Jenny Broomfield, and then by definition into the rest of the murders. The time had come to pass this on. It needed someone of higher rank to investigate, and if what Sanderson said was true about there being no senior investigating officers available, then either he had to reinstate Forrester, do it himself or bring someone in from another force.

He was still attempting to formulate his demands to the ACC into words when Ali appeared, a smile lighting up his angular features. 'We've got the forensics back on the hairs and sweat,' he said. 'Definitely Dwayne Varley's. I'm waiting for his solicitor, then we'll see if we can't improve his memory. Find out who suggested he kill Michael Braintree.'

'That's great. We might get Varley, Johnson and Azam at one go. Keep me informed.'

'You don't want to be in on it, then?'

'No, Khalid, I'll leave it to you. You've done all the hard work. You might as well have the glory.' He paused to pull papers out of his briefcase, then asked, 'Get anything worthwhile from The Project?'

When Ali described the meeting, Handford wasn't sure whether to be grateful to Paula Townsend for her information, sparse though it was, or angry with her for not coming forward earlier.

'Just who does she think she is, to make the decision as to what is important and what isn't?' he grumbled.

Ali defended her. 'I don't think she thought of it like that, John. It's just that she wasn't willing to have us trampling all over the women at The Project. Also she felt she had nothing to add to what had been in the papers, except that the girls were working, and she assumed we knew. And anyway, most of what she has is confidential between her and them.'

But Handford refused to be mollified. 'Bloody social workers. Didn't you remind her they were dead? Confidentiality doesn't come into it when someone is dead,' he said.

Ali frowned. When Handford was in this mood, discussing anything rationally was like swimming through soup.

'She's not a social worker, John,' he said with restrained patience. 'She's just someone who's trying to do her best in a very problematic area. And, yes, actually, she does feel confidentiality doesn't cease when a person dies. I talked with her for a long time. She's a caring woman, desperately worried for the young ones. Her feeling is, if we really wanted to, we could kill two birds with one stone and investigate what's happening to the girls while we're working on the murders. The two are linked after all.'

'And how does she suggest we do that, unless she can tell us for sure who is pimping them? Or is that confidential too?' There was a tinge of petulance in his tone.

'No, it isn't, John, and no, she can't. Like the women, the girls would never grass on their pimp. Most of them think of him as their boyfriend.'

'What, all of them? The same pimp?'

'Seems so, yes. Anyway,' Ali hesitated, 'I said I would do my best – give it a try.'

Handford glared at him. He was on firmer ground now. 'You're doing it again, Sergeant Ali, agreeing to something you're not in a position to agree to. We've got Sanderson as senior investigation officer now. Everything goes through him and I'm not about to flout that, and I would hope you're not too.'

'No, sir. I'm sorry. It's just that she made out a good case.'

'I'm sure she did, and in fact, I'm inclined to go along with her and you on this. Someone's got to get to these girls. They're part of the whole picture. See if you can persuade Varley to talk and I'll let Sanderson know, see where he wants us to go from here.'

'Thank you, sir.' Grinning, Ali pulled himself from the chair and turned towards the door where he hesitated. 'Oh, there was some-thing else came from my meeting with Mrs Townsend.'

'What?'

'It isn't much, but Paula – Mrs Townsend – said that the woman who looks after the girls is called Alice. If we can find Alice, we might be able to find out where they're being held and put a stop to it. And you never know, if this is where the killer is picking them up, we might put a stop to him.'

'Serial killers are notoriously hard to stop, Khalid. He'll probably turn his attention to girls who are not on the game.'

'And they matter more than the young kids in Alice's clutches?' Ali was visibly angry.

'I didn't say that and I didn't mean that, Sergeant.'

'No, I'm sorry. It's just having learned how badly abused these kids are . . . and what with Deepak being involved . . . well, you know.'

Handford did know, but he also knew that like most parents he wanted his daughters safe, and if the killer was targeting a certain section that didn't include them, then he felt safe as well. It didn't mean, however, that the Trash Bag Killer might not eventually become fixated on the killings rather than the victims – perhaps he had already done so with Jenny Broomfield.

'Find Alice, Khalid,' he said. 'But you work with Warrender on it. He may well have ideas as to who she might be.'

Handford watched his sergeant's back retreat into the corridor. It concerned him Ali had been so affected by the plight of the girls; he normally kept his emotions well in check. Could it be that he was, emotionally, attempting to right the wrong perpetrated by the man he had considered his best friend? He hoped not, because it would mean the case was becoming personal – although how you prevented that in circumstances like these, he wasn't sure.

Handford pondered the question as he put a call through to the Winchester police and asked for Chief Inspector Greenaway. As he listened to what the chief inspector had to say, his spirits plummeted. When the call ended, he picked up his now cold coffee, rested back in his chair and let the information swirl around in his brain, information that skewered Russell even more firmly to a serial killer's mission to rid the world of prostitutes. A wave of tiredness engulfed him. He couldn't believe the man he knew, the placid, unobtrusive, restrained man who was hardly ever provoked to anger, let alone violence, could turn into the monster who beat girls to death and then raped them in such a vile and brutal way. There had to be something, some small piece of information, which would rupture the vortex of incriminating evidence. But he was damned if he knew what it was.

So deep in his own thoughts was he that he jumped at the sound of the telephone, spilling his coffee over himself and his desk.

It was Noble.

'I'm in the viewing room,' the inspector said, a tremor of excitement lacing his words. 'I've got something you ought to see.'

'Give me two minutes.' Handford replied, frantically attempting to soak up the brown liquid with paper tissues before it swamped the mail and the statements spread out in front of him. Then, regarding the soggy mass with distaste, he dropped it in the waste basket, set the answerphone to pick up any messages and dashed out.

He arrived at the viewing room out of breath. Noble was alone, staring at the flickering images on the screen in front of him. At Handford's entrance, he glanced up and paused the tape.

'John, it occurred to me yesterday there might be something on the videos we took at the girls' funerals. You know the kind of thing, the killer enjoying his success and all that. Anyway, last night I took them home to have another look.'

'And there's something there?'

'I watched each one, one after the other, rather than we had done before, separately after each funeral. Doing that, I found something we missed.' He pressed the play button on the controls. The static image began to move on the screen. A clergyman and four people stood round the grave, their clothes caught by a wind that blew unimpeded across the plains of the churchyard. The priest clung on to his cassock with one hand and his prayer book with the other, its pages frolicking

'This was Beverley Paignton's funeral.'

'Not much in the way of family there to send her off,' Handford remarked.

'No, but look at her.' Noble pointed to a slim, waif-like woman desperately trying to keep her balance while she restrained her dark curly hair from blowing across her face. 'She isn't family, but she is on all the videos.'

'Who is she?'

'I don't know, but she's always at the graveside, and she chats with the families afterwards.'

'It may be Paula Townsend, manager of The Project. I'll ask Ali later. He's questioning Dwayne Varley at the moment. The DNA has come back positive.'

Without averting his eyes from the television, Noble said, 'Good. Are we going to be able to tie Azam in to Michael Braintree's murder?'

'I don't know. Depends on how afraid of Azam Varley is. But I don't doubt Ali will do his best.'

Noble pointed at the screen again. 'Look, there, in the corner of the picture; the woman standing to the left of the new headstone.' He paused the tape again.

Handford peered at the image. Another woman stood huddled in a long cape, her face hidden by the large collar she held against her cheeks.

'Who is she?'

'I don't know, but again, she's on all the other videos as well, and always in the background.' He pressed the stop button and ejected the cassette. 'Now, look at this one,' he said, placing another tape in the machine. 'This is Janice Thurman's funeral.' Again, a picture of a graveside scene filled the screen; this time several mourners stood in front of the mound of soil, the majority holding up umbrellas to shield themselves from the rain. Noble paused the tape. 'There's the first woman with the family, but look over there.'

The same woman as before, this time wearing a raincoat and hood, but her face clearly visible, was lingering metres away from the group of mourners.

'She's at Carla Lang's as well. Who do you think she is?'

Handford leaned back in his chair and clasped his hands at the back of his head. 'Alice. I'd bet a pound to a penny that's Alice.'

'Who's Alice?'

'According to Paula Townsend she's the woman who looks after the young prostitutes – a kind of madam, if you like. Unfortunately, Mrs Townsend has no idea where she's working the girls. Have you made a still of her?'

'Yes, it's here.' Noble held up a brown envelope.

'I've told Warrender and Ali to trace her,' said Handford. 'If this is her photograph, it'll make identification easier.' He stood up. 'Look, I've got something I need to discuss with you, but not here. Come back to my office; we'll drop this off on the way.'

'You weren't the only one busy last night,' said Handford when they were settled. He described the religious, historical pattern associated with the crime scenes as well as what he had learned from Collingham.

'That looks bad for Russell,' Noble mused.

'It gets worse. I talked to Chief Inspector Greenaway in Winchester just before I came down to you. He told me Russell's father has been picked up for kerb-crawling more than once. Never prosecuted though. According to Greenaway it was thought circumspect not to prosecute because of his importance to the town and the large number of people he employed. It seems, however, that not only did he put it about a bit, but he could give his wife quite a hiding if he was that way inclined. No proof of course, but, according to Greenaway, if he didn't, she was a very clumsy woman walking into so many doors. Not that it would have made much difference in the seventies and eighties, it would have been considered a domestic and we'd not have got involved. However, much later, they learned Mrs Russell had been having an affair with a local lad for some time before Stephen and his sister were born and for quite a long time after. Not surprising, given what her husband was like. From then on, Mr Russell senior made it known it was his right to sleep with anyone who would have him, usually prostitutes. Apparently he taunted his wife and his children with this all the time and with the possibility that neither Stephen nor his sister were his.'

'Nice man.'

'Yes. When he wasn't taunting, he was violent, and when he wasn't violent he was domineering – remember how he tried to get Catherine to terminate the pregnancy? – and according to Neilsen, it was Russell senior who insisted Stephen went to Cambridge, even though he would have preferred another university. It seems to me that the moods that both Neilsen and Catherine Mellings described had something to do with his parents. He disappeared for days, possibly back to Winchester, and when he returned he locked himself away, refusing to see or talk to anyone. Russell is a proud man, he wouldn't have wanted any of this to get out.'

'Or he could have been killing prostitutes as a way of getting back at his parents,' Noble suggested.

'He could have, but since we have no datal evidence, we'll find that hard to prove.'

'So if he hated his parents so much, why did he go back to work in the family business? Why didn't he leave home after graduating?'

'I think he probably had to in order to keep the peace. Then when his sister went off to university, and his mother divorced, he left both the business and Winchester. He must have come up to Yorkshire and joined the police almost at once. Obviously that was the personal reason for leaving the family firm.' Handford leaned back in his chair. 'I hate to say it, Brian, but Russell has the perfect background for turning serial killer.'

Noble turned a quizzical eye on Handford. 'And do you believe he did?'

'I don't want to. But honestly, everything I learn leads me to the conclusion he could have done. We just don't have any evidence to support it.'

Noble took out his handkerchief and wiped the sweat from his forehead. 'Okay, let's assume you're right,' he said. 'We're saying that, thanks to his father, he has an inbred hatred of prostitutes, possibly considers his mother as one, and that was why he killed the three in Cambridge. Why not in Winchester? There's nothing reported while he was living there.'

'I don't know, perhaps he was too busy keeping an eye on things and fending his father off.'

'And finally, when he left home, he was free to take his hatred out on prostitutes again,' Noble contemplated. 'So why not in 1993 when he came here as a DS? Why leave it until now to start a killing spree?'

'I don't know. Something must have triggered it. It's not unknown for serial killers to take a rest and then suddenly begin again.'

'All right, but why young girls? Those in Cambridge were seasoned prostitutes.'

'Not the last one,' said Handford. 'The last was fourteen. Perhaps, he found he got more of a buzz out of killing the younger girl than he did the older ones, and decided to stick with them.'

chapter twenty

Once Noble left him, Handford's intention had been to talk to Russell. Go through his statements with a fine-tooth comb. Every word, every phrase, every sentence. Try to find the elusive piece of information that would put him in the clear. But Russell was out and no one seemed to know where he'd gone. Unsure of what to do next, he rang Sanderson to fill him in with the latest developments.

When Handford had finished his explanation, Sanderson said, 'We've probably got enough now; if we need any more, I've got a chief superintendent from North Yorkshire standing by. He can take over as and when. The Chief Constable insisted. I got a right drubbing from him this morning for not passing it over straight away. Definitely knew my arse had been tanned when I came out.'

Handford murmured something about being sorry; it was difficult to know how to handle that kind of personal disclosure from such a senior officer. But it didn't seem to worry the ACC.

'Aye, so was I. He wanted to know why he hadn't been informed sooner, given it was a senior officer under suspicion. I told him he wasn't easy to contact in the Far East, but he wasn't having any. He wasn't happy either that I'd given you the job of researching Russell's background . . .'

Me and the Chief Constable both, sir.

'. . . but I told him you'd done a cracking job and I couldn't have wished for anyone with more discretion than you. He said if you were so bloody good, why were you still only a DI at your age. A good question, Handford. Why are you still only a DI? I've checked and you've passed the Board for Chief Inspector.'

'Yes, sir, a couple of years ago. But the inquiry into the Jamilla Aziz case got in the way, and I think after that Mr Russell felt I wasn't ready.'

'Then Mr Russell was wrong and I'll tell him so. He can have some of what the Chief Constable gave me. I'm just about in the right mood. It's a pity I have to suspend him afterwards, but there you are – that's seniority for you. I'll be with you this afternoon, Handford. Make sure that constable of yours has some chocolate digestives in; I think I deserve them after this morning.'

Handford replaced the receiver as he glanced at his watch. Five to twelve. He tried Russell's number again. No answer. He rang his mobile. Switched off. Where the hell was he? He had to talk with him before he was suspended; once that had happened he'd have the devil's own job getting near him. Punching in the number for the front desk he waited for Jensen to answer. The moment he heard the sergeant's voice, he said, 'What time did Mr Russell go out, do you know?'

There was a moment's silence, then, 'About ten to eleven, sir, according to the book, but there's no indication as to where he went. Just says "mobile".'

'It's off, I've tried it. Let me know as soon as he comes through the door.'

'The very moment, sir.'

'Oh, and Jensen, give me a buzz when Mr Sanderson arrives too, will you?'

Joe was early. The Square stretched in front of him, busy with people going about their business, ignoring him, as they ignored each other. He wasn't sure from which direction Leah would come; probably down the hill from the shopping centre or from the Interchange. Impatiently, he twisted around on the bench, letting his eyes skim the area. Standing up for a better view, he manoeuvred himself to try to catch sight of her. Behind him stood the City Hall, in front of him the demolition site, which had once housed the modern concrete and glass building. He'd come to watch it disappear in a cloud of dust one Sunday morning. It should never have been built in the first place. His preference was for the older structures. He glanced again at the civic building with its Gothic-type architecture. To its right had once stood the Bradford Unitarian Chapel, gone now, bulldozed in 1969 to make way for the law courts and Central Police Station. He often thought about that when he stared out of the window in the station. It was where he would purge his final victim.

The final victim. The whore. The whore who deserved more than any other to die. The whore who had called herself his mother. He would bring her here.

He had caught her at her whoring. In bed with her lover, when she thought he was at school. Graphically, he remembered the raw sensations searing through him, as he stood, mesmerised, watching the two of them writhing and rolling; first her on top of him, then him on top of her, until the sheet slid off them, so that the man's naked body was uncovered. And he watched as his buttocks jerked in an ever increasing frenzy. Then the man pushed himself into her, thrusting rhythmically, harder and harder, more and more urgently, grunting and groaning as he did so. Suddenly she screamed out loud, and the man stopped, collapsing exhausted on top of her. His first inclination had been to run into the room and hit out at the man for maltreating his mother, but then he saw her kiss him, passionately, fervently, and he knew that not only had she not been hurt, but that she had also been a willing partner, and for the first time, he recognised that what he had witnessed was reality and not a version of the smutty playground images he had leered over with his friends.

So complete had been the involvement of each with the other, he might as well have been invisible. When it was over, they lay next to one another in pleasurable silence, until the man stretched out his arm to pick up a packet of cigarettes from the bedside table. He took out two, lit them both with his lighter and handed one to her. For a moment they lay savouring the heat and the bitterness. Then his mother sat up and clasped her knees to her breasts. It was then she noticed him. She gasped and gave the man beside her a shove. He held the cigarette between his teeth, one eye closing as the smoke curled upwards, and he struggled to sit up. Almost in unison, they pulled the sheet around their bodies, covering their nakedness.

He saw himself back away from the door, then turn and run into the bathroom where he was violently sick. He could still feel the digested food in his mouth and on his tongue, still taste the burning acidity as he retched it into the toilet basin.

She had run after him, her dressing gown fastened loosely, so that it fell open revealing her white breasts. But she hadn't soothed him as she usually did when he was sick; she hadn't said she was sorry for making him sick. All she'd done was plead with him.

'Don't tell your dad, son. Please don't tell your dad.'

He hadn't told his dad. He wouldn't tell his dad anything, he hated his dad. Instead he'd made her pay. There were all kinds of ways a boy of ten could make his mother pay, and he'd become a grand master at the game. Throughout his boyhood and his teenage years he'd continued to control her until eventually he'd left. But being away from her didn't make her any the less damned; she would remain cursed, condemned to live with the fear that one day he would be there, sneaking up on her, ready to punish her again. And now, as each girl died, as she watched him clear the path to her door, she would be growing more and more fearful, never sure whether it would be her turn next. He'd keep her afraid of him; not let her rest in peace, not until she gained absolution amongst the rubbish.

The clock in the tower chimed eleven. Leah should be here by now; he'd said eleven o'clock. Perhaps she hadn't been able to get away; perhaps Alice had changed her mind. No, she'd said she'd come and she would. He'd got her a present; it was something she'd like. The others had; it gave them their freedom as, simultaneously, it tied them to him. He'd given it to the other four girls, then taken it back when he was tidying up so that he didn't leave anything to help identify them – or him. Now it would be hers – for a while at least.

Then he saw her, her blonde hair flowing behind her as she ran towards him.

'I'm not late, am I?' She was out of breath.

'It wouldn't have mattered if you had been, but no, it's only just struck eleven.' He stood up. 'Come on, let's get a drink.'

She turned towards him as they walked, concern clouding her features. 'What's happened to Deepak? Did you find out?'

'He's been released. Last night. He's all right.'

They crossed over the road and walked towards the café. Joe pushed open the heavy glass door for her. 'Do you want a coffee? Or would you prefer something cooler?'

'I'd like a Coke, please.'

'Anything to eat? I'll bet you've had next to nothing since last night.'

Leah scrutinised the cakes in the cabinet. 'Can I have a piece of apple pie?'

'One Coke and one slice of apple pie coming up. You go and get a table.'

He watched her as she made her way to the smoking area of the café. He preferred to be amongst the non-smokers, but for the moment she could have what she wanted. Placing the order, he continued to watch as she took a packet of cigarettes from her pygmy-sized shoulder bag and lit up.

She looked in his direction and smiled.

He paid for their slices of apple pie and their drinks, and carried the tray over to her. Setting it down on the table, he passed her her order and placed his own opposite, then sat down.

'I'm surprised you can get anything as big as a packet of cigarettes in that bag of yours,' he said.

She smiled at him and cut the pie with the spoon, then scooped it into her mouth, then said, 'You're having apple pie as well?'

'I thought I would.'

She picked up her glass of Coke and took a long drink, never taking her eyes off him. He found it disconcerting and turned his attention to spooning sugar into his coffee.

'I'm not sure I want Deepak free,' she said 'He's not always nice to me.'

'But I thought he was your boyfriend?'

'He is . . . well, he was. He might blame me for him being arrested.'

Joe reached over and placed his hand over hers. 'Now, why should he do that?'

'He just might, that's all.'

'Do you want me to find out why he was arrested, put your mind at rest?'

Her face lit up. 'Can you do that?'

'Mm, I think so. I know plenty of people who can tell me.' He glanced over at her. 'Do you live with Alice?' he asked.

She pulled a face. 'Yes.'

He laughed. 'I gather from that look you don't like living there. Am I right?'

'I hate it, but there's nowhere else.'

They ate in silence for a few moments.

'I'm worried about you,' he said, his voice filled with concern.

'Why?'

He ignored the question. 'I want you to have this,' he said, and pulled a small parcel out of his trouser pocket.

It was wrapped in blue paper, the same colour as the dress she was wearing at the leisure centre. She looked up at him, her eyes alight, as though no one had ever given her a present before.

'Go on, open it.'

Her fingers faltered as gingerly she nailed off the Sellotape and unwrapped the parcel, careful not to tear the paper.

'It's a mobile phone,' she cried in delight. 'The same colour as the wrapping.'

'And the same colour as the dress you were wearing yesterday.'

He smiled at her. He had every coloured cover at home. He would always get it right.

'I want you to have it so that I can get in touch with you and you can get in touch with me whenever you need to. If you decide you can't stand being at Alice's any more, you can give me a ring, and then I'll know to find you somewhere else.'

She turned it over in her hands, as cautious as if it were made of porcelain.

'Look,' he said. 'I've programmed in the number of my mobile. All you have to do is to bring up my name in the address book, then press the button with the little green phone on and wait for me to answer. At least then, I'll know when you need me.'

Handford was in the middle of scrutinising Russell's statement, when Warrender knocked on his door.

'I think I've found Alice,' he said as he walked in.

'That was quick work. How did you manage it?'

'It wasn't difficult, guv. It made sense to assume that if she's looking after the young prostitutes now, then at one time she had to have been a hooker herself. So, I went through all past records and came up with three Alices, one whose real name was Alice and two who used it as a working name. The rest was easy. I've been out showing the women the photograph you gave me, and a couple of the older ones came up trumps.'

'*You* have? Wasn't Sergeant Ali with you?'

'Yes, guv, but I told him to stay in the car.'

Handford raised an interrogative eyebrow. He hoped that didn't spell trouble.

Warrender pre-empted him. 'No problem, guv,' he said, 'it's just that the women won't speak to two of us at once, too intimidating. So I told him to stay put . . . and anyway,' a smile curled along the detective's lips, 'he's a bit nervous around prostitutes.' Warrender's eyes glazed over. 'Surprising really, given one of his friends is a pimp.'

'Warrender!' Handford's voice held a warning note.

Warrender smirked again. 'Sorry, guv,' he said without conviction.

Handford let it pass. He said, 'Is Sergeant Ali's friendship with Azam canteen gossip?'

'Not that I've heard,' Warrender said seriously. 'But it's bound to be eventually, particularly if Azam is charged and it goes to trial. The defence could have a field day, especially if Azam insists Ali knew.' He hesitated for a moment. 'All he had to do was to tell us and let us take it from there, then nobody would have known, least of all Azam. Instead of which he had to go and investigate himself. That can be construed any way.'

Handford had to agree, but he kept his own counsel.

Not Warrender. He was enjoying himself. 'That's the problem with his sort, they're arrogant.'

Handford bristled. He had given Warrender too much of a platform. 'Which sort is that, Warrender?'

But Warrender wasn't worried by his boss's tone. 'Fast-track sergeants, sir. They act before they think. It's lack of experience.'

And much against his better judgement, Handford had to agree with that too. Better to get back to the matter in hand before he and Warrender found themselves allies. 'So, tell me about Alice.'

'Apparently, she didn't work the streets. She had her own premises and charged the earth for her services – anything between fifty and five hundred pounds a go, depending on what the punter wanted. Twenty-odd years ago that would have been a lot of money.'

'It's a lot of money now, Warrender,' Handford said with feeling. 'So how long has she been off the game?'

'About ten, twelve years. Alice isn't her real name, by the way. She's Cynthia Houldsworth, forty-five or thereabouts. I'll check her out properly with the Inland Revenue later. Anyway, one of the women said that she'd only gone on the game to make enough money to start up in her own business. Once she'd done that, she jacked it all in and set herself up.'

'In a brothel for young girls? Some business.'

'No, guv, that's a side-line, although it's probably been up and running for most of the ten years. No, she set herself up in business all right – but legit. A bakery.'

'In the city?'

'Yes, guv.'

Handford could feel his annoyance with Warrender rising. 'Are you going to let me in on it then, or do I have to guess?'

'No, guv. I thought I'd leave the best bit till last. The bakery's in the south of the city, right next door to The Mount.'

Handford's eyes widened. 'The Mount police station?'

'Yes, guv, the whole bloody workforce there have been picking up their sandwiches from Alice since she opened, and not one of them has cottoned on to what's going on in the house behind.'

257

chapter twenty-one

'I'll give them bloody sandwiches,' stormed Sanderson. 'You're telling me that this woman has been running a brothel of young kids right under our eyes for the past five or ten years and nobody knew?' He stared unremittingly into Handford's eyes.

The inspector cleared his throat. 'It would seem so, sir.'

The three men were in Handford's office, Handford and Noble standing, Sanderson striding the room, puce with an anger that he pitched like a spear straight at the inspectors. The drinks and bis-cuits the constable had brought and placed on the desk remained untouched.

Sanderson walked over to the window and looked out. The sky was a deep blue and cloudless, the midday sun as bright as ever. All in direct contrast to the thunderclouds that had gathered in the small office.

After a few moments he spun round. 'Christ Almighty,' he seethed, 'have they been asleep for the past ten years or is it that half of them in that nick are getting their leg over?'

The question didn't seem to require an answer and the two men remained silent. Noble, who had had more dealings with the ACC, seemed to be coping better than Handford; he leaned against the filing cabinet, his elbow resting on the top. Occasionally his fingers fiddled with some papers. Handford stood in the centre of the room, his eyes firmly fixed on the floor. He knew about Sanderson's temper, everyone did, but this was the first time he'd been on the receiving end of it. The heat in the room was impregnable and Sanderson's anger rode its surface like a solar flare.

He glared, first at one then the other. 'Have you any idea what the press will make of this if it ever gets out? It'll give a whole new meaning to a sausage roll.'

Handford coughed and Noble spluttered as they tried to suppress their laughter. Sanderson glowered, then, suddenly his anger was released in loud guffaw and he squeezed himself behind the desk to sit in Handford's chair. He indicated that they, too, should seat themselves. When he spoke, his tone was lighter.

'Right,' he said. 'Damage limitation time. What have you done, if anything?'

Noble answered. 'At the moment DS Archer and DC Warrender are on surveillance close to the shop, sir. It's not official because we're out of our patch, but we didn't feel we could sit back and do nothing.'

'So The Mount isn't aware of what you're doing?'

'No, sir, not yet.'

'Good. Let's leave it like that. I'm going up there later to meet with the Divisional Commander and by the time I've finished with him he's not likely to complain about two officers doing what his should have been doing years ago. More to the point,' Sanderson continued, 'can you trust the two you have on surveillance? I don't want them mouthing off to the whole of the canteen.'

Handford and Noble exchanged glances.

'Well?'

'You'll have no problem with Archer, sir,' Handford said. 'But Warrender, well, he's not the most discreet of officers.'

'You mean he'll love it and the more salacious the better?'

'Something like that, sir, yes.'

'Has he had any opportunity to pass this on, do you know?'

'No, sir,' Noble interjected. 'As soon as he told us we sent him and Archer out on surveillance. I went down to the car with them.'

Sanderson relaxed. 'Good, then tell him I'll have his balls if he so much as utters one syllable about this. In fact, no, I'll tell him myself, when I get back. I want him up here the minute he's out of that car and he goes nowhere until he's seen me. Not even for a leak. Understood.'

'Sir.'

'Anyone else besides us know?'

'Just Child Protection, I told them almost immediately,' Handford said. 'At some point we're going to have to raid the place – and sooner rather than later – so they need to be in on it.'

'Social Services?'

'Not yet, but I can't see how we can avoid it. We don't know how many girls are in that house and they're going to need time to sort out places of safety.'

A quiver of excitement played on Handford's nerves as the

predator in him smelled action, which might take them somewhere or nowhere. The important thing was that now they weren't sitting around on their hands waiting for something to happen. He saw a problem, however.

'Child Protection want to go in tonight, sir. Brian and I think it's too soon. We'd prefer to know just what we're dealing with first. We need at least one night of surveillance, two if possible.'

Sanderson agreed. 'It's not going to make much of a difference to the poor little buggers, is it? Two more nights.'

A viscous silence enveloped the room, thick with misgiving about what they were expecting of these children. Sanderson's words had personalised the girls; it was better not to do that, better to forget them and stick to what you understood best; in that way you were less likely to be hurt by the knowledge that these 'poor little buggers' were thinking, feeling human beings.

An image of Nicola swam into his mind and for a moment Handford wished himself back at home with his daughter. He swallowed the craving, then said, 'I would appreciate it if you could have a word with the chief inspector at Child Protection, sir. He seemed to think this is nothing to do with us. He said we ought to stick to investigating the killings. I could hardly tell him if it hadn't been for our investigation, his team would have been none the wiser.'

The tension eased further and Sanderson allowed himself a smile. 'And I can?'

'It would be better coming from you, sir, if you don't mind. He may well be right and we ought to stick with our investigation, but the girls, Deepak Azam, Michael Braintree and the killer are interlinked, and if we break the chain we might lose all of them. Currently, Deepak Azam refuses to co-operate; Dwayne Varley has put his hand up to killing Michael Braintree, but won't implicate Azam; Michael Braintree is dead and can't help, so all we're left with are the girls. This is the first time we've been able to get anywhere near them, we've got to be in on it.'

'You don't need to convince me, Inspector. I'll tell him. But I'll have to give him something in return. A promise of no more than two nights of surveillance, one if possible, and then we go in. That do you?'

'Yes, sir, that'll do me.'

Russell's file lay unopened on Handford's desk. For most of the morning, he had felt like he was working in Centenary Square, the amount of human traffic that had passed through his office. But at last it was quiet. Noble had returned to his own room to organise the surveillance teams and the raid, taking Ali with him. Sanderson had called his driver to take him up to The Mount, and according to Jensen, Russell was not yet back in the station. Time now to concentrate on his own thoughts, such as they were.

In the vain hope he might gain inspiration from its official beige cover, he stared at the closed file. What was he missing? He'd know when he found it, some small point he ought to have picked up on earlier, and he would kick himself for not having done so. He also knew it would either strengthen the case against Russell, or it would blow it wide open and the DCI would be in the clear. That's how it worked. He opened it up and reread the statement. Like its author, it was short and succinct.

I left Central Police Station at seven-thirty; I can't remember saying goodnight to the desk sergeant, but I may have done so. From the station I went to the leisure centre for a massage. I would leave there at about a quarter past eight and arrive at the Claremont Clinic some ten minutes later. I parked my car in the clinic's car park. My appointment with my counsellor was for half past eight. I consider my session confidential and at this time I am not prepared to explain why I need the services of a counsellor. I was with her until nine o'clock, after which I went home, arriving at about half past nine. We had guests that evening and because I was so late, I went straight into the garden to offer my apologies, then showered and changed. I would be back with my guests within a quarter of an hour. I was the last to arrive, except for Andrew Collingham who had had to attend a council meeting.

Handford stretched himself out into a more comfortable position, his feet resting on the open bottom drawer of his desk, his body angled backwards against his chair, his hands clasped behind his head and his eyes riveted on the ceiling. He gazed at the water mark left by the leak during the heavy rains of the winter, a leak that had found its way through the flat roof of the building, into the top storey and eventually through the lower floors to his office. It was an irregular circle, darker at the edges than in the middle. A metaphor for Russell perhaps – his life currently darker at the edges than it was in the middle. He didn't know, imagery had never been his strong point. His mind wandered, a metaphor equals a resemblance equals a likeness equals a correlation. Correlation, now that was more his language. He'd been trained as a mathematician and if ever there was a time to think in a logical and mathematical way, this was it.

He slid his feet off the drawer and sat up. Inspiration had had its five minutes, now it was time for perspiration to take over. He pulled several sheets of paper from his drawer and picked up a pen. On the top sheet he wrote down the names of the current suspects. Stephen Russell, Deepak Azam, Tony Forrester, Other Pimps and Stranger. Taking five more sheets he headed each with one of the names. Underneath, he wrote, on the left, For and on the right, Against. Then on an impulse he pulled forward another sheet and wrote Location. For a mathematician, the methodology was crude, but it was effective. He had suggested it to Nicola as a way of organising her thoughts on her pregnancy.

He read through the statements given to police officers by all the suspects he had listed, writing down the 'fors' and 'againsts' as they presented themselves to him.

First, Russell. The 'For' list was long. Handford picked up the statement again for the night of Jenny Broomfield's death. Jenny Broomfield had his photograph in her purse. She had been looking for him. She was posing as his daughter, may be a daughter he didn't want anyone to know about. He had lied about his movements at the relevant times. He asked Andrew Collingham to firm up his alibi for that evening. He was in the vicinity of the last killing and at the right time. He refused to discuss his reasons for consulting a counsellor. (It could mean something or nothing.) He was in Cambridge at the time of the killings of the three prostitutes. His background was a textbook description for a killer who hated prostitutes, and he had access to garden equipment. The only 'Against' Handford could think of was that he found it difficult to believe he had a serial killer as a DCI. It didn't look good.

Then there was Deepak Azam. His only reason for killing Beverley, Janice and Carla would be that, as their pimp, they had displeased him in some major way, perhaps by gaining The Project's help to escape his clutches. Jenny Broomfield, on the other hand, had tried to get away prior to her being fully groomed, or at least Michael Braintree had made the attempt for her. In the 'Against' column, Handford posed the question as to why he should kill both Michael and Jenny. Without Michael, Azam could have worked his considerable charm on Jenny and had her working for him within weeks. So it didn't make sense for him to kill her as well, particularly as, according to Daniel, he had considered her a better class of girl. In the same column also was his alibi that he had been at the leisure centre. Statements taken from the staff on duty suggested that while no one had seen him at the relevant time, it didn't mean he wasn't there; certainly they couldn't prove he wasn't.

There was also the point that killing his girls would be like deliberately sending his own business into receivership. Even if they wanted out, Handford was sure Azam would have his own methods of maintaining obedience; their need for drugs, the combination of fear and love for him, or the fear that one of his minders might cut or even kill them. Indeed, killing one girl could be construed as a warning to the others, a kind of marketing exercise, but not three in quick succession. Finally, if the rape instrument was something like a gardener's dibble as the pathologist had suggested, then he didn't have one; they had checked on that. He employed a gardener, who liked to use his own equipment. That had been verified by the gardener in question, and he had nothing missing.

Handford turned next to Tony Forrester. As far as he was concerned, they had little on him except that he used prostitutes, preferably young ones (For), but no evidence they were under sixteen (Against). He had certainly asked for a young girl when Archer and Warrender had seen him (For), but he seemed to have been satisfied with the youngest there at the time (Against). He had knowledge of the dead girls being prostitutes when the information was supposed to have been kept under wraps. (For). Handford reread the interview transcript.

DI NOBLE	You knew the girls were prostitutes?
FORRESTER	MY WIFE TOLD ME.
DI NOBLE	That was classified information, Mr Forrester, she wouldn't have told you.
FORRESTER	I DON'T CARE IF IT HAD A 'D' NOTICE ON IT, SHE TOLD ME.
DI NOBLE	When did she tell you?
FORRESTER	AFTER THE SECOND GIRL HAD BEEN KILLED.
DI NOBLE	Can you remember exactly what she said?
FORRESTER	SHE SAID THAT IT LOOKED LIKE THEY HAD A KILLER WITH A MISSION IN THE CITY. I ASKED HER WHAT SHE MEANT AND SHE SAID THAT HE WAS KILLING PROSTITUTES. I SAID THAT I THOUGHT THE VICTIMS WERE YOUNG GIRLS AND SHE SAID YES THEY WERE. I TOOK THAT TO MEAN THEY WERE

FOURTEEN- OR FIFTEEN-YEAR-OLD PROSTI-
TUTES.

DI NOBLE   Had you used these girls?
            (Mr Forrester consults with his solicitor)

MR JOHNSON Mr Forrester has answered this question many
            times. He has admitted to using prostitutes, but
            he emphatically denies using under-age girls.
            Either charge him with kerb-crawling, Inspec-
            tor, or let him go.

And that was as far as they had got. Until they could talk to either
the girls or Alice, they would be unlikely to go any further with that
line of questioning. On the night of Jenny Broomfield's death he
had been out with a prostitute, he said (Against if true). But so far
there was only his word for it. Archer had driven him round the
designated area, but he had failed to identify the girl he alleged he
was with (For). They were still checking his movements on the
nights the other girls were killed. He did have access to a dibble,
to oil-stained pieces of rag, which he used when he was working on
his vintage cars, and a series of lengths of wood, which could have
been used to beat the girls (For). All had been sent to Forensics for
analysis, but they were still awaiting the results.

Handford felt it unlikely any of the other pimps would be responsible for the killings. They were too busy living off the girls and
keeping their heads down to be serious suspects. None of those
interviewed would admit to pimping, let alone being in conflict
with other pimps; none of them knew where they were on the
nights in question and none of them were about to be helpful if it
meant implicating themselves. And all threatened to sue for racial
harassment and unlawful arrest. While they were quite likely to kill
off one another's girls, particularly those who, to the detriment of
the others, gathered the most punters and made the real money, the
MO of the killings suggested a signature killer, rather than someone
ridding the streets of girls who were earning too much.

Then, most important of all, in the case of all suspects, there was
one very big 'Against' and it would prevent them from making a
case strong enough for the CPS to take on board. They had no
witnesses or useful forensic evidence. They needed semen or
blood, something that they could match to the killer, something
that would link him with the girl.

Handford put down his pen and studied the sheets. What was it?
What was he missing? He took up Russell's statement again.

We had guests that evening and because I was so late, I went straight into the garden to offer my apologies, then showered and changed.

That was it. He went straight to see his guests.

That and blood.

Shit. That was it. Blood.

Whoever had killed Jenny Broomfield would have splashes of blood on him, not much but some. As he hit her the sticky bodily fluid would spray on to him, on to the ground and on to anything that got in its way. There was some on the ground, mainly from the drag marks as he had moved her from where he killed her to the rubbish where he had thrown her, but at the point of the killings, there had been blood splatters, both on the ground, and, where there had been a wall, on the wall. Splashes from the same source would also have landed on the murderer's shirt and his shoes. They would have been minute, not visible necessarily to a casual passer-by, but certainly to someone he stood and talked to as Russell had to his guests when he returned home. Unless it was a half-light, when they might not have been easily visible.

Handford grabbed at his diary. He flipped though the pages until he came to the chart of sunrise and sunset times. Sunset last Thursday: 20.42 in Manchester. It would be about the same here. So half-light. Unless the garden lights had been on. They were on when Noble and Forrester had visited, like Blackpool illuminations, Noble had said, but that had been around midnight. If they were on at nine-thirty, which was likely, then surely the first thing anyone who had just committed a murder would have done would have been to shower and change, not go into the garden and talk to guests. Russell would never have taken that risk.

He glanced at his watch. Twenty-five past twelve. Where *was* the man?

He rang Jensen. 'Any sign of Mr Russell yet?'

'No, sir, not yet. I'll let you know as soon as he comes in.'

'Tell him, will you, that it's imperative I see him as soon as he arrives.'

'Yes, sir, I will.'

Handford rang Forensics.

'DCI Russell's clothes, have you got any results yet?'

'Not back yet.'

'Let me know as soon as they are, will you?'

'The very minute.'

Handford looked at the notes he had made. If none of the

suspects he had listed was their murderer, then who was? Could they be looking at someone entirely unknown to them? If so, they were back at square one and Handford didn't feel like being the one to tell Sanderson. The only other lead they had was the location of the crimes. Who, apart from Russell, knew of these? Presumably anyone who had read the pamphlet written by Collingham, anyone who had been taught by him and any of the teachers at the schools involved in his lectures. He wouldn't get the lists from Collingham until tomorrow, so he couldn't begin to check them out until then.

There was Collingham himself, of course. Perhaps they couldn't discount him. He knew better than anyone the locations of religious significance in the city. And according to Russell, he'd been late to the party because of a council meeting. No, it was ridiculous. There was absolutely no evidence against him. Nothing. Never had been.

Nevertheless, he pulled the sheet marked Stranger towards him and under the heading wrote Andrew Collingham's name.

'That's the third man to go into the bakery and come out of the house next door half an hour later,' Michelle Archer said. 'Do you think both houses are being used?'

Warrender focused the video camera. 'I'd say so, yes.'

'One for the ordinary punters and one for those who want to be more discreet?'

'Probably.'

'I've not seen anyone from The Mount go into the shop and stay for any length of time, though. Well, not long enough for a session.'

'It doesn't always take that long.'

Archer frowned. 'Wish it was you, do you, Warrender?'

Warrender lowered the camera, a flush of anger surging into his cheeks. 'No, I bloody don't,' he snapped. 'What do you take me for? I don't go with fourteen-year-old prostitutes. I don't go with fourteen-year-old girls, full stop.' He pointed to the bakery. 'The kids in there are not in there because they want to be; they've been forced into it. I don't force anyone into doing anything. God, Michelle. Don't you think any more of me than that?'

Surprised by his outburst, Michelle Archer shook her head in mute apology. 'I'm sorry, Chris. My mistake. It's just that . . . well, you've got to admit you've always managed to disappear for half an hour or so when we're on surveillance up near the factory.'

'Yes, for a quickie against the wall. That's different, those girls are older, and they know what they're doing. It's their choice. And anyway,' he gave a sheepish grin, his anger dissipating with the smile, 'if you've bothered to look, you'd know it's always with the same girl. Jade and I have an arrangement.'

'Oh, yes, and what's that? She gives you a screw and you don't nick her.'

'Something like that.' He slid down in the car seat, and folded his hands over the camera on his lap.

'You do know if you're ever found out, Chris, it would be a disciplinary?'

Warrender shrugged. 'Who's going to tell?' He glanced at Archer. 'The trouble with you, Sarg, is you've got me all wrong.'

Michelle Archer paused and considered. 'I don't think so, Warrender.' She regarded him narrowly. 'But just in case you've got *me* wrong, you need to know that when someone shops you, and eventually someone will, I'm not going to lie for you.'

'Don't worry, Michelle, I don't expect you to.'

Silence closed in on them as they continued to survey the road in front of them. Any man who seemed to take an inordinately long time to choose his sandwiches or who emerged from the house next door was caught on video, to be identified later. Registration numbers of all cars passing and stopping were written down, their drivers also to be identified as soon as the two of them were back at the station.

Warrender glanced at his watch. 'It's twenty-five past twelve. Any idea how long the boss wants us to stay here?'

'He'll let us know, he said. They want twenty-four-hour surveillance, so there'll be someone to take over at some point.'

'It's just that my stomach's beginning to feel that my throat's been cut. Do us a favour and go and get a sandwich.'

'Don't be ridiculous, Warrender. It'll look good if I go into that shop and later on somebody susses we're watching it. Anyway there's no need, I picked some up from the canteen before we set off.' She turned her body to lunge over the seat and stretched her arm out for her bag. 'Ham or cheese?'

'Neither for the moment.' He indicated towards the shop. 'Look over there.'

Archer unfurled herself from the back of the seat and turned to look where Warrender was pointing. A black Volkswagen Golf had driven up and parked immediately outside the shop. A young girl with long blonde hair got out, turned to wave at the driver and dashed up to the side gate. She opened it and disappeared inside.

Warrender pointed the camera at the car. 'Get his registration number,' he said.

Archer picked her notebook from the dashboard. 'You think she's one of the girls?'

'Don't you?'

'And the man in the car?'

'Either one of Azam's heavies, although I doubt it the way she smiled at him, or it's Azam himself, although I doubt that as well. Anyway, he looks white.'

'Russell? Tony Forrester?'

Warrender concentrated on the filming. 'Can't tell. It's not Russell's car. Not that that means anything. It wasn't Forrester's car on Saturday. Either way, I'll lay odds-on bets he's not her father or her uncle.' He lowered the camera. 'Nor is he a punter, unless the girls do deliveries, and I can't see that, can you? Not when they've got two perfectly good houses here and a front that has evaded a whole sub-division for years. No, it'd be too risky to do home visits. And anyway a punter would be taking a hell of a chance driving her back himself. He's going, you got his number?'

She nodded and they slid down in their seats as the car drove past. By the time it had turned into the main road which led down into the city, they had regained a sitting position, Archer said, 'If he isn't a punter, and it isn't Azam or one of his heavies and he isn't a relative – and I agree that's unlikely – then who else would be driving an under-age prostitute back to her place of work? Unless she's not a prostitute, but Alice's daughter, say.'

Warrender shook his head. 'Hasn't one.'

'Niece?'

'Would you bring your niece to stay while punters were roaming around the house?'

'No, I wouldn't.'

'And from what I've heard about Alice, neither would she, even if she had any close relatives, and I haven't been able to trace any. No, that girl lives here. Straight up through the side gate, not even through the shop. Alice'll have them well trained and they'll know not to get themselves noticed. The last thing she'd let them do is go through the shop.'

Archer placed her notebook back on the dash and picked up the sandwiches. She gave one to Warrender. Absentmindedly, he unwrapped it. 'You know, Sarg,' he said, 'I hope to God that whoever was in that car, it's not our killer making friends. Because heaven help her if it is, poor cow.'

Joe drove away from the shop. He glanced around him. There were a few cars parked alongside the kerb, but all seemed unoccupied. He hoped he hadn't made a mistake bringing her home, but she'd missed her bus and the next would have got her back at least half an hour late. There was no saying what Alice would have done to her then. Beaten her probably, but worse as far as he was concerned, prevented her from leaving the house again. He couldn't risk that; he'd got his mind set on her and he needed her free. They'd tried for a taxi, but the rank was empty and there was no way of knowing how long the next one would be.

In spite of the heat, she'd begun to tremble, although stopped short of crying.

'Ring Alice and tell her what's happened,' he'd suggested.

'I can't. She'll kill me.'

It was against his better judgement, but, if she was to get back on time, all that was left to him was to drive her. 'Come on then, I'll take you back.'

It was five to one when they arrived at the shop. She pulled herself out of the car, then turned and waved at him.

As she disappeared through the gates at the side of the building, he let the brake off and slid out into the road. No one, as far as he could see, had taken any notice of him, but then no one ever did. People were far too busy with their own business to notice him – even though they all knew of him.

The Trash Bag Killer.

He smiled. If only they were aware just how close he was.

chapter twenty-two

One of the rules of police investigations, particularly those involving a serious crime, is that officers keep their superiors up to speed with what they are thinking, what they are doing, or what they are about to do. With that rule come dire consequences for anyone who breaks it. It was a rule Handford knew well, and it was a rule he expected officers in his team to keep. Hadn't he rebuked Ali often enough for cutting his own path, for making decisions that weren't his to make? Yet any moment now he was about to break it himself. He should, he knew, talk his suspicions over with Sanderson and Noble before doing anything, but since he hadn't a gram of evidence, let alone proof, it was unlikely either of them would agree to him taking up any more time on what could be construed as nothing more than a whim and a desire for Russell to be innocent.

It was two o'clock when Jensen finally rang to say that the DCI was back in the building. It was four minutes past when Handford knocked on his door.

'Can I have a word, Stephen?' he said as he stepped into the office. Then, feeling the need to explain, he continued, 'There's something I need to know about the night of Jenny Broomfield's death.'

'In that case, no. Not without my solicitor and an officer of my rank or higher present.' Russell returned to the paper he had been reading.

Handford took a deep breath and tried again. 'Please Stephen, I have to know exactly what you did when you arrived home last Thursday.'

Russell looked up. 'I said no, Handford and I meant no.' His eyes were as cold as his tone.

Handford stood his ground. 'For God's sake, Stephen, we're

under pressure here. The press, the authorities, the public, everybody wants an arrest and most of them don't care whether we get the right man or the wrong one. All they want to hear is the word arrest to make them feel safe again.'

Russell sought to break in, but Handford continued, trying to keep his voice steady.

'No, you listen to me for once.' He pointed out of the window. 'Not only are the people out there afraid for their daughters, they're also afraid of it becoming another Ripper fiasco. They want to know the police are getting somewhere, they want a suspect, and like it or not, as far as Sanderson's concerned, you're the only one in the frame. He's close to suspending you, for God's sake!'

The colour drained from Russell's cheeks.

'*I* don't believe you killed her,' Handford went on, 'but that doesn't matter because there's enough circumstantial to arrest you on suspicion. It doesn't matter there's little or nothing to say you *did* kill her, because there's plenty to suggest you *might* have done. Nor does it matter if, eventually, we have to let you go without charge, or if it goes to trial and you're acquitted; the damage will be done. The press will have a field day and it'll be a good story while it lasts. Can you imagine the headlines? "City's Detective Chief Inspector arrested as the Trash Bag Killer". You'll be hounded, your wife will be hounded, and again it won't matter because even if you're innocent, smoke and fire will spring to the public's mind, because after all, everyone always knew the police were corrupt and looked after their own. And so far as the job is concerned, Stephen, as blameless as you might be, you'll be put in some backwater where you'll stay at Chief Inspector level for the rest of your career. I know, I've gone through it.'

While he'd been talking, Russell's eyes had not left his. Now that Handford had stopped, the DCI stared instead at the papers on his desk. A harsh silence reverberated throughout the room. The fan hummed subliminally and a fly buzzed silently against the glass of the window. For what seemed an age, time fell into a state of paralysis and they all – Russell, Handford, the fan and the fly – became a tableau, a picture freeze-framed.

Eventually, Russell lifted his head, a haunted look on his face. A man plagued by his past, his present and an unknown, unimaginable future.

Finally, he met Handford's gaze. 'What's your question?' he asked.

Handford breathed a heavy sigh of relief. 'Thank you,' he said.

'Tell me again exactly what you did when you got back home on Thursday night.'

Russell's voice was without inflection; no light, no dark, just a flat line on the sound monitor. 'I arrived at about nine-thirty. I was late so I went directly to the garden to apologise to my guests for my belated arrival, then I went to change and shower.'

'How long would you say you were in the garden?'

'Four, five minutes, no more.'

'Tell me, Stephen, were the lights on or off?'

'On.'

'You're sure about that?'

'Yes, they're timed to come on at dusk. I'm not sure exactly what time dusk was on Thursday, but they were certainly on when I got home.'

Handford sighed. 'Thank you, Stephen. I'm sorry I had to put you through that.'

Russell gave a brief smile. 'Are you going to explain?'

'Not yet. But trust me, please, just trust me.'

Stephen Russell wasn't the only person to have to put his trust in Handford. He had to maintain his trust in himself. He had to trust that his gut feeling was good and not suffering from belief in his boss overriding common sense. If he got it wrong he would find himself in the same backwater as Russell.

The trick in this situation was to move slowly, scoop up each trickle of information, conserve it and then move on. According to his statement, Andrew Collingham had arrived at the party after Russell, his excuse being that he had been kept late at the police committee. If that proved accurate then it would be the devil's own job to disprove that he had gone home to shower in order to rid himself of the heat of City Hall before going on to the Russells'.

It took some time to get through to the council department he needed and Handford sat, receiver to his ear, his fingers tapping impatiently on the desk as he was passed from one person to another. Finally a voice said, 'Inspector Handford, how can I help?'

'I wonder if you can tell me what time the police committee meeting ended last week. I know it seems an odd request, but I can assure you it is important to an on-going inquiry.'

'Just a moment. I only typed up the minutes this morning – a bit late, I'm afraid, but you know how things are.'

Through the earpiece he could hear papers being rustled. 'Yes,' she said. 'Meetings are supposed to end at nine, but this went on a bit late. I don't know why it is that it's always the police committee that runs over. Still. It's minuted as ending at nine-twenty.'

Handford felt disappointment shower over him. 'You're sure, are you? The police committee on Thursday last?'

'That's right, except – no. The meeting wasn't held on Thursday. It should have been, but both the Chair and Vice-Chair were unable to attend so it met the day before. Yes, that's right, Wednesday the sixteenth.'

Handford could have kissed her, would have, had there not been multiple air waves between them. He asked if there were any other meetings on the Thursday evening, to be told that no, the police committee was the only one scheduled for then, but she'd verify it with the caretaker and get back to him.

The next call was to the college. He was put through to CDT immediately. He asked if Mr Collingham had left yet.

'Left,' said the weary voice at the end of the phone. 'He hasn't been in this morning.'

'Oh, I'm sorry,' said Handford. 'I thought he was attending a departmental meeting regarding the GCSE results.'

'Why should we have a meeting about GCSE results? They don't come out until tomorrow. I'm only here because we've had a delivery of wood and if it doesn't go under lock and key straight away it disappears. You wouldn't believe the things people pinch.'

Handford's tone was smooth, smoother than it felt. 'So Mr Collingham's not helping you with the wood?'

'You've got to be joking. Lecturers get their hands dirty? I don't think so.'

Handford laughed as though he understood exactly what the man meant. 'Thank you for your help and I do apologise for disturbing you. I must have misunderstood Mr Collingham.'

Thoughtfully, he replaced the receiver. He had to tread cautiously. Two lies didn't make a serial killer, merely a liar. The question was why? Why had he lied so unnecessarily? There could be lots of reasons. Perhaps he hadn't wanted to attend the Russells' drinks evening. Unlikely, since he'd been a friend of Stephen Russell for some time. But even more strange was why he should lie about the GCSE meeting. It couldn't be that he hadn't wanted to talk with Handford, because he'd agreed, albeit reluctantly. Perhaps he had council business that was being kept under wraps before being put before an unsuspecting public as a *fait accompli*. Perhaps he was having an affair, had been with her last Thursday and was going to meet her again this morning and didn't want to be late. There could be a lot of innocent or semi-innocent reasons for the lies.

He would like to have found and questioned Collingham there and then, but he had little on which to base his questions except two lies and the man's knowledge of the religious sites. Not enough. He needed more information about him, and he knew just who to ring to get it quickly. Peter Redmayne. Peter was a journalist on the local paper. He and Handford had become good friends after he had handed him some useful material in a previous case.

'Peter.'

'John. Goodness me, I thought you'd died. You were going to keep in touch, remember?'

Handford laughed. 'Now, come on, Peter, you know as well as I do that a police officer is taught how to avoid returning phone calls in basic training. It's the first thing we learn.'

'Yes, I know, so you've told me – often. Me, I'm not so sure. It couldn't simply be old age and a bad memory, could it?'

'Sadly, Peter, you may be right. But I'll try to do better in the future.'

'Yes, I'll believe you, even though a thousand others wouldn't. In the meantime, what can I do for you? You *do* want something, I suppose?'

'Please, but it's a bit tricky. I want information on one of our councillors. I can't tell you why, and before I divulge who, you must promise to hold tight on to those word-processing fingers of yours. No by-lined copy for tomorrow's paper. Not unless you want to see me cut up in to small pieces.'

Redmayne's tone became conspiratorial. 'Now, let me see. Rumour has it you're on the serial murder squad.' Where did he get his facts? 'And you're asking me for information on a particular councillor. I wonder, could he, whoever he is, be involved in some way?'

In spite of himself, Handford smiled. 'Come on, Peter, you know better than that.'

'Okay, but it's always worth a try. Go on, then, I promise. Same terms as before? When anything breaks I'll be the first to know.'

'The very first.'

'So who is this councillor?'

'Andrew Collingham.'

Redmayne whistled. 'When do you want it?'

'Today.'

'I'll get you what we've got here. But you'll have to wait for anything else I can dig up. Do you want me to fax it over?'

'Better not. Let's meet at the Globe. Seven o'clock?'

Handford was in his office with Khalid Ali when Warrender brought a print-out of the registered owners of the cars that had passed or stopped at the bakery. There was an asterisk against the car that had dropped off the blonde girl. It was registered to Mayfield Nurseries.

'I'm still trying to get in touch,' Warrender said, 'but the phone's been engaged every time I've rung. I think I'm going to have to go up there. It's the garden and landscaping centre on the Harden Road.' He fiddled with the print-out. 'I've got a nasty feeling about this, guv. That blonde knew the place too well; she's got to be one of the working girls. She didn't go in through the shop like you would expect, she went straight through the side gate and up to the back of the house. If she was anything other than a prossie, a relative or the daughter of a friend, say, she'd have gone in through the shop. And I don't think the man in that car was a casual punter either.'

'Evidence?'

'None, guv. Just a feeling.'

Handford knew all about feelings; he allowed Warrender to flow with his.

'Those kids, they're vulnerable,' the detective went on. 'Otherwise they wouldn't allow themselves to be conned into prostitution. All they need is some smoothy like Azam to pamper them, look after them, be nice to them and they'll do anything for him, because most of their lives they've missed out on all those things. The killer comes from the opposite end of the same mould, that's all. He'll work the same way – stalk, get to know, be nice, build up their confidence in him – it's just that his objectives and motives will be different. One uses for money; one kills. Either way they both destroy.'

Handford looked on in amazement as Warrender talked. He'd never seen this side of the constable before. That he was a good detective had never been the issue, more that he was a self-opinionated, sexist, racist bigot. But this was new. He let him have his head.

'Go on,' he said.

'Our killer likely uses a gardener's dibble for raping. Where better to get your hands on one but at a garden centre? And if it's anything like the centres I've been to, there'll be lots of good strong lengths of wood too. He takes some away with him, kills and rapes with them, then in to work where he pops them back where he got them from and some poor sod of a gardener buys them. It's about the most foolproof way of getting rid of the evidence that I can think of.'

Handford turned to the sergeant. 'Ali?' he asked.

'It makes sense,' he said. 'Everything Warrender's mentioned about the way the girls are lured into prostitution equates with Paula Townsend's version. What amazes me is that in spite of everything, they're just as easily lured by the next man who shows them friendship. Vulnerability isn't something that dissolves when some pimp is nice to them, it's permanent. They'll pick up on anyone who seems to care about them.'

Handford nodded; he knew all about vulnerability.

'If the scientists are right about the rape instrument,' continued Ali, 'then it makes sense that the killer might work at a garden centre. And now with the car we have a link with one.'

Handford remembered Susan Forrester's gaff and he wasn't about to be caught out by the same mistake. 'True,' he said. 'But before we go rushing in, let's find out who was driving that car. Then at least we'll have some questions to ask. Warrender, try the number again; if it's still engaged, you and Sergeant Ali go up there. Oh, and Warrender, find out who owns the place.'

Warrender was gone only a few minutes. When he returned he said, 'The car's registered to the garden centre all right. I spoke to the owner – a Mrs Rachel Collingham. But she said she hadn't realised it was out. The staff are able to use the two cars they've got as and when they want. There doesn't seem to be any system there of signing in and out, but she says she'll ask around and let me know when she finds out who's been using it. She seemed a bit out of it, to be honest, probably the type who prefers talking to flowers than to people. Anyway, if I haven't heard anything by tomorrow I'll go up and question the staff myself.'

Handford tried to keep his excitement to a minimum. There was no doubt in his mind who could have been driving that car. But he didn't want to influence the others until he was absolutely sure.

Instead, he said, 'Do that, but in the meantime make sure everyone on surveillance is aware of that particular registration number. If he picks up the blonde girl again, they must forget the surveillance and arrest him. I'm not prepared to take any chances with her safety. I'd rather be wrong than that.'

*

By the time he arrived at the Globe a little after seven, Handford wasn't sure whether he was right or wrong to be doing what he was doing now. Peter Redmayne was waiting at one of the tables outside. Quite unlike the popular concept of an investigative journalist, he was a small man in his mid- to late thirties, slight and angular, with dark bushy hair, which looked as though it hadn't seen a comb in years. The silver-framed glasses he wore were too big for his face and periodically slid down his nose, forcing him to push them back, which he did with unexpected vehemence. Beneath his uninspiring exterior, however, Handford knew there was a brain as sharp as any academic and a persistence second to none. Once on a story, he clung to it like a ferret until he was sure he had everything, and when he wrote it he was logical and literate as well as hard-hitting and persuasive.

On the way to the pub, Handford had decided that a story of under-age girls being lured into prostitution, then kept in a brothel, complete with pimp and madam, was just the kind of challenge Redmayne would relish. If the journalist went along with him over Collingham, he would let him in at the ground floor with news of the brothel and give him the nod when the raid was to take place. It would be good copy; Redmayne would be fair in his reporting and circumspect in preserving his source. With his psychological fingers crossed, Handford had concluded that whatever the police ethics of him leaking the information, these girls were the victims of their pimp, their punters and, more frighteningly at the moment, the killer. Such abuse warranted the maximum publicity – and Redmayne was the best person to give it. Susan Forrester had been concerned that the girls were out there and that not only did the police not know where they were working from, but the powers that be were not that interested in them finding out. 'What can you do,' she had said, 'short of leaking it?'

Nothing.

Redmayne broke into his thoughts. 'Usual?'

Handford nodded.

'I'll get our drinks; you go in to the garden. Do you want anything to eat?'

'No, better not. Gill will have something ready.'

The garden was almost empty, although it would certainly fill up as the evening wore on. One of the few free houses in the district, the Globe had gained in popularity over the years, offering as it did a variety of ales, including real ale, as well as a passable restaurant and a menu of bar meals. Handford looked around to find a table that would give them privacy. The garden was immaculate. The owner had obviously taken as much care with the external design as he had with the interior décor. He chose a table in a shady area as far away as possible from the building and sat down. His eyes wandered over the well-designed lawns and flowerbeds and he wondered if perhaps it was Mrs Collingham and not the owner who had landscaped them. As his thoughts settled on the councillor's wife, he speculated as to whether she was ever suspicious about her husband's lifestyle.

He found it difficult to believe wives didn't know what their husbands were up to. How could they not know they were living with a monster? Didn't they get even the slightest clue? A hint, a suggestion? Perhaps they did, but put it out of their minds as being too horrendous to contemplate. Indeed, he conjectured, who would believe him if he intimated that Collingham could be the killer? If the man in the white shirt, the suit and the tie, the man who looked after their interests at local level could be a killer, then who could they trust?

'Here we are.' Redmayne passed the half-pint of lager to Handford and placed his own beer opposite, then climbed over the wooden bench to sit down.

They drank for a moment without speaking, then Redmayne pulled a buff folder from his briefcase. 'I've got what you want,' he said. 'I might be able to find more, but it'll mean a bit of digging. Do you want me to?'

'Let's see what you've got first, then I'll decide.'

'Right. Andrew Joseph Collingham. Born 10 January 1963, third of four children. The others are Joshua Benjamin, Michael Samuel and Abigail Ruth.' Redmayne glanced up at Handford. 'Note the biblical names. Collingham senior was a devout Christian, but cruel with it if the people I spoke to are to be believed. He was a textile worker and his wife a teacher. Andrew left school in 1979 and was apprenticed to one of the big multi-national firms. Went all over the country on jobs.'

'Do you know where?'

'No, but I might be able to find out. Do you want me to?'

'Please. Go on.'

Redmayne flicked over to the next page of his notebook. 'He began a change of career in 1989 when he became a part-time lecturer in building studies at the college. In 1990 he was taken on full-time, and rose to head of department in 1994. He also married his wife Rachel then. He'd met her through the college; she was lecturing in horticultural studies. Shortly after their marriage her father died and she came into a sizeable fortune, some of which she put into the house they now own and the rest into the nursery and landscape gardening business on the Harden Road. She's been very successful. They're a successful couple.'

'When did he go into politics?'

Redmayne took a long drink of his beer. 'It had been an ambition of his for some time, but he had to wait until the college opted out of local authority control. Prior to that, the fact that he worked for the education authority prevented him from taking up public office. Anyway, he was elected to the council at his first attempt and became Labour councillor for Little Horton. He's been there ever since.'

'He's on the police committee, I believe.'

'Yes and a member of the planning group. He's also involved in some kind of charity work, although he keeps that quiet.'

'He's on the management committee of The Project.'

'The voluntary group that looks after the prostitutes?'

Handford nodded.

'Well, I'm amazed. I wouldn't have thought he was the type. He's always seemed to have quite outspoken views on the prostitutes in the city. He helped Deepak Azam have them moved to a designated site, you know.'

Handford didn't know.

'What about his family?'

'His father divorced his wife when Collingham was twenty-three. His parents' marriage couldn't have been brilliant because his mother moved in with another man shortly afterwards, together with her daughter who would be about thirteen or fourteen at the time. They married quite soon after. It was said his father had been something of a bully and that Collingham often turned up at school with bruises. Nothing was done then, of course. It was nobody's business but the family's.'

'Where's his father now?'

'No idea.'

'Does he see his mother at all?'

'I've never seen her at any of the functions, but she still lives in the city, up at Bierley where she and her new husband moved. I think she went back to teaching for a while. She's retired now, of course.'

'And the daughter?'

'Don't know.'

Redmayne drained the last dregs of his drink.

'Another?' Handford asked and took the glass as it was handed to him. The garden was busy now, and he had to struggle his way through the drinkers and the waiters and waitresses as they sidled past tables with plates of food. Collingham's past was fairly neutral, though not entirely, which meant he needed more. More on the bullying, more on the mother's second marriage, more on Abigail Ruth who he had described as the 'product of my mother and her lover'. The period in Collingham's life that most interested Handford, however, was when he was working away. Where had he been? Was it too much to ask that at some time he was in Cambridge? Probably. He ordered their drinks and carried them back to their table. Could Collingham really be a prime suspect? Handford chastised himself for forging ahead too quickly. He had to be careful, make sure he wasn't doing a Forrester by trying to prove the councillor a killer in order to prove Russell wasn't.

Redmayne picked up his glass. 'Are you going to tell me what all this is about?'

The question was hardly unexpected, but Handford knew he couldn't give it an answer. He remained silent.

Redmayne's face tightened with exasperation. 'I've spent enough time with the police to know what that silence and that look mean, John. It means there's something going on and it doesn't take a genius to work out what. So, if you won't tell me, I'll tell you. You're on the serial killer murder; you're asking about Andrew Collingham, therefore you think he's involved somehow.'

Still Handford remained silent. Redmayne took his silence as a yes.

'You can't mean it?' He returned Handford's stare. 'My God, man, you do, don't you? I can tell by your face. So, if you suspect him you must have something on him that you're not telling. Come on, John, give.'

Still Handford said nothing.

'Answer me this, then. Would it be worth my while digging deep into his background? So that I'm well in front of everyone else when the story breaks.'

Handford yielded. 'You haven't heard this from me, Peter, but my gut feeling tells me that you wouldn't be wasting your time if you did.'

As much as Handford wanted to get home, he drove instead to the office. The Cambridge file was in his desk and he needed to look at it.

The cleaner was in when he arrived. 'I thought you'd be gone by now, Inspector Handford.'

'I'm on my way soon, Beryl,' he said. 'I just need to check some information.' He pulled the Cambridge file from the cabinet. The collator, Ted, had been thorough, giving him any information he thought might be of use. Lindsay Jefferson, the fourteen-year-old victim, had been found on the site of a former chapel. The builders were clearing the site to begin the work on a supermarket.

Lindsay's body was dumped there for all to see, curled in the remaining vestiges of rubbish burnt by the workmen.

Handford flicked through the papers until he came to one he had initially thought irrelevant and had only half scanned. It was a list of workmen from the same multi-national for which Collingham had worked. They had been contracted to clear the site and build the supermarket. All had been questioned as a matter of course. All had been eliminated. He let his eyes run down the list.

Allen, C.
Ambler, D.
Ash, F.
Beddoes, L.
Carver, S.
Chilcott, T. R.
Collingham, A. J.

Yes.

He tried to stop himself trembling.

It may be coincidence, he knew that, but whether it was or it wasn't, he couldn't keep his concerns to himself any longer; he would have to pass them on to Noble and Sanderson. He picked up the phone and dialled the ACC's number.

chapter twenty-three

At the next morning's nine o'clock briefing they consolidated what they had on Andrew Collingham.

It was accepted now that the crime scenes were part of the killer's scenario and that Collingham knew more about them than anyone. If they were to pre-empt another murder, it was logical to check on all other locations of religious significance, particularly those sheltered from public gaze with wheelie bins close by. So far all victims had been found within a radius of one and a half miles of City Hall. In the evenings councillors parked their cars in the Jacob's Well car park only a short walk away. That would be the optimum place for Collingham to leave his car and would account for the fact that it had not been picked up by CCTV cameras in the crime areas. A couple of detectives were given the task of locating and checking out all such sites within a similar radius from City Hall, certainly no more than two miles. Further than that, it was suggested, he would have to take his car and that would leave him open to it being seen or, if he left it at Jacob's Well, a long walk.

Once that was agreed, Handford bought them up to date with what they had learned. The detectives for the most part listened to him in silence, but once he had finished, he insisted that nothing had altered and all that they had was circumstantial. There wasn't a shred of physical evidence to put Collingham or anyone else at any of the scenes. Without that they'd never get a conviction.

Sanderson, who had been sitting behind one of the tables, showed his impatience. 'This is all very negative, ladies and gentlemen,' he said. 'It seems to me that there's little point in moaning about what we can't do. It would be far more profitable to look at what we can do.' He moved over to the map and pointed to the location of the bakery. 'We keep up surveillance on the bakery, continue to take and check registration numbers. Watch for the blonde; if she's picked up again, follow her, because she's the best lead we've got at the moment. If it's evening or night-time, stop the car and get her out because that's when the killer strikes. Even if we're wrong, it's better to be safe than sorry.'

Sanderson was enjoying his role as senior investigating officer. 'Sergeant Ali you go back to The Project. Talk to Paula Townsend, verify Collingham's exact role there, and check whether the blonde girl has visited them in the last few weeks. And don't let her fob you off with that confidentiality crap. If she tries, make sure she realises this girl is likely to be the next victim. If she has anything, we want it. Threaten her with a charge of obstruction if she refuses to come across.'

Handford and Noble smiled at each other.

'Right, you, Warrender,' continued Sanderson, 'go to the garden centre and find out who used the car.'

'If it was Collingham, sir, what do I do? Do I question him or leave him alone?'

'He'll wonder why, if we don't question him, sir,' said Handford. 'He must know by now that he's been seen either because he noticed the officers on surveillance, or his wife's told him.'

'I don't agree that we should question him,' argued Noble. 'If he is the killer, it will warn him off. Once he knows we suspect him, he'll go underground, and we might never find him. It could be months, years even before he reappears.'

Although admitting there was sense in what Noble was saying, Handford wasn't convinced that leaving Collingham was the best way to tackle the problem. 'Collingham's no fool; I still say he'll be expecting us to question him. This man is arrogant. If we bring him in, question him, appear to accept his answers, then let him go, he'll think he's won and has beaten us again.'

'Then he'll go straight out and pick up the first girl he sees and kill her,' someone said.

'I don't think so,' said Handford. 'There's nothing random in what he does. He chooses his victim carefully, talks his way into her life, then decides on the time and the place of her death. After he's killed her, he spends time tidying up, robs her of her identity. SOCOs say the scenes of crime are the cleanest they've ever seen. He'll not go straight out and kill. Whoever it was in that car, I'll bet my pension on him being our killer and the blonde girl being the one he wants. If it was Collingham, we question him, let him go with our apologies and follow him. We don't let him out of our sight. If he tries anything, we'll have him.'

'I hope to God you're right,' said Noble.

Handford, too, hoped to God he was right. The consequences if he wasn't didn't bear thinking about.

The heat hung heavy and he could feel the sweat running down his back. According to the forecast the weather was about to break and last night's thunderstorms in the south were heading northwards. They were expected in Yorkshire in the late evening. Nicola hated thunder; she had ever since she'd been very small. No story, no white lie had ever been enough to erase her fear. Even now, she would come to him to cling on until the worst was over. Tonight he wouldn't be with her to comfort her during the storm nor to reassure her while she fought to resolve the dilemma of what to do about her pregnancy. She hadn't yet come to any decision, and he feared that in spite of her assurances, time would make it for her.

At half past ten, Warrender rang in. 'It *was* Collingham in the car, guv. His wife has verified it. Apparently his was in for a service, so he used one of the business's cars. What do you want me to do now?'

'Where are you?'

'Still at the nursery.'

'Find out from his wife where he is, then pay him a visit and ask him politely but firmly to come back with you to the station. The chances are he's at the college; it's GCSE results' day.'

Warrender's call was followed by one from Ali. 'I've spoken to Paula Townsend,' he said. 'She's absolutely sure our young blonde hasn't visited The Project. So, if she is the next victim, he didn't pick her up from there.'

'And Collingham?'

'He's on the management committee, which means that he attends eight meetings a year. However, Paula said he does much more. You remember I told you about the computer system? Well, it appears he was the far-sighted benefactor she talked about. He takes a real interest in the women, apparently, tries to help as much as he can.'

'The youngsters as well?'

'Everyone. He likes it to be kept quiet, though, because, according to Paula, that's the kind of man he is.'

I bet he is, Handford thought as he replaced the receiver.

Collingham, the dichotomy. On the one hand he goes out of his way with Deepak Azam to have the women moved into a designated area, and on the other he gives not only of his time to

The Project, but also his money. Collingham, the benefactor, or Collingham the serial killer? Time would tell.

It was afternoon before Collingham arrived at Central Police Station. He had refused Warrender's request when he had found him at the college. He was far too busy, he said, but was quite prepared to stop by when he had finished with the results. It wasn't just a matter of handing them out, he had explained, there were students to interview, both those who were to take their studies further and those who had failed at the first hurdle. *They* couldn't wait; the police could.

'I had to agree to it, guv,' Warrender said. 'It was like Leeds City station when Leeds are playing at home. There were students milling round all over the place. It might have warned him off if I'd been too pushy.'

Collingham was full of apologies when he met Handford in the foyer, his Yorkshire accent left firmly behind at his house. The DI shook his hand and said that DC Warrender had explained and not to worry, he was here now. They climbed the steps to Handford's office, exchanging pleasantries about the weather as they went. Once inside he offered him a chair.

'Now what can I do for you, Inspector?' Collingham asked when he was settled.

Handford had to admire the man, the way he immediately claimed the advantage. He must know where he'd been seen and what he'd been seen doing, yet he showed no sign of nervousness, only a desire to assist.

Handford decided to reclaim what should have been rightfully his and said, 'Yesterday at twelve fifty-five you were observed by a surveillance team stopping outside the bakery next to The Mount police station. You dropped off a young girl who went into the house behind the bakery. Can you tell me who she was, and why she was in your car?'

If Collingham was taken aback by the abruptness of the question, he didn't show it.

'Why, yes, Inspector. The girl lives there.'

'Who was she, sir?'

'If I tell you, you are to promise me she will not be picked up by the police and nor will she be harassed by you.'

No wonder Collingham was voted on to the council at the first attempt; he was good. He had varied the rules, modified their respective positions and hijacked the interview in one sentence.

Handford had two options; one was to distance himself from the request, the other was to go along with it. He decided on the latter.

'I can't make any promises, Mr Collingham, as I'm sure you're aware, but I'll do my best to do what you ask.' The words stuck to his tongue.

The councillor uncrossed and recrossed his legs as he made himself more comfortable.

'Do you know The Project, Inspector?'

'Yes, sir, I have heard of it. Something to do with helping prostitutes, I believe.'

'That's right. Well, I'm a member of the management committee. I was up there yesterday; I go up as often as I can – to help, you know.'

'Which is why, when I tried to contact you at the college, you weren't there, and the man I spoke to said you hadn't been in?'

Even that didn't faze Collingham. He gave a slight laugh. 'A little white lie, I'm afraid. I prefer to keep my work at The Project quiet, so I use the college as an excuse. Anyway, the girl was there. Her name is Leah, and that's as much as I'm prepared to say. It's a question of confidentiality, you know. After talking with Mrs Townsend, she was very distressed and I offered to drive her home.'

'To the bakery?'

'Yes, she lives there with her aunt, she said.'

'Why was she at The Project, do you know?'

'No. What any of them discuss with Mrs Townsend is confidential, and quite rightly she wouldn't tell me, even if I asked, which I wouldn't dream of doing.'

'The girl isn't a prostitute then?'

'I don't know. As I have repeated more than once, conversations at The Project are confidential.'

Handford pushed. 'And you couldn't make an educated guess?'

'I could put two and two together, Inspector, but I'm not sure what good that would do. She has been to The Project, she will be getting help with whatever her problem is.'

'Do you expect to see her again?'

'Possibly, but I doubt it. We just happened to be at The Project at the same time.' Collingham was showing signs of boredom. 'Now, if that's all, Inspector, I'm a busy man.'

'Of course, sir.' Handford stood up and smiled. 'Thank you for coming in, Mr Collingham. You've been very frank. My apologies for bringing you here, but we are questioning all drivers seen in that area.'

Collingham stood up. 'No problem, Inspector. I'm only too glad to be of help.'

Handford made for the door. 'I'll get someone to show you down,' he said.

While they waited Collingham flicked into councillor mode. 'May I ask,' he said, 'this surveillance, is it anything I should know about as a member of the police committee?'

'I don't think so, sir. Just part of an on-going inquiry.'

As soon as he had gone, Handford radioed down to the waiting car. 'He's leaving,' he said.

Once Collingham had left, Handford joined Noble to put the finishing touches to the raid on the bakery and the house next door. According to Michelle Archer there were probably ten or eleven youngsters working at the two brothels and the busiest time appeared to be between nine and eleven-thirty at night. A team comprising detectives and uniformed officers was set to raid them simultaneously at a quarter to ten. The chief inspector from Child Protection rang to let them know that he had already contacted Social Services who were currently preparing places of safety. The women on the team were to be consigned to gather up the girls, the male officers the punters, and uniformed officers posted at exits from both houses, back and front, to detain any defectors. Michelle Archer was assigned to take care of the blonde girl. It was Noble's job to arrest Alice, a job he admitted he would relish.

Once they'd all been gathered together, prisoners and girls were to be taken to Central Police Station where the latter would be checked over by a doctor and transferred to places of safety. The men would be questioned immediately, charged and bailed. It was going to be a long night.

Every night was a long night for Leah, and this one she anticipated would be the worst and the longest yet. She closed her eyes and squeezed out the tears, then checked in the pock-marked mirror that her mascara hadn't run.

She was on to her fourth punter of the night. The first was a regular and, as punters went, a decent man. He was gentle with her, and when he had finished, thanked her. The other two were not so nice. They wanted their money's worth and cared little how they got it. The easy way or the hard way. The easy way was her protection and she allowed them the easy way. Or that was what she let them think; they'd find out when they got home the easy way wasn't always what it seemed, for she'd managed to roll both of them, getting more than fifty pounds from one. And this money she would keep, because tomorrow she was going to contact Joe and ask him to help her get away from here, find her somewhere safe.

But she still had to get through the night and if the rest of the girls were to be believed, her fourth punter was a pervert, but harmless. He liked to tie the girls up, wrists at the bedhead, legs splayed out and feet harnessed to the bottom. What was important was she made him think she'd enjoyed him. If she did that, she'd be all right. Alice had trained her in pretending enjoyment, but Leah wasn't sure. What if she couldn't? It was easy when she'd some control over the situation, but by tying her up, he would take the control from her. There were macabre stories, too, as to what happened if he believed they hadn't enjoyed him. One way was to leave the girl tied to the bed. If she was lucky, the next punter would untie her, but there'd been this one girl, she'd been told, who'd been fucked by nine more punters before she'd been released. Alice hadn't cared. It had served her right; she should have pretended harder. How hard was harder?

Tonight, he'd asked for Leah specifically. He liked beginners and Alice couldn't see any reason why he shouldn't have her. They'd all got to get used to the perverts and the weirdos, and the sooner the better because the streets, when they worked them, were full of them.

The weather had broken and thunder was rumbling close to the house. Storms frightened Leah. When she'd lived at home, before the new boyfriend moved in, she used to crawl into her mother's bed to cling on to her until it was over. Then, when she left to live in the squat, and there was no one to cling to, she would roll herself into a ball, clasping her hands over her head like a helmet as the thunder resounded throughout the fragile building. Now, like this, she could do nothing more than close her eyes as each explosion burst overhead.

Tying her up had been part of the ritual, his depraved kind of foreplay. First he fanned her long blonde hair over the pillow, then sitting astride her he licked and caressed her wrists and ankles before winding the cord around them, to pull it tight as he harnessed her to the bed. Once satisfied, he slid off the bed and moved slowly backwards, feeling for the wall with his outstretched hands.

She turned her head, the only part of her she could move. Twenty to ten. He yelled at her to look at him. She turned back. When the red numbers showed ten past ten it would all be over. But now at twenty to ten, Leah was trussed tight and frightened. The cord with which he had fastened her was blue and cut into deep into her flesh. She wanted to go to the toilet. She clenched her muscles and hoped that she could hold out long enough. She'd no idea what he would do if she couldn't.

The man, naked, was pacing backwards and forwards now, oblivious of the storm raging outside. Groping his way along the walls he paced up and down, around the three sides of the bed, like an animal guarding its prey, gradually moving closer, his penis erect, his excitement mounting. His eyes never left her. When she closed hers to shut out the thunder, he demanded she open them again. She had to watch him all the way, concentrate only on him. He was close now, almost ready to climb on the bed. He lifted one knee, resting it on the edge, then pushed himself up with his other leg. His movements were graceful and smooth, like a ballet dancer's. Once he was balanced, he crawled towards her, his eyes still boring into hers.

The thunder roared, reverberating through the room, shaking the ornaments and toiletries on the dressing table.

He moved closer. Almost there. Almost over.

Out of nowhere came a clamour of voices, shouting and yelling, but she couldn't make out the words. Doors banged. Footsteps clattered on the stairs. Frantically, she turned her head from right to left. The devils had broken through the storm. The devils were coming to get her, like her mother's boyfriend had said they would. The punter kept coming, creeping like a cat towards her. His shadow covered her and his hot breath whispered over her body as he climbed upwards.

A triangle of light fanned across the room, increasing as the door was pushed open.

'In here, sir.'

It was too late for the man; he was coming, he needed her.

The swatch of light expanded, and a figure stood, silhouetted in the half-darkness. A woman. The punter turned his head and groaned. Leah felt the heat of his semen as it sprayed on to her bare midriff.

Another man was in the room. He made a grab for the punter, throwing him off her and off the bed. Relief surged through her and she felt the warm flow between her legs as her bladder opened and emptied.

'See to her, Michelle. Get her out of here.'

The woman leaned over her, her fingers fiddling with the knots of the cord. As she became free, the thunder crashed against the window pane, and Leah grabbed the woman, holding on to her as she had with her mother.

The other man snatched at the punter with his bear-like hands, lifting him onto his feet. He was visibly angry and even in the half-light, Leah could see his jaws working and the veins in his neck pulsating.

'I ought to cut it off, you pervert.' He brought his knee up towards the man's groin. He missed, but the punter doubled up in a reflex action.

A voice from the corridor thundered, 'Handford, leave him.'

Breathing heavily the warring man shoved the punter away.

The same voice, harsh. 'Out of here. Wait on the landing.'

He moved slowly out of the room, his shoulders hunched. Leah could make out his shadow as he leaned against the wall.

'I'll make a complaint against him,' the punter stammered.

'I don't think so, sir.' There was a recognition of danger in the older man's voice.

He grabbed at the punter's clothes and pushed them towards him. 'Now, you get dressed and go downstairs. A police officer down there will take your name and escort you to Central Police Station. After that – well, we'll see.'

He moved towards Leah and touched her on her arm. 'It'll be all right, love, don't worry. Michelle here will see to you.' Then turning to the woman, he said, 'Look after her, Sergeant.'

'I will, sir.' And Leah felt the comforting arm of the police officer around her shoulder.

The house was quiet now. The punters and Alice had been transported to Central in police vans, the girls driven off in separate unmarked cars. Handford wandered from room to room. Each door had a name on it; this one, the blonde girl's room, read Jasmine. It wasn't her real name. According to Collingham her real name was Leah. Unusual she'd given him that; normally they kept it a secret.

He pushed at the door and walked in. The room stank of sex, sweat and urine. Sparsely furnished, it could have been any hooker's workplace. The double bed took up most of the space in the centre, its headboard hard against the back wall; next to it a small table. To the side of the door was the dressing table with a stool. Opposite, an old-fashioned wardrobe fitted into the space to the left of the window. He opened its doors. Skimpy skirts and tops hung limply from their hangers. Handford picked them out. They were cheap, the uniform of the prostitute. But to one side, in the corner, was a pale blue dress, more expensive than the rest. Hidden away for no one else to see.

Closing the wardrobe doors, he moved across to the dressing table where he searched skilfully through the drawers. Underclothes, make-up and at the back of the bottom one an envelope. He opened it and counted out the money. Five pounds twenty pence. Her fortune; a fortune she felt the need to hide. Then back to the small table by the bed. He slid open the single drawer. Another wad of money – seventy pounds – probably stolen from one or more of the punters. Since no attempt had been made to hide it, it would no doubt be passed onto Alice, and minus her percentage, from her to Azam. Jasmine would be unlikely to see any of it. Handford took a small plastic bag from his pocket and placed the money inside, then pulled out the drawer fully to tip the contents onto the bed. Cigarettes; a wrap of heroine, a mobile phone and some packets of condoms. He counted out six.

The man he'd pulled off her hadn't worn a condom, he remembered; no doubt he'd paid more for that privilege. He hoped Jasmine used her own form of contraception.

Suddenly, Handford could take no more. He sat down heavily on the edge of the bed. For how long had the girl in this room had to endure such abuse? And the girl before her? And the girl before that? And all the other girls they had taken away from here tonight? He scanned the detritus scattered on the counterpane. The sum total of the life of a fourteen-year-old, seventy pounds from some abuser, a few cigarettes, a wrap of heroine, six packets of condoms and a mobile phone. There was hardly anything there she could call her own, except five pounds twenty pence and a few clothes. Even the name wasn't hers.

He picked up the phone. It was blue, almost the same blue as the dress in the wardrobe. Pressing the button, the small screen lit up. He waited for it to boot up, then pressed on the address book symbol. A number appeared. There were no others, just that one. Azam's? Doubtful. He rang it, but a voice broke in. 'The mobile phone you have rung is turned off. Please try again.'

He shut it down and dropped it into an evidence bag. This was one for the scientists.

A sound from the doorway pulled Handford from his thoughts. He glanced round. It was Ali.

'What are we doing, Khalid?' he asked. 'This poor kid.'

'I know.'

'I wanted to kill the man in here. I probably would have if Sanderson hadn't intervened. He'd tied her to the bed, for God's sake. She is fourteen years old and half his size, and he'd tied her to the bed. What sort of man gets his kicks like that?'

Ali was more practical. 'The kind of man we're going to get locked up for child abuse and then put on the sex abuse register.'

Handford shook his head. 'Look around you, Khalid.' He waved his hand over the articles on the bed. 'This is Leah, or what's left of her. A kid who is a nobody to the men who use her and to those of us who ought to be protecting her.'

'Then let's go back to the station and make her into a somebody again. Let's make those men suffer. Charge them so that their wives and families know how they spend their nights and their money. Let's make sure the whole world knows.'

'Not me, Khalid. I don't think I want to do this any more.'

'Yes, you do, because if you turn your back on it now, you'll have failed them, Jasmine and all the rest. Alice will be in the magistrates' tomorrow, along with half the punters. She'll probably be remanded in custody. It will get into the press.'

An image of Peter Redmayne in the pub garden flashed into Handford's consciousness. He remembered their murmured conversation and allowed himself a slight smile. There was a God after all, he thought. It was just that sometimes He needed a little shove.

'Come on, then,' he said, pushing himself off the bed. 'Let's leave this to SOCO. See what damage we can inflict back at the station.'

It was the early hours of the morning when Handford finally arrived home. The wall lights were on in the lounge. In the half-light he could make out Gill's sleeping form on the settee.

Tiptoeing over to her, he crouched down and watched her as she slept, her breathing smooth and rhythmical. Seeing her there, so peaceful, went some way to dissolving the depravity of the past few hours. Eventually, he kissed her lightly on the forehead and at the same time brushed her arm with his fingers. She roused, opened her eyes and pushed herself slowly into a sitting position.

'You've been waiting up for me,' he said. 'You haven't done that for a long time.'

She caressed his cheek with her fingertips. 'You look awful,' she said. 'Was it bad?'

'As bad as I've ever seen it.'

'Do you want to talk about it?'

'Tomorrow, perhaps.' Tomorrow when the visions were less vivid.

Gill slid off the settee to crouch with him and folded her arms around him.

'Nicola's decided,' she said. 'She's going to terminate. We have an appointment at the clinic tomorrow.'

Relief flooded over him and he closed his eyes for a second. Tears welled up behind the lids and when he opened them he was unable to prevent them from spilling over. Rightly or wrongly, it was the decision he had wanted her to make.

Gill wiped the tears from his cheeks with her thumbs. 'She wants to go to university and then follow in her father's footsteps by joining the police force. She can't see herself doing that with a baby.'

Handford glanced at his wife, but there was no animosity behind her words, no bitterness in her eyes. 'And that's all right with you?' he asked hesitantly. 'I know how much you hate the service.' He didn't want to spoil the moment he'd just had with his wife.

'I don't hate the service, John. I just hate the way it elbows into our lives without so much as a please or a thank you. But it's her decision, and they're her reasons. And to her they're sound reasons.' Gill smiled. 'She asked me if I minded, just as you did. What could I say? I said no. But honestly, looking at you tonight, I think she might have been better off with the baby.'

chapter twenty-four

For Handford, the night had been a chimera of visions, smells and sounds. Images of the girls lingered with him in his dreams, black and white, except for the blue cord tied around Jasmine's wrists and ankles. A deep sky blue that penetrated his psyche, imploded in his brain. Eidetic images, eidetic thoughts – a blue cord, cavorting with the blue dress and the blue mobile phone. Then Nicola's baby, scraped from her, lying blue in the kidney dish. Visions and images swirling in his brain, so that when he awoke, he did so with a start, drenched in sweat. And once awake, the yeasty smell of sex combined with the acrid scent of urine that characterised Leah's room permeated his nostrils and caught at his throat.

He left for work at the usual time, greeting his neighbours on the way with the usual good morning. Everything normal, yet nothing normal.

He had spoken to Nicola before he left, hugged her and told her not to worry, everything would be all right. He had to believe that or else what was the point?

'Mum will ring me when it's over.' He hugged her again. 'I wish I could be there with you,' he said.

'Don't worry, Dad, it's your job. I understand.'

He wished he did.

The storm of last night had abated, but grey clouds hung low over the roads and the fields, the sun and blue skies of the past month no more than a memory. The tarmac glistened wet and the drive into the city was treacherous.

Not wishing to see or talk with anyone, he stayed at his desk, reading statements, making notes, trying as he did so to make sense of yesterday's events.

The girls had said very little; they had been taught well how to avoid police questions, and last night hadn't seemed the time to push them. Alice, too, had invoked her right to silence and during the hour-long interview she had neither admitted anything, nor made an attempt to defend herself. The solicitor who had been pulled out of bed to represent her had been unable to alter her stance. In the end they had charged her under her real name of Cynthia Houldsworth, with living on immoral earnings, keeping a brothel, and causing or encouraging prostitution of minors, with the promise of more to come once their inquiries were complete. She was appearing in the magistrates' court this morning and it was expected the bench would remand her in custody.

Azam, too, had been brought in first thing to be questioned yet again about his possible involvement in procuring young girls for prostitution. They had no more evidence than at the previous interview, but hoped that once he realised the brothel had been raided he would admit his part in it. It was a vain hope. Even the trick of an accidental meeting between Alice and him in the custody area hadn't fazed him. Both had acted as though the other was a complete stranger.

Handford asked Ali to check Missing Persons, nationally and locally. Leah was the only girl so far for whom they had a partial name and she might have been reported as missing by someone. After that, he feared, there would be the long trawl in trying to unearth the identities of the other girls. It would be easier if they would just tell them.

'Work with Child Protection on it,' he said. 'But make it clear that for the moment Leah is ours. As far as we know, she's the only one who has met Collingham. And we need to know how he works.'

He hoped the mobile phone he had found in her room would provide some clues in that direction. It needed logging in for forensic analysis, but before that, he wanted to try the number in the phone book again.

This time it rang.

A man answered.

'Hello, Leah?'

Handford cut the connection. The voice was unmistakable. Collingham's. He'd given Leah the means to keep in touch with him. Why, if, as he had insisted, he had done no more than drive her home? Certainly, he hadn't seen her last night. After his interview he'd gone straight home and stayed there, and only examination of the mobile would show whether he had rung her or she him. The phone had to be part of his strategy; to Leah, the outward sign of the mask of sanity, which he wore to befriend and manipulate; to him the means of knowing where she was at any one time. A girl as vulnerable as Leah would accept him and his presents at face value. Had he done the same with the other girls? Given them a phone, this phone? Almost certainly, if it worked once, it would work every time. None had been found at any of the crime scenes or on the bodies, not even Jenny Broomfield's, so if this had been his method of keeping in touch, then it had to have been removed after the killings.

He sent for Michelle Archer, then rang through to Forensic. 'I'm sending you a mobile phone,' he said. 'I need to know who it's registered to, and to whom and when calls have been made. Can you do that?'

'If the SIM card is intact, yes. When do you want it?'

He tried to sound hopeful. 'Yesterday?'

The man at the other end chuckled. 'So you're not in a hurry, then? Go on, I'll see what I can do.'

Archer popped her head round his door. 'You wanted me, guv?'

'I need Leah in here now,' he said.

The sergeant made to argue. 'I'm not sure she's ready . . .'

'She's going to have to be ready, Michelle. I think we've got the connection between her and Collingham. Take her to the soft interviewing suite and let me know when you've arrived.'

Shortly after eleven o'clock, the CPS solicitor called to verify that Alice had, as expected, been remanded in custody until the end of the month. The girls were safe from her for the moment at least. The men, all of whom had been named, had, however, been granted conditional bail until mid-September.

Handford would have preferred the men in custody as well, but you couldn't have everything.

He glanced at his in-tray. Still full. Most of it stuff from other cases and nothing to do with the serial killings or the raid. As important as it was, he wasn't sure his brain could cope with more of the written word until he had made pathways into the frothy mass of information already there.

He rang down to Brian Noble. 'Coffee time,' he said.

'We're going to have to let Azam go. Again.' Noble banged his fist on the desk, dislodging a pen, which scuttered to the floor. For a moment he ignored it, then bent down to pick it up. He resumed his seat and swirled the pen between his fingers like a majorette's baton.

'Not one of those girls will make a statement against him. He's put them through all that, all the indignities we saw last night and they still won't grass him up. It makes you wonder what he's got that we haven't.'

'Give them time, Brian,' Handford said wearily. 'When they've had time to get used to living normally, perhaps with normal families, they'll talk then.'

'I doubt it,' Noble said scornfully. 'They're in care and that's what most of them ran away from in the first place.'

'Archer is bringing Leah in. We may get something more from her. She was badly frightened last night. Like it or not we're going to have to use that.' He shook his head. 'To be honest, I can't get the picture of her out of my mind. The cord he tied her with was blue. I can't get that out of my mind either, but don't know why it worries me so much.'

'Probably because it was our fault. We left it too late. We should have gone in when Child Protection wanted us to. Two nights won't make any difference to them, that's what Sanderson said. Well, perhaps two nights made a big difference to that girl. All I know is we should have gone in earlier.'

'It was one night.'

'What?'

'It was one night, not two.'

'And what the hell difference does that make?'

'None.'

The silence settled uncomfortably. They were both tired and their tempers were fraying in equal proportions to the level of their weariness. Handford walked over to the window and looked out. Rain clouds were gathering again.

'Last night's storm has done some good,' he said, 'but we're in for some more.'

'We are when Sanderson reads this.'

Handford turned. 'What?'

'Today's paper.' He threw it to Handford. The front page was taken up with a photograph of a policewoman leading one of the girls wrapped in a blanket out of the side gates of the bakery. Another officer was protecting her from the rain with a large umbrella, which served the added purpose of hiding the young girl's face. In the bottom right-hand corner overlaying the larger picture was a smaller one of Alice covered in a coat being escorted to the police van. No one had thought to shield her with an umbrella. The headlines screamed out in large black type BAKERY BROTHEL, and Peter Redmayne had his by-line.

Handford scanned the opening paragraph. It said everything there was to say.

A forty-seven-year-old woman was arrested last night and charged with a number of offences, which are purported to have occurred over the past ten years at the bakery close to The Mount police station. In the shadow of the police sub-division, the woman, Ms Cynthia Houldsworth, is alleged to have controlled a number of schoolgirl prostitutes in two houses. According to sources, she prepares girls as young as twelve for the streets.

Handford read on. There was a vivid description of the raid, Peter Redmayne making the most use of the weather conditions to add to the horror and degradation of the occasion. He ended with:

Councillor Andrew Collingham, labour councillor for the Little Horton ward and a member of the police committee, commented, 'It beggars belief that this kind of thing is going on in our city and under the noses of the very people who should be there to put a stop to it. We feel for the young girls, but are happy in the knowledge that they are now safe in our care.'

'Bloody hypocrite,' Handford muttered, slapping the paper down on the desk, although he had to admit Redmayne had pulled quite a stroke getting a quote from him.

'Who?'

'Collingham.' Handford slumped into the chair beside the desk. 'In one breath he's giving time and money to an organisation set up to help prostitutes, and in the next is moving the older women on and driving the young ones back to their brothel. Not content with that, then he's setting about to kill them one by one. Then,' he picked up the paper. 'Then, he has the cheek to make statements like *"We feel for the young girls, but are happy in the knowledge that they are now safe in our care."*'

Noble smiled grimly. 'A bit of an exaggeration, John, but I know what you mean and it makes me angry too.'

Handford leaned over the desk. 'We can't leave it like this, Brian, we've got to get him in to question him.'

Noble agreed, but advised caution. 'Talk with Leah first; she might give you more to go on. There's no point you going in while you're in this mood. Calm down first. Collingham's a clever man and you need to be as quiet and controlled as he is.'

Handford rubbed his hand over his face. 'Yes, you're right.' He threw Noble a smile. 'Our councillor is right about one thing, though. Leah's safe from him at the moment.'

A silence developed, to be broken a few moments later by the shrill ring of the telephone.

The skin tightened apprehensively round Noble's eyes. 'Sanderson?' he mouthed. Handford shrugged his ignorance.

'DI Noble.' Relief flooded his features. 'It's for you,' he said, passing the receiver over.

'DI Handford.'

'It's Doctor Jessop. I thought you'd better know that one of your little girls from last night is pregnant. Very early stages yet, I doubt she'll know herself. Can you pass it on to whoever she's living with? I ought to tell her myself really, doctor–patient confidentiality and all that, but in the circumstances it might be better coming from the Residential Service Manager or the foster parent or whoever.'

Handford closed his eyes; as if they didn't have enough to worry about. 'I'll pass it on, doctor. Who's the girl?'

'The name she gave me was Jasmine, but I think you said her real name was Leah. Anyway she's the one.'

Leah looked tired. Her face seemed to have shrunk overnight and her eyes were dark-ringed, as though she hadn't slept.

Michelle Archer threw Handford a stony look which said, 'I told you she wasn't ready.'

'Do you want a coffee, sir?' Her voice was icy enough to freeze any drink she offered him.

'No,' he said. 'Thank you.' Then he turned to Leah. 'I want a word with Michelle here. Will you be all right on your own?'

Leah nodded in reply.

Once outside Handford rounded on Archer. 'I know how you feel, Sergeant,' he said, 'but we have a killer out there and that girl is the only lead we have. Would you rather he finds someone else to kill, while we're pussy-footing around?'

'I just think she needs more time, sir.'

'We don't have time,' he said angrily. He took a step backwards. 'And neither has she. She's pregnant, Michelle. Dr Jessop rang earlier to tell me. She's in the very early stages apparently, but she needs to know. So, who tells her? Me, you or the manager of the home?'

'I will, sir. She trusts me I think. But later.'

'Whenever you think it's best. But try to remember your role here. You're a police officer, not a social worker. Leave the counselling and the caring to them.' He gave her a warning nod. 'Right, let's get on with it.'

The two went back into the room. A soft interviewing suite, meant to soothe traumatised adult victims and alleviate the fears of the younger ones, it was decorated in subtle pastel shades and furnished with upholstered chairs and sofas, a sideboard and a rectangular coffee table on which there were magazines and a vase of fresh flowers. To one side, and partially hidden, was a kitchen, which allowed them to make drinks and sandwiches.

Leah was sitting exactly as they had left her, hands clutching her mug like a comfort blanket. Michelle Archer was right; she wasn't ready, traumatised as she was. The feelings she was experiencing were not induced just by last night's events, but more a culmination of weeks of abuse.

Michelle Archer spoke first. 'This is Inspector Handford, Leah. I don't know whether you can remember him from last night.'

'He was the copper who threw the punter off the bed. The one the other copper shouted at.' Her voice was flat, the events recited in a monotone as though she had learned the answer by heart.

Handford smiled. 'That's right.' He sat down in the armchair opposite her. 'I'm not here to talk to you about last night, Michelle will do that later when you're feeling better. I want you to tell me, if you will, about the man who dropped you off at the bakery yesterday.'

For a moment her eyes lit up. 'You mean Joe?' Then the brightness was overlaid with suspicion. 'Why do you want to know about him?'

Handford ignored her question. 'Do you know him well?'

'He's not one of the punters if that's what you think.'

Handford's voice softened. 'No, Leah I don't think that.' He turned to Michelle Archer. 'I'll have that coffee now, Michelle.'

The sergeant got up and moved over to the kitchen area. They heard water running into the kettle and the click of the switch. Then she reappeared to lean against the partition wall.

'Do you know him well, Leah?' Handford asked again.

'Not very, but he's nice.'

'In what way is he nice?'

'He listens to me when I talk. He doesn't tell me what I should do and shouldn't do.'

'Anything else?'

'No.'

Handford sighed inwardly. What had happened to these girls to make them latch on to the first person who was nice to them? 'Nothing? Are you sure?'

'He doesn't want to have sex with me, if that's what you mean.'

'He doesn't?' Handford's tone suggested he didn't believe that.

'No, he doesn't.' Her tone was defiant. 'In fact,' she became more sure of herself, 'he's going to find me somewhere to live, somewhere where the punters can't get at me.'

'Did he say that?'

'Yes.' She stared straight at Handford, her expression brooking no argument. 'And I believe him.'

'Did he tell you where?'

'No, he said he'd ring me and let me know once he had sorted it.'

Handford took the mobile phone out of his pocket. 'Did he give you this?'

She lunged for it like a spoiled child. 'Give it to me. I want it!'

Handford swerved his hand away from hers. 'Did he give you this, Leah?' His tone suggested he needed an answer, and she wouldn't get the phone back until she gave him one.

'So?'

'When?'

'Yesterday. He said I could ring him whenever I wanted. We're not allowed to use the phone at Alice's, and he said he wanted to be able to get in touch with me as well. There's nothing wrong with that.'

His assurances were bleak. 'No, Leah, there's nothing wrong with that.' He paused. The click of the kettle as it switched off resounded in the silence. Michelle returned to the kitchen.

'I'm afraid I can't let you have it back straight away,' Handford said. 'We have to keep everything we found at the bakery for a little while.'

'Even my clothes?'

'No, there are police officers up there at the moment, but when they've finished, Michelle will take you back to get your clothes. I've got this for you though.' He handed her an envelope. 'Count it if you want; it's all there.'

Five pounds twenty pence.

Michelle handed him his coffee.

'I should have left it really, but I decided not to. All I ask is that you don't tell the man who shouted at me, otherwise he'll shout at me again.'

She smiled at him, lighting up her face. 'I won't,' she assured him, and she put the envelope in her pocket. When she looked at him again, her eyes were filled with fear. 'What's going to happen to me?'

'What do you want to happen to you, Leah?'

'Am I going to prison because of what I was doing with those men? That's what Alice told me would happen if I told anyone.'

Handford wanted to go over to her and put his arms around her, just as he had with Nicola this morning. Instead he allowed his compassion to transform into anger, which he directed at Alice. 'She's wrong and she'd no business telling you that. You're not in any trouble at all. None. You're not to think about that again; you're not to worry about it. Promise me you won't.'

She nodded, then said, 'Can I go now?'

'Soon. Did he give you any other name besides Joe?'

'No, just Joe.'

'That's all? No last name?'

'No.'

'Can you describe him to me?'

'He's old like you,' Handford felt rather than saw Michelle Archer smile, 'and he's tall and his hair's dark and his eyes twinkle all the time.'

Could it be? Andrew Collingham? He was fairly sure the person who had answered the phone earlier had been him and Leah's description matched.

Andrew Joseph Collingham. Joseph. Joe.

Was this man two sides of the same serial killer?

Handford and Ali walked into interview room three where Andrew Collingham was waiting with his solicitor. He stood up, his arrogance more discernible than ever. But this time, Handford wasn't about to allow him to gain the advantage.

'Please sit down, Mr Collingham.'

The solicitor, however, was more used to police interview rooms. His greeting was cold. 'Inspector,' he said, his Yorkshire accent pronounced.

'Mr Robertshaw.' Handford made no attempt to shake hands. Robertshaw was an old adversary. Born and bred in the county, he was nearing retirement, but for all that, was not to be trifled with. A man with a mercurial mind, he allowed no one to get the better of him. Yet, to look at, dressed as he always was in tweed jacket, beige shirt and trousers and tartan tie, he could have been mistaken for a farmer visiting the city. A stereotypical *One Man and His Dog* country sort. It wasn't difficult to imagine him walking the cows in for milking or rounding up the sheep. But, as Handford knew well, they underestimated him at their peril. He and Sanderson came out of the same mould and it was as well to accept that.

'I would like to know why you have brought my client in for questioning.'

'You know why, Mr Robertshaw. I have information that leads me to believe he is involved in some way with young prostitutes and I need to know how involved.'

Ali unwrapped the tapes and slipped them into the recording machine, which, once they were settled, he switched on. At the familiar beep, Handford went through the preliminaries, reminding Collingham that at this moment he wasn't under arrest. He asked him if he understood. Collingham agreed that he did.

Handford's first question was straight to the point.

'I would like you to tell me how you met the girl known to you as Leah.'

If it took Collingham by surprise, he didn't show it. 'I met her at The Project; she was distressed and I offered to drive her home. I told you this yesterday.'

'What is your interest in The Project, Mr Collingham?'

'I'm on the management committee and I help out up there sometimes.'

'Which means what exactly?'

'I attend eight meetings a year and give of my time to help the women. Sometimes that means no more than handing out condoms or clean needles. Sometimes it means listening to them when they want to talk.'

'I understand you donated a computer system?'

'Yes. They wanted one; I was able to get one. The two went together.'

'So, you met Leah at The Project and offered to drive her home?'

Collingham sighed. 'Yes.'

'Did you know that Leah's "home" was in fact her place of work, and that she was being used as a prostitute?'

Again the question didn't throw the man into confusion. 'I assumed that, because she was up at The Project, she was involved in prostitution, why else would she be there? But I didn't know the bakery you raided last night was where the work, as you call it, was taking place.'

'Do you know of any more young girls who are working as prostitutes?'

This seemed to upset Collingham. He whispered to his solicitor. 'Where is this leading, Inspector?'

'It's leading to me finding out, sir, just how much your client knows about what has been going on in our city for the past decade.' Handford was on the verge of adding, 'And why he hasn't done anything to stop it' but he held back. That was a question for later.

Robertshaw nodded at Collingham to answer the question.

'I was aware of some young girls who were desperately trying to get out of prostitution. I didn't know where they worked and nor did I feel it necessary to come to the police. What we do up at The Project is confidential; if I come running to the police every time I hear or fear something, it would close down in a week because the women would no longer trust us.'

'What about the girls, those under sixteen?' asked Ali. 'Shouldn't The Project be protecting them?'

'Do you know anything about the Children's Act, Sergeant? Once a girl is fourteen she is deemed to be able to make her own mind up about what she can and can't do. We are tied by that.'

Handford marvelled. The man was good.

He countered. 'So, how do you equate that interpretation with the law governing the age of consent?'

Collingham smiled. 'I don't. The law, as you well know, is a confusion of rules and regulations, many of which conflict. As a result legislation doesn't always protect. This is one instance.'

'Are you suggesting then that the young girls we took from the bakery last night have given their consent to work as prostitutes?'

Collingham was beginning to show signs of stress. The deep timbre of his voice moved up a notch, so that it became less of a bass and more of a baritone. 'I don't know. They might have done; they're not all young innocents, you know.' His eyes blazed into Handford's and for a moment he struggled to retain his composure. Eventually, he said, 'All we do at The Project is help those who want to be helped. Perhaps the rest don't.'

'And that includes Leah?'

'Yes, no, I don't know.' He turned to his solicitor again.

'This has gone far enough, Handford. Ask your questions if you have to, but don't blame my client for the state of the law.'

Handford conceded. 'So, Mr Collingham, you drove Leah home from The Project?'

'Yes.' His voice was more high-pitched, moving towards tenor and his eyes were showing an emotion that was more than fear.

Handford pushed home his advantage. 'How do you account for the fact then, that Mrs Townsend is insistent that Leah has never been up to The Project and that she has no knowledge of the girl.'

Collingham began to fragment. Handford leaned back to give him time to collect himself and to work on his answer. Collingham's eyes darted between the two officers opposite him, wondering, no doubt, how much they knew.

When he thought he had had long enough, Handford regained his position, this time resting his forearms on the table, his face closer to the councillor's. He repeated the question.

Hostility bruised Collingham's features, but he was back on safer ground.

'Confidentiality, Inspector, is the most important concept at The Project. Other than that, I can only assume she has either forgotten or she doesn't know the girl as Leah.'

'How do you know her as Leah? The girls never give their real names, only their working names. It's their protection against the punters and the police. So how did you know her real name?'

'She told me.'

'What did she call you?'

He was calmer now and he paused to weigh up his answer. 'I'm sorry, I don't understand.'

A reply that gave him more time to work out how much Handford knew. The inspector refused him his unspoken request.

'How did she address you? By what name?'

'Joe, all the women did.'

'Why Joe? Why not Andrew?'

Suddenly Collingham's patience snapped again. 'I could hardly use my own name with a girl like that.'

'A girl like what?'

'A prostitute, a whore. Would you want her to know who you were? You can't trust that kind; they use you, then let you down.' His voice lifted another octave and suddenly he was slipping into soprano. 'My mother called me Joe when I was little.'

'And that's why you referred to yourself as Joe with the women, because your mother used it sometimes?'

Collingham's anger was beginning to get the better of him and the look in his eyes was bordering on the feral. 'What difference does it make? I could have used any name, providing it wasn't the one people knew me by.'

Robertshaw placed his hand on Collingham's arm. 'Take it easy, Andrew.'

But Handford didn't want him to take it easy. He wanted him in a state in which he would make mistakes. He measured his words.

'Look, Mr Collingham. You know and I know you didn't meet Leah at The Project. I also know you've been aware of her for some time. Now, let's start again, shall we? How and where did you meet Leah?'

Collingham glared at him. 'The first time I met her was in a department store. She was running away from someone.'

'Who?'

'She didn't say, but she was obviously frightened. Then I bumped into her outside the leisure centre.'

Ali and Handford exchanged glances.

Ali asked. 'Deepak Azam's leisure centre?'

'Yes.'

'Why were you there?'

'Why does one normally go to a leisure centre?' Collingham's confidence had returned, his voice was back to normal and his eyes were almost smiling. Almost. 'I like to make the most of the college holidays.'

Handford wasn't to be drawn. 'Go on,' he said.

'It was the morning Azam was arrested. She was distressed at his arrest and I took her for a cup of coffee while she waited for the woman she said was coming to pick her up.'

Ali took over. 'Why was she at the leisure centre?'

'She'd spent the night there, with her boyfriend, she said.'

'Her boyfriend?'

'Deepak Azam, I imagine.'

Handford heard Ali draw in his breath. Stay calm, Sergeant, he willed him, just stay calm.

'Anyway, she was worried about him,' Collingham went on, 'and I said I would try to find out what was happening. We arranged to meet yesterday morning in Centenary Square. I took her for a coffee and told her what I'd found out. As a result she missed her bus and I drove her home.'

'So, why didn't you tell us this before? Why lie?'

'Because I knew she was into prostitution.'

'How?'

'An educated guess, Inspector. She'd spent the night with Deepak Azam.'

'He uses prostitutes?'

'So I've been led to believe.'

Ali broke in. 'Does he work them?' He was breathing heavily, his disgust close to the surface. Handford glanced at Ali. The man's face was set, his expression implacable and he hoped he wouldn't lose the sense of professionalism he had held on to during the last few minutes and allow this to become personal. If he did that, they would lose the advantage.

'I really don't know,' Collingham responded. 'All I know is that from time to time he sleeps with young girls. They come to him; he doesn't go to them.'

Collingham was calm again now that the spotlight was off him and on to Azam. It needed to be refocused.

Handford asked, 'Can you tell me then, why you gave Leah a mobile phone?'

Collingham's composure slipped once more. The question had unnerved him and he ran his tongue over his top lip. 'I was worried about her.'

'Worried enough to keep in touch? With a girl like that?' He could barely keep the sarcasm out of his voice.

'Yes.'

'Why didn't you simply take her up to The Project and let Mrs Townsend look after her, or come to us? It seems to me that there's little point you telling a reporter that the police ought to put a stop to this kind of thing, if you, as a member of the police committee, aren't going to play your part.'

'Handford, really.' Mr Robertshaw gave a good impression of a charging animal.

This time it was Handford's turn to lift his hands in mute apology. But he had made his point and was happy to forego the answer.

'Do you have any more questions for my client, Inspector? Because it seems to me that from what I've heard here, he is not involved with this prostitute in any way except as a member of The Project, as a councillor and as a concerned citizen. You have no reason to detain him any longer.'

'Just a few more, sir.' He turned back to Collingham. 'Beverley Paignton, Janice Thurman, Carla Lang and Jenny Broomfield, do you know them?'

This time Collingham was not caught out. '*Did* I know them, Inspector? They're the victims of our Trash Bag Killer. No, I didn't know them.'

'You said that on the evening of Jenny Broomfield's death you were at a police committee meeting and then at a party held by Detective Chief Inspector Russell?'

'Yes.'

'Mr Collingham, there *was* no police committee meeting that night. It was held the previous evening because neither the Chair nor the Vice-Chair were able to attend. Indeed there were no meetings at City Hall that night. I've checked.'

Collingham smiled. He was totally in control now. 'I think I told you yesterday that I often use the council meetings as an excuse for my work at The Project. I was up there.'

'And Mrs Townsend will verify that?'

'I doubt it, it was her night off. I was there on my own.'

'Can anyone verify it?'

Collingham's smile widened. 'Only the women who visited and it's unlikely they'll talk to you.'

Handford let Ali take over.

'You say you didn't know the dead girls, Mr Collingham. I find that difficult to believe because Mrs Townsend certainly did. In fact she went to their funerals. Even if you didn't join her there, surely their deaths were discussed by you all as a management committee?'

Collingham gave his interrogator a pitying look. 'I knew *of* them, Sergeant, of course I did. But that's a very different thing from *knowing* them.'

Handford changed direction again. 'What about the nights the other girls were killed? Can you remember your movements on those nights?'

'Is there any reason why I should?'

Handford smiled. 'Humour me, Mr Collingham.'

'I have no idea. I'm a busy man, I need my diary to tell me what I've been doing on any specific evening.'

'But not those nights, surely? Those nights are fixed in everyone's minds.'

'Not mine.'

'Yes, sir, even yours. In fact I would go so far as to say, especially yours.'

The meaning was tantalisingly clear. 'You think I killed them?'

'I don't know, sir. Did you?'

'Of course not. Do I look like a serial killer?'

'I'm not sure what a serial killer looks like, but I imagine he's very similar to you and me.'

Robertshaw broke in, his ruddy complexion on fire. 'Enough, Inspector. You brought my client here because you had information that made you believe that in some way he is involved with young prostitutes. Now you are suggesting he is killing them. Do you have any evidence to substantiate this accusation?'

'I wasn't accusing him, sir, just asking.'

'I repeat, Inspector, do you have any evidence for asking him?'

Handford remained silent.

Robertshaw continued. 'Are you going to charge him?'

'No, sir, not yet.'

'In that case, my client is leaving.'

Handford nodded and Ali made to turn off the tape. 'Interview terminated at sixteen twenty-three hours,' he said and flicked the switch.

Handford pushed his chair back. 'Sergeant Ali will seal the tapes and then show you out. Good afternoon, gentlemen.'

His eyes met Collingham's and for the first time that afternoon he saw nothing but fear. Collingham was guilty all right and Collingham knew that Handford knew.

chapter twenty-five

Handford pushed open the door of the incident room, empty of detectives. A couple of civilians glanced towards him as he entered, but then returned to the mound of paperwork and interview tapes still to be transcribed. They would finish for the day within the next quarter of an hour and what wasn't completed would be left for another time.

Wandering over to the window, he took a bite of the chocolate bar in his hand, then, as he chewed, let his eyes take in the scene below. It was the end of the day and the public square between the police station and the magistrates' court was almost deserted. Occasionally a sombrely dressed man carrying a briefcase skipped down the steps from the courthouse, or someone passed from Channing Way to the Tyrls and from there to the bus stops that lined the main road. To the west, the sun was fighting to breach the rain clouds, occasionally throwing bright shafts of light over the mellow brickwork of City Hall. A temperate south-west breeze blew across the area, teasing the leaves of the trees lining the pavements and catching the water from the fountain, spraying it in a fine mist over the edges of the rectangular pool it served. The geraniums and busy Lizzies housed in the two wooden boxes glowed flame red, adding some brightness to the physical and psychological darkness of the day.

Although the look of fear in Collingham's eyes after the interview had initially given Handford a certain satisfaction, it now haunted him. A frightened serial killer who knew time was running out was a dangerous threat. That he was poised to kill again, Handford had no doubt; he had been preparing Leah, befriending her, gaining her confidence and had given her the means by which they could both keep in touch. But with his prize plucked away from him, he would have nowhere to go to satisfy his urges, except perhaps to a complete stranger. Handford had considered momentarily letting Leah have the phone back so that she could contact him. A knee-jerk reaction he should never have contemplated, wasn't worth the risk and wouldn't have been sanctioned anyway.

The truth was that he was more than concerned that not only was Collingham frightened, but that he was also slipping over the edge. Andrew was slithering into a permanent state of Joe. Andrew, the stable and reliable councillor, had for whatever reason allowed himself to become Joe the unpredictable, Joe the prostitute hater, Joe the murderer. Handford had listened to the interview tape over and over again, and his nerve ends coiled each time Joe took precedence.

I could hardly use my own name with a girl like that.

A girl like what?

A prostitute, a whore. Would you want her to know who you were? You can't trust that kind; they use you, then let you down.

Someone had let him down. His mother perhaps. She'd been the one who'd called him Joe, and Joe was the name he used with the prostitutes. There had to be a link. According to Redmayne, she'd had a lover and once the divorce came through she'd left the house she'd shared with her husband to live with him and then married him. Perhaps Collingham's hatred of women stemmed from that? Except he was twenty-three. Hardly at an age when the effect would have been devastating. Earlier, perhaps, when he was much younger. Whatever it was, it had to have been something so traumatic that the only way to cope was to channel his anger into viewing every woman as a prostitute. Handford sighed; this was no more than supposition, amateur psychology. Nevertheless, it would make some weird kind of sense for Collingham to satisfy his need by substituting the cause of his paranoia for Leah, who was now out of his reach.

He would like to have updated Russell, but the time wasn't right. He had to be absolutely sure that Collingham was the killer before he talked to the DCI, just in case he was wrong. The poor man would have to live in suspense a little bit longer.

A phone rang. One of the women picked it up. 'It's for you, Inspector,' she said. 'Peter Redmayne.'

'Thanks. I'll take it in my office. Put it through, will you?'

Andrew Collingham's mind was not on his driving. Although he didn't like to admit it, the interview had unnerved him. Handford knew too much. The little bitch must have told him about the mobile phone. That was their secret, hers and Joe's. How could she betray him?

The police had betrayed Andrew too. Why hadn't he been informed about the raid? He ought to have been told as a member of the council and of the police committee. It was his right to know. He could have warned Joe, given him a chance to get her out of there. Now she had disappeared and no one was saying where she was. He'd tried to find out, gone to the top.

'This is Councillor Andrew Collingham. Put me through to the director of Social Services. Hello, Jim. These girls . . . yes, it's awful, I agree. Yes, I intend to make it a priority to find out why the police were not aware of what was going on . . . egg on their faces . . . yes. About the girls? Where are they? Keeping that quiet; need to know basis . . . yes, it is sensible.'

Handford knew where she was; he had to in order to question her. He would interrogate her like he'd interrogated him, frighten her into betraying Joe. Then, they'd hunt him down like an animal. Not Andrew, they'd not hunt him down. Andrew would leave, get out of the city; he'd done it before, three times in Cambridge. Joe was the problem; he couldn't leave immediately, not until he'd had his needs satisfied. And this time it had to be total satisfaction. So satisfied that he would never have the urge to kill again. That meant the queen of prostitutes. This had all been about her; the ultimate prize, the ultimate punishment. The Beginning, the Genesis. Destroy her, and the umbilical cord that gave all the others life would be severed. Leah was no longer, so it had to be her. His mother.

'You're sure this is true, Peter?' A current of unease sparked through Handford

'Positive. When I suggested that Mrs Collingham had rushed into marriage after the divorce, I got the whole story. Everyone I spoke to, neighbours, friends, family even, couldn't wait to blacken the old man's name. According to them, Mrs Collingham had been having an affair with her present husband for at least fifteen years. The youngest girl was his, although Collingham senior never knew. It was no surprise to anyone that his wife had turned to someone else, the old man was a bully. Textbook case. Beating the boys, molesting the girls. Nobody blamed her.'

'Why didn't she report him or leave him?'

'We're talking about the sixties and seventies here, John; you didn't tell the authorities that that sort of thing was going on then. It was too shameful. You kept it behind closed doors.'

'What about Andrew?'

'Everyone's proud of him, the way he's turned out – college lecturer and respected councillor. He could easily have gone the other way, they said. He'd been a docile kid until he was about ten apparently, wouldn't say boo to a goose, then he turned, became a bully like his father and a bit of a cruel lad – animals, younger kids, his mother – he didn't seem to care.'

'Do you know what triggered this?'

'According to Mrs Collingham's best friend who made me promise not to tell a soul, since Letty had told her in confidence, it all seemed to stem from Andrew coming home from school early one day to find his mother and lover boy in bed together. She was beside herself, the friend said, worried sick that he would tell his father. But he never did. Took it out on her instead. Called her a slag once in full view of the street.'

'And now he's killing prostitutes. Makes some kind of bizarre sense, I suppose. Anyway, thanks a lot, Peter. I'm not sure how you do it, but I'm glad you do.'

'Oh, it's just my natural charm. You know, the one that gets me first on scene when a brothel of child prostitutes is raided. Did you like the piece, by the way?'

'I did, but I can't say the same for the Assistant Chief Constable. He tore a hell of a strip off both Noble and me. Said if he ever found out who'd leaked it, he'd have – well, I'll leave it to your imagination as to what he'd have.'

Redmayne sucked in his breath. 'Ouch, painful. Don't worry, John, he'll not hear anything from me. My sources are as private to me as – as what he was going to tear off you.'

Handford laughed. 'Good, that makes me feel a lot safer. Oh, Peter, just before you go, give me the mother's married name and address, will you? We may need to talk to her at some point.'

'It's Mrs Letty Walker, 23 Knowles Crescent, Bierley.'

There was little to do now but wait and Handford had never been very good at that. Sanderson had sanctioned surveillance on Collingham and two officers were assigned to follow him. They were told to keep in constant radio touch, leaving Handford with little to do but listen to the commentary over the airwaves.

From Central, Collingham had walked to his solicitor's office where he had spent about half an hour. From there he had dashed into City Hall, to emerge a short while later clutching a wad of letters, after which he had returned to Jacob's Well to pick up his car, then driven home, arriving at a quarter to six.

The area around the house, Handford knew, was not designed for surveillance. Standing alone, the renovated chapel was in a hollow about half a mile from a hamlet of four or five houses and a pub. The B-road wound through the moor to lead down to Ilkley, or in the other direction to the village of Baildon and from there to the main route to Bradford, Leeds or Skipton. But here, where Collingham lived, it was pure countryside. Miles of moorland, fields, dry stone walls and little in the way of population.

Along the road at varying intervals were rough grass lay-bys where hikers and ramblers parked their cars to set off on the long trek across the hillsides. Warrender and Clarke had stopped in the nearest to the house then, to give themselves a better view, moved higher up the moor. They were currently making their way through the bracken, still wet from last night's thunderstorm and today's drizzly rain.

'It would be quite pleasant here, if it wasn't so bloody wet.' Warrender oozed irritation. 'Just look at my trousers.'

'Stop moaning, you two, and keep your eyes on the house,' Handford warned them over the radio.

It was difficult to know just how long this would go on. Whether Collingham would go for a stranger, or for a substitute, or whether he would wait and pick up another older prostitute was anyone's guess. Handford didn't know; all he could be sure about was that Collingham had lost the girl he had intended to kill, but not the desire to kill.

'He's on the move, guv,' Clarke's voice crackled over the radio. In spite of the area, reception wasn't brilliant. 'He's dressed in a tracksuit and carrying a large sports bag. Probably going to the leisure centre. He's got some nerve, I'll give him that. Suspected of murder and he's off for a game of squash.'

Handford could hear the two pushing their way through the undergrowth as they ran down the moorside to the car. He glanced at his watch – half past six.

'Got him, guv. He's in his car on the B6151 heading in to Baildon.'

Silence.

'We've just passed Ian Clough Hall.'

That meant they had gone straight across the roundabout and were still moving in the direction of the city.

'We're at the bottom of Baildon Road now and through the lights on to the A6038 and into Shipley.'

Silence.

Then, 'Through the traffic lights, first set . . . second set . . . come on, Clarke, get through the next lot or we'll lose him. Third set and we're turning left into Canal Road.'

Silence.

Come on, come on, keep me in touch.

'Still on Canal Road. Coming up to the city centre turn-off. He hasn't taken it. We're now on the Shipley–Airedale Road. He's probably going down to the leisure centre via Otley Road. No, he's moved into the Wakefield lane. Where the hell is he going?'

Handford turned to the map and fingered the route. Wakefield Road. He wasn't going to the leisure centre, nor to the designated area for prostitutes. He'd missed the turn off for the first, and the second was miles away. Wakefield Road, to the left Dudley Hill, to the right East Bowling and straight on – Bierley. He was going to Bierley. He was going to his mother.

The radio crackled. 'We've lost him, guv.' There was panic in Warrender's voice. 'We've bloody lost him. Some idiot driving an HGV pulled in front of us on the roundabout. We lost sight of him. No idea which turn-off he took.'

'He's going to Bierley, Warrender. For God's sake, get there. He'll be going to his mother's. Mrs Letty Walker, 23 Knowles Crescent.'

Handford grabbed at the door and dashed along the corridor to the incident room. 'Ali. With me. Now.'

Joe drove carefully. There was a purge on motorists at the moment. He'd checked when he'd left home and there was no sign of anyone following him, so it would be stupid to allow himself to be picked up by the traffic police. Better to concentrate on getting to his mother. From home to Bierley it was eight and a half miles, or thereabouts; fifteen, twenty minutes, no more. Park up by the side of the house, by the gate. Don't forget the bag. He could bring her out by that gate where there'd be no one to see him; the house opposite was offset and the windows faced a different direction.

In by the front gate.

She's got it nice, I'll give her that. A semi, ivy clinging to the wall, beginning to hide the bedroom window; trees in the garden, too many for its size, but they give privacy.

The front door. She never locked it. He opened it and went in, closing it quietly before turning the key in the lock.

'Hello, Mum.'

She was sitting in one of those high chairs that make it easy for old people to get out of. Next to her was a square table on which was an open packet of fruit gums. The television was on – *Emmerdale*. She'd watched the soap from the beginning when it was *Emmerdale Farm*. No one had been allowed to disturb her when it was on. *Make the most of it, Mum, it's the last one you'll see.*

She glanced up at him. 'Andrew.' Her eyes reverted to the screen.

She didn't seem surprised to see him, even though he hardly ever visited. He walked around the chair to stand close. Her arthritis was getting worse. Her clawed fingers and gnarled hands rested on her lap. Her permed hair was thinning; he could see the pink of her scalp. She smelled; the house smelled. She was too crippled to look after herself. What was *he* doing? The man she'd let screw her; where was *he* when she needed him?

'Where is he?'

Her whole body shifted into a position in which she could see him. 'Tom? He died six months ago. I wrote and told you.' Tears swelled in her faded blue eyes. She turned back to the television.

He remembered. The letter painfully scrawled. He'd had a heart attack. It had been sudden, nothing anyone could do.

It didn't matter.

'What are you doing here?'

'I've come to see you, got something for you.' He wanted to give it to her there and then; the punishment, the beating and then the final blow, but he couldn't. The chair had a high back and she was small, seemed to have shrunk since the last time he saw her. He couldn't get close because of the chair.

'What?' Still her eyes never left the screen.

He had to make her stand, so that he could get to her. 'You make us a nice cup of tea, and I'll show you.'

'When the adverts come on.'

The stupid silly bitch. Everything was more important than him. It always had been. Tom, screwing, 'don't tell your dad', even when he was being sick.

He waited. Now, not later. Now. He ran twitching fingers through his hair. His heart raced; adrenaline flooded his limbs; it had to be now. He bent down to open the bag, the sound of the zip resounded in his ears. But the chair was in the way. The wings hid her face, and her head rested against the back, only a tuft of greying hair visible over the top.

'*I'll* put the kettle on.'

He walked into the small kitchen and filled the kettle, switched it on. It took only a few moments. Cups, saucers, milk, sugar. Another few seconds.

He wandered back in to the room. 'Do you want me to make the tea?'

'No, I need to get up, move my body. Otherwise I get stiff.'

Words ended, music began. The adverts. Letty pushed herself painfully from the chair.

He jerked the stick out of the bag.

Once upright, she took a few seconds to gain her balance, then slowly shuffled one foot forward, then the other.

Joe moved behind her.

'No, I don't need any help, I'll be all right once I get going.'

He lifted the stick above his head and brought it down hard on her back. She screamed, louder than any of the girls had screamed. It echoed round the room, from wall to wall to wall. He hit her again and again, the impact of the blows reverberating along his arms. By now she was on the ground; the small table she had caught hold of as she went down at her side and the fruit gums flung out of their packet. Lying on her stomach, moaning, blood seeping though the weave of her blouse. There hadn't been so much blood from the girls. He lifted the stick for one last blow.

Then, as an urgent rapping came at the front door, his hand was held as if in an iron grip.

'Letty? Letty? Are you all right in there?'

His mother moved, attempting to stretch out her arm as though to catch hold of the help that was too far away. He brought the stick down on her head and suddenly there was silence. She was no longer moaning. She was almost at peace; he was almost at peace. But not quite.

He pushed the stick back in the bag and pulled out the garden dibble. To gain absolution she had be punished in the only way whores understood, in the only way she understood.

The banging, more urgent this time.

'Letty!'

Another knock, then, 'Ring the police. Now.'

No time. He'd do it later. He replaced the dibble, slung the bag over one shoulder, then turned her over and grabbed at her shoulders. Her eyes stared up at him, unquestioning. She was light, even in death she was light. He dragged her through into the kitchen. It was small and his bag kept catching on the furniture, slowing him down. Holding her with one hand, he groped for the door with the other. As he found the knob, he pulled at it. Locked. He let her fall to the ground while he grabbed at the key and turned it. The door opened smoothly. Pray that the neighbours haven't come round the back. No. Deserted. Probably too frightened at what they might find. Leave it to the police. Didn't they know there'd be nothing once he'd gone?

Lifting his mother to hold her under her armpits with one arm, he pulled the gate open with the free one. Then to the car. He half walked, half dragged her across the pavement, opened the back door and bundled her in, then ran round to the driver's door, threw in his bag, jumped in, turned the key. The engine fired and his tyres screeched as he drove off down the road.

For Handford there was an ominous inevitability about what he expected to find at Letty Walker's. A small crowd had gathered around the house. Handford had the car door open, almost before Ali had stopped. Two uniformed officers were keeping back the small crowd that had gathered. Warrender and Clarke came through the gate. 'The front door's locked,' Clarke said.

'Check round the back,' Handford yelled at Ali as he ran over to the knot of neighbours.

Waving his warrant card, he said urgently, 'What's happened?'

A woman explained. 'We heard screaming through the wall. We live next door,' she said, pointing towards the semi's twin. 'It was awful. We thought a burglar had got in. Then it all went silent. We banged on the door, but there was nothing. So my husband rang the police.'

'Did anyone try to get in?'

'No, not with all that screaming. We thought it better to leave it to you lot.'

The front door opened and Ali emerged. 'Back door was open, boss, this was locked from the inside. There's nobody there, but something's happened.'

Handford followed him back in. The room was empty, there was no sound except that which came from the television which was still on. Wherever Letty was, it wasn't here. The witnesses, the stars of *Emmerdale*, had seen everything, yet nothing. The high-backed chair was skewed away from the set, a small table had been upturned and a packet of sweets spilled. On the carpet was a scraping of blood, as though someone had rubbed a weeping wound against the pile. In the kitchen two cups and saucers stood on the work surface, together with a jug of milk and a sugar basin. The kettle was hot.

There was no sign of Letty Walker.

'He's taken her,' Ali said, then added hopefully, 'Hospital?'

'I doubt it, but get someone to check. No, she's the reason for his killing spree. And now she's probably dead. I shouldn't have waited. I should have come up here when Redmayne gave me the information he did. Warned her.' His face was bruised with guilt.

Ali looked round, as if for inspiration. 'So what do we do now?'

'We find him and hope to God we're not too late.'

Ali's brow furrowed. 'That's all very well, John. But where do we start looking?'

'I don't know, except that it's unlikely he'll change his routine now. He'll be taking her to some place of atonement. One of the sites he lectures about.'

'Somewhere where he'll want her found easily, like the others,' Ali broke in. 'Where there are wheelie bins?'

Handford wasn't sure. There was more to this killing than the others. It was more personal. 'No, I don't think so. This is his mother. And she's his prize. He'll want to parade her in full view of everyone. And there's only one place I can think of where he can do that.'

'Where?'

'The focal point of the city. There used to be a church close to where Central and the magistrates' court are now, the Bradford Unitarian Chapel. They pulled it down to build them. That's where he'll be taking her. Somewhere between City Hall and Central Police Station.'

It took Ali only seven minutes to reach Central Police Station. Collingham's car was parked next to City Hall on Channing Way. Ali pulled up behind it. It was empty. A hubbub was coming from the concourse. A small group of people had gathered by the water, straining to look at whatever was in there. Police officers were racing down the steps from the station.

Handford pushed his way through the crowd. There, at the opposite end of the rectangular pond was an old lady face down in the water, which was steadily turning red around her. Handford could make out her grey hair, like a halo as it floated gently on the surface. Beside her was a man in a tracksuit. He was clinging on to her, prodding her, screaming at her.

'Mummy. Mummy. Wake up.'

'Oh, my God.' Handford yelled at the police officers, 'Get these people away. Now.'

The crowd backed off, refusing to turn around, their eyes continuing to be drawn to the spectacle in front of them.

Handford pulled off his shoes and socks and jumped into the water. It splashed around him, on to the flags. A shiver ran through his body; it was bitterly cold. The bottom was rough with grit and stones and once or twice he lost his balance as he paddled his way through discarded rubbish and over to the two of them. A swift glance told him that there was little he could do for the woman, but the man needed help.

It was Collingham, but he didn't know whether he was looking at Joe or at Andrew. Joe the killer, or Andrew the son. Either way, whoever he was, his speech suggested he had regressed to his childhood, and because of that Handford had to get the name right.

He took a chance and touched him on the shoulder. 'Andrew,' he said quietly. 'Come with me.'

Andrew Collingham looked up at him, 'Look what Joe's done,' he wailed.

He pushed at her again and when she didn't respond, he refocused on Handford, his eyes pleading. 'She won't wake up,' he cried, tears falling. 'My mummy won't wake up.'

Handford lifted him up gently. 'I know,' he said. 'You come with me and I'll get someone to look after your mother.' He eased Collingham out of the water. An officer threw a blanket over his shoulders and Handford held him steady as the two men walked up the steps of Central Police Station.

epilogue

It was some days later when Sanderson visited Handford.

'Just been to see Russell,' he said. 'Had to eat a bit of humble pie. Anyway it's good to see him off the hook. A bit shocked though about Collingham. They were good friends, you know.'

'Yes, sir, I did know.'

'He's very grateful to you.'

Handford made no reply. He felt like saying, 'And so he should be.'

'A lot of this was his own fault though, and I've told him that. Even so, I've had to offer him a bit of a carrot. Stop him suing us for all we've put him through. You know, Handford, I can remember the day when sue was no more than a word that came between suds and suede in the dictionary; now it's the first thing we have to consider before we get out of bed each day. Anyway, Detective Superintendent Slater is due to retire next year sometime and it's very likely Russell will get his job. That will mean there'll be a DCI post up for grabs.' He leaned over the desk. 'I want you to be the one who grabs it. I can't see Mr Russell refusing to back you now, and I most certainly will. I've been very impressed with you during this investigation. Even Mrs Forrester has thrown her hat in the ring, so to speak.'

Excitement flooded Handford. 'I'll give it some consideration, sir.'

'You'll do more than that, man, you'll put in for it. And that, Handford, is an order.'

Handford smiled. 'Yes, sir.'

Sanderson's expression became serious. 'You know, we would never have suspected Russell at all had it not been for the photograph. A real coincidence that. It begs the question as to whether Collingham found it on the girl and deliberately left it behind to incriminate Russell, or whether he had no knowledge of it at all until it was mentioned to him when he was asked to firm up the alibi and decided to use it for his own ends.'

'I don't suppose we shall ever know, sir; certainly Collingham's in no fit state to tell us. One thing is for sure, without it we would never have caught him. However he used it, it contributed to his downfall.'

The two men sat in silence for a moment, then Sanderson stood up. 'I'll be on my way, John; get down to some real police work, you know, the kind that involves a lot of paper.'

He held his hand out to Handford who took it with a smile.

When he had gone, John Handford returned to his own paper-work. For the moment, Collingham hadn't been considered fit to be charged, but they still had to get everything ready for the CPS. He was in the secure ward of a psychiatric hospital undergoing tests, but was said to be in a state of regression. They had searched his car where they had found the weapon he had used on his mother, and the garden dibble, which he didn't have time to use. Both had gone off for forensic examination. His house had been searched also. There they had come across a locked cupboard in his shed, which contained the bags he'd taken from the dead girls, all carefully labelled. In Beverley Paignton's they'd also found the address of the bakery. Had Forrester had that information, the brothel would have been shut down, Collingham would have been denied his victims, perhaps even apprehended, and she would have been saved the embarrassment of being taken off the case and posted to the training division.

'Better in the long run,' she said when she and Handford had met up after Collingham's arrest. 'I've got a marriage to repair.'

It seemed, too, that inquiries into the deaths of the prostitutes in Cambridge might be cleared up at last. Ted had come up with the information that the multi-national for which Collingham had worked had indeed been in Cambridge in November 1982 and May 1983 when Jenny Marsden and Kate Jennings had been murdered. Fortunately, one of the directors was an amateur historian and had kept all information since the beginnings of the firm. It was, he said, his intention when he retired, to compile it in a book. Collingham's name had been amongst the list of workmen in the relevant months.

'That'll give him something to put in his book,' Ted remarked.

Cambridge police asked to be allowed to question Collingham when he was fit enough. Handford didn't hold out much hope.

For a time, it looked as though Deepak Azam would evade

prosecution. Conspiracy to murder Michael Braintree was a non-starter. Dwayne Varley insisted it had been an accident, that he had only meant to teach Michael a lesson. The boy was too lippy by far. Azam had nothing to do with it. Fortunately for Mr Braintree and Mr Emmott, Azam had left them alone after the fracas at the leisure centre. It had always been on the cards that he would exact revenge, but had obviously decided the wisest course in the circumstances would be to forget it. Handford had talked to Daniel who had agreed if necessary to act as a witness against Azam, although given his information was hearsay, it was possible he wouldn't be called.

Unfortunately, not one of the girls at the brothel nor the women on the street was prepared to name Azam as her pimp. The CPS refused to agree to a prosecution with so little evidence. It wouldn't be in the public interest, they said; what they meant was that they were afraid of stirring up racial unrest if they did. Azam was too important in the community for that. So again they had to release him and this time he made an official complaint of racial harassment through his solicitor and for a while it looked as though he would get away with it.

But his arrogance was his downfall. He was sure of the girls' loyalty, but he hadn't reckoned on Alice. A sixty-forty split was what he had always had, and she couldn't see any reason why that shouldn't continue. She asked to see Handford with her solicitor. Deepak Azam was as much involved with the young girls as she was, in fact more so, she said, because he was the one who groomed them ready for her. He slept with them before he passed them on and he slept with them whenever he felt like it afterwards and he got them used to other men. He took forty per cent of everything they earned and none of the risks. When the girls reached sixteen, he introduced them to the streets or, if they had worked in Alice's other house, he gave them a flat, expected them to charge more for services rendered and took most of what they earned. For that, they lived rent free. She gave the police names, addresses and dates. She had kept records, she said, for this very eventuality. Why she'd changed her mind, no one was quite sure, but she was having a rough time on remand with the other prisoners and presumably couldn't see why her partner shouldn't suffer too.

Azam was arrested shortly afterwards. Ali had wanted to make the arrest himself, but Handford refused. It might make the sergeant feel better, dissolve his guilt, but the chances were the community wouldn't see it that way. Azam would become a martyr to the cause and Ali the traitor. Who would say what would happen? Neither Handford nor Sanderson was prepared to risk it and the ACC had felt the need to make sure Ali understood that. Whatever was said in the confines of Russell's office where the interview had taken place, Sanderson had come out red in the face and Ali, in contrast, as pale as his pigmentation would allow. It certainly kept him quiet for a couple of days. Handford said nothing, but hoped on the one hand his sergeant had learned his lesson, but on the other that it hadn't crushed him so much that it had knocked out of him the quality that made him the good detective he was.

As for Leah, instead of the pregnancy giving her the opportunity to rid herself of Azam by making a statement, she suddenly wouldn't hear a word said against him. She'd rationalised every-thing in her own mind. Once he knew she was having his baby, he would look after them. He always said if she got pregnant, it would be a baby made in love, so what else would he want to do? Michelle Archer had even suggested the baby might not be his, but Leah had been adamant. All the punters had worn condoms, Deepak hadn't. He never had with her. When he made love, she said, he didn't want anything coming between them. They could add the charge of unlawful sexual intercourse with a minor to the rest, but it was doubtful it would go anywhere, even with the baby, because Leah would insist she consented. In spite of the law on consent, it would more than likely be considered that at fourteen she knew her own mind. Handford feared for her.

Thank God Nicola had him and Gill. Physically, she was getting over the termination well, but Handford wasn't so sure about the mental or emotional scars. She cried a lot, but whether that was a case of hormones or grief it was difficult to say. Either way, she would always have her family's support. Leah, on the other hand, had no one.

A soft knock on his door broke into his thoughts. He looked at the pile of papers in his in-tray and wondered if he would ever get through it all. He sighed and called, 'Come in.'

Catherine Mellings stood in the open space. He could just about make out Hannah behind her. She was small like her father, with the same dimpled chin. Her dark hair was pulled back in a slide and she looked pale. The death of her friend had affected her badly and would no doubt continue to do so for some time.

'I don't want to disturb you, Inspector Handford,' Catherine said, 'but we're leaving tomorrow, taking Jenny's father home.

We'll return for the full inquest of course, but for the moment he'll be better back with us in Norwich.'

Handford rose. 'Please,' he said, 'come in, sit down.'

'Only for a moment.'

'How is Mr Broomfield?' A silly question, but a necessary one.

'As well as you would expect. Two years ago, he had a wife and a daughter; now he has neither. I'm not sure how you get over that.'

An embarrassed silence followed, until Catherine asked, 'Is Stephen in?'

'I think so, do you want to see him?'

'No, I don't, but Hannah does. I'm not ready to talk to him yet. Partly, I think, because I treated him shabbily by not telling him about Hannah, and partly because I don't want to open up all the old feelings I had for him or he for me. It would be unfair to both my husband and his wife to do that. We've all moved on, made our own lives. One day perhaps, for Hannah's sake, but not yet.'

Handford felt for her.

'When you part from someone you love in the way Stephen and I parted, it hurts, Inspector. A physical pain in your chest. So you turn that love into hate, because, believe you me, it's easier to handle. The love doesn't go, it just becomes hidden. That's the way I coped. Until now Stephen had been hidden and life has piled its detritus on top.'

'And Hannah?' Handford couldn't help asking.

Catherine put her arm round her daughter. 'We all have a lot to come to terms with, Hannah most of all. She feels responsible for Jenny's death, but I think we all hold some of the responsibility. I thought, perhaps I hoped, Hannah wasn't interested in her natural father. I was wrong. I should have looked deeper, seen that she didn't want to upset me or Paul by asking to meet Stephen. I should have offered her the opportunity and not relied on her reaction when she was young. I couldn't see her pain, and if I'm honest, I didn't want to be hurt any more myself. However, it's now apparent I can't let Stephen fester under my blanket of hate. Hannah must meet him and get to know him, otherwise what was all this about? She has our permission, mine and her father's, to make whatever arrangements she wants with Stephen, except that she must come back with us tomorrow, and they mustn't interfere with her school work.' She pulled a face. 'GCSEs next year.'

'Don't remind me,' smiled Handford. 'My daughter is Hannah's age. We've all got that delight to come.' *Thank God.*

He turned to Hannah. 'Do you want me to take you to see Stephen, now?'

'Please.' She looked at him, her eyes open and assessing. So like her father.

He pushed back his chair, but she hesitated. 'Do you think he wants to see me?' she asked.

Handford's voice was soft. 'I don't think it, Hannah, I know it. Come on, let's do it now.'

They walked along the corridor together until they reached Russell's office.

'You ready?'

She nodded.

Handford knocked and pushed open the door as Russell called, 'Come in.'

'Sorry to bother you, Stephen,' he said. 'But there's a young lady here keen to meet her father.'

Russell slowly raised himself from his chair.

Handford stood to one side to allow Hannah through, then quietly closed the door behind her. If it hadn't been Detective Chief Inspector Stephen Russell he'd been looking at, Handford would have sworn he'd seen the glint of tears in his eyes.